UNEMPLOYMENT AND INFLATION

INSTITUTIONALIST AND STRUCTURALIST VIEWS

A Reader in Labor Economics

UNEMPLOYMENT
AND INFLATION

INSTITUTIONALIST AND STRUCTURALIST VIEWS

Edited by Michael J. Piore

M. E. SHARPE, INC.
WHITE PLAINS, N.Y.

Design: Laurence Lustig

Library of Congress Catalog Card Number: 79-55274
International Standard Book Number: 0-87332-143-X (hardcover)
                                    0-87322-165-O (paperback)

Printed in the United States of America

Contents

PART THREE

Labor Market Structure

Preface

THIS VOLUME IS THE OUTGROWTH of a project on employment and inflation which was funded by the Ford Foundation through the National Committee for Full Employment. Most of the recent work presented here was discussed and debated in seminars sponsored by that project, and a number of the papers in the volume were originally written for the Committee. The project was initiated by Arthur Gundersheim, Executive Director of the Committee, with William Spring, Director of the Regional Institute on Employment Policy at Boston University, and myself. Gundersheim has since left the Committee to work for the Amalgamated Clothing and Textile Workers, and Spring has moved to the staff of the White House Domestic Council. These present affiliations may make it difficult for them to take a position on the controversies this volume addresses, but they were instrumental in creating the institutional structure and intellectual climate that fostered debate about these ideas, and thus they deserve much of the credit for what strength the arguments acquired in the process.

It was the hope of all of us when we undertook this project that it would contribute in a modest way toward rebuilding relations between the academic community and the trade union movement. For helping us believe that this is an important and achievable goal, we are indebted to Murray Finley and to Coretta Scott King, co-chairpersons of the National Committee, and to Mitchell Sviridoff, Robert Schrank, and Basil Whiting at the Ford Foundation. Finally, much of the impetus for this project came from Eden Weinmann, Julie Kerksick, John Gardner, and Richard De Haas, who have committed themselves to careers working for full employment in local communities and have pestered us to provide a specific program around which to organize. I wish we had been able to provide them with something that came closer to a program. I hope that they will be able to see this volume as a step in that direction.

My own work on this material was also facilitated by a grant from the Sloan Foundation to the Department of Economics at M.I.T. for the study of economic institutions, and by discussions with students and faculty involved in this project, particularly Paul Temin and Paul Joskow.

Michael J. Piore
Cambridge, Mass.
March 1979

vii

About
the Contributors

Eileen Appelbaum is Assistant Professor of Economics, Temple University.

Clint Bourdon is Assistant Professor, Harvard School of Business Administration.

John T. Dunlop is University Professor, Harvard University.

Bennett Harrison is Associate Professor of Economics and of Urban Studies and Planning, Massachusetts Institute of Technology.

Roger Kaufman is Assistant Professor of Economics, Amherst College.

E. Robert Livernash is Professor Emeritus, Harvard School of Business Administration.

Paul Osterman is Assistant Professor of Economics, Boston University.

Michael J. Piore is Professor of Economics, Massachusetts Institute of Technology.

Arthur M. Ross was Professor of Economics, University of California at Berkeley.

Charles F. Sabel is Assistant Professor in the Program for Science, Technology and Society at Massachusetts Institute of Technology.

Lester C. Thurow is Professor of Economics, Massachusetts Institute of Technology.

David Wheeler is Assistant Professor of Economics, Boston University.

Introduction

THE CENTRAL ISSUES in discussions of national economic policy are unemployment, inflation, and the relationship between them. The economics profession in the United States has developed a particular set of views about these issues. There is not, it must be said, a consensus about the precise causes or cures for either unemployment or inflation. Indeed, most economists would admit that neither is fully understood. There is, however, widespread agreement that understanding is to be built by working from the premises that unemployment and inflation are related and that that relationship is mediated by the labor market. These premises are built into a network of theoretical beliefs and understandings to which most American economists subscribe, and out of which have been woven the various theories of inflation and unemployment debated within the profession in recent years.

There is, however, a divergent set of views about these policy issues, held by a small minority of professional economists. From time to time these views too have surfaced in the policy debate, but the number of people espousing them is so small and their appearance in public debate and professional journals so irregular, that they often seem to be the idiosyncratic ideas of single individuals. In fact, however, the views are not idiosyncratic in that sense. They have a fairly long intellectual history, have been more or less shared by a number of economic analysts (albeit a decided minority of the economics profession), and grow out of a definite theoretical perspective upon economic processes. The purpose of this volume is to introduce that perspective. It is designed for the informed layman, for students, and for policy makers. However, the readings may also be of interest to professional economists, particularly the younger members of the profession educated in more recent years, when the range of theoretical perspectives presented in graduate classrooms seems to have narrowed.

The essays should speak for themselves. My first essay provides the introductory framework for the volume as a whole. The other essays in the first section discuss related developments in economic thought. The remainder of the material is grouped in two sections, one concerning wage determination and inflation, the other, labor market structure and un-employment. This division reflects the basic argument of the book: that wage determination and unemployment are two distinct processes that are largely independent of each other and must be understood separately.

Since the readings are for the most part self-contained, these remarks are designed less to introduce the readings than to place them in the context of broader debates about theory and policy. Basically, this introduction undertakes three tasks: first, to discuss the dual labor market hypothesis, and through that discussion to identify the broader theoretical problems raised by the particular issues of inflation and unemployment as conceived in this volume; second, to relate the perspective developed here to recent developments within orthodox economic theory; and third, to illustrate the contrast to orthodox theory by assessing the implications of the present perspective for understanding current macroeconomic events. A last section briefly distinguishes these selections from similar work inspired by Marxist theory.

The dual labor market hypothesis

Most of the contemporary selections in this volume are conceived in terms of the dual labor market hypothesis. None of these, however, explicitly develops the hypothesis itself. Moreover, they embody an interpretation of that hypothesis which differs significantly from that dominant in the profession (although it is, I think, widely accepted among those responsible for the original formulation). Thus the first introductory task is to present the dual labor market hypothesis and to clarify its theoretical implications.

The original hypothesis is that the labor market is divided into a primary sector and a secondary sector. Jobs in the secondary sector tend, relative to other jobs in the economy, to be menial and low paying and to connote inferior social status. They are unskilled, insecure, and offer little opportunity for advancement to better-paying, more prestigious job opportunities. The relationship between supervisor and subordinate is direct and personalized, unmitigated by work rules and customs, and there is no grievance procedure or due process in the administration of discipline. The secondary sector tends to be populated by the underprivileged and disadvantaged, by ethnic and racial minorities, and by groups with a marginal commitment to the labor force, such as housewives and youth. The argument of this volume hinges on the distinction between the two sectors. The bulk of unemployment is associated with movement in and out of the labor market and among a set of basically undifferentiated short-term jobs by the groups that populate the secondary sector. Wage inflation is a process that originates in "the other," or primary sector, where employment involves a long-term, institutionalized commitment and where the social and institutional structures through which this commitment is secured entrain a fixed wage structure.

Since originally developed, the dual labor hypothesis has been expanded to recognize a division within the primary sector between a lower tier and an upper tier that is composed of professional, managerial, and certain craft jobs. Very little use is made of this distinction in the readings presented here, but it is important for other economic problems and in the development of an understanding of why divisions within the labor market arise. Given the recognition of this third sector, the term dual labor market is now something of a misnomer.

For present purposes, the more significant shift has to do with the focus of the hypothesis. The original hypothesis was formulated in an attempt to understand the problems of black workers in urban ghetto areas. As such, it was directed at economic mobility, and within the economics profession the debates concerning the dual labor market hypothesis have centered around that issue.[1] However, as a general hypothesis about labor market structure and as an explanation of patterns of wage determination and unemployment—as it is used here—it is not a hypothesis about mobility at all but rather one about economic behavior.

In essence, the argument is that the behavior of the critical economic variables changes systematically as one moves across market segments, and that this variation is a reflection of differences in the behavioral patterns of workers and their employers. Interpreted in this way, the hypothesis would remain a useful analytical tool even in the face of substantial mobility among strata so long as behavioral patterns of mobile workers changed as they crossed the relevant boundaries. Lack of mobility would help to *explain* differences in behavioral patterns, but there are other explanations for these differences which are consistent with quite a bit of intersectoral movement.

The behavioral patterns in the different strata correspond to what Peter Temin, developing a distinction that originated with John R. Hicks, calls *instrumental, customary,* and *command* behavior.[2] Conventional theory builds upon the premise that all economic behavior is instrumental, i.e., a clear distinction is drawn by the economic actors between means and ends, and decisions involve the selection of the most efficient means for the achievement of given ends. The theoretical structure which follows assumes that this is true, if at all, only for professional and managerial workers (i.e., those in the upper tier of the primary sector). These people constitute a small minority of the work force and are important in neither wage inflation nor unemployment. In the remainder of the primary sector, behavior tends to be customary. The work community becomes attached to certain patterns for their own sake, and these patterns act as binding precedents independent of their effect upon the ends presumed in conventional analysis. With respect to wages, for example, workers are committed to maintaining fixed wage relatives, although that commitment may impose wage rigidities that have a detrimental effect upon the worker's income—the presumed goal of the work process from the individual's point of view. That commitment may be literally customary, as I believe it is (see selection IIB-2), or it may be the product of political processes within trade unions, as Ross argues (in selection IIA-3), or of a commitment to long- as opposed to short-term economic and technical constraints, as Dunlop argues (in selection IIA-1). In the context of the problems examined in this volume, the results are similar. In the secondary sector workers behave on the job in response to the *command* of the supervisor. The patterns of unemployment and wage determination grow out of the processes of recruiting and maintaining a labor force which will tolerate the relationship to the industrial workplace that command behavior seems to entail.

The ultimate analytical questions raised by the dual labor market hypothesis are those of why the economy seems to generate jobs of these very different kinds and why these different jobs are associated with radically different behavioral patterns. The readings that follow do not really address these questions. At best they hint here and there about what the answers might be. Hopefully, they also indicate that it is possible to understand a good deal about the way the economy operates and to formulate a number of policies for dealing not only with inflation but with a variety of labor-related problems without resolving these more basic issues. Nonetheless, the viability of the approach as an alternative to conventional economic analysis does depend upon their eventual resolution, and for this reason it seems worthwhile to summarize some conjectures about what that resolution might be.

My own thinking centers around the division of labor and the process of specialization associated with it.[3] There is a long tradition in economics that argues that these are the critical processes in economic growth. There is a certain mystery about why this should be the case. I would argue that such specialization is critical to the intellectual processes through which more productive techniques evolve. For example, in order for an engineer to mechanize an operation on the assembly line, he must be able to separate that operation from the logic of assembly and consider it in relation to the logic of a machine. Similarly, the advantage of placing accounting tasks and production tasks into separate departments is that the two kinds of tasks can then be thought about and organized according to distinct logical systems, appropriate to each.

This process of specialization has two effects upon the job structure. First, it makes each productive unit much more sensitive to the flux and uncertainty inherent in productive activity and the demand for output. In an unspecialized, subsistence economy, each unit engages in a variety of activities. When people for some reason cannot work at one activity, they simply switch to another. When it rains, people do indoor work; if they decide to become vegetarians, they leave the cattle and concentrate on the corn. In a specialized economy, such adjustments are not as readily made: rain leads to unemployed construction workers; vegetarian fads produce unemployed cowboys. Thus, the increased susceptibility to unemployment limits specialization. It also encourages a form of economic organization in which that proportion of demand which can be sustained over a long period of time is separated out and met with specialized productive resources. The residual demand, which is uncertain and highly sensitive to flux, is then met with different, less-specialized resources, capable of switching easily to other activities when demand turns down. Charles Sabel, in his essay on marginality (III-2), suggests how this is likely to produce a secondary sector of the labor market manned by marginal workers. What is from this perspective industrial "marginality" is from another perspective a polyvalent organization in which industrial work is only one of several productive activities in which the worker is engaged. If specialization is indeed the engine of economic growth and yet increases the susceptibility to unemployment, it is easy to see why, as economic development proceeds, unemployment should become an increasingly central issue, the focal point of political clashes between labor and management and among different groups of workers. Job security arrangements in industrial societies appear to be the outcome of such clashes, a point to which I will return below.

The second effect of the division of labor is that at any given time it generates an employment structure composed of jobs involving various different combinations of tasks. Some of the jobs are exceedingly broad, others very narrow. One might think, for example, of the contrast between craftsmen who put together a whole automobile, and assembly workers, each of whom does a couple of jobs on the line. The craftsman's job is sometimes thought of as a vestige of the early stages of industrialization, but it is not. Even in the automobile industry there are segments of production, such as Rolls Royce or specialized racing cars, for which demand is so small or so variable that assembly production is unwarranted. The prototype engineers in the newer electronic industries of today are the modern analogue of the automobile craftsmen at the turn of the century.

Workers with broad jobs, like the craftsman or the engineer, will tend to think about and understand their work in a very different way than do workers performing a few narrow operations. These differences in modes of thought and understanding, which grow out of the characteristics of the jobs themselves, seem to underlie the instrumental, customary, and command behaviors that characterize the various labor market strata. The craftsman's job will appear to the worker who performs it as holistic; he will be able to see the basic processes which are generating the work and determining the tasks he is asked to perform. The fact that he does so enables him to understand his work as a means toward particular ends, to see the job in instrumental terms. The assembly-line worker, on the other hand, has a job which is so narrow that he cannot possibly perceive in his work the principles (or ends) toward which it is directed. He has no choice, therefore, but to understand his work as a set of routine procedures, customs, or habits, which he memorizes and repeats in the appropriate setting. Hence the customary behavioral patterns observed in the lower tier of the primary sector. When jobs are narrow and their composition is unstable as well, people tend to hold them only a short time, and the relatively small number of stable workers operate in an environment of extreme labor turnover. Under these conditions even a customary understanding is impossible, and the work must be performed in response to the specific commands of somebody who does understand what is going on. This gives rise to the command behavior of the secondary sector. In this way the division of labor provides an explanation both of how the distinctive behavioral patterns exhibited in different sectors of the labor market arise, and of the distribution of jobs across the different sectors.

This interpretation of the variation in behavioral patterns as reflective of differences in ways of understanding work grows out of a number of ideas about cognition developed in the postwar decades in developmental psychology, structural anthropology, and philosophy.[4] The notion of the division of labor as an intellectual process critical to technological development and economic growth is rooted in a similar set of theoretical ideas. It is not possible to develop these ideas here, but it seems important to note the connection. The hope is that these developments in cognitive theory will provide the ultimate analytical foundations for the kind of approach which the readings in this volume present.

Keynesian economics and the neoclassical synthesis

Because it originally focused upon mobility, the dual labor market hypothesis is often contrasted to the theory of human capital, which has become the dominant theoretical framework in economics for the analysis of that issue. When the focus is shifted to behavior, and behavioral hypotheses are directed at the questions of inflation and unemployment, the relevant theoretical debate also shifts: the argument must be understood in the context of the debate surrounding Keynesian economics and macroeconomic theory. That relationship is suggested in part in the selections by Eileen Appelbaum and by David Wheeler in Part I. But it is important to supplement the understanding suggested there by reference to the historical evolution of the Keynesian problematic.

Keynes' contribution to economic theory was adopted by most professional economists in the United States in the form of the "neoclassical" synthesis. This was a theoretical attempt to marry a Keynesian approach to macroeconomics, which explained unemployment and inflation by systematic rigidities in certain prices (in particular, wages and interest rates), with a microeconomic theory that continued to assume that variation in prices was the principle mechanism for the allocation of resources among various commodity markets. The "synthesis" thus involved a basic theoretical contradiction. It was accepted despite this contradiction because it provided an explanation of the Great Depression, which was the central economic experience of the generation that dominated the profession in the 1950s and 1960s. As a new generation entered economics in the 1960s and 1970s, the experience of the Depression receded from the consciousness of the profession. An explanation which derives so much of its power from its ability to explain that singular event has lost much of its attraction, and the contradictions it entails have become increasingly troublesome. Much of the work in economics in the last fifteen years has been directed at the development of an understanding of economic processes that escapes the neoclassical synthesis.

The body of the profession has done this by rejecting the Keynesian model and attempting to reformulate macroeconomic theory in a way that is consistent with the traditional understanding of individual behavior and particular commodity markets. The theoretical agenda implicit in the selections that follow is the opposite: it accepts the Keynesian framework for an understanding of macro behavior and attempts to develop an understanding of microeconomics which is consistent with it.

The main—but hardly the only—theoretical question upon which these various approaches can be joined is that of the rigidity of wages. In conventional micro theory, wage rates are flexible and vary so as to equate supply and demand. When the demand for a given type of work falls off and workers who perform it are unemployed, their wage falls; at the lower wage some workers find other kinds of work more attractive; some employers find it more attractive to hire the remaining unemployed than they did before and substitute them for machines or for other workers; consumers find the output that these workers produce cheaper and buy more of it. All of these responses to a lower wage tend to restore full employment in the particular market.

The same reasoning, extended to the behavior of the economy as a whole, implies that wage variation should be a mechanism for the maintenance of full employment. When demand for labor falls off in a recession, the wage should decline. This should encourage some workers to leave the market; encourage certain employers to use labor in place of capital or to prevent raw materials wastage, product spoilage, and the like; and induce consumers to shift to commodities that use more labor relative to other factors of production. If this were actually to happen, we would observe relatively wide variations in wages over the business cycle and small variations in employment and unemployment. Instead, what we observe (or at least what we think we observe) is the opposite: relatively stable wage rates and relatively unstable levels of employment and unemployment. In Keynesian theory this is attributed to "wage rigidity."

Keynes himself had a particular explanation for that rigidity.[5] His explanation was that people were interested in *relative*, not absolute, wages: we care about what we earn relative to the other people we know. But in modern capitalist economies with decentralized wage setting, Keynes argued, there is no institutional mechanism through which the level of wages relative to the prices of other productive resources can fall without most people perceiving that decline as a fall in their wage relative to other wages. Each wage reduction, in other words, must be separately negotiated in a way that makes it appear to the workers involved as if their wage alone were declining.

The neoclassical synthesis skirted the issues raised by this argument. There was no formal statement or direct refutation; rather, this was done through the manner in which Keynesian economics was taught. Keynes' basic insights were identified as, first, the notion of wage rigidity, and, second, the recognition that the rigidity is so deeply rooted in the nature of the economy that policy must accept it as given. Particular explanations of wage rigidity, however, were generally ignored in the classroom and the textbook. Keynes' own explanation, this seemed to suggest, might be correct; but there were a number of other equally plausible possibilities.

In fact, however, it is not so easy to find an explanation of wage rigidity that is consistent with the way in which economists are predisposed to model behavior, and the models developed in the 1950s and 1960s by people who even now consider themselves to be staunch Keynesians contradicted Keynes' own explanation. One example of this is the debate about the consumption function, in which a hypothesis by James Duesenberry, which incorporated the idea that people's behavior was motivated by a concern about relative income (analogous to Keynes' hypothesis about relative wages), was rejected in favor of the permanent income hypothesis of Milton Friedman and the life-cycle income hypothesis of Franco Modigliani, both of which built upon more orthodox assumptions. [6] Another example is provided by structural inflation theories, such as that developed by James Tobin, which model local markets on the assumption of wage changes, implying a tolerance for the very changes in relative income that Keynes himself argued were not acceptable to workers. [7]

The theory of inflation developed in this volume is in this respect much more in the spirit of Keynes: it is a theory in which relative wages do not change. It does not make explicit reference to *The General Theory* and derives in large measure from a rather different impetus, but it is, I believe, the line of inquiry which would have developed had the profession taken seriously Keynes' own theory of wage rigidity and attempted to explore it systematically and work out its theoretical implications. Similarly, the views about the operation of the labor market for particular social and demographic groups that underlie the selections in the third section of this volume are consistent with the hypothesis of fixed wage relatives. They depend upon direct labor allocation by employer recruitment rather than upon the response of individual workers to wage signals.

In contrast, the approach of the main body of the profession to essentially the same theoretical problem in recent years has been either to deny that employment fluctuates more than wages, or—when the greater variability of employment is admitted—to explain it along lines consistent with conventional micro theory. My own reading of these efforts is that they have not been very successful even on their own terms; certainly it is true that the profession has moved rather rapidly from one to another over the last several years. But it is useful to review some of them and suggest how they might be viewed from the theoretical perspective of this volume. This will serve both to heighten the contrast between the two approaches to the Keynesian dilemma and to clarify the points at issue between them.

The most recent, and at the moment the most prominent, explanation of the variability of employment relative to wages is "implicit contract theory."[8] The idea is that a large proportion of the unemployed are on temporary lay-off from jobs where they have long-term contractual relationships that guarantee their eventual recall. The theory attributes this contractual relationship to an agreement between workers and their employers to maintain rigid wages and variable employment. The agreement is in turn understood in terms of assumptions about the different attitudes of the two parties toward risk. Given these assumed attitudes, the contracts are shown to be consistent with a rational, deliberate calculus on all sides. The contracts, and the wage rigidity to which they lead, are thus "explained" by rational behavior.

The theory embodied in the essays that follow is in certain respects built around the institutional arrangements upon which implicit contract theory focuses. It, however, looks for the origin of these institutions in other places: in union politics, in custom, in the technology, or in the way people learn and understand their jobs. This approach, moreover, builds upon certain additional institutional and behavioral details that the implicit contract theory ignores. One of these is that the institutional arrangements involving lay-off and recall characterize the primary sector of the labor market, whereas the great bulk of unemployment that has to be explained is associated with the secondary sector, where by-and-large such institutional arrangements do not prevail.

Second, as the reading by Roger Kaufman (III-1) suggests, the institutional arrangements associated with employment security vary substantially from country to country. In the countries of Western Europe, for example, workers have tried—and to a very large extent have succeeded—in creating arrangements that guarantee both wage stability and employment stability. Thus the institutions that the implicit contract theory is designed to explain are nowhere near as universal as the motivation which the theory uses to explain them.

Finally, the institutions of job security in industrial societies do not seem to have arisen through processes characterized by deliberate, rational economic behavior. Quite the contrary, they emerge in sudden social explosions and seem to be the product of abnormal political processes perceived by the people who live through them as bordering on revolution and anarchy. Prominent examples of these are the sitdown strikes of the late 1930s in the United States, May 1968 in France, and the hot autumn of 1969 in Italy. Such processes, as Charles Sabel's selection (III-2) suggests, appear to be much better understood in terms of shifts in individuals' perceptions of who they are, what they want, and the roles they are playing within the industrial world. These are the things that are taken as the fixed parameters in the process of rational decision making as modeled in implicit contract theory.

The implicit contract theory has come under a certain amount of criticism from conventional economists, and therefore it is worth emphasizing the structure as well as the content of our critique. It proceeds by expanding the list of "stylized facts"—in this case, institutional characteristics—that appear together and with which a theory that purports to explain any one item must at least be consistent. The conventional criticisms focus on the logical consistency of those postulates about rational behavior upon which the theory is built.

Before implicit contract theory, the popular effort to incorporate wage determination and unemployment into conventional microeconomics was *search theory.*[9] This theory started from two observations: first, at any given time there is a relatively wide dispersion of wage rates paid for essentially the same type of work, and second, workers possess relatively little information about the alternatives available. Unemployment in this theory becomes a period during which workers collect information about alternative employment opportunities. Under various assumptions about the rational strategy of workers and employers in such a world, the theory is then extended to explain the relationship between wages and unemployment and the behavior of these variables over the business cycle.

From the perspective developed in this volume, the basic failing of search theory is that it, like implicit contract theory, divorces various institutional features from the larger reality of which they are a part. It is true that there is a rather wide and persistent disparity among wages offered for essentially the same work, but as Dunlop points out (in selection IIA-1), many of the higher-wage jobs are not available to unemployed workers. Many workers, it is also true, have poor job information, but most of these workers are in the primary sector of the labor market. Workers in that sector do not need to be unemployed to search for work, and both workers and employers report that unemployment is the worst condition from which to search. Workers claim that it forces them to accept jobs prematurely, and employers tend to be suspicious about the quality of unemployed job candidates. Primary workers, moreover, describe the experience of unemployment as psychologically debilitating in ways that impinge upon search activity. Finally, unemployment is associated primarily with work in the secondary sector, where there is much less wage dispersion, where there is so much mobility among jobs that workers can obtain information about relative wages either from their own experience or by asking fellow employees and thus do not need to search, and where jobs are of such short duration that it generally would not pay to "invest" in a search for information one did not have.

Again it is worth contrasting the difference between the perspective out of which search theory developed and that from which it is being criticized here. The contrast is brought out sharply by one proponent of this approach, who draws upon a series of interview studies of the behavior of unemployed workers during the Great Depression to estimate the distribution of actual unemployment between two activities—leisure and search—and the way in which that distribution shifts with the duration of unemployment. He uses the fact that workers do not begin to search for some time after becoming unemployed to support an argument that the rational unemployed worker will first prefer leisure but then gradually spend more and more time searching.[10] What the workers actually report, however, is that the experience of unemployment is at first so psychologically shattering that they are unable to leave the house, let alone look for work. This suggests that unemployment, at least of the kind experienced in the 1930s, cannot be modeled as the outcome of a rational, deliberative process. Indeed, it is destructive of the capacity to make the very kind of calculation that conventional models assume explains its existence. A truly powerful theory of unemployment would explain why it tends to have this effect.

A third attempt on the part of conventional economic analysts to deal with the issues of unemployment and inflation has been to deny the reality of observed unemployment. The basic analytical implication of this denial is that because what we call unemployment is "unreal," the analyst should not be surprised that it fails to correlate with, or control, wage movements in the manner predicted by conventional theory. The principal evidence adduced to support this position is the concentration of measured unemployment among groups with a marginal commitment to work, such as women and youth, and its apparent association with the frequent exit from, and reentrance to, the labor market, which is a product of the marginality of their attachment.

Again, this argument builds upon an element of reality also highlighted by the selections in this volume. These studies, however, see this feature of reality in the context of a variety of other features that do not sit so easily with the theoretical structure upon which conventional theory is built. The secondary labor market is composed, not simply of women and youth, but also of ethnic and racial minorities. Some of their unemployment may be the product of a commitment to other activities, but a good deal of it is associated with the inability of black and other minority youth to escape the secondary sector, and a frustration with, and resentment of, this work to which they seem to be condemned. Moreover, it is apparent that the presence of these groups in the secondary sector is the historical outgrowth of a process in which a parental generation is deliberately recruited to perform economic functions which the primary labor force will not accept, and produces a second generation who feel trapped in their parents' jobs (see selection III-5).

The nature of this process strengthens the obligation of the society to respond to the demands for upward mobility—of which unemployment is a symptom. It also raises the possibility that the manner of labor force participation by women and youth is less an outgrowth of inherent tastes than a social constriction imposed by the requirements of the economy; that the attitudes of these groups have also changed historically through participation in the labor market; and that part of their unemployment too is now symptomatic of an inability to move into the primary sector, rather than the inherent marginality of their commitment to work.

All of this points to a range of questions about why the economy might generate secondary jobs and need marginal workers to fill them, which the conventional approach, by focusing upon the fact of marginality *per se* and taking as representative of the category as a whole those members for whom work is truly a secondary activity, ignores. The other analytical difficulty with this approach is, of course, that while it may explain why observed unemployment fails to control wage behavior, it does not explain what does.

The current economic situation

Although this volume is designed to suggest a general theoretical perspective, several of the selections are addressed to the particular economic conditions prevailing at the time they were written, conditions that are only tangentially related to present issues of economic policy. For this reason, and as a further illustration of the broader framework we are attempting to sketch, it will be useful to say something about the present economic conjuncture.

There is general agreement about the characteristics of the present economic situation which economic theory is called upon to interpret and explain. These are generally presented in contrast to the post-World War II economy prior to the Vietnam War: relatively high rates of unemployment, with particular concentrations among minority and secondary workers; relatively high and persistent rates of inflation; a general failure of long-term capital investment to reach levels anticipated on the basis of projections built out of the experience of earlier postwar decades; and a rate of growth in labor productivity which is extremely low by long-term historical standards. [11]

The dual labor market hypothesis suggests that the patterns in unemployment, in long-term capital investments, and in productivity growth may be attributed to a tendency to tilt economic expansion disproportionately toward the secondary sector. Apparently, employers in the late 1960s and in the 1970s have chosen to avoid permanent commitments to expanded productive facilities and an increased group of permanent employees. Instead they have attempted to meet expansions in demand through temporary arrangements which are easily reversed. They have thus responded to economic expansion with greater utilization of existing equipment; with retention of older facilities that are already depreciated and which might under other circumstances be scrapped; with methods of production intensive in labor, which is variable, as opposed to capital, which is not, and have preferred for this labor marginal groups who do not impose long-term employment commitments, who can be counted on to quit before too long, and if necessary can be fired.

The greater long-run flexibility and reversibility obtained in this way is purchased, however, at the cost of improvements in labor productivity. Workers in marginal employment relationships are probably less efficient than even the same people hired on a permanent basis. By definition, labor-intensive techniques are less productive than capital-intensive ones. Productivity is further depressed by other expedients such as postponed maintenance, increased overtime, and the like. At the same time, the reliance upon marginal workers explains both the expansion of their employment relative to the primary labor force and—because their marginality is valued for the ease with which they are disemployed—their high rates of unemployment.

Why has the expansion been tilted in this way? The answer that follows from our analysis of the causes of duality is—increased uncertainty. In seeking the causes of this uncertainty, two periods can be distinguished. The first of these is the late 1960s and very early 1970s, when the uncertainty was associated with the Vietnam War. The outstanding characteristic of that period from an economic point of view is that the economic expansion was generally attributed to war expenditures (an attribution which in fact was only partially correct), and that throughout the period the war was expected to end within four to six months (this belief proved of course to be completely wrong). The expansion itself and the particular structure of demand being generated were thus believed to be transitory, and employers saw no reason to make permanent accommodation to it. These factors have been little noticed by economic analysts of the period, but they were evident in virtually all the field interviews we conducted with employers at that time.

Economic analysts have been much more sensitive to sources of uncertainty in the most recent expansion, and my own views here are more or less coincident with theirs. The main generators of uncertainty since 1973 have been the energy crisis triggered by the OPEC oil embargo, and the continuing confusion about the relative prices of different sources of energy, the unprecedented inflation which the energy crisis appears to have engendered, and the variety of efforts to regulate economic activity. It is important to emphasize that in this analysis such basic factors as energy, inflation, and regulation are important not in themselves but because of the uncertainty which surrounds them. This leads to policies very different from those that conventional analysts derive from an apparently similar diagnosis. What is important, our analysis implies, is not that we solve the energy crisis or halt inflation or eliminate regulation, but that we stabilize these processes and make them and their impact upon business decisions predictable and, if possible, routine.

From this perspective, many of the policies that have been urged out of a concern over uncertainty are simply wrong. Thus, in the area of regulation, what is required is not less regulation but stable, certain, firm regulation. It is not, for example, the imposition of emissions controls on automobiles that discourages long-term investments in the auto industry, but the fact that the industry knows it can get the regulations changed through the political process—and is uncertain what the amended regulations will be. By the same token, the deregulation of controlled industries cannot be expected to increase long-term investment in them until the companies affected learn to live with and understand the new climate that deregulation creates. In the short run, lack of familiarity with the new environment is likely to discourage investment. And if the unregulated market turns out to be more volatile than the controlled one, investment may be permanently reduced. Similarly, it is not inflation *per se* which discourages investment—indeed, since inflation makes it better to purchase now rather than later, quite the opposite—but uncertainty about the future rate of inflation. Persistent talk about reducing inflation to some low, but unpredictable rate (to the extent that anybody takes it seriously), must simply aggravate uncertainty. By the same token, from this point of view the problem is not the content of energy policy but the failure to agree upon any particular policy at all.

One further important implication of this interpretation is the sensitivity of the character of an economic expansion to the announced goal of government employment policy. Think, for example, of business managers deciding between two different ways of meeting an employment expansion: One involves heavy capital investment and permanent employment commitments; the alternative is a relatively more labor-intensive technique and, if possible, high-turnover marginal workers who will make no long-term claims upon the enterprise. This choice will surely depend upon whether or not the decision maker thinks the expansion will last. And that in turn will depend upon the government's announced target for unemployment. If that target is 4%, a drop in unemployment from 5 to 4% will be met through the strategy of permanent accommodation. But if the target is 5%, the same drop from 5 to 4% will be viewed as very temporary. All of this suggests that the shift in the employment target from 4% in the Kennedy-Johnson years to the 5.5% of Nixon and Carter has itself probably contributed to the deterioration in the American economic performance.

The preceding discussion has focused on investment, productivity, and unemployment. One might attribute the high rates of inflation in recent years to disproportionate expansion of the secondary sector as well. There is a sense in which an effect of this kind follows directly from the preceding analysis. Because productivity increases provide a margin through which firms can absorb higher input costs, the inflationary impact of a given increase in wages and prices will be greater the lower the rate of productivity growth. Thus, by dampening productivity, the tilt toward the secondary sector has an adverse impact upon price stability. It could be argued, however, that the tilt has a direct impact upon wage inflation as well; that the rigidities in the wage structure of the primary sector make it much more resistant to market pressures than the secondary sector, where the institutional and customary norms that create such rigidities are absent.

Two factors militate against this diagnosis, however. First is the finding (suggested in selection III-4) that the process of wage determination in the secondary sector, while distinctive, is no more clearly responsive to the competitive market forces of conventional theory than is the process in the primary sector. Second, while an incomes policy may be justified at the present time by the fear that distortions in wage patterns may begin to aggravate inflationary pressures already present, there is little evidence that wage controls will be able to bring that process to a halt. Rather, the current inflation appears to originate with shocks to the price structure generated by the Arab oil embargo in 1973. Those shocks set off an inflationary process. That process has in turn come to be built into the expectations of virtually all economic actors and is anticipated in long-term transactions between labor and management, but also between borrowers and lenders, and among firms contracting for materials, processed goods, long-term capital equipment, and construction projects. The way in which the oil crisis set off the inflationary spiral is suggested in selection IIB-3, on price inflation. The Iranian political crisis may have a similar impact upon pricing. But the relevance of an analysis of shocks of this kind for the achievement of price stability is limited. Once the shocks have been accommodated, the proximate cause of the inflation becomes expectations, and it is these which must be dealt with to bring the inflationary process to a halt.

In the emphasis upon expectations as the major source of contemporary inflation, this diagnosis coincides with the standard economic analysis; but again, the conclusions for theory and policy to which this seems to point are not those generally accepted by the profession. If inflation is indeed anticipated and allowed for in advance in economic decisions, then the economy must behave in terms of resource allocation and income distribution very much as it would in a world of stable prices. It is thus not clear that expected inflation should be the central concern it has been made by the Nixon and Carter administrations. But to argue that inflation is really "expected" and that the expectations are uniform across socioeconomic groups, and certainly, to attempt to revise those expectations through public policy, we would need a theory of how expectations are in fact formed. Orthodox theorists have been attempting to meet this need with the theory of rational expectations. The basic premise of this theory is that the economic agents utilize efficiently all of the information available to them.

The problem with this approach is that it treats "information" as bits and pieces of experience which have a definite meaning to the relevant economic agents. In so doing it jumps over a prior step in the epistemological process: experience only achieves meaning in terms of some analytical framework, and one needs to know what that framework is before one can talk about how new information is absorbed. Adjustment to the Arab oil embargo, for example, might simply involve people's assimilation of new data in terms of their old framework of thought. Or, the adjustment could involve the development of new conceptual frameworks through which people who never looked at oil prices at all suddenly become sensitive to changes in the political climate and see those changes as having a direct impact upon their personal welfare.

A theory of knowledge must explain not only the bits and pieces of experience that individuals receive but also the analytical framework through which that information is interpreted, how that framework arises, and how it changes over time. This is the basic lesson of structural and developmental psychology, in which, we suggested above, the dual labor market hypothesis can be grounded. Our explanation of market strata may be rephrased in these terms as follows: The instrumental behavior presumed in economic theory, wherein the individual actor makes a clear distinction between means and ends, presupposes a causal model of the processes concerned. The experience of workers in the lower tier and in the secondary sector does not enable them to develop or maintain such a model, and the customary and command behavior which we observe is the product of the ways of organizing their experience that are utilized in its place. This line of reasoning suggests not only that the universal assumption of instrumental behavior is misplaced but that instrumental behavior itself may not be all of one piece. Some people may be unable, given their limited experience, to develop any causal model at all; even people who can generate such models may have sufficiently diverse experience that the models they utilize are different, even inconsistent with each other.

Radical changes in economic conditions may thus affect similar people very differently, revealing inconsistencies and forcing adjustments in their basic understandings. In a world of stable prices, for example, an analytical framework that allows for inflation will be equivalent to one that does not: only when inflation is injected into such a world will a divergence between the two models become apparent. The behavior of an economy where people were originally operating with both models will then depend critically upon the response to this difference. The rational expectations theory avoids this problem by assuming that all people operate with the first model. Prior to the advent of that theory, economists tended implicitly to assume that people operated with the second model and, moreover, that they continued to operate in this way for some period after inflation had begun. In fact, both of these alternatives are real possibilities, and the issues raised by the choice between them are open questions, capable of exploration not only in empirical terms but also by reference to theories of learning. In other words, to resolve the issues raised by inflation and rational expectations, economic theory must turn toward cognitive psychology. To the extent that it does so, it joins the theoretical problematic of the dual labor market.

The origins of the selections

Ideas about how to solve intellectual problems are generally attributed to "hunches" or "intuition," but ultimately they must come from somewhere. The judgment of conventional economists is heavily influenced by training in a theoretical apparatus that assumes purposive decision making in a world of perfect information. The empirical techniques of the discipline place a premium on the estimation of formal models built out of this apparatus, and discourage the reformulation of the model in the light of the data. The operating experience with actual economic decisions which informs and tempers judgments arrived at in this way is essentially *ad hoc*, depending almost exclusively upon the limited career and consumer decisions of the economists themselves or upon cataclysmic events which economists share with the rest of the society, such as the Great Depression of the 1930s and the inflation of the last decade. A set of ideas fundamentally at variance with the conventional assumptions must come either from a different set of experiences or from a different theoretical structure.

The impetus behind the selections that follow is a different set of experiences. The early writings on wage determination grew out of experience in the administration of wage controls during World War II. The more recent writings on employment are the outgrowth of participation in inner-city manpower projects, poverty programs, and civil rights activities. These experiences, which were largely fortuitous, have been supplemented by research projects whose most distinctive feature is their use of open-ended interviews with participants in the activities being studied. Such interviews are not unlike the experience of direct participation. The latter places the analyst into a situation in which he cannot impose his own analytical framework but must, in order to gain acceptance and control, understand and communicate within the analytical framework of the economic actors themselves. Open-ended interviewing may be thought of as an attempt to recapture the experience of direct participation: what is important in such interviews is not particular answers to particular questions but the framework in which those answers are conceived and to which every answer, whether true or false, is a clue.

This approach, unfortunately, has generated a number of apparently *ad hoc* theoretical constructs. The dual labor market hypothesis, as we have developed it above, is an attempt to pull those constructs together into a coherent analytical system; but, as the earlier discussion indicates, it is far from complete. An alternative approach to much the same set of problems has grown out of the Marxist tradition. If the impetus for the first approach is the experience of the analyst, the impetus for this alternative is theoretical. Marxist economists have been especially important in the formulation of the dual labor market hypothesis.[12] Because this work opens a range of additional issues which cannot be adequately dealt with in a reader of this kind, it is not represented among the selections which follow. Nonetheless, a few comments are warranted.

The special relevance of Marxist theory to the problems at hand derives, I believe, from a combination of two factors. First, Marxist theory, like conventional theory, comprehends economic behavior as part of a comprehensive analytical system. But, second, it views that behavior as part of a larger social process. Since the constructs that arose out of the participant observation which underlies the work represented here are also rooted in social processes, Marxist theory seems to promise the integration of those constructs into a framework with the analytical cohesion of conventional theory. The effect of custom upon wage relationships, for example, is not unlike the role of convention in the determination of the value of labor power in Marxist theory. Similarly, the marginal groups of the secondary sector might be interpreted as Marx's reserve army. Thus, the way in which Marx links the value of labor power and the reserve army to the laws of motion of the capitalist system suggests what it would mean to escape the *ad hoc* character of the customary wage or the secondary sector as initially formulated and to give them broader analytical significance.

Marxist economists, of course, believe that their theory can do more than this: that it can itself constitute the broader framework into which the constructs fit. A fair selection of their work in the domain covered by this volume would make such a claim plausible but not commanding, and I personally doubt that it can be made commanding within an orthodox Marxist framework. The difficulty is that orthodox Marxists root social processes very tightly in the material conditions of production and assume that people's ideology and politics are a direct reflection of these conditions. Thus, for example, revolution is brought about by changes in the mode of production. These changes operate through their effect, first upon the perceptions of the workers, and then upon the kinds of political action to which those changed perceptions lead. But the motive force on which the analysis focuses is always the material conditions themselves. The cognitive assumption implicit here is precisely the assumption made in conventional economics in the theory of rational expectations: that economic reality is automatically reflected in a unique and essentially complete and correct way in the understanding of actors.[13]

Postwar developments within the Marxist tradition, however, have departed rather markedly from this analytical approach. Marxist thinkers in the last several decades have been preoccupied by the question of why the revolutionary change which Marx foresaw as inevitable in the last stages of capitalism comes most often in relatively underdeveloped countries and has proved so elusive in mature nations. Their answers have focused on the independent role of systems of ideology and belief, and this has forced them to turn to a set of analytical questions about how people understand their world. These are essentially the same analytical issues that, we have just argued, are entrained by the hypothesis of rational expectations now preoccupying conventional economics, and by the notions of cognitive structure in which we have attempted to root the dual labor market hypothesis. If these analytical ideas were to be pursued, this suggests, these three apparently different understandings of economic activity would begin to converge.

Notes

1. For examples of standard interpretations of the dual labor market hypothesis by conventional economists, see Glen G. Cain, "The Challenge of Segmented Labor Market Theories to Orthodox Theory: A Survey," *Journal of Economic Literature* (December 1976), pp. 1215-57; or Michael Wachter, "The Primary and Secondary Labor Market Mechanisms: A Critique of the Dual Approach," *Brookings Papers on Economic Activity*, no. 3, 1974, pp. 637-80.

2. Peter Temin, "Modes of Economic Behavior: Variations on Themes of J. R. Hicks and Herbert Simon," M.I.T. Department of Economics Working Paper #235 (March 1979); John Hicks, *A Theory of Economic History* (London: Oxford University Press, 1969), pp. 9-24. Actually, Hicks first recognized the role of customs in the context of his theory of wages, where it functioned precisely as it does in the selections in Section IIB of this volume. See J. R. Hicks, *The Theory of Wages* (London: Macmillan, 1963), pp. 316-19.

3. The material that follows is developed at length in my essays in Suzanne Berger and Michael J. Piore, *Dualism and Discontinuity in Industrial Society* (forthcoming).

4. For a layman's introduction to these issues see: Howard Gardner, *The Quest for Mind: Piaget, Levi-Strauss and the Structuralist Movement* (New York: Vintage Books, 1974). See also: Gerame S. Halford, "The Impact of Piaget on Psychology in the Seventies," in *New Horizons in Psychology 2*, ed. P. C. Dodwell (London: Penguin Books, 1972), pp. 171-96; Hans G. Furth, *Piaget and Knowledge: Theoretical Foundations* (Englewood Cliffs, N. J.: Prentice Hall, 1969); and Lawrence Kohlberg, "Stage and Sequence: The Cognitive-Development Approach to Socialization," in *Handbook of Socialization Theory and Research*, ed. David Goslin (Chicago: Rand McNally, 1969). pp. 374-480.

5. John Maynard Keynes, *The General Theory of Employment, Interest and Money* (New York: Harcourt, Brace, 1958), pp. 13-14; 264-67.

6. James Duesenberry, *Income, Savings, and the Theory of Consumer Behavior* (Cambridge: Harvard University Press, 1949); Milton Friedman, *A Theory of the Consumption Function* (Princeton, N. J.: Princeton University Press, 1957) Albert Ando and Franco Modigliani, "The Life Cycle Hypothesis of Savings: Aggregate Implications and Tests," *American Economic Review* (March 1963).

7. James Tobin, "Inflation and Unemployment," *American Economic Review* (March 1972), pp. 1-18.

8. See, for example, Martin Baily, "Wages and Unemployment under Uncertain Demand," *Review of Economic Studies* (January 1974); and Costas Azariadis, "Implicit Contracts and Underemployment Equilibria," *Journal of Political Economy* (1975), pp. 1183-1202.

9. Edmund S. Phelps et al., *Microeconomic Foundations of Employment and Inflation Theory* (New York: W. W. Norton, 1970).

10. Robert J. Gordon. "The Welfare Cost of Higher Unemployment," *Brookings Papers on Economic Activity*, no. 1, 1973, pp. 133-96, esp. 155-62.
11. See, for example, *The Economic Report of the President and the Annual Report of the Council of Economic Advisors*, January 1978 and January 1979.
12. For a discussion of Marxist and radical interpretations of the dual labor market hypothesis, see David Gordon, *Theories of Poverty and Underemployment* (Lexington, Mass.: Heath Lexington Books, 1972); and Richard Edwards, Michael Reich, and David Gordon, eds., *Labor Market Segmentation* (Lexington, Mass.: Heath Lexington Books, 1975).
13. For a development of this point see Marshall Sahlins, *Culture and Practical Reason* (Chicago: University of Chicago Press, 1976).

Wage Rigidities, Employment Opportunities, and Labor Market Stratification   AN OVERVIEW

Editor's Introduction
to Part One

THE MATERIAL IN THIS SECTION is designed to provide an overview of the theoretical perspective upon wage determination and labor market processes that is developed in this volume. The first selection presents the framework in which the volume as a whole is conceived. It was written for a project on alternative views of wage inflation and unemployment sponsored by the Committee for Full Employment, and constituted the focal point around which that project was organized. Several of the other readings in this volume develop in detail points introduced in this essay.

The remaining readings in this section have been selected to suggest the connection of the argument developed in this volume to related theoretical ideas. The second selection, by Lester Thurow, presents the distinction between "job competition" and "wage competition" models of labor market behavior. Thurow's approach is very similar to that of the dual labor market hypothesis (in terms of which the first reading is conceived) in that it rejects a uniform model of labor market behavior and identifies one market sector with fixed wage relatives, but it relies more heavily on conventional variables and processes to determine the outcomes in the different markets. Thus, for example, while wages are rigid in the job competition sector, the distribution of jobs among workers is still determined by a cost calculus, and workers are allocated on the basis of their "productiveness" or "trainability." This assumption is not built into the model that is implicit in the first reading, and the meaning and analytical utility of the concept of "productiveness" is in fact called into question in subsequent readings. Similarly, Thurow assumes that outside the job competition sector, the process of wage determination does conform to the conventional competitive model, an assumption questioned in selection III-4.

The third reading, by Eileen Appelbaum, examines the relationship between the dual labor market model and post-Keynesian economic theory. This relationship is also discussed in the essay by David Wheeler. The major reason for including this last selection, however, is to establish that existing quantitative evidence leaves ample room for the alternative theoretical approach to which the volume is devoted.

Unemployment and Inflation: An Alternative View

1

BY MICHAEL J. PIORE

AN OVERWHELMING MAJORITY of academic economists holds that there is a functional relationship between the rate of wage (and price) inflation and the level of unemployment. That relationship is known as the Phillips curve. It implies in the simplest, most straightforward, and most brutal terms that full employment *causes* inflation. Thus, the fundamental conflict between two basic goals—price stability and low unemployment—has become the central dilemma of American economic policy.

But there is an alternative view of inflation and unemployment that grows out of two bodies of thought and research. One of these is the tradition of institutional labor economics, particularly the theories of wage determination which emerged from that school in the 1940s and 1950s. The leading representative of that way of thinking today is John T. Dunlop, and the kind of policy it suggests to cope with inflation is very close to that which Dunlop advocated and tried to pursue within the Nixon administration. The other important school of thought is that of labor market stratification, which developed in the context of the civil rights experience, the black revolt, and the war on poverty in the 1960s. Many—although not all—of the proponents of the stratification theories are political radicals. The conflict between their political views and those of older institutional economists like Dunlop has served to obscure a shared intellectual perspective and is undoubtedly one of the factors underlying the complete domination of the debates about economic policy by other views of economic processes.

The conventional view that there is a functional relationship between unemployment and inflation is based, at root, on the notion that the wage is set by supply and demand in a market process. Inflation is generated when demand exceeds supply, and the demanders drive up wages, competing

From *Challenge*, May-June 1978, pp. 24-32. © 1978 by M. E. Sharpe, Inc.

with each other to attract labor that isn't there. Unemployment, in this view, is supposed to measure the gap between supply and demand. When it is very high, supply exceeds demand and wages are stable or falling. Were the term "unemployment" taken literally, the unemployed would always represent unutilized resources, and wage inflation would begin only at zero unemployment. In fact, however—the argument runs— unemployment is an imperfect measure of the gap between demand and supply. There are always some people between jobs; not all people who want work are qualified for the jobs available; not all people who claim to be unemployed really want to work. At some level of unemployment greater than zero, demand actually begins to exceed supply, and it is at this point that wage inflation begins. As unemployment is driven further below that level, the inflation accelerates.

Those who hold the alternative view challenge this basic notion. They assert that wage determination and unemployment are two essentially distinct processes which must be understood independently of each other, and can be attacked through separate policies.

The wage determination process

The distinction between wage determination and unemployment arises because in most contexts the wage does not, and cannot, function to equate supply and demand. Instead, wage rates perform certain basic social and institutional functions. They define relationships between labor and management, between one group of workers and another, among various institutional entities (the locals in a national union, the various branch plants of a national company, the major employers in a local labor market, the major international unions which compose the American labor movement), and last, the place of individuals relative to one another in the work community, in the neighborhood, and in the family.

The role of wages in this respect results in a series of fixed relationships among the wage rates of certain groups of jobs and workers; these relationships are known as wage contours. The economy is composed of a series of these more or less self-contained contours. The boundaries of the contours evolve over time, as do the relationships within them. But at any given moment of time, the boundaries and the internal wage relationships are fixed. When a wage breaks out of line, distorting one of these fixed relationships, immense pressure is generated to restore it. The pressures emanate directly from rank-and-file workers and take the form of job action and strikes. They also generate political and organizational conflicts among various branches and divisions of such bodies as trade unions and corporations.

The most prominent example of the operation of these forces at present is New York City. There, as in most cities, the various municipal employee wage rates form a single contour. In 1976, the police attempted to distort the traditional relationships among these different groups of workers, demanding a special accommodation in the city's budgetary crisis. The city's resistance resulted from the fear that any special settlement with the police would lead to pressures from the other workers to restore the traditional wage pattern by granting equivalent wage increases, and the resulting wage adjustments would undermine the city's fiscal stabilization program. This year, conflict has centered around the negotiating structure. The city has sought to bargain with the unions as a group, but the police and firefighters have insisted upon separate negotiations. These disputes have national implications, because New York is loosely linked to a national wage contour comprising the major American cities.

In the last round of major negotiations, there were several other prominent examples of the same process. The rubber workers had fallen behind industrial wage patterns in steel and automobiles, to whose wage contour they belonged, and their long strike with its high ultimate settlement was an attempt to restore the traditional pattern. The teamsters, too, have had a relatively self-contained wage contour; in that case, disruption emanating from the Chicago local has been the focal point of wage determination. In the construction industry, a national contour is formed out of a patchwork of settlements in which there are traditional relationships both among different crafts within a given city and among the same crafts across cities. Thus, one out-of-line local settlement will generate ripples through these interlocking wage relationships that spread out across the national economy.

The inflationary process

This view of wage determination suggests that inflation is a two-part process. It is triggered by external shocks which drive a wage within a stable contour out of line. Individuals and institutions then react to restore the original differentials. The process of restoration generates the bulk of the actual inflation. But the initial shocks are the strategic factors.

These shocks appear to come from any number of sources, and it is probably not possible to formulate a single theory about how they are generated. In the examples cited above, many of the disruptive elements are, in fact, accidental. The New York police won a fortuitous court victory which gave them negotiating leverage; the rubber workers' old contract had no escalator clause, other settlements in the contour did, and an unprecedented inflation made such a clause the central determinant of the wage. Other disruptions are more systematically related to social and economic events: for example, the opening of a new plant in a community with a well-defined wage hierarchy; the organization of a new trade union (in recent years, very important in the public sector); political contests among union leaders (important in trucking, in construction, and also in the New York City police case); labor supply problems; product market

7

bottlenecks. Inflation, on the national level, appears particularly responsive to shocks which hit a number of contours simultaneously. To the extent that there is a relationship between full employment and wage inflation, it is because full employment, or the levels of economic activity which produce it, have a tendency to produce shocks of this kind. But the shocks that produced inflation earlier in the 1970s appear to have been connected with the oil crisis and with food costs. Such shocks are virtually impossible to predict. I would guess that if there is a single set of national pressures in the next few years, it is likely to be connected with the retirement of George Meany, the emergence of younger, more militant labor leaders, and the effect of insurgent challenges to established union leaders over wage demands.

Anti-inflationary policy

This view of the inflationary process suggests that, in the short run, wage policy must be directed at controlling the initial shocks and the process through which the shocks spread within fixed wage contours. Over the long term, the policy might also be concerned with changing either the composition of the contours themselves, or the relationship among wage rates within them.

To develop such a policy in detail would require an extensive analysis of each of the component elements. It is not possible to present that analysis here. The important conclusions and the incomes policy which follows from them may be summarized in the following brief points:

1. It appears possible to forestall most, if not all, of the shocks that generate the initial distortions through persuasion, pressure, and control directed by a national wage board. The basic leverage for this policy comes from the recognition by rank-and-file workers that the distortions are unjust and inequitable, however advantageous they may be from a personal point of view. Employers and trade union leaders also consider the distortions troublesome, because they know the countervailing pressure which will follow. Hence, there is a predisposition to accept government intervention, so long as it is confined to forestalling disruptive shocks.

2. It is not possible to forestall attempts to restore traditional relationships once they have been distorted. The pressures for restoration tend to be commanding. Attempts to stop them are likely to produce resistance in the form of wildcat strikes and a black market for labor. These attempts also undermine the political support for wage policy. Most of the current political opposition to incomes policy is generated by the failure of public policy-makers in the past to distinguish between initial distortions and efforts at restoration.

3. The necessity of making the distinction between disruptive shocks and the restoration of traditional relationships means that labor and management must participate extensively in the policy machinery; it

cannot be run by "neutrals" or by government officials alone. Only people intimately involved in labor-management relations are capable of supplying the detailed information which will distinguish the boundaries of the various wage contours of which the economy is composed, and will separate the two types of wage changes. Incidentally, the participation of labor and management may also be required for the political success of the program.

4. This type of wage policy implies that there cannot be a single national wage guideline or even a technically determined set of wage standards. Instead, wage policy must be tailored individually to each wage contour. The institutional structure through which policy is implemented should probably reflect this as well. Thus, a national wage board would have to operate through a series of subsidiary bodies which specialized in the control of particular wage contours.

5. The machinery described above can be distinguished from a long-term strategy designed to eliminate systematic sources of wage distortion and to change the dimensions of existing wage contours or the relationships within them so as to make them more consistent with the surrounding economic and social environment. Again, the precise content of such a policy would depend upon the peculiarities of each sector, the nature of its individual problems, and the actual leverage which government can bring to bear upon a solution. In construction, in trucking, and among municipal unions, for example, it can be argued that union mergers and centralization of power within national unions would operate over the long run to foster wage stability. In the medical care sector, it appears that adjustments in job structure and manpower policies are required. The most troublesome wage problem in the immediate future is undoubtedly the adjustments that must be made in the public sectors due to the conflict between the pressures of unionization, and the financial crises of state and local governments. Here the role of the federal government is extremely varied and complex and ought, at the very least, to be coordinated in a more studied and deliberate fashion.

Unemployment

The view of unemployment which complements the foregoing view of wage determination is less fully developed, and its specific public policy implications are less clear. Though this makes it somewhat more difficult to present concisely, it does nonetheless constitute a coherent alternative perspective.

First, a sharp distinction must be made between the level of unemployment and its distribution among various demographic groups. The level of unemployment is determined by the aggregate demand. Demand, in turn, can be regulated by the government through monetary and fiscal policy. The techniques for doing so have been clear since the publication of Keynes' *General Theory* in the 1930s. The chief constraint upon reductions in the level of unemployment in the postwar period has thus been the unwillingness of the federal government to pursue more expansionary policies. Since the 1960s, the ostensible reason for the government's reluctance has been that this course was alleged to generate inflation. As we have just seen, this supposed relationship between inflation and unemployment is questionable, which leads one to wonder if there is not some other, more fundamental constraint upon economic expansion. These are matters which will be discussed further below. In the present context, the basic point is simply that the level of unemployment is directly controllable by the government through known and generally accepted techniques.

This brings us to a second related point: the conventional interpretation of unemployment seems to imply that labor supply constitutes an absolute barrier to expansion; the barrier is indicated by some level of measured unemployment greater than zero. Those who hold this view argue that the intuitive idea of unemployment as unutilized resources which can be brought into production is wrong because the measured figure is "contaminated." Presumably, there is an irreducible residual level of unemployment composed of people who don't want to work, who are moving between jobs, or who are unqualified. If there is in fact some such residual level of unemployment, it is not one we have encountered in the United States. *Never in the postwar period has the government been unsuccessful when it has made a sustained effort to reduce unemployment.* On several occasions, unemployment has even fallen below the government target.

Third, the above interpretation of the level of unemployment does not explain why, at virtually any level, it is concentrated among certain demographic groups. In the United States in the postwar period, those groups have been youth, women, and black workers. There have been two basic ways of explaining this concentration. The usual approach has been in terms of the characteristics of the groups themselves. This has led to policies which are targeted at the specific groups, attempting to change their characteristics. The alternative approach is to account for the distribution of unemployment in terms of the functions which the groups perform in the economy. The result for policy would be a concern with two contingencies for which the conventional view does not allow: the possibility of changing the economic structure so that the functions of these groups would be eliminated; and the likelihood that if the functions are not eliminated, any success in dealing with the problems of one particular group will simply lead to the creation or discovery of some other group to take its place. The most graphic example of this latter contingency is the phenomenal growth of the illegal alien population since the late 1960s, which seems to be a response to the reluctance of black workers to play their traditional economic role and the resulting search by employers for alternative sources of labor.

What are these economic functions and why do they lead to high relative unemployment rates among those who perform them? The perspective I am developing here provides responses to these questions, but it is deficient in transforming those responses into operational policy proposals. It appears that the basic characteristics of the jobs held by the high unemployment groups are that they pay low wages, are often menial, and require little skill. In addition, many are also subject to seasonal variations, are sensitive to sudden shifts in taste and fashion, are in declining industries or marginal firms, and offer little prospect for continuous employment, let alone meaningful career opportunities.

It might be possible to reduce the number of such jobs but it is apparently not possible to eliminate them entirely without radical adjustments in the patterns of consumption and production of the rest of the society—perhaps without a fundamental change in the nature of the economic system. There are a number of examples of how these kinds of jobs are related to the broader economic structure. Here is one: the job security arrangements in many industries are predicated upon the ability of employers to transfer peaks in demand to other firms, or to sectors of the economy where firms are freer to hire and fire at will. Major nonunion employers who have "full employment" or guaranteed employment apparently fulfill their commitment in this way. Unionized firms in industries ranging from automobiles to blue jeans use subcontractors in a similar manner. But if the firms with freer hiring and firing patterns, and the sectors of the market from which they draw their labor, were eliminated, all employers would be forced to absorb the flux and uncertainty of economic activity themselves, and could not afford to provide the kind of employment security which most white males enjoy at prime age. Another example: without a low-wage labor force willing to bear economic flux and uncertainty, most of our declining industries such as textiles, shoes, and garments would be forced to move abroad much more rapidly. This would, in turn, threaten the employment of higher-paid, more secure workers who service these industries. It would also force adjustments in our balance of payments which would lead to a decline in our standard of living. A third example involves the direct effects of the elimination of low-wage menial labor upon the standard of living. The most dramatic effects would undoubtedly be to intensify the inflationary pressures and organizational problems in medical care, an industry which is already a focal point of social concern.

Why do such jobs generate high relative levels of unemployment? A partial reason is the characteristics of the jobs themselves. Obviously, jobs which are especially sensitive to economic flux and uncertainty are going to be most likely to end in people being thrown out of work. This cultivates a high voluntary turnover among the labor force: if the job offers no career prospects and is likely to disappear pretty soon anyway, there is obviously no incentive to make special sacrifices to hold it. But probably more fundamental is the fact that where there is a set of jobs so clearly inferior to other employment opportunities, social stability is possible only if the groups holding the poor jobs have special reasons for doing so. With the possible exception of blacks, groups which hold the inferior jobs have all had other, more basic social commitments. Work is often secondary or tangential; as a consequence, these groups frequently move in and out of the labor force. It is that movement which produces most of the unemployment. Thus, women have been committed to the home and children; youth to school and to adolescent pursuits before they settle down to regular employment; migrants from abroad and often from rural areas in the United States to a life in their home communities to which they return frequently. Blacks constitute an exception in the South where they were forced into their roles by a racial caste system. In the North, however, their acceptance of low-wage jobs and their high unemployment was more attributable to the fact that they were a migrant population, attached to the South and viewing their northern experience as temporary. When the black population in northern cities began to be dominated by second-generation, permanent residents who had grown up there, it rebelled against its assigned role in the labor market.

It has been argued that the social structure *creates* these groups in order to have people who will play these economic roles. But, again with the exception of the black workers in the South, it seems more plausible to argue that the society "finds" groups within an already existing social structure who are willing to play these roles. American society did not invent adolescents, or migrants, or housewives. But it has used them and, in the process, become dependent upon them. The difficulty is that precisely because it did not invent them, it has a very limited capacity to control their aspirations and self-conceptions. These are subject to an independent evolution, and, as they evolve, they create pressures for change. This happened with blacks and, to a lesser extent perhaps, youth in the 1960s. It is happening today with women. This is the policy problem—not the unemployment of the groups, but rather, the place of these groups within the economic system and their growing disenchantment with the roles and social organization which once made that place acceptable. This implies that relatively high unemployment among certain groups is a problem, first, of upward mobility for these groups in the labor market and, second, of the economic functions which these groups currently perform.

In sum, then, the basic explanation of the high relative unemployment of certain groups is that the jobs which they hold have relatively high rates of discharge and layoff, and the workers who hold these jobs have relatively high rates of entrance into and exit from the labor force. The two factors are related: in order to get people who are willing to accept the menial, low-wage jobs involved, one has to call upon groups with a marginal attachment to the labor market and these groups tend to have high rates of movement into and out of the labor force. The nature of these groups explains why their high relative rate does not impair our ability to reduce the *level* of unemployment: the groups are such that, with relatively little effort on the part of employers, it is possible to induce a large increase in the amount of labor they supply. At the same time, because of the character of the jobs to which they are confined, those members of groups who are already working constitute a reserve of people ready to move up to higher-level jobs. Thus, for practical purposes, there is an infinite supply of labor both for menial and for better-paying jobs. This also explains why institutional and social factors are so important in wage setting. Supply is not a constraining factor, and in terms of conventional theory, which relies on the forces of supply and demand to set wage rates, these rates are indeterminate. This way of looking at the problem leads to the conclusion that the fundamental economic problem is neither unemployment nor inflation, but economic opportunity and social mobility.

Public policy for upward mobility

The problem of upward mobility must in turn be considered not simply in terms of the workers holding the jobs, but also of the social function which these workers now perform; if they are to be upwardly mobile, their current jobs must either be eliminated or filled by others. How are policy-makers dealing with this problem?

1. *Administration.* The United States already has a substantial number of public policies designed to promote the upward mobility of minorities and women. These include equal employment policies to insure that opportunities are open to qualified workers, and education and training policies to equip workers to fill newly opened jobs. The major difficulties with this range of policies appear to have been internal administration and coordination. Of particular concern was the administration of the Equal Employment Opportunities Commission (EEOC). Until now, no president has ever given top priority to staffing the agency with good administrators; the appointments were always dominated by short-run political considerations. Hence, the new administrators will be faced with a history of poor practice, and of failure on the part of the agency to act as the key instrument of economic policy which it ought to have been. As for coordination, at least three distinct aspects of the problem may be distinguished: coordination between the EEOC and other agencies promoting equal opportunity, for example, the Labor Department, HEW, the Civil Service Commission; coordination between agencies providing education and those providing training (HEW and Labor); and coordination between equal opportunity policy and education and training policy.

2. *Planning.* The policies for both equal employment and education and training need to be conceived in terms of a broader framework which takes account of available job opportunities. Few have ever asked the

elementary question whether there are going to be enough "good" jobs to promote the upward mobility of women and blacks without displacing white workers and if not, what can be done about it. There are a number of policies which would reduce conflicts if there did indeed turn out to be a scarcity of "good" jobs. We could delay the entrance of white males into the labor force by expanded education and training, for example, or promote early retirement in certain sectors by adjustments in the social security system.

3. *The vacuum.* Conversely, there is the question who will perform the jobs vacated by upwardly mobile workers. As noted earlier, what appears to be happening now is that undocumented alien workers are filling these jobs by default. This raises issues which should be the subject of study and ultimately of policy. First, are the aliens subject to special exploitation because they are illegal? Are minimum labor standards being violated? Second, will the children of alien workers want upward mobility, and is the society capable of providing them with job opportunities?

4. *Elimination of low-wage jobs.* This area is one which needs special study, planning, and experimentation. There is now no policy, and virtually no base of knowledge upon which policy could be built.

The Phillips curve, the evidence, and the determinants of economic policy

The foregoing suggests that the central issue of economic policy is the upward mobility of discontented low-wage workers. In fact, the problem of discontent and frustrated aspirations is a good deal more widespread, and the policy problem more complicated, than we have indicated here.

In light of this alternative view of inflation and unemployment, the total acceptance of the Phillips curve in recent debates about economic policy becomes astonishing—so astonishing that an explanation is called for. In fact, the evidence for the existence of such a relationship is very weak. There are virtually no grounds for assuming a simple functional relationship between the level of unemployment and the rate of wage (or price) inflation in the last ten years. A simple plot of unemployment and inflation would show that the points lie all over the map; in no way would they trace out the regular relationship which the theory postulates.

The notion of such a relationship has been rescued in academic debate by introducing two principal refinements into the theory. First, it was argued that measured unemployment did not represent true unemployment, and the unemployment rate was therefore adjusted in various ways. When these adjustments proved insufficient, a second refinement was introduced—the notion that inflation gets built into expectations. To account for this effect, past rates of wage inflation were used along with unemployment in the estimating equations. Both these refinements have been handled in such a way that one is unsure whether the theory is being used to explain the data or the data reworked to fit the theory. Indeed, in the case of the expectations variable, there is almost certainly a good deal of the latter effect: the estimation techniques have allowed the researcher to pick out from a range of possible data precisely those which best fit the theory. What is surprising in all of this is not that it occurred, but that there has been so little discussion of it among economists and econometricians, who are normally so careful to avoid such procedures and so quick to point out their dangers when others use them. It is also surprising that there have been no independent attempts to define and test the theories of either "true" unemployment or of expectations. All of this leads one to suspect that the Phillips curve is really a rationalization of something else. But of what? One must suspect that for economists, the use of the curve is designed, consciously or unconsciously, to rescue the notions of supply and demand, which constitute the central ideas of the discipline. But what about the rest of society? Is it simply being "taken in" by the economists?

The intellectual history of economic debate in the postwar period indicates that just the opposite is the case. The Phillips curve and the lessons it teaches won widespread public acceptance only in the middle sixties. Before that time, the intellectual obstacle to full employment was a completely different but equally effective notion: that of the need for a balanced federal budget. That idea had very little support among professional economists, but it was almost universally accepted by politicians and by the public at large. The push for a balanced budget was abandoned early in the 1960s by President Kennedy, and its intellectual respectability in informed political debate declined very rapidly thereafter. It is at that point in history that the concept of the Phillips curve, which until then had been largely confined to professional discourse among economists, became prominent in public discussions of economic policy. The coincidence of the growing acceptance of the curve and the declining commitment to a balanced budget can hardly be accidental. It seems to suggest that Americans have always had some intellectual construct which served as an obstacle to an economic policy for full employment. This leads one to suspect that the arguments which justify the dampening of employment are actually rationalizations of policies decided on other grounds.

Economic policy is the outcome of a political process. The important actors in the process are, on one side, the trade union movement and organized minority groups pushing for expansion and a low rate of unemployment and, on the other side, the business and banking communities which have been infinitely more cautious and conservative. Actual policy is the outcome of the balance of pressures exerted by these two groups and one can almost say that the target rate of unemployment, indeed even the rate of unemployment itself, shifts continually as that balance is adjusted. The debate is conducted in a vocabulary supplied by economists and through professional economic spokesmen, but the result is the outcome of direct political pressure. The change in economic policy from aggressive expansion in the 1960s to the recessionary conditions of the 1970s was produced by a large shift in the balance of these political forces.

And an analysis of that shift is critical to an understanding of the factors which really act to undermine full employment in the United States.

What I find most impressive in the climate of the period in which this shift occurred is not so much the gain in the power of the business and banking communities—although after the Republican election victory there certainly was such a gain—but the weakening of will and conviction among trade union leaders on the full employment issue. The trade unions did not actually abandon their commitment to full employment but they certainly expressed themselves with a lot less fervor. Their changing attitudes were, in turn, attributable to incipient problems with the rank-and-file. In the late 1960s, trade union officials and lower level management shared a general feeling that rank-and-file workers were becoming increasingly aggressive, difficult to manage, and restive about existing organizational structures, and that these attitudes were the direct result of a prolonged period of low unemployment which taught workers, especially the younger ones, to "undervalue" what they had already achieved and to aspire to "unrealistic" improvements in employment and working conditions. If prolonged full employment was spurring these feelings, a taste of unemployment and recession, it was felt, would help cure them.

It would seem that full employment generated among the favored members of the American labor force a set of discontents and desires not unlike those expressed by disfavored groups like minorities and women: discontent with existing employment opportunities and desires for improvement and upward mobility. If this is true, it implies in turn that there is a systematic tendency in the United States at full employment for aspirations to outrun opportunity. In a country such as ours, whose national ideology is built around its self-conception as the land of opportunity, this is bound to be a very difficult thing to face. And it is easy enough to understand why we would prefer theories which located the limitations upon full employment elsewhere, in events and processes such as inflation or the need for a balanced budget, which have nothing fundamentally to do with the national ideology. By the same token, however, so long as we conceive the problem in these terms, we will never be able to achieve full employment. More important, we will never be able to meet the ideological commitments upon which the country was founded and upon which our identity as a nation rests. To meet the goals we have defined for ourselves as a people, we must make the issue of the quality of economic opportunity central to our thinking about economic problems and the direct focus of our economic policies.

In what direction should we move? Unfortunately, because our mode of economic discourse has served more than anything else to obscure and suppress these issues, it is very difficult to move directly to operational policy. The immediate steps are rather to encourage a new mode of thinking, an alternative line of research, and a different political rhetoric.

A Job Competition Model

2

BY LESTER C. THUROW

GOVERNMENT EDUCATION and training policies have to a great extent been based on a "wage competition" view of the labor market. They have not had the predicted impact since they have ignored the "job competition" elements in the labor market. Instead of competing against each other based on wages, individuals compete for jobs based on background characteristics. As a result, this section outlines the role of job competition in the American economy and its implications for programs designed to alter the distribution of income.

To make the presentation as clear as possible and to highlight the differences between a wage competition economy and a job competition economy, the argument will be advanced *as if* job competition existed without wage competition. In reality there is a continuum between wage competition and job competition. The real American economy lies somewhere on the continuum between these two extremes. Both types of competition exist. The "as if" assumption is made to clarify the role of job competition by isolating its impacts from those of wage competition.

In a job competition model two sets of factors determine an individual's income. One set of factors determines an individual's *relative* position in the labor queue; another set of factors, not mutually exclusive of the first, determines the actual distribution of job opportunities in the economy. Wages are paid based on the characteristics of the job in question and workers are distributed across job opportunities based on their relative position in the labor queue. The most preferred workers get the best (highest real income) jobs. (In this context a job is best thought of as a lifetime sequence of jobs rather than a specific job with a specific employer.)

Given the factors that determine an individual's position in the labor queue and given the factors that determine the distribution of lifetime

Excerpted from Lester C. Thurow and Roger E. B. Lucas, *The American Distribution of Income: A Structural Problem*, a study prepared for the Joint Economic Committee of the Congress of the United States, March 17, 1972, pp. 19-26, 33-39.

17

income ladders, it becomes possible to formulate a technique for calculating the impacts of education and training.

The labor queue

In neoclassical theory the labor market exists to match a vector of labor demands with a vector of labor supplies. In the matching process, or in the mismatching process, various signals are given. Businesses are told to raise wages or redesign jobs in skill shortage sectors. In surplus sectors they are told to lower wages. Individuals are told to acquire skills in high-wage shortage areas and discouraged from acquiring jobs and skills in low-wage surplus areas. In the process each skill market is cleared with increases or reductions in wages in the short-run and by a combination of wage changes, skill changes, and production process changes in the long-run.

In a job competition model labor skills do not exist in the labor market. New workers come into the labor market with a variety of background skills and characteristics. These background characteristics (education, age, sex, etc.) affect the cost of training a worker to fill any given job, but they do not in general constitute a set of skills that would allow the worker to enter directly into the production process. Most cognitive job skills, general and specific, are acquired either formally or informally through on-the-job training after a worker finds an entry job and the resultant promotional ladder.

Such a training process is evident in the American economy. A survey of how American workers acquired their cognitive job skills found that only 40 percent were using skills that they had acquired in formal training programs or in specialized education. In addition, most of these reported that some of the skills that they were currently using had been acquired in informal casual on-the-job training. The remaining 60 percent acquired *all* of their job skills through informal casual on-the-job training. Even among college graduates over two-thirds reported that they had acquired cognitive job skills through informal casual processes on the job. When asked to list the form of training that had been the most helpful in acquiring their current job skills, only 12 percent listed formal training and specialized education.[1]

Thus the labor market is not primarily a market for matching the demands and supplies of different job skills, but a market for matching trainable individuals with training ladders. Except for background characteristics, the demand for job skills creates the supply of job skills since the demands for labor determine which job skills are taught. In marginal productivity terms, marginal products are associated with jobs and not with individuals. The operative problem is to pick and train workers so that they can generate the desired marginal product of the job in question with the least investment in training costs. For new workers and entry level jobs, background characteristics form the basis of selection. Those workers with the background characteristics that yield the lowest training costs will be selected. For workers with job experience, existing job skills (including skills like reliability and punctuality) are relevant to the selection process to the extent that they lead to lower training costs. Training ladders or job progressions emerge when job skills are complimentary.

Workers are ranked in a labor queue based on their training costs regardless of whether the job skill in question is general or specific.[2] Even if the job skills in question are basically general and workers pay for their own general training, employers are still interested in training costs. Several factors determine this interest. First, every job has some specific skills for which employers must pay training costs. The most universal are where and when to report, locations of tools, and the experience of working with a specific set of individuals as a production team.

Second, non-marginal inereases in the quantity of any one factor will raise the marginal productivity of other factors. The marginal product of capital depends on the quantity and quality of labor with which it is working. Consequently, employers will want to generate more job skills, general or specific, than individuals will be willing to buy. Individuals simply are not able to appropriate all of the indirect benefits of the additional skills.[3]

If employees pay training costs by accepting wages below their marginal productivity and if all workers in a given job are paid the same wage, the difference between wages and marginal productivities will be adjusted to reflect average training costs. To the extent that employers can hire workers with less than average training costs, they will be able to earn extra returns. The difference between wages and marginal productivities simply exceeds actual training costs.

In addition many firms will find that they must pay for all or part of the general training costs that might be absorbed by the employee. Assume for the sake of simplicity that there are two types of labor—trainable and untrainable. The wage rate for trainable labor may be such that it exceeds marginal productivity minus training costs for many general job skills. Due to the complementarity between skilled labor and other factors of production it still pays firms to undertake such training, but it also pays them to minimize training costs. By the same token the wage rate for trainable labor need not be less than that for untrained labor even during training. As a result, workers do not necessarily pay for their training by accepting wages less than their opportunity costs of working as untrained laborers.

Based on the background characteristics and skills acquired in previous jobs, potential employees are ranked by employers on a continuum from the best worker to the worst worker. Although it is possible to place groups with the same background characteristics and skills at some specific point in the queue, this is not to say that each individual in that group falls into the same specific position on the labor queue. Each group could be characterized by some distribution around its own mean.

Such distributions arise for a number of reasons:

(a) Since there are many relevant background characteristics, classifications based on any one characteristic, such as education, will lead to a distribution of workers around the group's mean.

(b) If job search procedures resemble Markov chains, there is no guarantee that employers and jobs will be perfectly matched. Employers may fill with less than the best available employee since time and other search costs are necessary to find the best available employee. Similarly laborers may take less than the best available job. The result is nonequal incomes for identical individuals.

(c) A host of other market imperfections (transition costs, etc.) may generate distributions of income for individuals with identical characteristics.

(d) Some characteristics that are unmeasurable or difficult to measure (willingness to take risks, personal motivation) will generate observed distributions of income around group means since it is never really possible to distinguish homogeneous groups based on generally available background characteristics. The net result is income distributions where some individuals with preferred background characteristics will make less than some individuals with less desirable background characteristics.

(e) Different employers order their labor market queues differently. A background characteristic of relevance to one employer may not be of relevance to another. Thus a group's national position is merely a weighted average of its position with each individual employer.

Training costs are the basic determinants of the rank order in the labor queue, but lacking direct evidence on specific training costs for specific workers, laborers are ranked according to their background characteristics —age, sex, educational attainment, previous skills, psychological tests, etc. Each is used as indirect measures of the costs necessary to produce some standard of work performance. (Training costs, as the term is used here, include the costs of inculcating norms of industrial discipline and good work habits and the uncertainty costs associated with hiring workers whose training costs are more variable or unknown.)

Subjective elements may also enter the labor queue. If employers discriminate against blacks, blacks will find themselves lower in the labor market queue than their training costs would warrant. To some extent the smaller the objective differences in training costs the more subjective preferences can determine the final ordering. If every individual had identical training costs, blacks could be placed at the bottom of the labor queue with no loss in efficiency.

The national labor queue depends upon the distribution of background characteristics and employers ranking of different background characteristics, but it also depends upon the distributions within each background class. (See Chart 1.) An individual may belong to a class with a set of characteristics preferred to the characteristics of another individual, but still end up

Chart 1

The Labor Queue

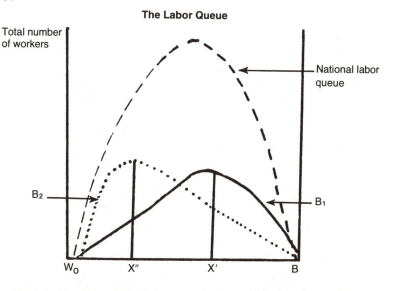

Notes: Ranking number of workers from least preferred to most preferred. B_1 and B_2 are sets of background characteristics where B_1 is generally preferred to B_2. The National Labor Queue is derived by vertical addition of the underlying distribution for each background class.

with a lower position in the national labor queue. While no two workers may be exactly alike, the costs of discovering small differences are so large that individuals are ranked based on a finite number of background characteristics. This means that there are a finite number of rankings in the labor queue and that many individuals have identical rankings.

Based on such a labor queue, jobs and their corresponding training ladders are distributed in the labor market with employers working down from those at the top of the queue to those at the bottom of the queue. The best jobs will go to the best workers and the worst jobs will go to the worst workers. Given a need for untrained (raw) labor, some workers at the bottom of the labor queue will receive little or no training. In periods of labor scarcity, however, training will extend farther and farther down the labor queue as employers are forced to train more costly workers to fill job vacancies. If there are an inadequate number of jobs, those at the bottom of the labor queue will be left unemployed. [4]

Differences between these expected values will depend upon the size of the random fluctuations around the group's expected value. As a result, groups have expected positions in the labor queue, but individuals do not. They are subject to random fluctuations around their group's expected position.

To the extent that education and formal training are an important background characteristic used for screening individuals into different job opportunities, alterations in the distribution of education can have an important impact on the shape of the labor queue. Less dispersion in education leads to less dispersion in the labor queue. The relevant empirical question is the weight that is attached to education in screening relative to the weight attached to other factors. This obviously differs from job to job, but educational screening tests are ubiquitous if not universal.

Even given a labor queue, however, there is still the problem of determining the actual distribution of job or income opportunities. Since the labor queue is used to distribute individuals across job opportunities, the labor queue determines a group's relative position in the distribution of job opportunities but it does not determine the shape of the job distribution. Individuals compete for job opportunities based on their relative positions in the labor queue. The best jobs (highest real income) go to the best workers, etc., but the shape of the job opportunities distribution need not be similar to that of the labor queue. An equal group of laborers (with respect to training costs) might be distributed across a relatively unequal distribution of job opportunities. After receiving the resultant on-the-job training, the initially equal workers would have unequal marginal productivities since they now have unequal skills. As a result, the distribution of income is determined by the distribution of job opportunities and not by the distribution of the labor queue. The same factors that affect the shape of the labor queue may, however, affect the distribution of job opportunities (see note 4).

Consequently, the income or job distribution for each set of background characteristics is related to the income or job distribution for every other set of background characteristics. All of the underlying component distributions of income must, by definition, sum to a given national distribution of income. As a result, increases in the numbers of individuals in more preferred background groups can lead to a deterioration in the mean and/or distribution of income for less preferred groups. Every additional college worker may mean a deterioration in the position of the remaining high school workers.

Facilitating training

In a world where laborers acquire many of their cognitive job skills, general and specific, through informal training from other workers or their immediate supervisors, the labor market needs to be structured in such a way as to maximize the transmittal of knowledge and to minimize the resistance to new knowledge (technical progress). To some extent removing direct wage competition and limiting job competition to entry jobs is a necessary ingredient in the training system.

If workers feel that they are training a potential wage or job competitor every time they show another worker how to do their job, they have every incentive to stop giving such informal training. Each man would try to build his own little monopoly by hoarding skills, general or specific, and information. Job insecurity would also mean that every man had a vested interest in resisting any technical improvements that reduce the number of job opportunities in his occupation. Conversely, in a training system where no one is trained unless a job is available (this is what on-the-job training means), where strong seniority provisions exist, and where there is no danger of some competitor bidding down your wages, employees can more freely transmit information to new workers and can more readily accept new techniques. If anyone is made redundant by such techniques, it will be a clearly defined minority—new workers.

As a result, the types of wage and job competition that are the essence of efficiency in simple neo-classical models may not be the essence of efficiency in an economy where the primary function of the labor market is to allocate individuals to on-the-job training ladders and where most learning occurs in work-related contexts. Here wage and job competition (above the entry level) becomes counterproductive. Wage and job competition might allow the economy to approach its efficiency frontier more closely, but movements toward the efficiency frontier might also lower its rate of growth. Since the potential long-run gains from movements in the efficiency frontier completely dominate the potential short-run gains from moving closer to the efficiency frontier, the labor market needs to be structured to maximize long-run movements of the frontier rather than short-run approaches to it.[5]

What is the impact of limited wage competition for government policies to alter the structure of income? What is the implication of limited wage competition for education and formal training policies? To the extent that educated labor is distributed across non-competitive lifetime income ladders (job sequences), equalization of the distribution of education will have a correspondingly lesser impact on the equality of the income distribution. The dispersion in the labor queue will be lessened, but a narrower labor queue will still be distributed across a wide distribution of jobs or incomes. Education may equalize incomes through its direct impact on the distribution of job opportunities, but it will not equalize incomes by increasing the supplies and lowering the wages of high skill workers while lowering the supplies and increasing the wages of the low skill workers. More potential plumbers will not lower the wages for plumbers since the market is structured in such a manner that individuals cannot learn plumbing skills unless there is a job opening available. Such a job will not exist unless it can generate enough marginal product to pay the current wage.

Job competition in the American economy

It is beyond the scope of this paper to determine exactly where the American economy falls on the continuum between a wage competition economy and a job competition economy.[6] Seniority provisions, the stability of wages when excess supplies of labor develop, the extent of on-the-job training, the existence of highly structured internal labor markets, the intensity of relative wage bargaining, and a host of other factors would go into such a determination. Readers can judge for themselves exactly where they would place the American economy on such a continuum and whether they think a job competition model can aid in answering the relevant questions and puzzles. In any case there does seem to be a substantial element of job rather than wage competition in the American economy. To the extent that it exists it must be considered in any set of programs to alter the structure of American incomes.

If at the beginning of the postwar period, an observer had been told that the composition of the adult white male labor force was going to change from 47 percent with a grade school education, 38 percent with a high school education, and 15 percent with a college education, to 20 percent with a grade school education, 51 percent with a high school education, and 28 percent with a college education (the actual 1949 to 1969 changes), expectations about the distribution of income would have been very different depending upon whether the observer subscribed to a job competition model or a wage competition model. Assuming for the moment that there were no offsetting changes on the demand side of the market, the observer subscribing to a wage competition model of the world would have predicted a substantial equalization of earnings as the extra supplies of more educated workers drove down their relative wage rate. But what would the observer subscribing to a job competition view of the world have predicted?

According to a job competition model the most preferred group (college laborers) would have experienced an equalization of income within their group, a rise in incomes relative to other groups, but a fall in incomes relative to the national average. As the most preferred group expanded, it would filter down the job distribution into lower paying jobs. This would lead to a fall in wages relative to the national average. As it moved into a denser portion of the national job (income) distribution, it would however, experience within group equalization of income. By taking what had previously been the best high school jobs college incomes would rise relative to high school incomes.

Such a prediction would have been correct. The proportion of college incomes going to the poorest 25 percent of white male college laborers rose from 6.3 percent to 9.0 percent from 1949 to 1969 while the proportion going to the richest 25 percent fell from 53.9 percent to 46.0 percent. While the median income of college laborers was rising from 198 percent to 254 percent of the incomes of grade school laborers and from 124 percent to 137 percent of high school laborers, it was falling from 148 percent to 144 percent of the national average.

As the least preferred group (grade school laborers) contracted in size, a job competition observer would have expected it to be moving out of the denser regions of the income distribution and to become more and more concentrated in the lower tail of the income distribution. Given the shape of the lower tail of the American income distribution, such a movement would have led to falling relative incomes and increasing income equality.

In fact the incomes of grade school laborers have fallen from 50 percent to 39 percent of college incomes and from 63 percent ot 54 percent of high school incomes. The income going to the poorest 25 percent of all grade school laborers has risen from 2.9 percent to 6.6 percent of the group's total and the income going to the richest 25 percent has fallen from 53.5 percent to 49.4 percent.

Predictions of the position of the middle group (high school laborers) would have depended upon an analysis of the relative densities of the income distribution at the margin with college laborers and grade school laborers. Since the American income distribution is denser on the margin with grade school laborers than on the margin with college laborers, an expansion in the size of the middle group, should have lead to more within group equality, an income rise relative to grade school laborers and an income fall relative to high school laborers.

In fact the proportion of income going to the poorest 25 percent of all high school laborers has risen from 8.2 percent to 10.2 percent while the proportion going to the highest 25 percent has fallen from 46.0 percent to 41.6 percent. High school incomes have risen relative to grade school incomes (from 160 percent to 185 percent) and fallen relative to college (from 81 percent to 73 percent).

Changes in the job distributions for grade school, high school, and college laborers have been quite dramatic in the postwar period. Table 1

Table 1

Distribution of Jobs Over Each Education Class (Adult White Males)
(In percent)

	Elementary (0 to 8 years)		High school		College	
	1950	1970	1950	1970	1950	1970
10 percent best jobs	4.3	1.7	10.5	6.5	28.9	25.6
2d best 10 percent	6.0	3.5	13.2	11.3	16.3	14.7
3d 10 percent	7.6	3.5	13.4	11.3	10.0	14.7
4th 10 percent	7.7	6.2	13.4	12.5	9.9	9.6
5th 10 percent	9.4	6.9	12.1	12.5	6.9	8.8
6th 10 percent	10.7	8.7	10.6	12.4	6.1	7.1
7th 10 percent	11.8	11.3	9.0	11.5	6.0	5.9
8th 10 percent	13.1	15.6	7.0	9.3	6.2	5.0
9th 10 percent	14.8	19.6	5.2	7.1	4.6	4.7
10 percent worst jobs	14.4	23.0	5.6	5.5	5.1	3.8
Total	100.0	100.0	100.0	100.0	100.0	100.0

25

Table 2

Job Probabilities (Adult White Males)
[Figures for: 1950—Money income in 1949, population in 1950; 1970—Money income in 1969, population in 1970]

| Quality of jobs (determined by income of total males with income 25 years and older) | Percent of total people in each job class, in 1950 and 1970, with the following education | | | | | |
| | Elementary | | High school | | College | |
	1950	1970	1950	1970	1950	1970
10 percent best jobs provide incomes of—1950, $5,239.3 and up; 1970, $15,000 and up	21.8	4.8	37.0	30.2	41.0	65.0
2d best 10 percent provide incomes of—1950, $4,028.84 to $5,239.2; 1970, $12,506.26 to $14,999	30.6	9.9	46.4	52.7	23.0	37.3
3d 10 percent—1950, $3,519.7 to $4,028.83; 1970, $10,012.9 to $12,506.25	38.8	9.9	47.0	52.7	14.2	37.3
4th 10 percent—1950, $3,025.2 to $3,519.6; 1970, $8,752 to $10,012.8	39.0	17.4	47.0	58.2	14.0	24.4
5th 10 percent—1950, $2,553.6 to $3,025.1; 1970, $7,573.9 to $8,751	47.8	19.4	42.4	58.3	9.8	22.4
6th 10 percent—1950, $2,101 to $2,553.5; 1970, $6,449.6 to $7,573.8	54.2	24.4	37.1	57.7	8.6	17.9
7th 10 percent—1950, $1,530 to $2,100; 1970, $5,148.3 to $6,449.5	59.9	31.6	31.6	53.5	8.5	14.9
8th 10 percent—1950, $706 to $1,529; 1970, $3,576.6 to $5,148.2	66.7	43.8	24.6	43.5	8.8	12.7
9th 10 percent—1950, $270.6 to $705; 1970, $2,008.2 to $3,576.5	75.3	54.9	18.3	33.2	6.5	11.9
10 percent worst jobs—1950, $0 to $207.5; 1970, $0 to $2,008.1	73.2	64.5	19.6	25.8	7.2	9.7

shows the actual probability distributions for grade school, high school, and college white adult male laborers in 1949 and 1969. In 1949 a grade school laborer had a 4.3 percent chance of obtaining a job that would place him in the top decile of jobs and a 14.4 percent chance of getting a job that would place him in the lowest decile of jobs. By 1970 these probabilities had dropped to 1.7 percent and risen to 23.0 percent. Conversely, the probability of college laborers holding a job in the bottom decile of jobs has fallen from 5.1 percent to 3.8 percent. (The probability of holding a job in the highest decile also fell due to the vast expansion of college laborers.) High school graduates have become similarly disadvantaged. Their probability of holding high income jobs has fallen and their probability of holding low income jobs has risen.

An alternative method for looking at the same changes is to look at the fraction of jobs held by each educational group in each decile of jobs. (See Table 2.) While college laborers held 41 percent of the best jobs in 1950, they held 65 percent of the best jobs in 1970. Conversely, grade school workers saw their percentage of the best jobs drop from 22 percent to 5 percent.

The increasing economic segregation based on education can be seen even more clearly in Table 3, where each cell has been adjusted for changes in the proportions of college, high school, and grade school laborers. (The table is constructed so that each cell would have the number 1 if incomes were randomly drawn with respect to education.) In 1949, a college graduate was 6 times as likely to hold a job in the top decile as a grade school graduate (2.715/0.436), but by 1969 he was 15 times (2.549/0.1714) as likely to hold a job in the top decile. Conversely, the probability of a grade school graduate holding a job in the lowest decile has risen from 3 to 6 times that of college graduates. Similarly college probabilities of holding the best job have risen relative to high school graduates (from 2½ to 4 times those of high school) while high school probabilities of holding the worst jobs have risen (from 1.2 to 1.5 times those of college). Extrapolation of these trends for another 20 years would lead to a world where income was almost perfectly segregated based on education.

Although the job competition model seems to postcast accurately what would have happened to the American distribution of income in the postwar period, postcasting is not completely convincing and there are other explanations for what happened in the postwar period. One explanation would argue that increasing technical progress has simply made education more necessary to acquiring income producing skills. Training costs differentials have risen and this explains the increasing economic segregation based on education. Another explanation would argue that higher education has become more meritocratic in the postwar period (i.e., it is becoming more perfectly correlated with other income producing factors). Thus there is an appearance of more economic segregation based on education. Still another explanation would argue that

Table 3

Normalized Probabilities (Adult White Males)

[Figures for: 1970—Money income in 1949, population in 1950; 1970—Money income in 1969, population in 1970]

Quality of jobs (determined by income of total males with income, 25 years and older)	Percent of total males in each job class, in 1950 and 1970, with the following educational attainment (divided by percent of total males with that educational attainment that year)					
	Elementary		High school		College	
	1950	1970	1950	1970	1950	1970
10 percent best jobs provide incomes of—1950, $5,239.3 and up; 1970, $15,000 and up	0.436	0.1714	1.066	0.648	2.715	2.549
2d best 10 percent provide incomes of—1950, $4,028.84 to $5,239.2; 1970, $12,506.26 to $14,999	.599	.3535	1.337	1.130	1.523	1.468
3d 10 percent—1950, $3,519.7 to $4,028.83; 1970, $10,012.9 to $12,506.25	.772	.3535	1.354	1.130	.940	1.468
4th 10 percent—1950, $3,025.2 to $3,519.6; 1970, $8,752 to $10,012.8	.776	.621	1.354	1.248	.927	.960
5th 10 percent—1950, $2,553.6 to $3,025.1; 1970, $7,573.9 to $8,751	.952	.692	1.221	1.251	.649	.881
6th 10 percent—1950, $2,101 to $2,553.5; 1970, $6,449.6 to $7,573.8	1.079	.871	1.069	1.238	.5695	.704
7th 10 percent—1950, $1,530 to $2,100; 1970, $5,148.3 to $6,449.5	1.193	1.128	.910	1.148	.5629	.586
8th 10 percent—1950, $706 to $1,529; 1970, $3,576.6 to $5,148.2	1.328	1.564	.708	.933	.5827	.500
9th 10 percent—1950, $270.6 to $705; 1970, $2,008.2 to $3,576.5	1.500	1.960	.527	.712	.4304	.468
10 percent worst jobs—1950, $0 to $270.5; 1970, $0 to $2,008.1	1.458	2.303	.564	.552	.4768	.3818

the American economy has become more of a credential society where education is used as a cheap (or defensible) screening device. It is not very closely related to training costs but it is used as a pervasive hiring criterion.

Although it is not possible to disprove the hypothesis that technical progress is changing in a manner so as to offset precisely the impacts of rising and more equal educational distribution, the consistency in the distribution of income, the lack of acceleration in productivity increases, and the filtering of college laborers farther and farther down the income ladder all raise questions about offsetting changes on the demand side of the labor market.

To distinguish among rival explanations it would be necessary to look at training costs to see if training cost differentials have risen over time and to see if training costs are now more highly correlated with education. If they have not risen over time and are not more highly correlated with education, the economy must be becoming more credentially oriented. Alternatively, the wage competition model may be inappropriate. (Analysis of correlations between job performances and education would not provide the necessary evidence since training programs are used to equalize job performances in similar jobs. Training costs differ; but not job performances.) A question then arises as to why artificial credentials should have become more important.

Implications of a job competition view of the economy

If there is a substantial element of job competition rather than wage competition in the economy (as the author believes there is), education's impact on the distribution of income (both its level and shape) cannot be simply determined with rate of return calculations based in normalized income differentials between different levels of education. Although the exact impact of an alteration in the distribution of education can have different impacts on the distribution of income depending upon the factors outlined above, large observed income differentials could persist after the net social productivity of education was reduced to or below zero. An increasing supply of college laborers might lead to college laborers accepting jobs farther down the job opportunities distribution. In the process they would lower average college incomes, but they would also lower average high school incomes. This would preserve the observed wage differential between college and high school labor, but it would not have its neo-classical meaning. A differential would not mean that output was increasing as a result of more education; a differential would not reflect the productivity differential between the marginal college man and the marginal high school man.

As a result there is a need to be much more agnostic about the economic returns to education than current economic analysis would indicate. Education may or may not have the payoffs that are currently predicted. To determine whether it does or does not, a job competition model would lead to the analysis of who bears training costs, the exact movements in the distribution of education, the distribution of training costs across job opportunities, the elasticities of training costs with respect to education, and the other factors outlined above.

If true, the job competition model indicates that most of the current programs to improve the data base for estimating the economic returns to education are misdirected. They are focusing on calculating accurate normalized income differentials when they should be focusing on calculating the impact of education on training costs. Unfortunately, the types of samples and surveys for generating accurate incomes differentials are completely inappropriate for generating accurate data on the impact of education on on-the-job training costs. At the moment data on training costs by education class is almost completely nonexistent. Such data should be a key goal in the design of future expenditures to improve our knowledge of the market for educated labor.

If true, the job competition model indicates that education may become a defensive necessity to private individuals even if there are no net social returns to education. As the supply of educated labor increases, individuals find that they must improve their education simply to defend their current income position. If they don't, others will and they will not find their current job open to them. Education becomes a good investment, not because it would raise an individual's income above what it would have been if no one had increased their education, but because it raises their income above what it will be if others acquire an education and they do not. In effect education becomes a defensive expenditure necessary to protect one's "market share." The larger the class of educated labor and the more rapidly it grows, the more such defensive expenditures become imperative. Interestingly many students currently object to the defensive aspects of acquiring a college education.

Education may, however, have a payoff in terms of economic mobility even if it does not have a payoff in terms of increasing incomes or equalizing the distribution of income. If incomes are randomly assigned once an individual enters an educational class (acquires a particular background characteristic), increasing college laborers (particularly minority group college laborers) may be a powerful device for increasing economic mobility or equalizing the distributions of white and black incomes.

Both the postwar experience with impacts of education on incomes and the extent of job competition in the American economy lead to substantial doubts about the feasibility of altering the structure of American incomes with government programs that are exclusively focused on the supply side of the labor market. Background characteristics can be altered without altering the structure of incomes. Given the on-the-job nature of most skill acquisitions it is very difficult to design government training programs for altering the skills actually used. Even if skills can be taught in formal training programs, workers find that labor markets are not able to absorb them since normal entry jobs are not skilled jobs. Supply side programs may be necessary in any general program for altering the structure of American incomes, but they must be combined with programs to alter the structure of labor demands.

Notes

1. U.S. Department of Labor, *Formal Occupational Training of Adult Workers*, Manpower Automation Research Monograph #2, 1964, pp. 3, 18, 20 and 43.
2. General skills are skills that are useful to more than one firm (i.e., they can be sold in the market), while specific skills are useful to one and only one firm (i.e., they cannot be sold in the market).
3. The equilibrium wage rate for trainable labor can easily exceed that for untrained labor, yet workers may still be paying for training since the equilibrium wage rate is below the marginal productivity of the jobs that they hold.
4. To understand the labor queue it is helpful to view the market for labor from a probability perspective. Positions in the labor queue are distributed in a lottery, but it is a lottery with conditional probabilities. For each group of background characteristics there is some associated probability distribution that determines the position into which each individual falls. (See equation 1.) If the sets of background characteristics were ranked from the most preferred to the least preferred, the expected value of each group's position will fall in the same rank order as that of the background characteristics. (See equations 2 and 3.)

$$(1) \qquad \sum_{i=1}^{n} P_j(X_i/B_j)=1 \qquad j=1, 2, \ldots m$$

where X_i=the ith rank order where there are n possible ranks
B_j=the jth set of background characteristics where there are m sets of background characteristics.

$$(2) \qquad \sum_{i=1}^{n}[P_j(X_i/B_j)]X_i=E(X_{B_j})$$

and

$$(3) \qquad \sum_{i=1}^{n}[[P_1(X_i/B_1)]X_i]> \sum_{i=1}^{n}[[P_2(X_i/B_2)]X_i]> \ldots > \sum_{i=1}^{n}[[P_m(X_i/B_m)]X_i]$$

or

$$E(B_1)>E(B_2)> \ldots >E(B_m)$$

where $E(X_{B_j})$=expected value of position of individuals with the B_jth background characteristics.

5. Although direct wage and job competition may not be pervasive, strong indirect wage and job competition can occur in the external labor markets if final demands are marked by high price elasticities. If an industry or firm gets its average wages out of line, consumers force them back into line by shifting to alternative goods and services. The only comprehensive study of price elasticities by Houthakker and Taylor found that out

of 82 exhaustive consumption categories 54 had price elasticities that were not significantly different from zero, 9 had price elasticities between zero and 1, 8 had price elasticities between 1 and 2, and 11 had price elasticities in excess of 2. Thus there is some scope for indirect wage and job competition in the external labor market, but it is limited. In many areas it does not seem to exist. H. S. Houthakker and Lester D. Taylor, *Consumer Demand in the United States* (Cambridge, Mass.: Harvard University Press, 1970).

6. All of the data in this section including that used as a source for the tables comes from the U.S. Bureau of the Census, *Current Population Reports: Consumer Income: Income in 1969*, Page 101 and U.S. Bureau of Census, *U.S. Census of Population: 1950*, PE-No. 5B, GPO, Washington, 1953, pp. 5B-108.

The Labor Market in Post-Keynesian Theory

3

BY EILEEN APPELBAUM

THE LABOR ASPECTS OF post-Keynesian theory have yet to be systematically developed. Still, as this article will attempt to show, it is possible to combine some widely agreed-upon tenets of post-Keynesian thought, such as the importance of the oligopoly sector, the nature of technology in industrialized countries, and the process of price formation by firms, with the work that has been done by American institutional economists, particularly with regard to segmented labor markets. The result of this synthesis is a fairly comprehensive analysis of the labor market that largely follows Keynes in its approach to the demand for labor, and the segmented labor market theorists in its approach to the supply of labor. A post-Keynesian analysis of this sort leads to a conclusion radically different from the orthodox, neoclassical theory. This is that neither the demand for labor nor the supply of labor depends on the real wage. It follows from this that the labor market is not a true market, for the price associated with it, the wage rate, is incapable of performing any market-clearing function, and thus variations in the wage rate cannot eliminate unemployment.

The orthodox theory of wage determination and unemployment

The conventional analysis of the demand for labor by the firm proceeds on the basis of three fundamental assumptions. The first is that firms always act to maximize profits, even in the short run. The second is that firms are able to combine labor and capital in any proportion whatever, and that firms can alter the capital-labor mix every time the relative price of capital and labor changes. Finally, it is assumed that firms are price-takers in the market for labor and other factors of production, and that therefore they view wage rates as given. Under these circumstances it follows that the demand for labor by the firm is given by the familiar rule, "hire labor up to

From *Challenge*, January-February 1979, pp. 39-47. © 1979 by M. E. Sharpe, Inc.

the point at which the value of the output produced by the last worker employed just equals the money wage which he or she must be paid." The firm's demand for labor thus depends on the contribution to production of the last worker hired (reflecting the marginal product of labor); on the price which the firm receives for its output; and on the money wage which it must pay. Ignoring the aggregation problems involved in generalizing from the individual firm to the entire economy, orthodox theory utilizes the same method of analysis to derive the economy-wide demand for labor, which is viewed as varying inversely with the ratio of the money wage rate to the price level—that is, with real wages.

The conventional analysis of labor supply is based on the following assumptions: that work represents a sacrifice for which the worker must be compensated; that the individual's (or, in some formulations, the household's) well-being is related to the hours of leisure and to the purchasing power of income; and that each worker (or household) is attempting to maximize his, her (or its) well-being. Given their initial endowments of wealth, the money wage rates which they can command, and the price level, it is argued, workers will find that some combinations of leisure time and purchasing power will be attainable while others will not. Each worker will then choose to supply that number of hours of labor which maximizes his or her well-being. The individual's labor supply decision thus depends on money wages and the price level. If workers immediately calculate the full effect of price level changes on purchasing power, then the hours of labor supplied by the individual will be an increasing function of the ratio of the money wage rate to the price level (that is, of real wages). The aggregate quantity of labor supplied can then be obtained by adding up the individual supply curves, and it is positively related to the real wage rate.

Having thus derived both aggregate labor demand and labor supply as functions of the real wage rate, the standard macroeconomic analysis of employment proceeds to demonstrate that, in the absence of rigid money wages, supply and demand in the labor market would simultaneously determine real wages and the level of employment. It is convenient in arguing the point to begin with the commodity, money, and labor markets in balance and then consider the effects of a decline in autonomous spending. Immediately following the decline in spending, the amount of output sold in markets will be less than the full-employment level of output that firms have been producing. Initially, however, firms do not know this and continue to produce the full-employment level of output. With the supply of output greater than the demand, prices will, so the traditional argument goes, fall. With money wages unchanged, the real wage will rise. As a result, the demand for labor will fall while the supply of labor increases. If money wages were flexible downward, this excess of supply over demand would cause money wages to fall. The decline in prices and money wages would, in turn, reduce the demand for money. Needing less money for day-to-day transactions, households and firms would try to buy bonds, thus bidding up bond prices and forcing down interest rates. Lower interest rates would encourage an increase in investment spending, and output and employment would both rise. Ultimately, equilibrium would be restored in the vicinity of the full-employment level of output, with prices, money wages, and interest rates lower, and real wages virtually unaffected. The problem, as it is usually presented, is that money wages are not flexible downward, and thus involuntary unemployment must ensue.

The conclusion that some level of involuntary unemployment will have to be tolerated follows immediately from the "neoclassical synthesis" of Keynesian and pre-Keynesian arguments. If the money wage rate were flexible, this analysis suggests, real wage rates could adjust and would serve to equate the supply of and demand for labor. That is, flexible wages would act as a market clearing mechanism capable of eliminating excess supply or demand in the labor market. Market forces alone would tend to reestablish full employment; government policies to reduce involuntary unemployment would be unnecessary. However, with money wages rigid, even orthodox economists embrace the Keynesian view that government intervention in the economy is needed to offset any decline in autonomous spending and restore full employment. Fiscal policies to increase aggregate demand directly and monetary policies to reduce the rate of interest and thereby increase investment will, even according to orthodox analysis, reduce unemployment. Unfortunately, according to the orthodox economists, Keynesian economics is "depression economics"—Keynesian solutions can be safely utilized only during major recessions or depressions. At other times, policies that increase aggregate demand and reduce unemployment will raise the demand for labor, thereby driving up the money wage rate (which, according to the orthodox view, is determined in the labor market by supply and demand) and generating inflation. The result is a Phillips curve trade-off between unemployment and inflation. Thus orthodox economics suggests that some unemployment must be tolerated in order to keep inflation within reasonable bounds.

The post-Keynesian critique

As Sidney Weintraub observed, "Keynes' entire intellectual commitment was to use reason to eradicate economic ailments rather than to 'trade-off' one ill for another." Based on this heritage, post-Keynesian economists reject the view that the goals of stable prices and full employment are irreconcilable. As we have seen, orthodox economists view rigid money wages as the major cause of unemployment. They argue that if money wages would decline whenever aggregate demand fell, real wages would also be reduced, and the volume of employment would increase. Furthermore, orthodox economists contend that real wages must be increased in order to entice more people to work. Since they believe that bargaining over money wages determines real wages, they argue that firms that wish to hire more workers will have to pay higher money wages. Any increase in the demand for labor will, in their view, result in rising money wages. It is this argument that leads orthodox economists to the conclusion that price stability and low unemployment cannot be achieved simultaneously. Post-Keynesian economists, however, reject this theory of wage determination.

The arguments of modern-day orthodoxy were answered long ago by Keynes. Keynes objected to the twin ideas, (1) that real wages depend on the money wage bargain reached between workers and firms, and (2) that labor can reduce its real wage and increase the volume of employment by accepting a lower money wage. Even if the general tenor of orthodox theory were accepted, Keynes pointed out, these two propositions would not follow. A reduction in the general level of money wages, after all, will reduce marginal cost. At the going market prices for outputs, therefore, each firm will want to produce more. As the supply of products of all kinds increases, the orthodox view teaches that the general level of prices will fall. With both money wages and prices falling, the effects on the real wage are likely to be small. Even in the context of orthodox economic models, therefore, changes in money wages are not likely to be effective in altering real wages.

Keynes himself argued that in the short period money wages and real wages are subject to separate influences, and may even move in opposite directions. Post-Keynesians have argued that money wages depend largely on the respective bargaining power of business and labor, and on the normative factors reflected in what Eichner has termed the incremental wage pattern, or key wage bargain. Commodity prices, meanwhile, depend on the market power of firms and their need for internal funds to finance investment. Eichner and Kregel have argued that if investment is increasing, so that there is a greater need for internal funds, while at the same time firms are optimistic about their ability to maintain a higher margin above costs, prices will rise relative to money wages and the real wage will be depressed. The real wage, thus, depends on the rate of investment and the pace of economic growth. A reduction in money wages would, in general, not be effective in increasing employment, since money wages and real wages need not move in the same direction. Depending on the extent to which prices also fell, real wages might rise, fall, or remain unchanged. Moreover, a decline in money wages relative to prices would tend to reduce consumption demand and hence employment; while a decline in both money wages and prices would tend to undermine business confidence and reduce investment demand and employment. Post-Keynesians conclude that rigid money wages are not the cause of involuntary unemployment. Indeed, flexible money wages would subject firms to increased uncertainty and make planning more difficult without having much of an effect on either employment or real wages.

Keynes, in replying to the argument that an increase in the demand for labor can only be met through an increase in money and real wage rates, noted that in general the volume of labor forthcoming at a given money wage depends on the availability of jobs. Furthermore, he observed, in the real world the supply of labor does not necessarily vary with changes in the real wage for, after all, labor is not in a position to withdraw its services with every increase in the price level, even though its real wage has been reduced. Keynes also noted that there have been wide variations in the level of employment without any apparent change in either the real wage or the productivity of labor. These real world outcomes are inconsistent with the argument that the demand for and supply of labor are functions of the real wage, and appear to contradict orthodox economic theory. Post-Keynesians, accordingly, have developed alternative theories of labor demand and labor supply.

Production and the demand for labor

The post-Keynesian argument relating the demand for labor to production has three components: the first conceptualizes the institutional nature of the business sector; the second characterizes the prevailing technology; while the third describes the pricing decisions of firms with market power. The demand for labor can then be related to the level of output that firms plan to produce without reference to marginal productivity theory.

The simplest assumption about the industrial structure of the United States that is reasonably close to reality is Galbraith's view that there exists a dual economy. That is, the American economy may be viewed as consisting of (1) core industries characterized by oligopolistic market structures; high capital-to-labor ratios; the use of sophisticated technology; substantial training costs for skilled, supervisory, and technical workers; high wages; the need for a literate and stable labor force; and the presence of strong trade union organizations, and (2) a periphery in which industries are characterized by their lack of market power; archaic management techniques; low capital requirements; low skill requirements; low wages, seasonal employment and/or an unstable work force; and little or no labor organization. Firms in the core are more likely to belong to industries in which concentration is extensive and, as a result, are more likely to have some control over output prices than are firms on the periphery. Prices set by firms in the core are sufficiently high to permit the replacement of used-up capital and the internal financing of a major part of any planned expansion, the payment of wages to workers that include a share of the social surplus, and the realization of a rate of profit that is higher than the average rate prevailing in the economy. Prices of commodities produced in the periphery tend to be depressed below their "normal" level. Firms can only keep prices down, however, by not replacing used-up capital, by paying workers lower wages, and/or accepting a lower rate of profit. Thus we observe in the nonoligopolistic industries numerous workers who, despite the fact that they work full time, must receive welfare payments in order to subsist. At the same time, the rate of profit on capital employed is typically below average and the existence of firms in this category often is most precarious.

Firms on the periphery do not compete for workers of a given quality on an equal basis with the oligopolistic firms in the core. In addition to higher wage rates, firms in the oligopolistic sector are able to offer workers better fringe benefits, greater job security, more opportunities for advancement and the protections which trade union organization affords. As a result, oligopolistic firms have a relatively permanent labor force attached to them. Workers laid off by such firms may seek interim employment elsewhere, but if production returns to its original level at the plant to which they are attached, they will return to the job they held there. For similar reasons, in periods of rapid growth, the oligopolistic sector is able to attract workers from the nonoligopolistic sector as it needs them.

Based on the assumption that factor inputs can be combined in any proportion, the conventional theory of the firm holds that output can be expanded only by combining increasing quantities of the variable inputs (labor and raw materials) with a fixed input (usually the capital stock but sometimes management skills). As production increases, the firm experiences first increasing and then decreasing output per unit of input, so that variable and marginal cost curves eventually increase with the rise in output. Rising marginal cost both limits the expansion of output by each firm (since no firm will produce an output for which marginal cost exceeds marginal revenue) and necessitates price increases as production expands. Price changes, according to this model, result largely from changes in demand.

Despite the widespread use of this model, it is applicable mainly to firms engaged in the production of raw materials and foodstuffs. In other enterprises, even in the short run, output can often be increased by adding a second shift of workers. Full utilization of capacity is more often the exception than the rule; and output is increased or decreased by varying the degree to which the inputs—both "fixed" and "variable"—are utilized, without any significant change in the proportions in which capital equipment and the "variable" inputs are combined. Indeed, a great deal of production takes place within firms characterized by fixed factor, or technical, coefficients that are not subject to change in the short run. Thus, over a broad range of output levels, average variable and marginal costs are constant, increasing only when full capacity utilization is approached.

In the short run, then, most firms can meet an increase in the demand for their product simply by increasing output at the prevailing cost level. The supply of output is elastic as a result of existing reserves of productive capacity, and "supply curves" are therefore horizontal. Prices cannot be determined in the usual manner, nor can firms maximize short-run profits by producing the level of output for which the marginal revenue to be earned is equal to the marginal cost. Decisions with respect to price and output must be arrived at in some other manner.

Modern versions of the mark-up pricing model used by Weintraub, Eichner, and others owe much to the work of the Polish economist Michal Kalecki. In these models, average variable cost is constant, but average fixed cost decreases as production increases and overhead costs are spread over a greater volume of output. In setting price, therefore, firms must calculate average fixed and total cost per unit of output in advance, based on their estimates of the output that will be sold in the next period, or on some standard rate of plant utilization. Prices are usually established by adding to average variable cost a gross margin calculated to yield a target net profit should the firm actually sell the anticipated volume of output.

Variations in output, if they are moderate, leave price unchanged but do affect net profits. If the actual output sold is less than the estimated output, unit fixed costs will be higher than anticipated and net profits *ex post* will be less than the targeted amount. The reverse will occur if the output sold exceeds anticipated sales and the plant is operated more intensively than expected. While moderate changes in demand do not affect price, changes in money wage rates or in the prices of raw materials will generally cause prices to vary. Where a number of firms are engaged in producing for the same market, self-interest on the part of the firms commonly leads to the emergence of a price leader who effectively sets the market price of the product. This price will enable the leader to achieve its targeted profit when operating as anticipated, but other firms (which may be smaller or less efficient) may have higher costs and hence lower net profits.

Once prices have been established, the level of output which the firm produces in the short run is determined by the demand curve for the firm's output. Firms declare their price and they produce the output they believe the market will take. Firms motivated *not* by the goal of short-run profit maximization but by the wish to maintain or increase market share in a growing economy are likely to increase output rather than price when demand increases moderately or excess capacity is available. Of course, a large increase in anticipated sales for the products of a particular industry may generate a demand by firms for increased productive capacity. Firms in such industries may require more internally generated funds with which to finance investment, and may obtain such funds by increasing the margin above costs and setting a higher price. Thus a sustained increase in demand for an industry's output that is large enough to motivate firms to increase investment will eventually result in higher margins, if not higher prices. However, the usual marginal cost considerations do not enter here at all, and price does *not* vary with demand in a straightforward manner.

The various strands of the argument can be drawn together to explain the demand for labor. As part of the planning process, firms estimate expected GNP and project the corresponding level of anticipated industry-wide sales for the products they produce. Given the share of the market which it expects to command, each firm then estimates the level of output which it expects to sell during the period for which plans are being made. Prices are set by means of a mark-up over average variable costs that will cover fixed costs at the planned output and will yield a targeted profit if that output is sold. Fixed technical coefficients in production imply that the demand for production workers by firms in the core, if not the periphery, of the economy varies directly with the level of output that the firm plans to produce, assuming there is excess capacity available so that the firm is on the horizontal segment of its cost and supply curves. Managerial personnel and highly skilled technical and professional workers employed by firms in the core are usually viewed as quasi-fixed factors of production. Employment of these workers does not vary directly with the output the firm plans to produce. Instead, the firm requires some fixed number of overhead employees in order to operate each of its plants or plant segments. Utilizing a given plant or plant segment more or less intensively does not alter the number of such workers required by the firm. As production expands, however, so that additional plants are brought into operation, the demand for overhead workers will increase by discrete amounts. The aggregate demand for labor by the business sector can be obtained by summing up the demand by all individual firms, and it depends in a systematic manner on the expected aggregate demand for output.

Labor supply and underemployment

While much of the work that is performed in this society can be characterized as alienating or lacking in intrinsic rewards, the traditional analysis of the decision to supply labor ignores major dimensions of the labor supply process and yields conclusions that are at variance with observed reality. It is a somewhat distorted perspective which views the individual or household as weighing the disutility from additional work against the utility obtainable from the additional income thus earned, and offering fewer hours of labor or dropping out of the labor force entirely if real wages fall.

Eli Ginzberg has argued that work provides the individual with three essential kinds of satisfaction. First, whatever the level of real wages, employment of at least one family member is for most households the only available means of obtaining sufficient income to meet family needs. Necessity and the lack of workable alternatives compel households to continue to supply labor even in the face of a decline in real hourly earnings. Welfare payments, paid enrollment in manpower training programs, and the possibility of obtaining income via quasi-legal hustles or criminal activities do provide alternative sources of remuneration but, as

Bennett Harrison has argued, these are meaningful alternatives to paid work for only the most poorly paid workers. There is substantial mobility even then between the welfare rolls and low-wage employment. Secondly, employment provides the individual with purposeful activity and has a major impact on the individual's feelings of self-worth. Finally, though not all jobs give the individual a chance for development and training, employment nevertheless provides many individuals who are out of school with opportunities to utilize existing skills and develop new ones. Employment is important, therefore, for the income which the individual receives, for the contribution it makes to the individual's self-respect, and for its impact on the skill acquisition process. Very few households can afford to supply less labor as real wages decline; and an excess supply of labor cannot be eliminated in this manner.

The post-Keynesian analysis of unemployment draws heavily on the analyses of segmented labor markets advanced by radical economists like David Gordon, Michael Reich, and Richard Edwards, the analysis of internal labor markets by Peter Doeringer and Michael Piore, and the job competition model advanced by Lester Thurow.

The labor market, in which workers compete for the available jobs, is segmented into submarkets characterized by differences in wages, working conditions, and opportunities for advancement. To a large extent, labor market segmentation arose as part of the historical process which led to the development of technologically advanced, oligopolistic firms in industries at the core of the economy and smaller firms lacking technological sophistication on the periphery. The production processes of firms at the core have become increasingly complex, hierarchical, and interdependent. In this context many specific skills that workers need can only be learned through continuous tenure on a particular job or with a particular firm. Firms utilizing modern technologies thus have an incentive to encourage stable work histories for workers in jobs in which productivity is related to tenure both through adjustments in working conditions and monetary rewards and through a system of promotions to higher status jobs. Career ladders serve both to stratify workers and to keep them attached to the same firm for longer periods of time. It has thus become increasingly important for firms at the core to create differentiated job categories, whether they are required by technological change or not.

Encouraging stability on the part of the work force is costly to firms. Even firms at the core, therefore, have an incentive to restrict those extra expenses to as narrow a range of jobs as possible. Thus it is not surprising that even technologically advanced firms have created highly stratified internal job clusters with different entry requirements, with some strategic work sectors organized to encourage job stability and others to permit highly unstable work behavior. The labor market is, thus, segmented into a primary sector in which stable work habits are rewarded and a secondary sector in which turnover is high and stability is not required and often discouraged. Unemployment is concentrated among secondary sector workers and is related to the characteristics of their jobs rather than to wage rates.

Because testing new employees to determine potential job stability is difficult, employers have used superficial characteristics as an inexpensive screening device. They have tended, when filling the better jobs in which stability is important, to discriminate against those groups—blacks, women, teenagers—that historically have had unstable work patterns. Discrimination has set in motion a vicious cycle that guarantees that members of these groups will continue to experience high unemployment. Getting into the "right" job cluster has a critical effect on the training and advancement opportunities a worker receives. To the extent that skills must be obtained within the context of a specific job, discrimination against women, and against blacks and other minorities, restricts many of them to the lower strata of the labor market, denies them access to opportunities for job mobility and training, and confines them to the low end of both the skill and labor income distributions. The interaction between the characteristics of jobs in the secondary sector and the attitudes toward employment of workers with limited prospects has generated a high incidence of unemployment for women, as well as for blacks and other minorities.

Sex and ethnicity are not the only screening devices used to regulate entrance into the various segments of the labor market. Differences in class background and unequal access to educational institutions also function to limit entrance into jobs in the higher strata within the primary sector. Credentials requirements for those who are hired, together with subsequent promotions along an internal job ladder, serve both to shelter workers in the primary sector from the competition of other members of the labor force and to insulate the firm's wage structure from market forces. How rapidly workers are able to advance along their career ladders and how easily new graduates with the proper degrees and background will be absorbed into the primary sector depends on how rapidly the economy is expanding. Should the supply of highly trained and/or highly educated labor exceed the demand for such workers, it is not wage deflation but credentials inflation that will bring the supply of workers competing for jobs in the upper strata of the primary sector into line with existing job openings. Rising educational requirements for entrance into these jobs during periods of slow economic growth have the effect of thwarting the career aspirations of recent college and university graduates, who are bumped down into lower strata jobs in the primary sector and find few opportunities for advancement. Disappointment rather than unemployment is the price these workers pay.

The situation is quite different outside the primary sector of the labor market. With an excess supply of better educated young people, employment requirements for entry into the entire spectrum of jobs rise. Often, the level of certification has little to do with the actual requirements of the job; but certification is widely used by firms as an inexpensive screening device. The children of the poor, high school diplomas in hand, join the ranks of workers constrained by their own need for income and the limited number of primary sector jobs to seek poorly paying, unstable employment in the secondary labor market. Denied access to primary sector jobs, they can anticipate work experience marked by low earnings and a high incidence of unemployment. On the other hand, firms both on the periphery and at the core have available all the relatively unskilled manpower they need at the prevailing, low wage rate. No further reduction in wage rates is likely to reduce unemployment rates for workers in the secondary sector.

Summary

The labor market is not a "market" as that term is usually understood, for the labor market does not possess a market-clearing price mechanism. Variations in either money wages or in the real wage rate are unable to assure a zero surplus supply of labor, and thus eliminate unemployment. In the context of (1) an industrial structure that is largely oligopolistic, (2) fixed technical coefficients in production, and (3) mark-up pricing, the demand for labor depends on the level of aggregate economic activity. It has little, if anything, to do with the marginal product of labor. The supply of labor, meanwhile, depends largely on demographic and other sociocultural factors, though it is somewhat responsive to changes in employment opportunities. When aggregate demand falls below the potential output of the economy and unemployment increases, the personal qualifications required for entry into or advancement to a job in a given stratum of the labor market increase; and the educational gains of women, blacks, and others are devalued in the ensuing credentials inflation. The result is a queue of those awaiting access to the better jobs, or even to any job at all, that cannot be eliminated by a decline in real wages.

Conversely, while the demand for labor relative to the supply of labor plays a major role in establishing the level of money wages by strengthening or weakening labor's bargaining position, the growth of output and the solidarity of the trade union movement have an even larger impact. Of greater importance than the level of money wages, however, is the level of real wages. This, moreover, depends not only on money wages but on prices as well. When money wages increase faster than productivity, prices need to rise in order for the firm's margin above average variable costs to cover fixed costs and continue yielding targeted net profits. In periods of economic growth, if the margin above average variable costs rises as firms try to generate increased internal funds with which to finance investment, prices will rise relative to money wages. The growth of real wages may therefore be depressed below the growth in the average productivity of labor despite substantial gains in money wages. Thus, while conditions of slackness or tightness in the labor market play a role, neither money nor real wages can be said to be uniquely determined by the demand for and supply of labor.

Policy implications

The burden of the post-Keynesian argument is that wage determination and unemployment are two distinct processes and must be understood as such, and that wage rates do not serve, in most contexts, to equate the supply of labor with the demand for it. Thus, the labor market has no market-clearing mechanism—from which it follows that adjustments in wage rates cannot eliminate unemployment. The volume of employment depends on aggregate demand factors, not on wage rates. Techniques for regulating aggregate demand through government monetary and fiscal policies have been known at least since the publication of Keynes' *General Theory* in 1936. Reluctance to reduce unemployment through the use of such expansionary policies stems from the misguided view that a Phillips curve trade-off between inflation and unemployment exists. Increasing aggregate demand, it is feared, will lead not only to increases in the volume of employment but to higher money wages and prices as well. The fear of inflation has led public officials to pursue policies whose effect is to curtail the level of economic activity. It would seem that there has been sufficient experience with such policies in the last decade to convince even a skeptical observer that money wages and prices are largely unaffected by reductions in aggregate demand. Restrictive monetary and fiscal policies may keep unemployment high but they are ineffective in combating inflation. The resulting stagflation (high unemployment, high inflation) is an all too familiar outcome.

From the post-Keynesian perspective the primary cause of inflation is not excess demand for goods or labor, but rather the conflict over how the available income and output are to be distributed. Restrictive monetary and fiscal policies, by reducing the volume of income and output, merely heighten the struggle among megacorps, smaller firms, workers, and government over the distribution of income and output. There is clearly a need for public policies to assure that the economy continues to grow and that the national income is distributed in an acceptable manner. Implicit in this is the need for social and economic planning to determine the secular growth rate, to eliminate poverty, to improve the standard of living of workers and others, and to enable investment to take place at the appropriate socially determined rate. The difficult political questions raised by this approach should not be minimized. Safeguards would be required to insure that the development of goals and the implementation of plans would be subject to democratic control and responsive to social needs. Furthermore, such planning would result in socially imposed limits on the megacorporation's ability to determine its own margin above costs and to make investment decisions. But such policies are necessary if economic growth, full employment, and a rising standard of living are not to be sacrificed in the attempt to end inflation by conventional means.

Finally, it must be recognized that whatever the rate of unemployment may be, the burden is not shared equally by all demographic groups. Layoffs and firings are associated primarily with the deadend, low-wage jobs characteristic of the secondary labor market. As a result, blacks, women, and others who are overrepresented in the secondary labor market experience a disproportionate amount of unemployment as well. Ginzberg has calculated that between 1950 and 1976 the number of "poor" jobs increased much more rapidly than the number of "good" jobs: fewer than three out of every ten new jobs created by the private sector during that period were "good" jobs. Public policy to eliminate the poorest jobs and to create enough good jobs to allow for the upward mobility of women and blacks without displacing workers already in better jobs is clearly required. Again, difficult political and social questions are involved, for any substantial reduction in low-wage employment will require fundamental adjustments in consumption and production patterns throughout society.

Is There a Phillips Curve?　4

BY DAVID WHEELER

AMONG THE TWO-DIMENSIONAL diagrams so well known to students of economics, few are more familiar than the Phillips curve. As a descriptive device, this curve is nothing more than an approximation of the observed negative association between the inflation and unemployment rates during part of the postwar period. Association, however, has inexorably become causality in the minds of many Americans, so that low unemployment rates are thought to "produce" high inflation rates automatically.

Although such a notion is highly simplistic, it seems to have captured a powerful hold on public policy discussion in the United States. The consequences for national employment policy are obvious and unfortunate. Because it underlies this perception of a "tragic trade-off" in the economy, the Phillips curve should not be allowed to escape intense critical scrutiny. What sort of reasoning has led economists to impute causality to an observed association? And for that matter, how strongly observable is the association itself?

In thinking about these questions it is useful to understand the somewhat turbulent history of the Phillips curve. Its American genesis seems traceable to the work of two eminent economists in the late 1950s. Professors Paul Samuelson and Robert Solow had become interested in possible links between the movement of "real" variables in the economy (e.g., the unemployment rate, the output of manufacturing industries) and movements of prices. They were particularly interested in the work of A. W. Phillips, a British economist whose published scatter diagram of a century of British inflation and unemployment rates bore a remarkable resemblance to a negatively sloped hyperbola.[1] Samuelson and Solow plotted some equivalent points for the postwar American economy and produced the picture shown in Figure 1.

The negative association between the two rates was obvious (although the imposition of a negatively sloped hyperbola on the scatter undoubtedly required some exercise of the imagination). This initial observation

This paper was originally prepared for the National Committee for Full Employment and is based upon research funded by a grant to the Committee from the Ford Foundation. The views expressed here are those of the author and not necessarily endorsed by the Committee or the Foundation.

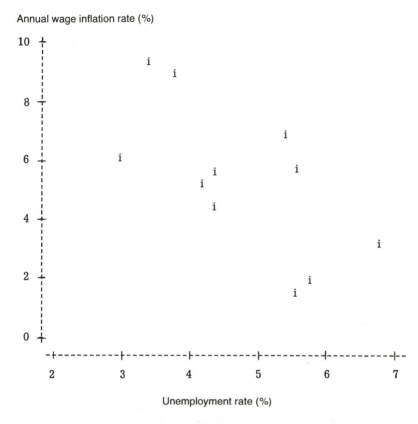

Figure 1

The U.S. Economy, 1948-1959

Annual wage inflation rate (%)

Unemployment rate (%)

inspired a series of articles which identified the inflation-unemployment relation as a crucial point of contact between movements in real variables and prices. In the Democratic Washington of the 1960s, macroeconomic "fine tuners" were quite receptive to this idea. The notion spread that there was in fact a stable inverse relation between unemployment and inflation, and that policy makers were therefore confronted with a "menu" of possible combinations.

Then something (or a series of things) happened to the economy. By 1976 Professor Milton Friedman could denigrate the whole notion of a Phillips curve by referring to another scatter diagram—this time for inflation and unemployment rates during the late 1960s and early 1970s (see Figure 2). Seemingly, the downward sloping hyperbola had been replaced by a cloud with a faint upward tilt. As Professor Friedman was quick to point out, this simple picture suggested that economists should look elsewhere for a satisfactory interpretation of the current inflation.[2] But

47

Figure 2

The U.S. Economy, 1965-1976

Annual wage inflation rate (%)

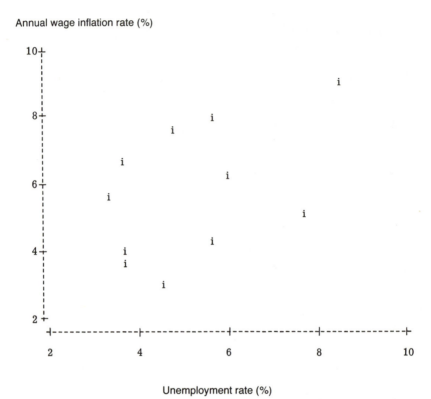

Unemployment rate (%)

Phillips curve advocates proved very reluctant to do so. Before long the believers had counterattacked with the assertion that the curve had simply shifted outward and gotten flatter, presenting policy makers with a much crueler menu in the 1970s (a given unemployment rate was now seemingly associated with a higher inflation rate). In defense of their position they pointed to the obvious dichotomy between points in the 1960s and 1970s (see Figure 3).

Thus was laid the groundwork for a spirited debate whose ultimate resolution has important consequences for the design of federal unemployment policy. The obvious need for careful statistical analysis in this context has prompted my own work on the Phillips curve. My research has focused on proper techniques for statistical estimation of Phillips equation parameters—that is, the numbers that determine the shape and position of the familiar hyperbola. My results seem to have relevance for the current controversy, but a fuller understanding of the argument itself should undoubtedly precede their presentation.

In the argument over the trade-off between inflation and unemployment in the 1970s, the contending factions are motivated by very different views of the American economy. On only one point would everyone agree: that wages are affected by extreme "tightness" or "slackness" in the labor market. In a period of extreme slackness (e.g., the Great Depression) there should be no upward pressure on wages at all, while in a period of extreme tightness a seller's market should ensure that wage demands are sympathetically entertained by business firms.

All the controversy, of course, is about what happens between these two extreme points and whether policy makers really have some choice in the matter. A Phillips advocate would suggest that the appropriate line connecting the extreme points (low employment–high inflation, and conversely) is a hyperbola of relatively smooth curvature. The reason? As the economy moves toward greater tightness in the labor market more skill shortages show up, the position of labor gets stronger, and the consequent wage demands higher. Policy makers are thus presented with a schedule of possible outcomes which depend on the degree of stimulation they choose to undertake.

Figure 3

Hypothetical Phillips Curves in the 1960s and 1970s

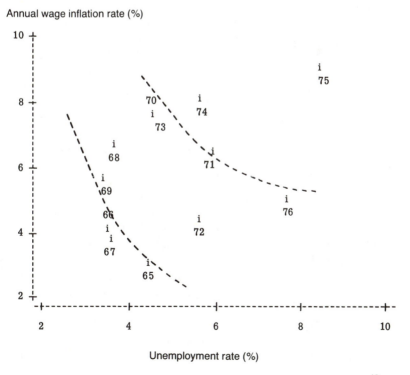

Annual wage inflation rate (%)

Unemployment rate (%)

Two opposing views, however, would deny that such a menu really exists. One view (espoused by Professor Friedman and many others) would argue that at any point in time there is a "natural rate" of unemployment which is dictated by such factors as the rate of capital formation and the demographic composition of the work force. Wage inflation in any given year should reflect two main forces: (1) the growth in labor productivity that workers are able to capture in the competitive bargaining process, and (2) the expected rate of inflation—which is incorporated in wage settlements because workers and owners are smart enough to be interested in purchasing power, not money income. Thus the only possibility for a trade-off between unemployment and inflation, in this view, would stem from a temporary failure by negotiants to predict the rate of inflation correctly. A short-run Phillips curve would be expected to prevail at any point in time, showing the consequences of unanticipated fluctuations in the rate of inflation. For example, if wage increases temporarily lagged behind price increases, the short-term effect might well be a reduction in the unemployment rate as labor seemed to become cheaper in real terms. In any steady inflationary state, however, real wage bargains would be maintained. Thus, in the natural rate view, the only long-run Phillips "relation" is a vertical line, and federal attempts to fine tune must ultimately prove fruitless.

The standard Phillips argument is also attacked from a very different perspective, which might be termed neo-Keynesian. In this view wage hikes can only reflect shifts in productivity, and the tightness or slackness of a competitive labor market should have no effect on wage outcomes in the long run. However, a sudden change in labor market conditions can result in the appearance of an unexpected pattern of excess demands and supplies in the markets for particular skills. If excess supplies do not lower money wages (and is there anyone who will seriously argue that *money* wages aren't sticky downward?) and if excess demands force them up (which is certainly a plausible notion), then inflation in the average wage level will persist as long as the mismatch continues. The labor force, however, is responsive to new opportunities. Given time, people retrain themselves and/or migrate in the search for higher wage-earning opportunities. Thus, inflation may be associated with a rapid *change* in the unemployment rate (since the market will take time to adjust to the new situation), but the *level* of this rate should not have anything to do with the process.

We can now see the width of the chasm between those who do not believe in the Phillips curve. To natural rate advocates the curve is vertical, while to neo-Keynesians it is horizontal! However, this difference should not be exaggerated. Even a neo-Keynesian would have to admit that a natural rate lurks down there somewhere, since it is really not credible to suppose that labor would not profit from a condition of zero unemployment. Thus, the neo-Keynesian Phillips curve is effectively L-shaped.

Now, one might think that such a controversy could be resolved by referring to "the facts." Indeed, all contenders would probably agree to a run-off between contending hypotheses using a multiple regression equation which separated out the independent effects of the unemployment rate, changes in this rate, and the expected rate of price inflation. Hoped for results could be summarized in the following way:

Phillips: A substantial role for the rate of unemployment; possibly some role for changes in that rate; a failure of money wages to fully absorb anticipated price changes.

Neo-Keynesian: An insignificant role for the rate of unemployment; a central role for changes in the rate; indifference with respect to the link between wage adjustments and inflation expectations.

Natural Rate: A substantial role for the rate of unemployment and full absorption of anticipated inflation by wages; indifference with respect to changes in the unemployment rate.

The strategic lines of divergence are clear here. Both Phillips and natural rate advocates would expect a negative association between inflation and unemployment in the short run, although they would differ about the severity of the long-run trade-off. Without *some* measurable short-run association, however, rethinking would clearly be necessary in both camps. The absence of such an association would not be at all troubling to a neo-Keynesian.

With all this in mind, we can easily imagine the rationalizations which the opposing schools would provide for the seemingly positive relationship between inflation and unemployment in the 1970s. Both Phillips and natural rate advocates would claim that the short-run Phillips curve has shifted outward in response to shifts in the demographic composition of the labor force and sluggish capital formation. Neo-Keynesians would assert that the simultaneous shifts of the inflation and unemployment rates have not been directly related at all, so that the best characterization of the relationship continues to be a horizontal line at whatever the current rate of inflation happens to be.

Problems of measurement

Hopefully, this brief summary has communicated the essence of the current dispute over the position and shape of the Phillips curve. From theory and casual observation let us now pass to problems of measurement, which are extremely thorny. The treachery of the path has not, of course discouraged potential entrants. As evidence, I can do no better than quote from the pages of *Fortune* (September 1976):

> It is clear that once the unemployment rate falls below a certain point, it becomes increasingly difficult, if not impossible, to control inflation. But for many years, economists thought that this point was around 4%—a figure that

got to be called the "full employment" rate of unemployment. Now it turns out that 4% is far too low. In fact, it has been too low for the past twenty-eight years.

According to an analysis done by M. I. T.'s Hall,* one of our leading labor-market economists, the sustainable rate of unemployment—the rate below which inflation starts accelerating—was around 5% as far back as 1948 and has gradually risen to between 5.5 and 6% in the last few years. (The rise reflects mainly the increased role in job markets of women and teenagers, who tend to have higher unemployment rates than men.) Calculations made by Franco Modigliani, also of M. I. T., more or less confirm Hall's findings. . . .

Hall calculates that wage inflation increases by about one-half percentage point for each full percentage point that the unemployment rate is held below its natural rate for a year. Suppose, for example, that the unemployment rate were somehow held at 3.5 or 4 percent in 1977-80 . . . . what is really involved in such low unemployment rates is a 12% increase in hourly earnings in 1980. Taking productivity gains into account, that figure means about 9.5% price inflation. . . .

These figures make it clear that unemployment must remain at much higher levels than conventional political rhetoric demands if we are to solve the problem of inflation. There is, however, a silver lining to this cloud. If economists have learned, to their chagrin, that unemployment should remain at about a 5.5 to 6% rate, they have also discovered that such a rate need not betoken great hardship.

This latter discovery is not due to personal experience, we may surmise, since professional economists have generally suffered from unemployment rates not much higher than those experienced by the readers (and editors) of *Fortune*. Are we to infer, then, that the entire economics profession would endorse these numbers as an accurate representation of reality? Obviously, the answer would be an immediate "no" from the neo-Keynesians. How then should we interpret these results?

It is important to realize at the outset that *Fortune*'s numbers are in no sense unique. They have been produced by econometric estimation, a process whose results depend crucially on the model of economic behavior chosen for investigation and the way in which the coefficients (or parameters) of that model are estimated statistically. As we have seen, the basic models of wage inflation posited by Phillips advocates, natural rate theorists, and neo-Keynesians all agree that some role in wage inflation can be played by the rate of unemployment, recent changes in that rate, and the expected rate of price inflation. The disagreement centers on the relative importance of those phenomena, and it is here that the question of statistical estimation becomes crucial.

Unfortunately, statistical methods in this particular context are subject to many pitfalls, and the use of different approaches to estimation can have

---

*The "Hall" in question is Professor Robert Hall, then of M.I.T. Professor Hall would undoubtedly regard *Fortune*'s treatment of his work as somewhat simplistic.

a drastic impact on the results. My own research suggests that this is precisely what has happened in the case of the Phillips curve. Much of the statistical work from which Phillips advocates have drawn their evidence has incorporated fundamental methodological errors. The result has been the assignment of illusory importance to the unemployment rate as a determinant of wage inflation.

Two particular problems have not been taken into account in much of the empirical work on wage inflation. First, while current price inflation certainly affects wage inflation through its impact on the expectations of labor and management, current wage inflation also affects current price inflation (over half the prices in the economy, after all, are wages). Econometricians call this "the simultaneity problem," because any equation which posits price inflation as one cause of wage inflation must have as an inevitable simultaneous counterpart an equation which identifies wage inflation as one cause of price inflation. To estimate a wage equation which pretends that the direction of causation is only from prices to wages is to engage in an ill-disguised sleight-of-hand. Since simple statistical estimation techniques are not designed to compensate for this phenomenon, they are quite likely to perpetuate the illusion. The resulting estimates of coefficient values can be very different from those which truly characterize the process being modeled.

A second problem which is inevitably encountered in this kind of work centers on the fact that the current rate of wage inflation is in part determined by its own past values. The logic of this assertion is quite easy to trace. It is reasonable to suppose that the role of the current inflation rate in determining expectations must be complemented by some role for inflation rates in the immediate past. But these rates are themselves significantly affected by past rates of wage inflation. Thus, the linkage: Past wage inflation generates past price inflation, which in turn contributes to the formation of present price expectations and the present rate of wage inflation.

A truly simultaneous model of price and wage determination must therefore incorporate (either explicitly or implicitly) the effects of past wage inflation on the current rate. This dependency is called "lagged endogeneity," since it concerns an endogenous variable (i.e., a variable whose behavior the model purports to explain) which is affected by its own past (or "lagged") values. Although lagged endogeneity seems innocent enough on the face of it, it creates additional technical problems which simple statistical estimation techniques were never designed to overcome. Again, the result of ignoring the problem can be coefficient estimates that are illusory.

Imagine the possibilities, then, when the coefficients of a wage inflation equation are estimated in a way which takes neither simultaneity nor lagged endogeneity into account. The "Phillips curve" that emerges from the results may be well be entirely illusory. Unfortunately, much of the work in the 1960s which led to the original belief in the Phillips curve did in fact ignore both problems. While simultaneity has frequently been taken into account in the 1970s, the problem of lagged endogeneity has continued to receive little attention. As a consequence, much of the evidence on which current Phillips advocates base their arguments is also untrustworthy. In interpreting reported results, it is extremely important to know whether the underlying statistical estimation procedure has been designed to compensate for both simultaneity and lagged endogeneity.

It is in this context that my own work becomes relevant, since I have used a fully compensatory technique developed by Professor Ray Fair of Princeton University to estimate the coefficients of a simultaneous model of wage and price inflation.[3] My results show a negligible role for the unemployment rate in determining the rate of wage inflation in recent years.

For purposes of illustration it may be useful to look at a graphical presentation of my results, which contrast strongly with those obtained when both simultaneity and lagged endogeneity are ignored in estimation. The curves in Figure 4 represent the application of a completely uncorrected estimation procedure to quarterly U.S. data for the period since the

Figure 4

Phillips Curves—Incorrectly Estimated Model

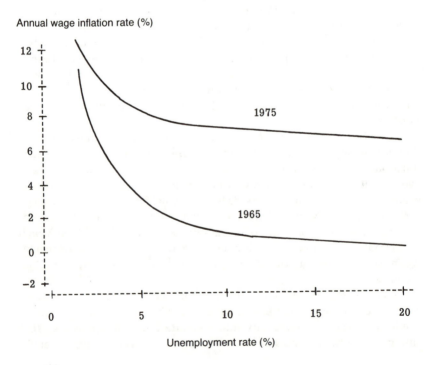

Annual wage inflation rate (%)

Unemployment rate (%)

Figure 5

Phillips Curves—Correctly Estimated Model

Annual wage inflation rate (%)

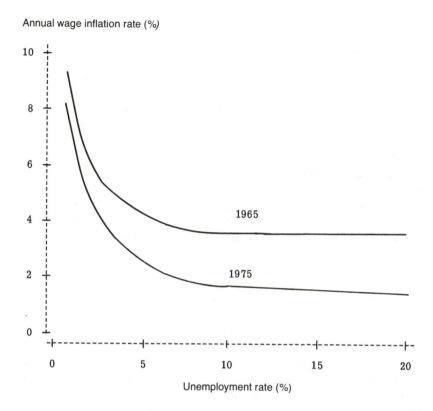

Unemployment rate (%)

Korean War. The result is an estimated Phillips curve for 1975 which is apparently much higher than that for 1965. The picture suggests, for example, that a 4% unemployment rate could be "bought" for about 4.7% in annual wage inflation in 1965, while the cost of the same unemployment rate had risen to 9.2% annual wage inflation by 1975. Here we seem to see substantial evidence for the crueler trade-off which has been so much with us in the press during recent years.

At this point, it is important to stop and recall the argument on which we have been dwelling. While the graphs in Figure 4 have a reassuringly scientific air about them, they represent econometric results that are essentially worthless. In the absence of any correction for the major estimation problems, they have no claim whatsoever to credibility.

This assertion is brought home forcefully when Figure 4 is contrasted with the picture produced by an application of the Fair technique to a simultaneous model of wage and price inflation. The results from the correctly estimated model are presented in Figure 5, and they could hardly be more different from their predecessors. In 1965, according to the corrected estimates, a 4% unemployment rate could be bought for 4.5% annual wage inflation. By 1975, things had apparently improved to the point where the same unemployment rate could be purchased for an annual inflation rate of 2.6%!

At first glance even these corrected results must seem suspect, since the current rate of unemployment is around 6% and the current annual rate of wage inflation is around 10%. Again, the curve itself can only be understood once it is recalled that it represents that part of wage inflation which can be traced to the strength of demand in the labor market. A concurrently high rate of inflation from other sources is perfectly possible, with a resulting sizable increment to the total observed rate of wage inflation from the impact on inflationary expectations. For our purposes, the important question here is whether the unemployment rate *itself* has had any measurable consequences for inflation in recent years. The answer given by the correctly estimated wage equation is "very little or none." This conclusion is reinforced by the fact that the parameter of the correctly estimated Phillips equation cannot even be distinguished from zero ("no effect") at any reasonable level of statistical confidence.

Thus, my work suggests that fears about a "crueler" inflation-unemployment trade-off have been misplaced, and that the two have recently had little or nothing to do with each other over the range of unemployment rates that are relevant for policy (down to, say, 3%). The results are certainly more comfortable for neo-Keynesians than for their opponents.

The reader must be wondering at this point whether my results are the last word on this subject. The answer, of course, is "no." I have corrected for two important estimation problems, but there are inevitably others. I think that my results are more defensible than most, but caution in interpretation (and policy prescription!) is always necessary in this domain. The final evidence is not likely to be in for some time. Meanwhile, we can be sure that the Phillips curve will continue to shift around in the newspapers as ideologically motivated shoppers pick and choose among available offerings. Hopefully, those who are seriously concerned with identifying the sources of inflation will not allow their attention to be monopolized by this spectacle.

Notes

1. See A. W. Phillips, "The Relation between Unemployment and the Rate of Change of Money Wage Rates in the United Kingdom, 1861-1957," *Economica*, November 1958, pp. 283-99; Paul A. Samuelson and Robert Solow, "Analytical Aspects of Anti-Inflation Policy," *American Economic Review Papers and Proceedings* (May 1960), pp. 177-94.

2. For a good summary of Professor Friedman's views on this question, see Milton Friedman, "Nobel Lecture: Inflation and Unemployment," *Journal of Political Economy* (June 1977), pp. 451-72.

3. See Ray Fair, "The Estimation of Simultaneous Equation Models with Lagged Endogenous Variables and First-Order Serially Correlated Errors," *Econometrica* (May 1970), pp. 507-16.

PART TWO

The Wage Structure and Wage Inflation

A. RIGIDITIES IN THE WAGE STRUCTURE: EARLY FORMULATIONS

Editor's Introduction
to Part Two

THE READINGS IN THIS SECTION are organized into two groups. The first group consists of early ideas about fixed wage relatives, most of which grew out of the experience of administering the wage-control program during World War II. Two contrasting approaches are presented here. The first, most prominently associated with John Dunlop, asserts the existence of rigidities in the wage structure (which he calls "wage contours") and their importance in macroeconomic analysis and for policy. Dunlop is not overly concerned with the origins of these structures, however, nor with the implications of their existence for microeconomic theory. He is content simply to list a number of factors that are responsible for wage-determination patterns. These include labor market and product market forces, which are stable over long periods of time, technology, custom and tradition, and organizational exigencies in companies and unions. To the extent that one gives priority to items at the beginning of this list, the notion of wage contours sits relatively easily with conventional economic analysis. The items toward the end of the list, however, suggest a very different theoretical agenda. That difference is argued and illustrated in the selection by the late Arthur Ross. His idea of "orbits of coercive comparison" is specifically linked to the internal politics of union organizations. While apparently a narrower concept than Dunlop's "contours," "orbits" are also purer theoretically, and Ross's piece makes much more explicit than Dunlop's the theoretical issues that may be at stake in assertions about wage rigidity. The selection by E. Robert Livernash, sandwiched between Ross and Dunlop, is also a bridge between them. Livernash develops the concept of internal wage structure, introduced by Dunlop under the heading of "job clusters," and the selection is of interest in part for the rich concrete material which gives flesh to some of these notions. But it is also clear that Livernash does not think these concrete details can be explained by conventional market forces, and that they thus constitute a more profound challenge to conventional theory than Dunlop seems willing to acknowledge.

The second group of three articles presents more recent formulations of the wage rigidities hypothesis. The first of these, by Clint Bourdon, describes contemporary patterns of wage determination in the private sector. It is based upon interviews with labor and management officials. It updates the patterns described by Ross and Dunlop, underscores the changes that have occurred in those patterns through the postwar decades, and identifies the issues that contemporary patterns seem to pose for the theoretical interpretation of contours and orbits. The following two pieces represent attempts to extend the theoretical foundations of wage rigidities by relating them to the ways in which people learn and understand their work. In this sense it connects the early work on wage rigidity to the more recent concerns with education and training which have dominated labor economics in the last decade and a half. The first of the two pieces is particularly concerned with the relationships among wage rigidity, custom, and on-the-job training. The second attempts to distinguish between wage rigidities and rigidities in the price structure introduced by so-called "rule of thumb" pricing. The theoretical ideas in these two readings are related to work in developmental psychology associated with Jean Piaget and Lawrence Kohlberg, which was alluded to in the Introduction. These selections may be treated as a third approach to the theory of wage rigidity, an alternative to Ross's emphasis upon organizational influences and Dunlop's focus on conventional labor and product market factors. But there are suggestions, particularly in the first of the two selections, about how the approach might be combined with a theory of organizational influences.

Wage Contours 1

BY JOHN T. DUNLOP

ALL WAGE THEORY is in a sense demand-and-supply analysis. A wage is a price, and the wage structure is a subsystem of prices. Prices and price systems are fruitfully to be interpreted in terms of demand and supply. There is no special or peculiar "demand-and-supply" theory of wages.

The notion of a "political" theory of wages involves confusion. In the absence of unions, firms or groups of managements make wage decisions; and under conditions of collective bargaining, the parties reach agreement on wage scales. It is indeed appropriate to study the processes, procedures, and influences which determine decisions in these organizations and the techniques which they employ in agreement making. Both parties ordinarily have some discretion, particularly in the short run and depending on whether they are wage leaders or wage followers, concerning the amount and the form of the wage settlement. But it does not advance understanding of decision making in organizations to label the process as either "political" or "economic." The decision-making process internal to a management organization or a union is an appropriate area of research, but this subject does not preempt the theory of wages. Moreover, a large part of the institutional study of decisions should seek to show the impact of external events, including market developments, on internal decisions.

It has been a problem in wage discussion from the earliest years to define the independent effect of a strike, of power, or of political action upon wage determination.[1] It is not a new issue. It is the old question which is revived under the guise of a "political" theory of wages.[2] The appropriate question is still what differences, if any, do unions make in wage determination? Are the net effects large or small, in the long run as well as the short run? Are the effects different for various components of compensation and on different types of wage rates in the total wage structure?

Wage theory has tended historically to disintegrate on the supply side. As has been noted, in the course of refinement of the wage-fund theory and the supply function associated with marginal productivity, the supply function tended to be pushed outside the analytical system. The amount of labor supplied and the wage rate came to be determined by social custom or institutional considerations. For purposes of economic analysis the wage rate came to be regarded as a given. In a sense the pivotal task of wage theory is to formulate an acceptable theory on the supply side.

It is not satisfactory to treat wage determination in terms of a single rate. In the past there have been various devices to reduce wage setting to the problem of a single rate. A single unskilled or common-labor rate has been envisaged into which all skilled labor may be translated as consisting of so many "units" of unskilled labor. This classical convention was followed by both Marx and Keynes. A single wage rate, out of the whole structure, is regarded as an index or barometer for all other rates. But all wage rates do not move together, either in the short run or in the long run. The wage structure is not rigid throughout a period of time. Moreover, the determination of the wage level and the determination of wage structure are closely interrelated.

Wage theory must operate with the concept of *wage structure*—the complex of rates within firms differentiated by occupation and employee and the complex of interfirm rate structures. The concept of wage structure, for the purpose of the present analysis, is a central concept; the analysis of wage determination will be approached through the wage structure. Indeed, the task of analyzing wage determination is not the problem of setting a single rate but rather the problem of setting and variation in the whole structure or complex of rates. While the general level of wage rates can be thought of as changing apart from variations in structure, they are not actually dissociated. Changes in the wage level, associated with changes in output levels in the system, are necessarily associated with changes in wage structure. The interrelation between the wage level and the wage structure is itself a major area of inquiry.

The wage structure within a bargaining unit, plant, firm, association, or other grouping in which wage differentials are set by the same authorities must be distinguished from the complex of interfirm or group structures each set by different agencies. From the point of view of the individual decision makers, the first wage structure is internal while the second is external. One of the central problems of wage analysis is to indicate the interrelations between the internal and external wage structure.

The analysis that follows utilizes two concepts which require explanation: *job clusters* and *wage contours*.

Job clusters and wage contours

A job cluster is defined as a stable group of job classifications or work assignments within a firm (wage-determining unit) which are so linked together by (1) technology, (2) the administrative organization of the production process, including policies of transfer, layoff and promotion, or (3) social custom that they have common wage-making characteristics.[3] In an industrial plant which may have literally thousands of jobs, each wage rate is not equally related and dependent upon all other wage rates. The internal wage structure, the complex of differentials, is not rigidly fixed for all time. Neither do relative rates change in random relation to each other. The internal wage-rate structure is to be envisaged as divided into groups of jobs or job clusters. The wage rates for the operations and jobs within a cluster are more closely related in their wage movements and wage-making forces than are rates outside the cluster.

Thus a tool room in a plant would ordinarily constitute a job cluster. The training and skill of the machinists who operate the various specialized machines—lathes, shapers, cutters, and so on—are similar. Their work is closely interrelated in the productive process. They may work together apart from others. They may have a common promotion, transfer, and layoff pattern. The wage rates within the tool room are more closely related to each other than they are to the rates for other employees in the power plant—on production lines, in the maintenance crew, in the office, or in the sales force. The wage structure of the ordinary plant is to be envisaged as comprised of a limited number of such job clusters, each with a number of rates.

From the analytical point of view these job clusters are given in the short period by the technology, the managerial and administrative organization of the wage-determining unit, and the social customs of the work community. Thus the employees on a furnace or a mill and the crew of a train or plane may constitute a job cluster (technology); so also may employees in a department (administrative organization), or the salesgirls in a department store or the stenographers in an office (social custom). These factors may reinforce each other in describing a job cluster, as in the instance of technological and administrative considerations defining the cluster of trucking rates in a department store or plant. In turn, certain job clusters may be more closely related to some rather than to other clusters. In this sense, clerical rates as a whole may be more closely related to other clerical rates than to managerial or factory rates. Wage theory, for the short period, does not seek to explain the configuration of particular job clusters. For the longer period, it is essential to show that the scope of a job cluster within a wage-rate structure may be expanded, restricted, or divided as a consequence of changes in the technology, administrative organization, or social customs, including union organization, in the plant.

The job cluster can be examined in more detail. Ordinarily a job cluster will contain a key rate, or in some cases several. The cluster consists of the key rate(s) and a group of associated rates. The key rate may be the highest paid, or the rate paid at the top step in a promotion ladder, or the rate paid for a job at which a large number of workers are employed. The rates set for a one-man streetcar or bus operator, a reporter at the top automatic step of advancement, a pilot of an airplane, a toolmaker, and a meat boner are illustrations of key rates. There may be several key rates in a single cluster and a number of clusters in one internal rate structure. Typically, the key-rate jobs show relatively less change in job content over a period of time and are often relatively more standardized among firms than are other jobs. The key rates are those which managements and unions typically have in mind and explicitly discuss in considering the internal wage structure.

The smallest building block in the wage structure is thus the job cluster comprised of a key rate, or several such rates in some cases, and a group of associated rates. The internal wage structure of the plant (wage-determining unit) consists of a number of these job clusters. Such is the anatomy of the internal wage structure.

The forces which determine the wage rates for the key jobs and the rates for associated jobs in a cluster are not confined within a firm. The "exterior" plays a very important role. The "exterior" consists of labor-market influences, including union and government wage policies, and forces in the markets for products. The "exterior" cannot operate directly on a thousand slightly differentiated jobs. The key rates play a decisive role in relating the exterior to the internal rate structure. Indeed, the key rates are affected by the exterior, and adjustments in these rates are transmitted to other rates within the plant, cluster by cluster.

Nature of wage contours

A wage contour is defined as a stable group of wage-determining units (bargaining units, plants or firms) which are so linked together by (1) similarity of product markets, (2) resort to similar sources for a labor force, or (3) common labor-market organization (custom) that they have common wage-making characteristics. The wage rates for particular occupations in a particular firm are not ordinarily independent of all other wage rates; they are more closely related to the wage rates of some firms than to others. A contour for particular occupations is to be defined in terms of both the product market and the labor market. A contour thus has three dimensions: (1) particular occupations or job clusters, (2) a sector of industry, and (3) a geographical location. The firms which comprise a contour constitute a particular product market; also, they may either be located in one labor market or scattered throughout a region or the country as a whole. The level of wage rates by occupations within the contour need not be equal, but changes in compensation are highly interrelated.

In the United States the basic steel contour for production jobs consists of the producers of basic steel products scattered in various communities throughout the country. The wage rates of the jobs in these firms—in their blast furnaces, steel works, and rolling mill operations—are closely interrelated. Some other operations of the same companies, such as cement mills or shipping, are typically excluded from the basic steel contour. While there are a variety of submarkets, and each basic steel producer may have specialized features resulting from its particular product market or from the particular locality in which it hires labor, nonetheless the basic steel wage contour is sharply defined and clearly distinguishable from others.

The meat-packing and rubber contours are further illustrations. But a contour is not to be identified with an industry. Many broad industrial groups of firms have such specialized submarkets that they are decisive for wage setting. In the paper industry, for example, kraft paper, newsprint, tissue paper, quality writing paper, and bank-note paper firms have such distinctive products markets, with some distinctive production and labor-cost problems, that they have separate wage-setting processes.

A contour should not be regarded as necessarily having a sharp boundary line. Some firms have such unique product markets that they fall among several wage contours. Specialized markets and competitive conditions may result in some firms "at the edge of the contour" being only slightly influenced by wage developments "at the center." The meat-packing pattern may spread from the major packers to other packing plants, then to some cutting plants for the hotel and restaurant trade, but not necessarily to all sausage makers. Indeed, in some localities such small plants may even constitute a separate wage contour.

Some major contours may constitute limits to the wage settlements within less significant wage-setting groups of firms. Thus, the flat-glass contour has been influenced both by the basic steel and the automobile contours. These larger patterns have provided limits conditioning the amount and the form of the flat-glass settlements.

A contour may be confined to a locality in its labor-market dimension. Thus newspapers in New York City constitute a contour for wage-setting purposes. The rates for various occupations in one newspaper are closely related to those in other newspapers in that city. Specialized product markets, for other types of printing or publishing, are a part of still other wage contours. In some localities wages in one group of firms may be so dominant as to spread that contour to firms which would ordinarily be in a different contour. The roles played by auto rates in Detroit, steel rates in Pittsburgh, and, traditionally, textile rates in Fall River are illustrative. Similarly, the role of some unions may be so significant in a locality as to expand a contour to include companies which ordinarily would be in separate contours or which would be relatively isolated.

A contour is confined to particular ranges of skill, occupations, or job clusters of the constituent firms. Not all types of labor hired by a firm will have wage rates determined in the same contour. Thus, a firm employing a professional chemist, a patternmaker, and a clerk may be expected to be part of three quite different contours. A construction firm hiring boiler-makers, operating engineers, and laborers will be a part of the construction product market in each instance, but three separate wage contours are

67

involved. The boilermaker's rate is set over the largest geographical area, while the laborer's rate is likely to be confined to a single locality.

A wage contour can be explored in further detail. In the ordinary case a wage contour contains one, or in some instances, several key settlements. The contour is comprised of the rates for the key firm(s) and a group of associated firms. The key settlement may be set by the largest firm, the price leader, or the firm with labor-relations leadership. Thus in the basic steel contour, the wages determined by the United States Steel Corporation generally have been followed by all other firms in the contour. The other basic steel producers have customarily followed the "pattern" immediately. In the meat-packing contour, the wage leader has been Swift, or in some instances Armour. In the rubber industry each of the "big four" has been the leader on occasion. In these cases, more time elapses between a change by the leaders and a change by the followers. Some firms may follow only at a distance, altering even the terms of the key settlement in some respects. The American Motors contract in 1955 provided such an illustration in the automobile contour.

A wage contour, then, can be envisaged as a grouping of firms, for a given range of occupations, in which some firms are very closely related to the leaders. Other firms are less directly associated. At the exterior of the contour, furthest from the key settlement, the firms may follow the leadership only remotely.

A variety of devices have been developed which relate wages determined by the key settlement to those of other firms in the contour. The existence of a common expiration date for the wage agreements in several firms or the sequence of anniversary dates is reflective of the relations within a wage contour. Some firms commit themselves in advance to pay the wages set by other companies; many commit themselves to consider a wage change when a "wage movement" has developed in the industry (contour). Specialized product markets or sources of labor supply or skill requirements or union organization may mean that a particular firm, remote from the "center" of the contour, will modify in some respects the "pattern" established at the key bargain.

The firms which comprise a wage contour may be organized into a formal employers' association rather than appear to make wage decisions without a common organization. In an association not all firms actually have equal weight in making decisions; wage leaders exercise the same functions within an organization as they would without one, although an association may mean that all wages are changed at the same time. In many instances, an association constitutes only a formal difference from the wage-leadership conditions that would be evident without an employers' organization.[4]

Wage-making forces are envisaged as concentrated on the key rates in the job clusters. These rates "extend" out from the internal structure of the firm to the "exterior" and constitute the focal points for wage-setting forces among firms within the contour. The key rates in the job clusters constitute the channels of impact between the exterior developments in the contour (and through the contour the larger developments in the economy) and the interior rate structure of the firm. Moreover, in an analogous way, the key bargains constitute the focal point of wage-setting forces within the contour and constitute the points where those wage-making forces converge that are exterior to the contour and common to the total economy.

A theory of wages is not required to treat each wage rate in the system as of equal importance. The view of the wage structure outlined above singles out a limited number of key job rates and key wage settlements or bargains for analysis. These particular rates are selected, at least in the short run, by the anatomy of the wage structure which is given by (1) the technology and administrative arrangements of firms, (2) competitive patterns in product markets, and (3) the sources of labor supply. Long-run forces affecting technology and competitive conditions in the product or labor market change both job clusters and contours given in the short run. Thus the spreading of large firms or unions with established wage policies into different product markets may change the anatomy of clusters or contours.

The concepts of job cluster and wage contour are analogous. In each case a group of rates surrounds a key rate. The concepts seek to relate the internal and the external wage structure; they focus attention on the mechanics by which the internal structure through job clusters is influenced by external developments in the wage contour. Wage theory cannot reduce all structure to a single rate; the limited number of strategic rates depicted by the job clusters and wage contours are to be the focus of wage theory.[5]

Wage structure in the short run

The concepts developed in the preceding discussion can now be applied to a particular case. Table 1 shows the union scale for motor-truck drivers in Boston for July, 1953. Each rate shows the wage scale established between the union and an association or group of employers engaged in selling transportation services. Each rate is to be interpreted as the key rate for truck drivers in a series of contours. Some small part of the differences in wages may be attributed to variations in the skill or work performed; some may be related to differences in the length of the work week and the timing of contract expiration during a year, and some may arise from differences in methods of wage payment. The teamsters who work at these various rates are essentially similar and substitutable. Essentially the same disparity in rates is found in most other cities, with a high similarity in the relative ranking of rates for various branches of the trade.

In a significant sense, the case constitutes a kind of critical experiment. One type of labor performing almost identical work, organized by the same

Table 1

Union Scale for Motor-Truck Drivers, Boston, July 1, 1953

Transportation service	Hourly rate
Magazine	$2.494
Newspaper, day	2.393
Oil	2.215
Paper handlers, newspaper	2.062
Building construction	2.00
Beer, bottle and keg	1.905
Railway express, 1½–5 tons	1.869
Meatpacking house, 3–5 tons	1.83
Grocery, chain store	1.819
Garbage disposal	1.725
Bakery, Hebrew	1.71
General hauling, 3–5 tons	1.685
Rendering	1.675
Coal	1.65
Movers, piano and household	1.65
Armored car	1.64
Ice	1.56
Carbonated beverage	1.54
Linen supply	1.537
Wastepaper	1.44
Laundry, wholesale	1.28
Scrap, iron and metal	1.27

SOURCE: *Union Wages and Hours: Motortruck Drivers and Helpers,* U.S. Bureau of Labor Statistics Bulletin 1154 (July 1, 1953), pp. 9–10.

union, is paid markedly different rates by different associations of employers in the truck transportation industry. Why the wide range in wage rates? Are the disparities temporary? Do they arise from "friction" or "immobilities" in the labor market? Are they primarily the consequence of a monopolistic seller of labor discriminating among types of employers? I believe the answer to these several questions is largely in the negative.

Basically each rate reflects a wage contour. Each is a reflection of the product market. Within any one contour the wage rates among competing firms will tend to be equal. Among individual beer distributors, construction firms, ice deliverers, or scrap iron and metal haulers there tend to be few differences in rates. But there are sharp differences in rates among contours. Fundamentally the differences in the product market are reflected back into the labor market.

But what are the mechanics? Why do not all teamsters move to the higher-paying contours? Or why do not the employers in the higher-paying contours set a lower wage rate, since similar labor seems to be available to other contours at lower rates? In a perfect labor market (a bourse) such changes toward uniformity would tend to take place.

Part of the explanation is to be found in the historical sequence of growth of the trucker's wage scale. Newer and expanding industries or contours, such as oil, have had to pay higher wages to attract labor in the evolution of wage scales. Part of the explanation is derived from the fact that this historical structure of wages has conditioned the labor supply so that the relative rates among contours are regarded as proper. A minor part of the explanation lies in the fact that these wage rates are influenced by the wages of the group of workers these employees tend to be associated with in work operations. Teamsters hauling oil and building materials come in contact with high-paid employees in their work operations, while laundry and scrap drivers have more direct contact with lower-paid employees. A larger emphasis is to be placed on the fact that competitive conditions permit higher pay at the top end of the list. Demand is less elastic and wages tend to be a lower proportion of the sales revenue. But do the firms pay more simply because they can afford to do so? If the union is considered a decisive factor, then an explanation can be made simply in terms of the union acting as a discriminating seller in dealing with different industries. While union influence may be significant in some cases, this type of wage spread is so general, apart from the union, that the principal explanation should lie elsewhere.

When the labor market is tight, the various contours are able to bid for labor so that a differentiated structure of rates reflecting the product-market contours and competitive conditions tends to be established. For a variety of reasons these differentials are not readily altered in a looser labor market. Making a wage change or changing a differential among sectors involves costs. Newer and expanding employers using the same type of labor have to pay more to attract a labor force, and a differential once established by a contour is not easily abolished.

For these various reasons the product market tends to be mirrored in the labor market and to determine the wage structure. The differentials are not transitory; they are not to be dismissed as imperfections. The differentials are not basically to be interpreted as a range of indefinite or random rates, although a community with a wide variety of firms in different product markets may present the impression of random rates. The wage contours and their relative rates reflect the basic nature of product and labor markets.

These arguments can be applied to most of the cases of interfirm wage differentials that have been reported. There are some differences in wage rates which reflect differences in job content; there are differences in costs and earnings in the way firms administer the same wage structure, and there are differences in methods of compensation (incentive and time rates). These factors account for some of the statistically observed variations in wage rates. However, the theoretically significant differences for similar grades of labor are those which reflect different product-market competitive conditions.

The long-term development of wage structure

The structure of wage rates of a country reflects to some extent the course of its industrialization and economic development. The supply of labor and the rate and pattern of industrialization are the crucial factors. A country with a scarcity of labor will probably require and establish larger wage differentials for skill than one with an abundant labor supply. A rapid rate of industrialization will produce larger skill differentials than will a slow rate. The sequence in the development of industries in the industrialization process will affect to some degree the structure of wage rates as differentials are used to attract a labor force to these industries from agriculture or from other industrial activities. A comparative study of the wage structures of various countries today reflects the imprints of the path of economic development.[6]

In an agrarian society, relatively small differentials are required to attract a labor force away from agriculture to industry. The first industries historically required simpler skills, and the levels of rates over agriculture were only slightly higher. As successive industries developed, higher rates were required to draw a work force, not primarily directly from agriculture, but from lower-paid industries. Successive industries appear to require more specialized skills, and higher wages result. The structure of wages thus reflects the pattern of industrialization.

Some of the same phenomena can be seen today when new plants are introduced into a particular community. There are a variety of circumstances which may result in new employers setting higher rates. The higher the general level of employment, the stronger these factors will be. The new industries may require higher standards of skill. The new plants may need several thousand employees as a minimum work force. A higher rate is needed to attract that number than if the plant were to grow gradually from a small figure. Labor costs are frequently a small fraction of total costs, and the product markets are often oligopolistic. These factors permit or encourage the enterprise to set a higher rate for the key jobs than would be paid for a comparable level of skill in other jobs in the community. The oil, chemical, atomic, and television industries provide current examples. All this suggests that there is a tendency for new industries to push the wage level upward.

The wage structure is to be approached as a reflex of the larger pattern of industrialization. The wage structure of an agricultural economy is largely undifferentiated by skill or product-market divisions. Increasing industrialization creates increasing differentiation by skill, creating many new occupations and job operations. Some of these occupations or jobs are key jobs and provide the basis for interfirm comparisons. Increasing industrialization also creates new groupings of products within which are unique types of competition. These product-market characteristics, combined with some features of the labor market, create wage contours within which wages tend to move under common forces, as opposed to wages outside the contour.

When a wage structure has been established, the labor supply tends to adapt itself to the relative structure of rates, as reflected in key rates, in a variety of ways. Preferences and relative ratings given to jobs by workers are not autonomous; they reflect the broad outlines of the established wage structure. The long-established rate structure, created as envisaged in this discussion, influences the choice of workers and may even take on normative elements. The labor force, for most occupations, would appear to be highly pliable over a generation. The established wage structure comes to shape labor supply over the long run. This is not to deny that supply may not adapt readily in the short period to changes in relative demand. Nor does it deny that relative wage rates may affect long-run supply for some occupations within some limits. The point is that the labor supply over a generation is clearly highly adaptable to the great variety of jobs created by modern industrialization and that the work force tends in important respects to adapt itself to the long-established rate structure for key jobs.

Conclusions

The questions that are posed for contemporary wage theory are quite different from those that challenged the wage-fund and marginal-productivity doctrines. The analysis of wage determination in each doctrine was at the very center of economics. As these earlier doctrines declined in usefulness and popularity, a tendency developed to treat wage rates as determined outside the system and as given for economic problems. Wage theory has shown a tendency to break down, particularly on the supply side.

A few suggestions have been made for the future of wage theory. A single wage rate or average concept is inadequate. The structure of wages, the whole complex of differentials, needs to be explained. Moreover, the determination of the wage level and the structure of wage rates are interrelated. In the analysis of wage structure, the concepts of job clusters and wage contours define the points at which wage-making forces are concentrated. The *anatomy* of the wage structure must first be understood if one is to explain changes in response to demand-and-supply factors. These concepts help to focus attention upon the operation of demand and supply. They suggest that product-market competition and conditions decisively influence the structure of wage rates. In the longer run, however, the wage structure is a reflex of the pattern and speed of industrialization.

Notes

1. See, for instance, Eugen von Boehm-Bawerk, "Macht oder Ökonomisches Gesetz," *Zeitschrift für Volkswirtschaft, Sozialpolitik und Verwaltung* (December, 1914), trans. by J. R. Mez, mimeographed (1931): "Nor could any sensible person deny that the existence of labor organizations with their weapon of strikes has been of pronounced influence on the fixation of wages of labor. . . . The great problem, not adequately settled so far, is to determine the exact extent and nature of the influence of both factors ['purely economic' and 'social' categories]. . . ."
2. See Arthur M. Ross, *Trade Union Wage Policy* (Berkeley: University of California Press, 1948).
3. See [the following essay] by E. Robert Livernash for a further development of the concept of job clusters and for much rich illustrative material. This concept has been developed in joint discussion and in common or similar administrative experience over the years.
4. While the impact of labor organization upon wage rates is frequently discussed in current literature, the question of the effect of employer organization upon wage rates is seldom explored. Frequently a formal employer organization merely sharpens relations already apparent.
5. For an imaginative discussion on the concept of labor market, see Clark Kerr, "The Balkanization of Labor Markets," *Labor Mobility and Economic Opportunity: Essays by E. Wight Bakke and Others* (New York: Wiley, 1954), pp. 92-110. The present discussion would add to that of Professor Kerr the emphasis that the scope of product markets is reflected back into the labor market, thus defining the scope of wage setting.
6. See John T. Dunlop and Melvin Rothbaum, "International Comparisons of Wage Structures," *International Labour Review*, vol. 71 (April 1955) pp. 347-63.

Job Clusters

2

BY E. ROBERT LIVERNASH

PRIMARY EMPHASIS IN this chapter is placed on the determination of wage differentials. No attempt is made to state a complete wage theory for the firm. The discussion and concepts of this chapter must be integrated with a more complete theory for the firm, with broader aspects of wage theory for the industry, and with more general concepts of economic and social behavior. However, the development of ideas on the wage structure of the firm may contribute to these larger aspects of theory and to the future study of wage structures.

The definition of the term "internal wage structure" is admittedly somewhat loose. As used in this chapter it refers primarily to single plants or establishments, but also to multiplant firms, depending upon their policy and environment. The term applies particularly to more complex structures, such as exist in many manufacturing plants, but also to simpler craft structures, with modifications in emphasis. This material must be read with qualifications as to particular points, depending upon the type of wage structure one has in mind.

The concept of the internal wage structure is a significant approach to wage-rate analysis. As thinking shifts from the more or less exclusive role of impersonal market forces to encompass union and management policies, procedures, and actions, some adaptation of approach is necessary. Abstracting the internal wage structure for consideration has the advantage of staying within a decision-making organizational unit and dealing with a problem having realistic administrative scope. In such an approach the discussion of "market," "administrative," and "institutional" forces can be blended in much the same way as they are in the other chapters of this book.

This approach necessarily puts in question the rather strong undercurrent and habit of thought of applying "demand and supply" independently to each wage rate in a plant as a subcase of the more general approach. At the very least, much of the richness of reality is lost by this process. More important, there simply is no compulsion of market forces adequate to explain the detailed determination of wage differentials.

Internal standards of job comparison, formal or informal in character, are a much more adequate explanation of many wage differentials than are market forces. From this point of view, the wage rate for one particular job in a plant cannot be divorced from the wage rates for other jobs within the same plant. Wage-rate and job-content *relationships* are a most important part of the explanation of each particular rate. Exploration of the nature and types of such relationships is an essential phase of wage theory.

To be sure, the standards of internal job comparison are similar in general character to those used in explaining occupational wage differentials in the labor market. But giving living reality to the wage structure in a plant as a going institution is quite different from relying upon a market-equilibrium concept as applied to each rate. Viewing the wage structure as a whole, in the light of both internal and external forces and adaptations, should supplement and clarify the total process of wage determination. Certain background considerations need to be discussed first, however.

Institutional and technological background

Most areas of production and distribution are dominated by a highly integrated process and a narrowly specialized labor force. The "job" is a narrow base for wage analysis, apart from its immediate technical reference. Many "occupations" have disintegrated with technical advance; remaining occupations are often subdivided over a wide range of skill.

The production process and the demand for and supply of labor

While some jobs still provide a reasonably distinct occupational category existing within various firms within a labor market, the great proportion of factory jobs are highly specialized as to industry and constitute a narrowly subdivided task within each industry. With such confined job- and wage-rate reference and with a highly integrated technical process, neither from the demand side nor from the supply side can one job typically be regarded as independent of related jobs.

The integrated production process creates a wide but variable area of joint demand for labor. An expansion or contraction of production is rooted in a technology which requires "balanced lines," with relative labor requirements on many jobs held to fixed ratios.

But this joint demand, while applicable to expansion and contraction of production and employment in a static sense, is also subject to continuous flux with dynamic changes in product design, product mix, and methods of production. By way of example, diesels altered the composition of maintenance work in railroad shops in part by expanding the electrical phases of the work and contracting the mechanical. Or again, the postwar style trend for men's shoes has considerably increased the proportion of stitching hours required to manufacture the average shoe.

For certain selected jobs and for some problems, demand for labor can be, and even must be, viewed with reference to the "job," but changes in the demand for labor commonly are with reference to a unit broader than the particular job. So common are these broader changes in the demand for labor, and so rooted in the productive process, that modern technology must be regarded as a force creating areas of joint demand with limited scope for the meaningful application of demand to highly specialized types of work.

There are similar difficulties on the supply side in attempting to conceive of independent supply curves for each particular job. With relatively small differences in the amount and kind of training, workers can shift over a fairly wide range of related jobs.

Within a group of jobs in a single plant related by a common pattern of promotion and transfer, not necessarily within a simple single sequence of jobs, wage differentials can be considered as premiums to compensate for added training and greater responsibility and to equalize disutility elements.[1] But if one adds the requirement that each job price must clear the market, contradictory facts arise. Within any such group of related jobs, the number of employees able, willing, and desirous of being promoted far exceeds the number promoted. The better-paying jobs appear at any given time to be rationed. This, of course, does not end the debate, as over a period of time some system of differentials would appear to be required to maintain the supply of labor on the more skilled jobs.

Modern technology has created a job structure which does not lend itself to a very satisfying explanation of internal wage differentials by a simple demand-and-supply approach. Fixed ratios of employment on so many jobs make it difficult to conceive of differentiated demand among these jobs. Joint demand blurs the demand concept for the purpose of the wage-differential problem. Discrimination from the point of view of relative supply is at least equally difficult, except as a dynamic concept of unknown normal magnitude to maintain an incentive for promotion.

Parenthetically, what is the appropriate economic concept to portray the reality of the promotion incentive and its wage magnitude? Leaving aside those professional fields which have large monetary costs borne by the individual and other specialized jobs for which there is no free training opportunity, most jobs in industry have no money cost of training to be borne by the individual. Both on-the-job and classroom training are provided by firms to create an adequate supply of skilled labor. Some company programs are outstanding in the opportunities they provide; other programs are more "catch-as-catch-can" but, nonetheless, meet the requirements of the firm. With some admitted exceptions, individuals are not prevented from taking higher-paid jobs because of the cost of training. A few workers have no desire for promotion, but most workers eagerly await the opportunity to move up the wage and job ladder. While a few workers are eliminated by inability, neither lack of ability nor lack of desire for better jobs limits the supply.

Workers in general simply do not have the opportunity to work at the skill level of their choice, nor are differences in job attractiveness, except for a few disutility elements, equated by wages. Jobs are rationed by the opportunities inherent in the productive process in relation to whatever selection policy may prevail in a given company. Over wide areas, selection is controlled primarily by seniority, in others, by managerial judgment of the relative abilities of individuals.

On the whole, a job-rate equilibrium concept seems a poor fit to these facts. An individual balancing of net advantages and disadvantages with no incentive at the margin to "move up" is an odd sort of notion. Realistically, the wage structure should, no doubt, continue to have a promotion-incentive factor with a continuous excess of workers able and willing to fill higher-paying job vacancies. While this is not well expressed by a wage diagram, it at least somewhat resembles a goal of "practical" wage administration. Perhaps a rapidly expanding economy operates best with a fairly large skill differential, but some economies appear to operate with a very small monetary incentive. This is no attempt at an answer. The question is merely posed of the meaning of a wage equilibrium concept in the allocation of workers within the skill hierarchy.

The seniority system and the labor market

The joint development of collective bargaining and personnel policies has disrupted the direct relation of many wage rates to hiring, so far as the labor market is concerned.[2] The wage rate is also a most inadequate and incomplete motivational explanation to account for an employee's willingness to remain in the employ of a given company.

The vast proportion of job vacancies in any plant or company is filled today, not by hiring from the outside, but by promotion from within the organization. There has been no sharp break with the past, for internal promotion has developed with the growing diversification and specialization of jobs. However, the growing importance of collective bargaining and modern personnel practices gave significant impetus to promotion from within. The policy avoids criticism of holding back those already employed in favor of outsiders, and is a basic part of increasingly elaborate programs to build morale and security by encouraging a lifetime view of employment with a given organization.

This policy and practice of promotion from within restrict hiring to a relatively small number of what may be called "hiring-jobs." While the list of such jobs is not completely static over a period time, these jobs are at all times a small proportion of the total and are typically at the bottom of the wage scale. By contrast, some hiring-jobs are above the lowest wage level. This is true where an entire group of jobs, including the bottom job in the group, is above the lowest level and has not been integrated with other promotion sequences. It is also true for certain unique jobs requiring training not provided within the organization.[3]

The pattern of hiring-jobs is one aspect of the particular wage structure. In broad view, however, the pattern would show these jobs grouped at the bottom of the wage scale and spread throughout departmental and organizational units as entrance spots from which most other jobs are then filled.

Probably a worker would not decide to leave one employer simply on the basis of a higher wage rate in another plant. While seniority is a strong influence in promotion, its almost unqualified application to layoff brings greatly enhanced job security with continued years of employment. This security against layoff is given added meaning by protection against arbitrary discharge. Standards by which the equity of discharge is judged, consciously and unconsciously, give weight to length of service. Each year also finds increasingly elaborate benefit plans related in amount to length of service. In this world of seniority, an employee would certainly be peculiar if he judged his economic position only in terms of his wage rate. Even here, his alternative choice is with hiring-jobs elsewhere. Above all, job security with its hedge against "hard times" is a most important retention influence.[4]

Most particular wage rates are thus not directly or closely related to a local labor market from an employment point of view. Employees enter and leave plants from the lower-paying "bottom" jobs. Expansion brings more rapid promotion. Recession brings layoff or demotion and downgrading for low-service employees. While seniority patterns differ, layoff schedules illustrate the indirect connection between many jobs and the labor market.

Wage administration and wage inequities

Particular wage rates are set by administrative decision within the firm. Neither union nor management policies, attitudes, and objectives toward the wage structure can be regarded as simply an adjunct to the employment process. Managements have increasingly worked toward a stable structure frequently based upon job evaluation in the local plant. Unions have increasingly accepted a stable structure, but have worked to broaden the base of comparison and are more qualified in their acceptance of evaluation. Union skepticism toward job evaluation has many facets. Perhaps the greatest fear is of the use of evaluation to freeze unions out of the wage-differential area or to restrict wage-differential policy too narrowly. Related to this is fear of an overly scientific, as contrasted with a looser equity, approach.

Real differences in philosophy may create administrative conflict in adjusting wage rates with technological change. It is not easy for a union to allow a job rate to be reduced, particularly with increased output per hour on a machine, regardless of the logic of the job analysis. Craft rivalry, traditional wage relationships, and the numerical significance of particular groups within the union may give a shallow ring to "logical" job relationships so far as the union leader is concerned.

On the other hand, with a reasonable voice in policy and administration, a union may find evaluation constructive and desirable from its point of view. Even in unions with official positions opposing evaluation, acceptance in particular situations is commonplace. There at least would appear to be a growing accommodation of management and union attitudes in this area.

Partly under government intervention, wage comparison has been facilitated by a large expansion in wage information. Establishing proper wage differentials has come to be a distinct administrative function with a defined general objective of maintaining equitable job-rate relationships.

The development of job evaluation has been a real force in the creation of simplified and improved rate structures. Apart from the impact upon the individual plant and company, job evaluation has had a more far-reaching influence. The widespread use of particular job-evaluation plans, such as the National Metal Trades plan, has created more nearly identical wage structures in geographically separated labor markets and has facilitated wage comparisons. Within communities, the increasing prevalence of similar evaluation plans has had the same effect. Finally, the use of job evaluation in collective bargaining on an industry basis, most notable in basic steel, has created nearly identical detailed wage structures throughout an industry or segment of an industry.

Collective bargaining, with or without job evaluation, has been an influence in creating and extending simplified and more uniform wage structures. While this influence is, perhaps, less obvious in the absence of job evaluation, many bargained structures are closely analogous to evaluated structures; and the "removal of inequities" is a common part of the bargaining process, as is the diminishing of differentials for the same job within and between labor markets.[5]

As collective bargaining first developed in the mass-production industries, wage inequities were an obvious avenue for union activity within wage structures that had not been subject to centralized managerial control and had more or less just grown. Nor were union representatives too concerned, during the organizational phase of union development, with just what constituted an inequity. As unions became going concerns, constant wage inequities were no more attractive to them than to management. Contracts began to restrict the area of wage grievances; wage-structure standards were developed.

In the light of our present knowledge neither the general impact of collective bargaining upon the wage structure nor the impact of management and union policies viewed separately can be stated simply. But attitudes and actions "for and against" such policies as job evaluation, wage incentives, rate ranges, automatic progression, freezing wage rates by contract, revising rates with changing technology, arbitrating wage rates and production standards, and other policies are clearly continuously influencing wage structures. Also significant are factors such as craft rivalries, the degree of conflict or accommodation in union-management relations, and the character of leadership in union and management organizations. As one example, the wage structure in a basic steel plant in 1955 could hardly be explained without reference to this range of considerations. While wage theory must of necessity abstract from many particulars, the usefulness of the theory may be judged in part by its potential supplementation in the light of these kinds of influences.

The discussion thus far has attempted to make clear that an operational type of wage-differential theory relating each plant rate to a market rate through the employment process is highly unrealistic. This is not to say that there are not "labor-market forces," both in an employment and a wage-comparison sense. It is to say, however, that not every wage rate is of equal significance and that systems of rates must be explained and related to their economic and administrative context and environment.

Some wage-structure generalizations

The background considerations previously discussed tend to support the view that the wage structure requires special analysis as such. Each single wage rate is not simply a subcase of the general case of demand for and supply of labor for the firm. But how can the process of wage comparison be analyzed to place this process within a meaningful framework? Certainly it is not adequate to regard the wage structure as nothing more than a process of internal job-content comparisons. It is equally discouraging to attempt to relate each wage rate to the labor market. Finally, it is not possible to ignore labor-cost influence and restrict thinking about the structure to wage relationships without regard to cost significance.

As a starting point in developing an analysis, three propositions are advanced and then discussed. These propositions are themselves related and each proposition can be, and is, of different significance for different firms in different economic environments. Needless to state, the propositions also require supplementation in various ways. They are as follows:

1. In internal wage-rate comparisons of job content and job relationships, any given job is not related to all other jobs in an equally significant manner. Some jobs are closely related as to wage significance, others more remotely related. While such job relationships have no simple, single basis, the larger relationships develop around key jobs.

2. In the external comparison of job rates in the firm to labor-market rates, each job within the plant structure is not related to a market rate in an equally significant manner. Not only are there obvious variations in the

"mix" of different types of plants and jobs in different labor markets but there is again no single, simple type of relationship. Joint integration to the market and to the internal structure, however, evolves around key jobs.

3. In relating the wage structure to labor cost, each job rate is not of the same significance as an element of labor cost. While most particular jobs are a small proportion of total labor cost, some are not, and employment at different wage rates varies widely in labor-cost significance—with the bulk of labor cost concentrated within a fairly narrow range of "production" rates.

The first two points are stated in terms of wage *comparison*. The significance of comparison is left open for development. Internal comparison is advanced predominately as an equity concept inherited in large part from valuation in the market place, but applied in its wage-administration and job-content context to create "fair" wage rates. External comparison is also meaningful in an equity sense relative to wage rates paid elsewhere, but is in addition related to the opportunity to hire and select as applied to groups of jobs and to some individual jobs.

As a broad framework, forces influencing the general wage level for an industry or for a wage contour are assumed. Also assumed are forces influencing the general level for the particular plant within its industry and labor-market context.

Internal job comparisons and job clusters

The basic premise here is that internal job-content comparison as a basis for wage-rate determination is stronger, and of a somewhat different character, within certain groups of jobs than between them. It is difficult to give a single name to the job groups within which internal comparison is most significant, but they may be called job clusters.[6]

As an elaboration of the basic premise, there are broad job clusters containing narrower clusters. Broad groups may be illustrated within manufacturing as (1) managerial-executive, administrative, professional, and supervisory; (2) clerical, and (3) factory. Within each broad group, narrower groups are obvious.[7] Within the factory group are maintenance, inspection, transportation, and production. Within production are certain smaller groups, varying with the nature of the industry.

Job-content comparison as a basis for wage-rate determination is felt to be strong within narrow clusters, somewhat weaker between narrow functional groups, and of least significance in relating broad clusters. An added notion must be introduced to this. Each cluster contains a key job, or several. Wage relationships within a narrow group and among such groups revolve around key jobs. Within clusters the primary determinant of non-key job rates is the job-content comparison with the key job. Among clusters, the basic consideration is the relationship among the respective key jobs.

Relationships among key jobs, and hence among clusters, cannot be outlined in simple form. The view has been stated that job-content comparison is somewhat weaker among narrow groups than within them, and weaker yet among broad groups. This does not necessarily imply that external forces become stronger as internal determination of wage differentials becomes weaker. In a broad way this is felt to be true, but the relationship between internal and external considerations is a separate, thought related, question, heavily dependent upon the particular environment. What is meant is that in so far as internal comparison continues to be the basis for wage determination, the relative compensation among broad groups is less rigorously determined by job-content comparison but depends more upon general judgment as to the appropriate relationship.

The nature of narrow job clusters

There is no single basis of classification for narrow job clusters. Geographical location within a plant, organizational pattern and common supervision, related and common job skills, common hiring jobs and transfer and promotion sequences, as well as a common production function, tie jobs together. The notion of a common production function deserves some emphasis, however. Departments frequently signify separate job groupings as they relate to different phases of production, thus constituting a functional group of related jobs.

Look quickly at a few industry structures. A shoe factory is divided into departments of cutting, stitching, lasting, making, and packing. We can recreate the historical process from the cobbler to the crafts to the specialized jobs. Today departments take the place of earlier crafts, but each department is organized around a phase or function of production. In textiles there is a spinning room, a weaving room, a carding room. Steel integrates coke ovens, blast furnaces, open hearths, and mills. On a ship, we find the engine room, the deck department, and the steward's department. Endless examples of the nature and organization of the production process reveal such job groupings, typically signified by "division" and "departmental" lines but based upon different production functions integrated into a larger whole. The reason for using the term "functional group" for these wage-related groups of jobs is to place primary, though not exclusive, emphasis upon this kind of job grouping.

Consider very briefly, as an example, the lasting and stitching departments in a shoe factory. One group "makes" the upper; the other "lasts" the shoe. Most, but by no means all, of the jobs in the stitching department are stitching jobs. These involve various special types of sewing machines. Some such stitching jobs are so closely related as to be almost (but not quite) the same job, as stitching straight tips and stitching fancy tips. Some stitching jobs require much more skill than others—in fact, the difference in training and experience required for these jobs may be greater than that required for many jobs with no common element of skill. In the lasting department, the specific element of common skill in operating similar machines is absent, but the tests of a well-lasted shoe are related among the jobs. As between these departments, transfer is virtually unknown. Each department has its own hiring-jobs and promotion sequences; one is predominately female, the other male; and wage comparison across the departmental lines, while not completely absent, is much weaker than within each department and is of a more general character.

Special job clusters

There are, however, at least the following meaningful special types of job clusters falling within the broad managerial, production, and clerical groupings:

1. The departmental functional group. This has been illustrated by the stitching and lasting departmental association of jobs with their respective hiring-jobs and transfer and promotion patterns.

2. The skill family. This has been illustrated by the stitching jobs within the stitching room. Other examples include (a) a craft job as in a steel plant with its apprentice scale and progression, then the job starting rate and class, the intermediate rate, and finally the full journeyman rate and class; and (b) many occupationally based jobs—typists, stenographers, semicraft machine operators, locomotive engineers, and so forth—with simple or complex levels and types of skill.

3. Related types of work. This can be illustrated by the varieties of "inspectors" in the New Hampshire state government. All these jobs relate to law enforcement: state troopers, game wardens, conservation officers, prison officers, probation officers, motor vehicle inspectors, theater and public building inspectors, aeronautical inspectors, food inspectors, factory inspectors, liquor inspectors, public utility inspectors, bank inspectors, etc. The differences among most of these jobs are far greater than their similarities. They also fall within many departments. They are related, however, as a wage group, though the relationships are not equally strong among all jobs.

Frequently inspection and assembly jobs in a factory are so diverse in character that they are not in any true sense an occupation or skill family, but are closely related for wage purposes and treated somewhat as though they were such a family. Various professional jobs—the "engineering" categories, for example—are closely related. Maintenance jobs constitute a similar category. Accounting and bookkeeping jobs might be described in part as a skill family and in part as related jobs. In various ways, jobs are thus pulled together through the performance of related kinds of work.

4. The work crew or closely knit work group. One of the clearest examples of such a group is a crew working on some large type of equipment—the open hearth crew, the rolling mill crew, the paper machine crew, the printing press crew. The jobs on an open hearth—

including first, second, and third helpers, the charging machine operator, the cranemen, the pourer, the stacker, and others—are clearly related by joint responsibility, level of responsibility, and the technical integration of work. Even small equipment frequently has operators, feeders, take-away men, and other kinds of specialized workers. A conveyor may create a closely knit work group. Various "gangs" may work at separate or remote locations. In an office, payroll jobs might constitute a closely knit work group.

In the above categories, the departmental functional group and the work crew or work group are, in wage terms, both "horizontal" and "vertical" in character. The skill group is predominately vertical and the related-job group can be either vertical or horizontal, but some of its most interesting impacts are horizontal. No exhaustive typing is possible, and there are groups within groups, as well as overlapping and tie-in relationships.

There can be no rigid classification of narrow job clusters. Sometimes a department is so large and diverse that it does not constitute a meaningful wage group. A related work group or a skill family may cut across departmental lines. In other cases, departments, skill groups, and related jobs may reinforce a single relationship. There is reality, however, in the concept of degree of wage relationship and job-content comparison in terms of groups of jobs.[8]

Job clusters and wage relationships

Within a narrow job cluster, wage relationships are predominately based upon a technical, though not necessarily formal, job-content comparison. The skill required (including job knowledge) is the primary differentiating factor,[9] but there are modifications in job placement relative to responsibility, working conditions, and physical effort (in the sense of heavy or light work). These relationships are influenced somewhat by custom and tradition and are mutually interdependent with promotion and transfer sequences. A wage differential of 5 cents per hour between two jobs within such a group is typically quite meaningless in terms of ability to hire or retain employees in a market sense and is also insignificant in terms of labor cost.[10]

Close association of employees on cluster-type jobs creates an environment that forces close comparison of jobs and allows a type of direct comparison more meaningful than where jobs are less closely integrated. Within such a job group, evaluation typically works out with reasonable precision and normally preserves a high proportion of existing wage relationships. Job content does not, however, create a completely rigid hierarchy.[11] Minor differences in placement can and do exist among the same jobs in different companies. Complete agreement as to the proper relationships would not be expected. These differences, however, serve only to emphasize the common-sense patterns in the major outlines of the relationships and the reliance upon judgment as to the relative wage significance of job content.

Normally there are one or a few key jobs within a job-cluster group. A key job may simply be a "good" cross-comparison job, because of similarity of job content, but usually a key job has significance because of its importance as to number of employees or key skill.

Primarily, key jobs are the more important jobs, the dominant jobs, within a group. Non-key job relationships are built around key jobs. A non-key wage rate may be adjusted with minor or major social disturbance within the group, but with little or no impact outside the group. This is a significant limiting aspect of wage relationships. Adjust a key job, and it may well pull all or most of the non-key jobs with it; and there will typically be repercussions outside the particular cluster—major or minor, depending on the strength of the ties with one or more other groups.

Internal comparison between key jobs in different clusters tends to be less precise and of a somewhat different character than comparisons within a group. As comparison is made among jobs that are very different in type and kind of job content, the area of judgment as to the "correct" relationship widens. Consciously and unconsciously, judgment leans more upon external market relationships or established internal relationships as the differences in job content and "social distance" increase.

Relationships among key jobs, and hence among clusters, must be qualified to admit differences in the strength and character of the association. Some relationships may be quite close in binding together internal groups. Two rival crafts forming key jobs in two groups may create a very close association. In other situations, the employees on one key job may hardly be aware of the existence of a second key job. The number of employees in particular groups, the traditional social position of a group, and other such considerations play a role in the relative strength or weakness of these relationships. Internal relationships may be reinforced or weakened by the existence and strength of external wage relationships. Cost considerations are also involved, as discussed later.

Key jobs and market comparison

While recognizing these differences among key-job relationships, the general point may be illustrated by the common procedure in applying job evaluation. The problem of rating the key jobs is quite different from rating the non-key jobs. The first step, creating the "skeleton" by placing key jobs within the evaluation scale, is much more difficult than filling in jobs once the skeleton is created. Where, for example, should the key maintenance jobs or the key office jobs be placed relative to the key production jobs? In the case of office jobs this direct question is typically avoided, since a different evaluation plan is almost always used. With the maintenance jobs there is a considerable area of judgment.

Putting the question even more broadly, certain jobs are "key" jobs from a market comparison point of view. This list of key jobs is not necessarily identical with the list of internal key jobs. Some wage structures are keyed to the labor market at only a few points. Not all companies or plants are in an identical market position. In a high-paying industry, reference to the labor market may be almost exclusively to other companies and plants within the industry. The steel industry inequity program appears to be a case in point. In a high-paying plant within an industry, existing plant relationships may be accepted as established relationships. In lower-paying plants and industries, market comparisons may be more directly related to local hiring conditions. But with all these relationships, the close association with job content becomes a weaker basis for wage determination.

Broadly speaking, there is, of course, a strong tie among all jobs in a plant. Stability of differentials, once established, is quite firmly maintained. Economic forces, both cost pressures and hiring considerations, apply in a major sense to the structure as a whole. A plant contemplating expansion from 20,000 employees to 40,000 in a city of modest size will have a different view of its "ability to hire" than will a small firm requiring an insignificant proportion of new entrants on the labor market to maintain normal employment. At the other extreme, the placement of one particular job is adjusted from time to time primarily with changes in job content. There are, however, adjustments of groups of jobs, such as all maintenance jobs, all office jobs, etc., demonstrating a degree of independence for broad and narrow clusters. This group movement of jobs is clearly shown under the impact of job evaluation. Study of such job-rate changes will demonstrate group realignment and a significant degree of preservation of narrow internal group relationships. Group adjustment is also shown in the historical evolution of particular wage structures. "Inequity" negotiations and the grievance procedure bring out responses between and within clusters.

While these various types of wage changes do not lend themselves to simple representation, they seem sufficiently clear to support the general proposition that all job rates, viewed through internal comparison standards, are not related with equal or similar significance, but are composed of a system of broad and narrow groups organized around key jobs. In rough outline, these groups can be analyzed in terms of joint demand and supply for particular types and kinds of labor. Perhaps, more appropriately, one should say that they reflect adaptations to labor-market conditions in which wage comparison and hiring considerations are blended. As part of this process, they change with modifications of job content as broad production processes are modified. No easy "causal" statement is possible; nonetheless, group wage movements are a significant aspect of the wage-determination process.

Issues arising from technological change

Before leaving the subject of internal wage comparisons, special mention must be made of the impact of technological change. Wage-rate grievances are most commonly associated with new or changed jobs; wage relationships are continuously forced to adapt to this dynamic factor.

Technological change may leave unaffected, may increase, or may decrease the skill and responsibility required in performing the job. It may also alter working conditions and physical effort. On balance, one can only speculate as to the total effect. "De-skilling" creates obvious headaches and problems and consequently attracts attention; upgrading, however, can certainly not be neglected.

One example of upgrading recently encountered has changed craft relationships in a particular printing establishment. All major craft groups have gained about equally from general wage increases in the period since 1940. Pressmen have gained, however, with the introduction of larger, more complicated, and faster presses. Technological change has been much more marked in the press department than in other departments. It has effected a change in group rate relationships by creating a significant proportion of more skilled and more responsible new and changed jobs. Product mix has also changed in favor of these jobs. Note particularly the group effect in raising average earnings and creating new promotional opportunities, as well as the specific effect upon particular jobs.

The troublesome wage problem arises when the skill content of a job is reduced. Workers are conscious of the advantage to the company of greater production per hour and lowered unit product cost. They wish to share in the gains of technology, or at least not to suffer a job-rate reduction. Industrial relations effects vary, of course, with the size of the group, promotion opportunities, layoff or demotion necessities, protections to present incumbents, and other factors. But sharing gains with all workers is "pie in the sky," and it is far easier to gain acceptance of new methods if the rate can be sweetened a bit. The logic of rate relationships may be submerged in such situations. A job-evaluation director nearly resigned recently in a plant making its first major move in the much discussed area of automation. On the other hand, an out-of-line rate can become the source of future grievances.

It is somewhat unrealistic not to expect technology to create continuously some proportion of preferred wage positions. While this does not alter the longer-term relationships which tend to mold the wage-differential structure, it must be given an important place in understanding day-to-day wage problems. General reviews of all jobs with differential wage increases may well continue as part of the process of gradual adjustment of a wage structure to technological change.

Wage-structure adjustment to market-rate influence

The influence of the labor market upon the wage structure can best be approached by a descriptive type of analysis. Individual firm and industry variations in the general level of wages are assumed to be a major source of rate dispersion. Consider in this setting the degree of dominance of particular market rates and the source of such dominance.

To start with some simple examples, in a small city one inquires of a high-paying firm what they pay an industrial nurse and why. The explanation is given that the job is evaluated and comes out at x dollars. Upon further discussion, we find that the personnel man feels that, in truth, the evaluation is definitely on the low side; but, after all, they're paying 25 percent more than the local hospitals. In a low-paying firm, we find that they pay the switchboard operator the identical rate paid by the telephone company. We ask whether that isn't high in terms of their other office jobs. The answer is yes, but they always hire a trained operator; the rate is really quite independent of other office rates; and it causes no "trouble." Consider an over-the-road trucking rate in a low-paying mill. Do they meet the trucking-firm rate? No, but they aren't organized yet and they do have the rate up so high that they would hate to have to argue it with some of their skilled production workers. In fact, they're not at all sure that they shouldn't sell their trucks and contract the work.

In all these examples the wages in question constitute peripheral rates for the companies discussed. These rates tend to be paid for hiring-jobs and they do not constitute internal key-job rates for significant clusters within the company (the trucking rate could be a key job in a warehousing department). They also have in each instance been pulled out of "consistent" internal alignment by market-rate influences. The market-rate influences are dominated by segments of industry in which the rates discussed are part of the central core of the general rate structure and subject to general rate influences in those industries. Consider a broader example: a paper box plant in Detroit in which the general rate structure is low by Detroit standards. How will this plant get maintenance and office employees and what will they be paid? We find that maintenance employees constitute a "tougher" problem than do office workers, but both are more difficult to obtain than the predominately female production employees. In this case, both maintenance and office rates are, the managers feel, on the high side relative to the firm's general level of wages. In fact, they have had to make "major" concessions to get and hold a maintenance staff.

In thinking of examples of market-rate influences, a series of considerations arises relating to how necessary it is to meet or at least come close to market rates and how difficult it is in terms of mutually interdependent wage relationships and cost effects within the firm. The pull of internal consistency through internal key jobs must be taken into account. This pull is around the central core of the general rate structure. There is also the pull of the market, which may be over a broad general group or quite specific as to a single job. The pull of the market may be essentially an equity comparison or quite directly related to hiring.

In the state wage structure in New Hampshire, a point was reached at which forty vacancies existed in the civil engineering series in the highway department. The implication was clearly either to revise the salary rates or curtail the department. A tapered adjustment covering the lowest three of six civil engineering categories was made, hiring being more critical than retention. Within a year most of the vacancies were filled. This local incident occurred in the midst of a country-wide shortage in all the professional engineering fields. Internal consistency, in a static sense, had to yield. On the other hand, a survey of civil engineering salaries would show the usual wide dispersion of rates and the presumed weakness of market forces.

Certain market rates may be highly structured within a community, ranging from a single rate to a narrow band. Other market rates are much more diffuse, covering a wide band with no central identifiable dominant source. A rate may be part of the central core of the general wage level, a key job in a broad cluster, a key job within a narrow cluster, or a peripheral, semi-independent rate. The position and meaning of the same job rate vary from industry to industry and company to company. The rate may be closely or more remotely connected to hiring.

Among these various wage examples, consideration must be given to firms and industries insignificantly influenced by "local" labor-market conditions. An oil refinery in a town or city may be slightly interested in local rates but not meaningfully so. The managers make "equity" comparisons within the industry, but there are no local-market rate compulsions. Their general rate structure is simply high enough to create an internally determined structure subject to equity comparison within the industry. The basic steel structure, as previously mentioned, was similarly relatively uninfluenced by rates outside the industry.

The diversity of actual markets in terms of geographic location, industrial mix, size, degree of union organization, and other characteristics explains the fact of rate dispersion. Employees are closely attached to particular companies, and hiring in most cases is predominately related to vacancies rather than closely to rates. Nevertheless, market-rate influences upon a wage structure do exist. The problem is one of formulating this influence in reasonable balance with other forces. The influence runs predominately by groups and categories of jobs through key jobs. It must be stated relative to the general level of wages for the firm, as associated with its industry, and to the total wage pattern in a community.

Only confusion results from attempting to draw a hard and fast distinction between market influences and internal-rate relationships. But there are differences in degree of influence. Internal relationships are strongest within narrow functional groups, though even here the amount of the wage differential is more a part of a broader picture than is the rank order of jobs. Among clusters, the internal ties are stronger: (1) in relating a narrow group to a larger group of which it is a distinct part; (2) within roughly comparable skill bands; and (3) where closely comparable or identical jobs are found in several functional groups. As concerns comparisons and ties between broader clusters, the internal forces grow weaker and the market ties, including historically established relationships, become stronger.

The influence of labor cost and broad market contours

The influence of labor cost is exerted primarily through the general level of wages. Within this context, jobs vary in their labor-cost significance. Jobs must be considered as to both their cost and wage relationship.

The general level of wages may be commonly associated with a fairly well-defined modal group of "production" employees and jobs. In manufacturing it consists frequently of a group of semi-skilled machine operators, assemblers, and other workers of this type. While for any one job within this skill band there is room for debate and adjustment without meaningful cost significance, total labor cost is fixed in large measure by the level of this band of rates. In other wage structures, the general level and modal group are associated with certain skilled jobs. In a printing establishment recently studied, the modal group and general level are clearly formed by the journeyman rates for the various crafts. Some structures may be bimodal and, indeed, some may have a single occupational rate as the key point in the general level. The general level is analytically related to the modal employee group and the concentration of labor cost. Wage-structure relationships are built around this central cost point.

Without exploring the ramifications of labor cost, it is clear that some industries and some firms are more confined by labor cost than are others. We recognize for industries and segments of industries the influence of differences in rate of expansion, variations in the proportion of labor to total cost, the degree of price competition in the product market, the greater or lesser strategic influence of labor cost within the product competition framework, and other factors.

Each firm is related by labor cost to a product and industry reference. Within any industry, the position of each firm varies; though there appears to be greater opportunity for independence in some industries than in others. However, in all industries some firms gain leadership positions by marketing performance, product and methods research and innovation, factory efficiency, and other ways. This leadership creates cost latitude within which they may respond to the labor market. While this side of the coin is a "permissive" factor, frequently allowing a favorable position in the local labor market, the reverse of the coin is not. Firms in an adverse position within their industry, particularly in industries tied by competitive cost to a low general level of wages, are frequently forced into an adverse labor-market position. These forced differences in the general level of wages override in large measure the weaker equalizing tendencies for most particular job rates. Broad differences within a rate band for a job can commonly be associated with general-level differentials of this character.

Aware as we are of the historical pattern of drawing industrial labor from agriculture, the complexity of the industrial wage structure must be imposed in detail upon the degree of industrialization of different areas. Superimpose upon various degrees of industrialization the factors influencing location of particular industries, historical and present, and the pattern of wage differentials among industries, national and local. Such diverse forces create the local labor markets with their steel cities, textile towns, and diversified but particularized metropolitan areas.

These broad contours are not the subject of this chapter, but they form the perspective from which one must view the "imperfect" market for truck drivers with its varied rates—the rate of the large oil company, the coal and oil wholesalers and retailers, the local warehouse, the large milk dealer, the beer concern, the soft drink company, the over-the-road rate, and so forth—and its differences in job content, cost significance, and industrial economics. These rate differences result predominately from "general level" rather than from "imperfect occupational" differentials.

As a different example, what do we mean by the market rate for typists in the city of Hartford? There are insurance companies in which this rate is part of the central core of the general rate structure; there are also financial institutions, retail and wholesale offices, and diversified manufacturing industries, with a heavy metal-trades concentration overlaid with a large airplane-engine manufacturing concern. The level of abstraction required to bring these many influences into a single rate (recognizing only differences in job content) is so extreme as to be quite misleading in the light of the total interplay of forces.

How can one put complex patterns into somewhat generalized form? It certainly is not labor cost that sets the rate for typists in a manufacturing firm. The rate could be doubled or tripled with no meaningful impact. The cost influence of all the office rates in such a firm becomes a significant but, typically, not a dominant consideration. The firm adapts its rate structure for office jobs to its general level of factory jobs *and* to the community pattern for office jobs. This adaptation may pull office rates down from a high level of factory rates or up from a low level of such rates. Each individual rate is part of a structure and held within tolerance limits within that structure. Substructures must be considered as being adapted to both the modal level of production rates and to the appropriate labor market from a cost and wage-relationship point of view.

As a major point in this labor-cost context, the "general level" has been associated, relative to the rate structure, with the modal group of production or factory employees. Latitude for wage adjustment for other groups needs to be viewed, in part, as a permissive degree of cost freedom not possible with respect to this central core.

Related to this discussion are some points connected with the broad problem of compression in rate structures and the narrowing of percentage skill differentials. In part this problem involves very general changes in the composition of the labor supply and the character of technological advance. In part it involves price and wage movements and the degree of inflation. But compression can also be seen in diverse wage movements among groups of jobs. General increases can be studied relative to special adjustments. For example, in a printing establishment general-level changes are essentially a skilled-level change, and special adjustments may be given to less skilled groups. More commonly, general changes have their primary impact on semiskilled jobs, and skilled groups may receive special adjustments. The main point is to note the group job character of the problem, as well as its complexity.

Notes

1. In particular cases, other influences may modify these commonly noted bases for wage differentials. Incentive jobs have a real or presumed effort—and output—premium. Variations in competitive conditions in different product markets may be reflected in job differentials. Special bases of payment, such as payment per mile in transportation, may have job and occupational repercussions.

2. A closely related discussion is to be found in Clark Kerr, "Labor Markets: Their Character and Consequences," *American Economic Review*, vol. 40, no. 2 (May, 1950), p. 278. The distinction between the wage and employment function is an essential one.

3. Variations in the extent and scope of internal promotion as contrasted with outside hiring are no doubt quite significant. Differences in the amount and type of training required on different jobs, differences in seniority units and customs, differences in management policies, as well as other factors, make this a complex picture. Within the same industry some firms do more "outside" hiring than others. Differences also exist among different labor markets. The trend, however, is presumably toward broader integration of jobs and more extensive training and promotion.

4. Statistics on labor turnover by length of service give clear support to this point of view. It would be difficult to maintain that ignorance of alternative employment opportunities is also a function of length of service. The resulting immobility is clearly a rational economic decision, though just how much immobility results is an open question. There may, on the other hand, be some enhancement of mobility through the seniority advantage of getting in on the ground floor in new plants and expanding industries. While seniority factors can be allowed for in explaining workers' job choices, they then obscure the explanation of wage differentials.

5. Inequity negotiations may combine the elimination of job inequities within the plant with the elimination of corporate interplant and industry geographical differentials. Union goals may include, but not be limited to, the traditional objectives of job evaluation.

6. The term *job cluster* follows Dunlop; the broad outline of this approach has been jointly discussed over a number of years.

7. Broad and narrow groups are somewhat arbitrary, but the distinction is essential relative to different types of structural wage changes. For example, for some structural problems one might find no need to break down the clerical group into narrower groups; for other problems, the subdivisions would be of primary importance.

8. Job-evaluation labor grades conceal the kind of job groups discussed and may appear to give an artificial simplicity to the relationships among jobs.

9. In some process-type industries it may be debated whether skill or responsibility is the primary differentiating factor.

10. It is related, however, to the previously mentioned, and difficult to define, concept of the promotion-incentive factor.

11. Technological change, which will be discussed briefly, is a constant disruptive factor.

Orbits of Coercive Comparison

3

BY ARTHUR M. ROSS

IT WILL BE WORTH examining in brief certain of the major questions to which current wage theory provides no answer or a poor one. These are no minor matters. They lie close to the heart of wage determination, and upon their satisfactory explanation depends our choice between resting with the hypotheses of current wage theory or seeking new and more efficient tools.

1. Why, in the bargaining process, is the size of the wage adjustment often more crucial than the amount of the wage which results? We have become accustomed to think of the wage bargain as a determination of the price of labor in the same sense that a sales bargain is a determination of the price of wheat. Nevertheless, the bargaining process is almost always directed toward an upward or downward change in a preexisting wage rate, and the greatest interest often centers on the magnitude of the change. The trade union leader must achieve a 15 percent increase for his group because most of the other locals affiliated with his international union have done so. The employer insists on a 10 percent wage cut, after other employers have been successful in enforcing it, so as to avoid competitive disadvantage. The fact-finding board suggests that an 18½-cent increase would be a fair settlement in the copper mining industry, in view of the fact that it has become the pattern of adjustment in the "related" iron and steel industry. Thus, equalizing tendencies in collective bargaining are directed toward equalization of adjustments as often as equalization of rates.

2. In economic theory, the market is the locus of the single price, enforced by competition among buyers and among sellers. Under competitive conditions, no buyer will offer more and no seller will accept less.

But wage rates are not equalized in the local labor market. Every competent survey establishes this fact. If it had never been established prior to 1941, the comprehensive area wage studies of the Bureau of Labor Statistics during the recent war would have provided a final and conclusive

From *Trade Union Wage Policy*, pp. 46-64. Copyright 1948 by The Regents of the University of California; reprinted by permission of the University of California Press.

demonstration. In order to promulgate schedules of "going rates" for wage stabilization purposes, the National War Labor Board found it necessary (with minor exceptions) to specify ranges or "brackets" for every occupation in every industry group and in every community.

Labor economists have expended much effort and exercised great ingenuity in a valiant endeavor to explain the observed differentials. This endeavor has proceeded along three lines. First, it is pointed out that comparisons are difficult because of variations in job content and methods of payment between one establishment and another. This is true enough, but it is yet to be shown that wage differentials can be explained away by these variations, and we can hardly afford to assume it by an act of faith. Secondly, it is argued that the concept of "wages" ought to be broadened to include vacation provisions, shift premiums and other nonwage benefits, regularity of employment and conditions of work. Here again, it has never been demonstrated that wages, even in this sense, tend to equality in the labor market area; and, as a matter of fact, better-paying firms usually provide better conditions of work and other nonwage advantages. Finally, economists have fallen back upon the discovery and description of multitudinous "imperfections" in the labor market. Workers are tied to their places of residence, employers and employees do not have complete knowledge of market conditions, job shopping and labor piracy are frowned upon, and so forth. But all this amounts merely to a reaffirmation of what has not been proved: that the equalizing tendencies in wage determination are composed of supply and demand operating in the labor market, and that equalization would be attained were it not for the imperfections. It implies that equalization is more likely to occur as the market is more competitive and less organized, but, as we shall see, the reverse is much closer to the fact.

3. One of the seemingly irrational phenomena of industrial relations is the fact that work stoppages frequently occur when the difference between the parties has been reduced to minute proportions. The general public finds it most exasperating to suffer the inconvenience of a stoppage when the parties are only 2 cents apart. Since the union takes the initiative in calling a strike, the public tends to put the blame on the callousness and arrogance of union leaders. Editorial columns are studded with mathematical demonstrations that the workers would have been much better off if they had accepted the employer's final offer and stayed at work. Legislators then propose that workers be required to accept or reject the employer's final offer in secret ballot before a strike can be called.

Strikes sometimes continue after an ostensibly reasonable basis for settlement has developed. In the 1945-46 General Motors strike, for example, the President's fact-finding board proposed a 19½-cent settlement in January; the company offered 17½ cents in February; and the parties finally settled for 18½ cents in March. Why was the extra penny so important to the Union? It will take the workers ten years to make up the loss of one month's work, at the rate of a penny an hour. And why was the penny so important to the company?

4. Another seemingly irrational practice of many unions (if rationality is conceived as the maximization of wage income) is their insistence upon a uniform wage rate throughout their jurisdiction. Every student of economics knows that a monopolist can increase his income by discriminating among buyers. There is little doubt that a union could achieve a higher average wage rate, and a greater total wage income for its members, if it were to extract from each employer the most that he could be made to pay. If this were done, wages would vary according to the importance of labor as an element in total cost, the elasticity of product demand, and the profit position of individual employers. Some organizations, such as the Musicians' Union, do make an elaborate classification of employers on the basis of ability to pay, and establish a different scale for each classification. Others, such as the Carpenters' Union, insist on a craft rate in all branches of employment in the local area.

There are difficulties in the way of price discrimination in the commodity market; buyers are likely to object to the practice, and the Robinson-Patman Act purports to prohibit it. But buyers of labor frequently object to the absence of discrimination; that is to say, they resent the imposition of a standard rate regardless of their wage-paying capacity.

The usual explanation is that unions seek a "standard rate" in order to "take labor out of competition." This follows the Webbs's classic chapter on the higgling of the market, describing the manner in which the pressure of competition in the commodity market becomes focused on the rate of wages.[1] But actually this is no explanation. "Taking labor out of competition" requires the organization of employees throughout the market in order to eliminate nonunion competition, and a policy of downward inflexibility, in order to prevent competitive wage cutting. It does not require uniformity of wages at any time.

5. One may also ask why it is that unions often press for consolidated bargaining structures, as represented by multiunion and multiemployer bargaining. Consolidation of bargaining structure is not necessarily attended by uniformity of wage rates, but equalizing tendencies are accentuated as equitable, and rational criteria are applied to larger areas of decision.

Why are multiunion bargaining units organized? In labor economics, "bargaining power" is often employed loosely and uncritically as a blanket explanation for decisions; here we are told that "joint bargaining on the part of craft unions may strengthen the bargaining power of individual crafts."[2] The assumption seems to be that the union's bargaining power varies directly with the size of the unit. Metz states that "generally speaking, the smaller the unit the less its bargaining power."[3] Actually, the opposite proposition is closer to the truth. A union's bargaining power is measured by its ability to win concessions from the employer. Other things being equal, bargaining power is greater as the percentage of total cost represented by workers in the unit and the monetary expense involved in meeting a given demand are smaller and as the demand for the services of the group is less elastic. A craft union representing only a minority of workers may have more bargaining power than a trades council representing all the workers. If the craft is indispensable and the workers are irreplaceable, the union can achieve the effect of a complete walkout by withdrawing its own members. Moreover, it can ordinarily depend upon the other unions to respect its picket lines. Therefore, there must be other reasons for the growth of multiunion bargaining structures.

If maximization of the total wage bill were the dominating objective of union policy, it would be most difficult to account for the frequent conflict between unions and management on the issue of multiemployer or industry-wide bargaining. It is highly probable that total wage payments are less under multiemployer bargaining than would be true if separate bargains were negotiated between the union and each employer. Unless high-cost firms are to be forced out of business, the wage rate must be set below the capacity of low-cost firms.[4] Notwithstanding the lesser wage bill which results, unions commonly strive for multiemployer bargaining, and management, on balance, opposes it.

Equalizing tendencies under collective wage determination

All these questions are addressed to the relationship between one wage rate and another, or between one wage bargain and another. They involve the structure and function of equalizing tendencies in wage determination. Economic theory does provide for equalizing tendencies, expressed in the Law of One Price and working through the interaction of supply and demand in the labor market area. It is not argued that the traditional market forces have no significance in a system of administered wages, but we have seen that they do not have compelling significance.

In collective wage determination the strongest equalizing tendencies emanate from forces of a different nature entirely—the force of organization and the force of ideas. Organizations are established for the very purpose of achieving mastery over market factors. The ideas are concepts of equity and justice which move in an orbit different from that of supply and demand.

The equalizing tendencies are of two kinds—comparison and consolidation. Equitable comparison links together a chain of wage bargains into a political system which displays many of the characteristics of an equilibrium relationship. Consolidation throws together previously separated bargaining units into the scope of a unitary decision. Both have the effect of integrating that portion of the wage structure in which they operate.

What is referred to here as the pressure of equitable comparison has been variously characterized in the literature as patterns of wage adjustment, wage leadership, key wage bargains, imitation, repetition, and diffusion. One author has constructed a cosmology of industrial relations in which master wage adjustments originate in "generating types" of bargaining relationships and spread into "satellite types."[5] Another observer suggests that "we have reached the stage where a limited number of key bargains effectively influence the whole wage structure of the American economy. When these strategic wages have been determined, for all practical purposes wage rates are determinable throughout the system within narrow limits. . . . The number of key bargains may be placed in the neighborhood of twenty-five to fifty."[6]

However we entitle them, comparisons play a large and often dominant role as a standard of equity in the determination of wages under collective bargaining.

Comparisons are important to the employer, whose greatest anxiety, in the absence of imperative economic pressures, is to avoid "getting out of line." One of the cardinal sins of business conduct is to offer a wage rate, or a wage increase, which proves embarrassing to other employers. In a period of aggressive union demands, there is a tightening of discipline in the business community; "getting out of line" becomes as criminal as grand larceny.

Comparisons are important to the worker. They establish the dividing line between a square deal and a raw deal. He knows that he cannot earn what he would like to have, but he wants what is coming to him. In a highly competitive society, it is an affront to his dignity and a threat to his prestige when he receives less than another worker with whom he can legitimately be compared. At times he is not sure what makes a legitimate comparison, and needs guidance on the point; this is one source of moral authority enjoyed by the union leader. The intelligent leader realizes what Whitehead, Roethlisberger, and other students of industrial psychology have often pointed out: that the worker's attitude toward the rate of pay is more significant, for many purposes, than the real income it provides, and that attitudes can be manipulated. The wage earner is not unique in his propensity for invidious comparison. The professor who has vegetated happily on $4,500 per year becomes morose when an associate professor is brought in at the same rate. The stenographer who celebrated jubilantly when she received an increase of $10.00 a month is disillusioned upon finding that an office mate received $15.00.

Comparisons are crucially important within the union world, where there is always the closest scrutiny of wage agreements in the process of negotiation as well as of those already negotiated. They measure whether one union has done as well as others. They show whether the negotiating committee has done a sufficiently skillful job of bargaining. They demonstrate to the union member whether he is getting his money's worth for his dues. A favorable comparison ("the best contract in the industry") becomes an argument for reelection of officers, a basis for solidification and extension of membership, and an occasion for advancement within the official hierarchy. An unfavorable comparison ("the best we could do under the circumstances") makes it likely that the rank and file will become disgruntled, rival leaders will become popular, and rival unions will become active.

Finally, comparisons are important to the labor arbitrator. The "going rate" and the "prevailing pattern of adjustment" are probably the most compelling criteria of wage determination. Anyone familiar with the realities of arbitration realizes to what extent the other standard criteria are subordinated to these and are employed as supporting rationalizations.[7]

There is an additional reason why going rates and going increases are likely to be followed. The ready-made settlement supplies an answer, a solution, a formula. It is mutually face-saving. The employer can believe that he has not given away too much, and the union leader that he has achieved enough. It is the one settlement which permits both parties to believe they have done a proper job, and the one settlement which has the best chance of being "sold" to the company's board of directors and the union's rank and file. One can understand why wage negotiations are often stalled until an applicable "pattern" develops, and why the employer is then reluctant to grant anything more and the union to accept anything less.

The proposition might be offered that "face" and prestige are bargained more closely than money, especially in a period of general prosperity. After all, the officer of a union, the official of a corporation and the representative of an employers' association are all dealing with other people's money. The fact that this goes on without noticeable damage indicates how loose are the ties which bind the economy together.

The ready-made settlement has other attractions. Negotiation, arbitration, strikes, and lockouts are costly, time-consuming, and unpleasant. They require specialized personnel. They often have a residue of ill will. If the "pattern" is not too outrageous, it hardly seems worthwhile to strive for a different settlement on the outside chance of gaining an extra penny or two. Wage leadership in collective bargaining recommends itself for much the same reasons as price leadership in the commodity market.

Finally, the availability of accurate knowledge has made bargaining settlements more interdependent. Union research offices devote much effort to keeping abreast of contract changes and to disseminating this information among the rank and file. The business community has been giving more attention to the enforcement of self-discipline since the end of the war. Personnel offices and commercial reporting services supply the employer with comprehensive data on levels and movements of wages.[8]

Orbits of coercive comparison

We have seen why equitable comparison plays a central role in trade union (and employer) wage policy, and why wage rates and wage changes are transplanted from one agreement to another. But the orbit of comparison is not infinite. There is no uniformity of occupational rates in local labor markets, let alone throughout the nation. There is nothing resembling an economy-wide pattern of adjustment. Even in 1945-46, when the 18½-cent adjustment was so popular, the average increase among manufacturing workers was 14½ cents; and among nonmanufacturing workers, 8½ cents.[9] And so we come to a group of central questions. Under what circumstances do comparisons have the most compelling effect? When does a difference become an inequity? What are the mechanisms integrating the wage structure under collective bargaining? In brief, what is the orbit of coercive comparison and the path of political pressure between one bargain and another?

Labor market competition

It has already been shown that the strongest equalizing tendencies in collective wage determination are removed from any spatial relationships with each other. Wages respond as much to factors which are independent of the labor market as to any influences within the market. The buyer and seller of labor do meet within some fixed geographic area, but the price at which the exchange takes place is often ultimately determined by other agencies hundreds of miles away, without necessary knowledge or concern for each of the particular markets affected by the bargain. Locality, an essential characteristic of the labor market so far as supply and demand are concerned, is of limited relevance for wage determination.[10]

Product-market competition

One might reason that wage changes would move from establishment to establishment within a single industry. Often they do: 97.9 per cent of workers in the basic iron and steel industry and 75.4 per cent of workers in the rubber products industry received 18½-cent increases in 1945-46. Often they do not, however: in the food products industry, 10.5 per cent received 5 cents, 16.8 per cent received 10 cents, and 29.0 per cent received 16 cents, with the remainder of the workers dispersed above, below, and between these levels.[11] Certainly the iron and steel industry is no more competitive than the food industry. Similar variations are apparent when absolute rates, rather than adjustments, are compared. Wage rates have virtually been equalized on a national basis in the coal industry, but the most sizable differentials prevail in the hosiery industry, the soap industry, and many other industries in which products compete in a national market.[12] Among local trade and service activities in San Francisco and presumably in other communities), wage rates tend to be uniform when the industry is covered by a master agreement and diverse when it is not.[13]

These facts suggest that the product market may have been the locus of equalizing tendencies in some instances, but only through its association with other influences and not in its own right; and that organization, rather than competition, is characteristic of those industries in which equalizing forces are apparent.

It may be that product-market competition will take on more significance in a depression. The trade union is primarily a political instrumentality and is not mechanically or continuously concerned with conditions in the product market. The business firm, on the other hand, is primarily an economic institution and is more clearly oriented toward costs, prices, and profits. Ordinarily the employer goes on the offensive in a depression.

It follows that product-market competition is a more significant mechanism for diffusing wage reductions than wage increases. One may note that Mr. Dunlop, in describing how "wage changes may spread by means of impacts on cost-price relationships," deals for the most part with reductions. "A decrease in wage rates may lead to product price reductions, aimed at securing a larger share of orders. These price changes may in turn force competing enterprises to reduce prices and enforce wage reductions. . . . A second variant may be initiated through the action of large buyers in the product market forcing price reductions after an initial cut. . . ."[14]

In a period of prosperity, when unions take the initiative, there are no similar compelling economic forces diffusing a wage increase throughout the product market. It is not particularly important to the employers, for the time being, if labor costs move out of line with each other. The product market is a significant "universe" to the union, under these circumstances, only when it is coterminous with the jurisdiction of a single organization, the scope of a unitary decision, or the locus of interunion rivalry.

On balance, it may be concluded that product-market competition is a more influential orbit of comparison than labor-market competition, but nevertheless not of decisive importance. It is of greater moment to the employer than to the union, but in a progressive economy the union is on the offensive during the major part of the time because money wages and real wages have a secular tendency to move upward.

Centralized bargaining within the union

We come now to a group of more compelling influences—centralized bargaining within the union, common ownership of establishments, participation by the government, and rival union leadership.

In many unions, particularly old-line AFL unions, wage bargaining is a function of the local units. Here the comparison between one bargain and another is often not especially sharp.

In other unions, particularly the newer CIO unions, bargaining has been taken over by the regional and central offices of the organization. This is characteristic of the Auto Workers, the Steelworkers, the Electrical Workers, and the longshore and maritime unions of the CIO. The international union not only requires that any settlement be submitted to it for ratification, but actively participates in negotiations. Under these circumstances, there is a much greater tendency toward uniform settlements. The local office may be little more than a membership-recruiting, dues-collecting, and grievance-adjusting outpost of the organization. The international union carries on all significant negotiations. Local officers and members look to the international union for fair and equal treatment and feel they should share equally in the benefits deriving from their common strength. The parent body feels a natural compulsion to deal evenhandedly between one unit and another.

Centralized bargaining is accompanied by consolidation of strategy within the union. By moving together under the leadership of the parent body, the different locals can achieve the effect of industry-wide bargaining (or more properly union-wide bargaining) even though the employers continue to negotiate individually. During the war, several CIO unions developed master contract proposals, or "uniform national programs," which every local union was instructed to serve upon its employers. The Mine, Mill, and Smelter Workers had a six-point program, the Steelworkers had a seventeen-point program, and so on.[15] Consolidation of strategy has lessened to some extent since the end of the war, but union-wide or industry-wide settlements have persisted, with minor exceptions, in the basic steel, rubber, meat packing, electrical, coal, railroad, maritime, and automobile industries.

When bargaining is centralized and strategy is consolidated, nonuniform adjustments are possible, but the international union must assume the burden of proving that they are necessary or desirable. It must guard against being accused of discriminating between local unions. In 1946 the meat packing unions, in order to reduce geographical differentials in the industry, negotiated higher increases for "southern" and "river" plants than for "metropolitan" plants. This was justified to the workers in the "metropolitan" plants on the ground that otherwise work would be shifted to low-wage areas. In the same year the Steelworkers had a similar problem. Employers in the steel fabricating industry demanded insistently that they not be governed by the uniform adjustment in the basic steel industry, as they had been in 1946. Desirous of reaching peaceful agreements throughout its jurisdiction, the union decided to grant the demand. It then took the position that the 15-cent settlement was not a "pattern" and should not stand as a bar to larger settlements in the fabricating industries.

Common ownership of establishments

When two or more establishments are brought under common ownership, "equal pay for equal work" becomes a persuasive slogan. The case is similar to that of the centralized union. The wage policy of a multiplant company is generally made in the central office, or at least is subject to central consideration.

A single decision-making agency of any kind finds it difficult to discriminate, because its employees, customers, or members demand that it deal equitably among them. The multiplant company is no exception. To the union, most wage differentials appear to be inequitable and irrational. Inequity and irrationality are less tolerable when they emanate from a single source than when they inhere in a multitude of separate decisions.

Thus, the Auto Workers are more incensed at wage differentials between various plants of General Motors than at those between Ford and General Motors. During the recent war, the union made a number of bitter attacks upon the War Labor Board's area wage stabilization program (which it called the "bracket racket") because the program made it impossible to apply "General Motors rates" to a large number of plants which had lately been acquired by the Corporation. In the union's long-range wage program, company-wide equalization has priority over industry-wide equalization.[16]

Another example is found in the California street railway industry. The Los Angeles Railway System and the Key System in the San Francisco Bay area, as well as a number of other local transit systems, were recently acquired by the National City Lines, a holding company. Transit wage rates in Los Angeles and the Bay area had not been equal prior to this consolidation of ownership. In its 1947 negotiations with the Key System, the Carmen's Union initially demanded a basic wage rate of $1.56 per hour. It was clear, however, that the real objective was $1.35, the Los Angeles rate; and the Carmen's Union soon offered to "compromise" on this figure. The Key System refused to pay the Los Angeles rate, and it was only after a strike of eighteen days (an unusually long stoppage in a public utility dispute) that the union leaders agreed to recommend a settlement of $1.31. Despite this recommendation, the rank and file accepted the settlement only by a vote of 837 to 532.

Participation by the government

When the government participates actively in the determination of wages, the pressure for uniform treatment is almost irresistible. It is a cardinal tenet of democracy that the government must exercise its powers evenhandedly and dispense justice impartially. To discriminate among unions and among employers is virtually impossible from a political standpoint, even if it were desirable. Subtle notions of equity permitting nonuniform treatment might be designed, of course; but it hardly requires demonstration that the government is in no position to enforce them against strong private organizations.

It is only natural that when the government steps into a labor dispute, it brings along its own concepts of right and wrong. The nature of these concepts is apparent from the government's own behavior as an employer. The Walsh-Healey Act provides that contractors doing work for the United States shall pay wages not lower than prevailing rates determined by the Public Contracts Board. The charter of the City of San Francisco requires that workers employed on the municipal street railway shall receive wages equal to the average of the two highest-paying transit systems in California. Since the government's own wage policy, developed in a political context, rests so heavily on the principle of equalization, it is not surprising that it should adhere to that principle with regard to private employment.

Throughout the war period, collective bargaining was dominated by the National War Labor Board. The Board enjoyed thinking that it operated strictly on a "case-by-case basis," with every dispute decided on its own merits, but in practical effect this was only a pleasant fiction. The "merits" of a case rested on the application of rigid and uniform policies which gradually developed during the first two years of experience. This was not the result of choice but of necessity. It would have been extremely difficult to grant more to one union than had been granted to another under similar circumstances. Moreover, the Board was engaged in the mass production of directive orders—twenty thousand before the job was done. As every sophomore knows, mass production demands standardization. There was a standard policy on general wage increases: the Little Steel formula. There was a standard policy on union security: maintenance of membership and checkoff if the union's strike record was not too bad. There was a standard policy on vacations: one week for one year's seniority and two for five. There was a standard policy on promotions: seniority governs when merit and capacity are equal. And so on.

The twenty thousand directive orders introduced much uniformity into collective bargaining contracts throughout the country, especially in manufacturing industries organized by the CIO. Also, they encouraged a widespread habit of thinking in terms of pattern, precedent, and prevailing practice. The effect of the Board on the thinking of labor and management was particularly influential in the case of new local unions and newly unionized firms. Union membership increased by almost 40 percent during the war, and several thousand additional bargaining units were established. To a considerable extent, the union and employer representatives in these new units had had no bargaining experience in the prewar period, when the bargaining table was better insulated from external influences and negotiations were more self-contained.

After V-J Day, it was decided to lay the Board to rest; the President's Labor-Management Conference of November, 1945, assembled to devise machinery for the adjudication of postwar disputes, developed into a prolonged ceremony of reverence at the altar of "free collective bargaining." Nevertheless, the government played an integral part in the "first round" of postwar settlements. The "first round" was conducted rather more clumsily than might have been possible and required the use of numerous expedients—presidential policy speeches, "leaks" from the Commerce Department, fact-finding and emergency boards, prolonged strikes, government seizures, threats of legislation, and so forth.

The pattern of uniformity was developed in the application of Executive Order 9697, setting forth the government's wage-price policy for the reconversion period.[17] It was necessary that wage increases be approved by the Stabilization Board before they could serve as the basis for a price adjustment from OPA. In practice, the most important of the numerous criteria in the Executive Order became (a) the "general pattern" already established within industries and (b) the elimination of "gross inequities" as between "related industries."

Diffusion of "general patterns" was facilitated by a broad definition of industries. Perhaps the most inclusive was the definition of the electrical products industry, which became coextensive with the jurisdiction of the United Electrical Workers.[18]

The identification of "related industries" by government fact-finding boards and by the Stabilization Board itself was even more instructive. The key wage bargain was made between the Steelworkers and the basic steel producers on February 15, 1946. Earlier settlements of 22 cents in the oil industry and 16 cents in the meat packing industry had been made, but after February 15, 18½ cents became the rule. On February 12, the Stabilization Board gave "preapproval" to any wage increases not in excess of 18½ cents per hour in the iron-ore mining industry and in "certain plants engaged in the steel processing or fabricating industry."[19] "Certain plants" was a means of designating the jurisdiction of the United Steelworkers of America among steel fabricators.

On March 2, 1946, the Stabilization Board approved agreements between the United Rubber Workers and the "Big Four," providing for wage increases of 18½ cents per hour, in order to correct "gross inequities in wage increases between related industries."[20]

Later in March the Stabilization Board approved the 18½-cent strike settlement between General Electric and the Electrical Workers. The parties had applied for approval on the ground that the increase "accords with increases recently granted by, and approved for, other industries." The Board rejected "the concept of any single pattern of increases which might be alleged to have developed generally throughout all industry," but added that "the actual facts of the case, as developed in a separate document submitted by the union and by the independent investigation made by the Board, do require the approval. . . ." The Board found a relationship between the electrical industry and the steel and automobile industries, indicated by the similarity of wage movements in the past, the existence of certain common job classifications in all these industries, the "considerable degree of geographical relationship," and the "limited interrelationship in terms of products."[21]

On March 18, 1946, the Board made a finding that a wage inequity existed between the refractory industry and the steel industry and approved wage adjustments to a maximum of 18½ cents.[22] On April 8, it declined to recognize an asserted relationship between dairy workers and automobile workers in Detroit,[23] but on May 24 it approved wage increases up to 18½ cents per hour for the nonferrous metals industry in eleven western states, on the ground that the industry bore "a close relationship to iron-ore mining, steel, and aluminum industries, in which 18½ cent increases were previously approved."[24]

The National Wage Stabilization Board and the Office of Price Administration did not have primary jurisdiction over the railway industry in the postwar period. Nevertheless, on May 22, 1946, an Emergency Board appointed under the Railway Labor Act recommended an 18½-cent wage increase for seventy thousand employees of the Railway Express Agency, represented by the Railway Clerks, the Machinists, and the Blacksmiths, Drop Forgers, and Helpers.[25] On June 22, a strike against the Hudson and Manhattan Railroad was settled by the same adjustment, as recommended by another emergency board.[26]

The two-day strike of the Locomotive Engineers and the Railway Trainmen throughout the nation's railroad system in 1946 resulted from mismanagement on the part of the government officials involved as much as from arrogance on the part of union leaders. Considerable dissatisfaction had developed among the railroad workers over the deterioration of their relative earning status. Once they were "the aristocrats of labor." By 1945, their annual earnings were surpassed by those in the automobile, ship-building, machinery, rubber, and petroleum industries.[27] Leaders of the railway unions had chafed under wage stabilization policies during the war. The CIO had chartered a rival railway union, and District 50 of the United Mine Workers had been raiding the Brotherhoods. Government boards and agencies had already awarded 18½ cents per hour to a large number of labor organizations which had neither the venerable history nor the political problems of the Brotherhoods. Sixteen railway unions had agreed to arbitrate and were bound to accept the decision of the arbitration board. The Locomotive Engineers and the Railway Trainmen, however, had not participated in the arbitration; and when the Emergency Board made an identical recommendation, they were free to repudiate it. Under the circumstances, it is difficult to understand how the two boards could feel that a wage increase of 16 cents per hour would be satisfactory. The President, attempting to mediate the difficulty, made a "compromise proposal" providing that the wage increases be advanced to 18½ cents on the condition that the seven rule changes also recommended by the Emergency Board be withdrawn. This was too clearly a restatement of the original recommendation to permit acceptance without loss of face, although it probably would have been acceptable if it had been proposed in the first instance.[28] The Locomotive Engineers and the Railway Trainmen finally accepted the proposal, but only after a disheartening debacle which might have been avoided if the two boards had recognized the necessity for an 18½-cent award in view of the prior involvement of the government in a large number of settlements at that level.

The extent of government participation in the "second round" of postwar wage increases was much less than in the "first round." For this reason, there was considerably more diversity in the settlements. The uniform pattern in 1946 was diffused throughout a solid nucleus of our economy: basic steel, steel fabrication, nonferrous metals, electrical manufacturing, automobiles, rubber, farm equipment, aluminum, ship-building, coal, and railroads. The 1947 "pattern" consisted of wage increases of 11½ or 12½ cents per hour, plus "fringe benefits" (most commonly, paid holidays) sufficient in value to bring the total to 15 cents. The scope of its application was much more limited, however. It was confined largely to establishments in the basic steel, automobile, farm machinery, and electrical industries; and even here, there were many more exceptions than in 1946. Steel fabricators were released by consent of the union; a large number of minor electrical goods concerns granted smaller or larger increases; and there were some variations in the farm machinery industry.

To be sure, 15-cent settlements were common in the clothing industry and in some other industries; and it is probable that the average increase of all manufacturing workers was closer to 15 cents in 1947 than to 18½ cents in 1946. However, the clothing agreements and others in the neighbor-hood of 15 cents were only coincidentally connected with the multi-industry settlement in the heavy industries. A true pattern involves a traceable relationship between one bargain and another, and not merely a coincidental similarity. It might be added that the Lewis-Fairless agree-ment in July could be characterized as a 15-cent settlement only by the widest stretch of the imagination.

Thus, when the government left the scene in 1947, a powerful influence making for uniformity of adjustments was removed; and the notion of a master wage bargain embodying a national wage policy receded into the background. It should be kept in mind, however, that if the government should again have occasion to participate actively in the determination of wages, it will doubtless serve once more as an instrument for linking together a multitude of separate agreements into a more closely integrated system.

Rival union leadership

It is strange that although controversy between political parties is valued and competition among businessmen is glorified, rivalry among unions and union leaders is regarded as strictly pathological.

From many points of view, rival union leadership is unmistakably an evil. It leads to jurisdictional disputes. It limits the extent to which unions can discipline their members and underwrite their commitments. It reduces the effectiveness of the labor movement in public affairs.

But there is another side to the coin. Leadership rivalry is the lifeblood of unionism in the United States. After all, the American trade union is pragmatic to the core, neutral in ideology, and weak in political purpose. In the absence of competition for the allegiance of workers, there would be little else to ensure its militance and guarantee its role as an agency of protest. Moreover, rivalry has been the most effective stimulus to organize the unorganized. Let the reader ask himself if the labor movement would be as far along as it is today, in terms of total membership, had there not occurred the split between the AFL and the CIO in the 1930's.

Union leadership rivalries are of three kinds. The first takes place within a single union. There are the ins and the outs, the Young Turks and the Old Reliables, the right wings and the left wings. All the familiar tactics of political mobilization are employed in achieving and holding power. The second is rivalry among the leaders of separate unions, striving for preferment in the upper reaches of the labor movement. The third is jurisdictional rivalry between dual unions claiming the same territory.

Regardless of the form of rivalry, the wage rate and the wage increase are paramount symbols of success. Mr. Taylor states, "The principal non-economic consideration in wage determination in these postwar years is not so much a struggle between employer and union for the loyalty of workmen . . . , but an intense competition between labor organizations based upon the magnitude of their demands upon the employer and upon the size of immediate wage increases."[29] The more intense is leadership competition, the more certain it is that comparisons will be played upon for all they are worth. Practical politics and personal animosities combine to make this the one situation in which workers are assured of "full knowledge."

Under these circumstances, wage comparisons are doubly coercive. They have an offensive aspect and a defensive aspect. The first serves as a disequilibrating force. In order to improve his position and that of his organization, the union leader is impelled to break the equilibrium when conditions are opportune, so that comparisons can be manipulated to advantage. The second serves as an equalizing force. When a rival group has been able to move out in front, the union leader is compelled to restore the equilibrium at a higher level. "Equilibrium" is used here in the technical sense, as a point of rest representing the balance of opposing forces. It is often a necessary condition for stable industrial relations, and therefore has more than academic significance. The equilibrium itself, however, is highly unstable. The motive to break it is fully as strong as the motive to make it.

Notes

1. Sidney Webb and Beatrice Webb, *Industrial Democracy* (London, 1920), pp. 654-703.
2. Florence Peterson, *American Labor Unions* (New York, 1945), p. 192.
3. Harold W. Metz, *Labor Policy of the Federal Government* (Washington, 1945), p. 99.
4. Wage uniformity is not the inevitable result of multiemployer bargaining; employers may be differentiated and classified on various bases. However, standardization is more likely to occur than under single-employer bargaining.
5. Frederick H. Harbison, "A Plan for Fundamental Research in Labor Relations," *American Economic Review*. Vol. 37 (May 1947), Supplement, pp. 379-82.
6. John T. Dunlop, "American Wage Determination: The Trend and Its Significance," a paper read before the Chamber of Commerce Institute on Wage Determination, Washington, D.C., January 11, 1947.
7. See George Soule, *Wage Arbitration* (New York, 1928), pp. 3-5. One arbitrator offers the following explanation of the usefulness of comparisons: "There is no magic formula for wage adjudication. Consequently one of the compelling considerations must be what has happened in free and successful collective bargaining. This indicates how experienced bargainers have evaluated the wage-influencing factors which have evidenced themselves, and what they consider to be 'just.' Arbitration . . . is a substitute for successful bargaining, and the 'pattern' or 'package,' indicates what might have evolved from successful bargaining had the parties acted like others similarly situated. Attention to the 'pattern' or 'package,' rather than adherence to any rigid formula, also reduces the risks of parties entering wage arbitration; but should also encourage their own free settlement. It tends to afford equality of treatment for persons in comparable situations. It also provides a precise, objective figure rather than an artificially contrived rate." Arbitration award of Clark Kerr, *In the Matter of Utility Workers of America and Pacific Gas and Electric Company,* May 27, 1947.
8. "With the advent of the trade union and the personnel department in their modern form, knowledge of wage variation . . . becomes much more inclusive and systematic. A wider and more accurate coverage of wage data results, and better records are compiled. . . . The impression is easily formed that sources for general knowledge of wage changes have multiplied very rapidly in recent years." Dunlop, *Wage Determination Under Trade Unions* (New York, 1944), p. 124.
9. These averages relate to the 79 per cent of manufacturing workers and to the 41 per cent of nonmanufacturing workers who received an increase of some size between August, 1945, and May, 1946. If *all* workers are considered, the averages fall to 11½ cents and 3½ cents. About 30 per cent of the manufacturing workers received increases of 18 or 18½ cents. This would be equivalent to about 45 per cent of *unionized* manufacturing workers. *Monthly Labor Review,* 63 (September 1946), pp. 342-46.
10. Mr. L. H. Fisher has suggested to the author that the term "labor market" is of dubious utility in describing the determination of wages today. As originally conceived, the labor market had spatial properties, but there are no geographical boundaries of the forces affecting the wage policies of unions and employers under collective bargaining. If the term is divorced from geographical content and is employed to represent merely the orbit of wage-determining influences, it becomes tautological. Wages are determined within whatever sphere of influence wages are determined.
11. *Monthly Labor Review,* 63 (September 1946), p. 344.
12. United States Bureau of Labor Statistics, *Handbook of Labor Statistics* (1941 ed.; Washington, 1942), Pt. II, pp. 162-79, 345-49, and *passim.*
13. See Clark Kerr and Lloyd H. Fisher, "Multiple-Employer Bargaining—the San Francisco Experience," in a symposium entitled "Insights into Labor Issues," edited by Richard A. Lester and Joseph Shister and published by Macmillan.
14. Dunlop, *Wage Determination Under Trade Unions*, p. 125. Mr. Dunlop adds that "a third variant of wage changes induced through the price mechanism operates through the cost of living," and that "the third variant would appear to be the most common avenue for the spread of wage increases." This, of course, is a very different kind of cost-price relationship.
15. In 1945 the author was chairman of a tripartite panel which held hearings on a dispute involving the Auto Workers and a parts company. After listening to a long and turgid

argument concerning the union's demand for a maternity-leave clause, the panel inquired how many women were employed in the plant. The company's personnel manager consulted his records and reported that two women, one aged forty-nine and the other fifty-three, were currently on the payroll.

16. "The first logical step in the carrying forward of such a program is the establishment of corporation-wide wage agreements in multiple plant corporations, and the equalization of wages within and between plants in such corporations. . . . The second logical step . . . is the establishment of wage agreements based on equal pay for equal work in all plants and corporations doing comparable work within a section of our industry. . . . The final culmination . . . must result in the establishment of an industry-wide wage agreement based on equal pay for equal work, regardless of the products manufactured or the geographical location of the plant." *A Program for UAW-CIO Members* (Detroit, 1946).

17. Section 3(a) of this order read as follows: "The National Wage Stabilization Board or other wage or salary administration agency having jurisdiction with respect to the wages or salaries involved shall approve any wage or salary increase, or part thereof, which it finds is consistent with the general pattern of wage or salary adjustments which has been established in the industry or local labor market area, between August 18, 1945, and the effective date of this order, or where there is no such general pattern, which it finds necessary to eliminate gross inequities as between related industries, plants or job classifications, to correct substandards of living, or to correct disparities between the increase in wage and salary rates in the appropriate unit since January, 1941, and September, 1945." *Labor Arbitration Reports*, III (Washington, 1946) p. 74. (Hereafter cited as *LAR*.)

18. This industry was defined as including all establishments producing one or more of the following items: "radios, radio tubes, phonographs; telephone and telegraph equipment and electric signalling apparatus; electrical refrigerators and refrigeration machinery, including compressors, evaporators, condensers, and other related mechanical devices essential to electrical refrigeration; complete electrical air-conditioning units; household electrical appliances, including heating, cooking, cooling, cleaning, and laundry equipment; lighting fixtures: wiring devices and supplies; carbon and artificial graphite products for the electrical industry; electrical measuring instruments; electrical prime movers and other electric power equipment (including motors, generator sets, transformers, switchboards, panel-boards, and other transmission accessories) for employment in the generation, transmission, or utilization of electric energy; wire and cable for the transmission of electrical energy; automotive electrical equipment; electric lamps; storage and primary batteries (wet and dry); or electrotherapeutic and electromedical apparatus." National Wage Stabilization Board, Release No. 37, April 11, 1946.

19. *Monthly Labor Review,* 62 (May 1946), p. 837.

20. *Monthly Labor Review,* 62 (May 1946), p. 838.

21. *LAR*, II, pp. 410-11.

22. *Monthly Labor Review,* 62 (May 1946), p. 839.

23. *Monthly Labor Review,* 63 (August 1946), p. 317.

24. *Monthly Labor Review,* 63 (August 1946), p. 318. The nonferrous metals adjustment had been recommended in the report of a presidential fact-finding board, which, after ten pages of logic-chopping over the concept of "relatedness," brought forth a new category of "fundamentally basic industries." Included in this category are steel, iron-ore mining, aluminum, and nonferrous metals. "All are engaged in producing the essential industrial metals—those sinews of our basic economy so vital to reconversion and other national requirements of today. All face similar problems in winning the ore from the earth; all must concentrate and purify the mined substance; all must reduce the chemical compounds found in nature to the useful metallic state; all melt, work, shape and cast these metals into useful forms; and all approach the solution of these problems with similar tools and techniques." *LAR*, III, p. 81.

25. *Monthly Labor Review,* 63 (August 1946), p. 318.

26. *Monthly Labor Review,* 63 (August 1946), p. 323.

27. *Survey of Current Business,* 26 (October, 1946), p. 32.

28. A further complication was that in 1941 and 1943 the unions had been able to secure better terms than those recommended by emergency boards. See Herbert R. Northrup,

"The Railway Labor Act and Railway Labor Disputes in Wartime," *American Economic Review*, 36 (June 1946), pp. 324-43. When the Administration persuaded the unions to postpone the strike in 1946, it was indicated that a better settlement would be secured. See verbatim transcript of telephone conversations among President Truman, Mr. Steelman, Mr. Whitney, and Mr. Johnson in *United States News*, Vol. 20, June 7, 1946, pp. 71-74.

29. George W. Taylor, "Wages and Industrial Progress," address delivered at the University of Pennsylvania, January 10, 1947.

The Wage Structure and Wage Inflation

B. RIGIDITIES IN THE WAGE STRUCTURE: RECENT FORMULATIONS

Pattern Bargaining, Wage Determination, and Inflation: Some Preliminary Observations on the 1976-78 Wage Round

1

BY CLINT BOURDON

JOURNALISTS AND GOVERNMENT officials, mainly following the comments of John Dunlop and others, denoted the bargaining that occurred in early 1976 as the beginning of a three-year wage round. This appellation, a throw-back to the early years of post-World War II bargaining, had long been out of favor. Indeed, Otto Eckstein found in a 1968 follow-up to his first wage-round study that the bargaining schedule was no longer so simple as to be described (or captured statistically) in that manner.[1] A look at the expiration dates of major contracts does, however, lend some credence to the wage-round terminology. Throughout the sixties and seventies there was a consistent three-year pattern of contract renewal in autos, steel, trucking, and a few other industries. Although the total bargaining calendar appeared to be fairly evenly balanced on an annual basis in the late sixties and early seventies (in terms of number of contracts being renewed), a more regular pattern of three-year contracts was again emerging by 1976 (Table 1). In 1976 there were agreements expiring in several major, visible industries (meatpacking, autos, rubber, and trucking), in contrast to only two agreements (in cotton textiles and cement) in 1975.

Of course, implicit in the basic idea of wage rounds is the assumption of an interrelation between major collective bargaining agreements. A series of three-year rounds provides, in this view, only triannual observations on the determinants of wages. All annual settlements in intervening years are

Table 1

Years in Which Wage Settlements Were Concluded in Most Major Collective Bargaining Units in Specified Industries or Industry Groups, 1964-76

Industry	Wage settlements[a] reached in													
	1964	1965	1966	1967	1968	1969	1970	1971	1972	1973	1974	1975	1976	1977
Meatpacking	+			+			+			+			+	
Cotton textiles	+	+				+	+	+	+	+		+	+	+
Apparel:														
Women's dresses	+		+	+		+	+			+			+	
Women's coats and suits	+		+	+		+	+			+			+	
Men's coats and suits		+			+			+			+	+	+	+
Men's shirts		+							+			+		
Paper and pulp:														
West Coast			+	+		+				+	+		+	
International Paper		+		+			+			+	+			+
Petroleum refining	+	+		+		+		+		+				
Rubber		+		+			+	+	+	+		+	+	
Cement		+			+			+			+			+
Basic steel and related industries		+			+			+			+			+
Aluminum		+			+			+			+		+	+
Farm and construction equipment				+b			+			+			+	
Automobiles	0			+			+	+c		+			+	
Aerospace		+			+				+		+			+
Longshoring:														
Atlantic and Gulf Coast	+d	+				+				+	+	+		
Pacific Coast		+	+					+	+	+		+		
Trucking	+			+			+			+			+	
Communications	+		+	+	+	+		+	+	+	+			
Bituminous coal mining	+		+		+			+			+			
Railroads	+		+e	+		+	+			+		+		
Total settlements by year	11	12	7	12	7	8	10	11	6	14	10	7	11	7

SOURCE: U.S. Department of Labor, Bureau of Labor Statistics, *Current Wage Development* (April 1977).

[a] A plus sign indicates that settlements (including those under wage reopening provisions) provided wage increases in the first contract year. A zero indicates they did not. A blank indicates there was no settlement in the particular year.

[b] Some settlements in late 1967. [c] Chrysler Corporation. [d] New York Harbor area only. [e] Trainmen and firemen.

simply reflections of the key agreements made early in the wage round. Thus, the identification of wage rounds cannot be based solely on fluctuations in the bargaining calendar but must extend to the verification of links between major agreements.

This essay looks at the sequence and characteristics of settlements in 1976 and 1977, with a brief synopsis of the various influences on those agreements. The information was gathered from published and unpublished sources and from interviews with union research staffs. After this chronological review of the settlements, an attempt is made to define some initial hypotheses on the nature of their interrelationships.

The national master freight agreement

The first major settlement of 1976 was the National Master Freight Agreement (NMFA) for local cartage and over-the-road drivers, negotiated between the Teamsters and Trucking Employers, Inc. (TEI), the major employer association. The agreement for substantial increases in wages, benefits, and noneconomic gains was signed on April 2 after a very brief strike and the virtual collapse of the employer association. The terms of the agreement were for a 65-cent increase in the first year and 50 cents for subsequent years plus an annual, uncapped cost-of-living adjustment (COLA). The contract also called for three additional holidays, substantial increases in health and pension contributions, and various work-rule changes (air-conditioned cabs, single rooms for over-the-road drivers, etc.). The terms of the agreement were costed out by the Council on Wage and Price Stability (COWPS) to be an increase of 31% in total compensation over three years, assuming a 6% cost-of-living increase. This figure of 31% was then cited by some as "the pattern" for other settlements to meet. In fact, the Teamsters thought the cost of the settlement could have been estimated at anywhere between 25 and 35%.

Various factors influenced the outcome and content of the agreement: First, the Teamsters had fallen behind cost-of-living changes due to a capped COLA in previous contracts. Because of this, as well as the auto settlement in 1973 and its uncapped COLA, the union leadership perceived a wider gap between auto and trucking wage levels and wanted to make this up. Second, 1976 was an election year for Frank Fitzsimmons, and membership demands for uncapped COLA and a catch-up increase were strong and particularly important. Third, there had been little preparation for bargaining by the employers or by the Teamsters and employers together. Before the contract expired a considerable amount of time was spent with lawyers from both sides discussing noneconomic issues and contract structure and language, leaving only two weeks for substantive bargaining over very complex economic issues like pension funding, cost-of-living formulas, and so forth. As a result, the agreement had to be forced through at the last minute to avoid a potentially long strike and greater federal involvement in its settlement. Finally, trucking is a regulated industry, and both the size and timing of the increases are issues the employers use to justify rate increases to the Interstate Commerce Commission (ICC). For example, the employers rejected the idea of splitting the 50-cent increase in the second year into two steps (thereby saving some wage payments for part of the year) since two 25-cent increments meant they would have to go to the ICC twice for rate changes. On the other hand, a large wage increase can be passed along in price due to its inclusion in the ICC's rate formula. This may make many employers less sensitive to large settlements.

As a pattern setter, the NMFA has considerable impact within transportation and associated industries organized by the Teamsters and other unions. The NMFA itself covers roughly 400,000 drivers directly and is followed immediately, and usually on identical terms, by a Chicago-area agreement which covers 40,000 additional drivers. Then there are various special agreements for particular cargoes (auto haulers, truck and bulk cargo trucks, and some individual company agreements) as well as thirty separate agreements with United Parcel Service in different areas of the country. All of these contracts explicitly follow the Master Freight pattern. (One important exception occurred in 1970. Fitzsimmons, in the early years of his presidency while Hoffa was away, settled the NMFA for an increase of $1.35 over three years. The Chicago-area locals refused to follow this and struck for a total increase of over $1.65. When they had settled for that amount, Fitzsimmons went back to TEI and got a new settlement, without a strike, with approximately a $2.20 increase.)

The Teamsters also cover 300,000 to 520,000 workers in food warehousing, and attempts are usually made—often unsuccessfully—to replicate some NMFA gains in these contracts. (In particular, in 1976 they copied the uncapped COLA and its formula.) Other Teamster locals try to use the NMFA gains as examples in bargaining in manufacturing, airline ground service, and miscellaneous other contracts. So the NMFA apparently sets a very strong pattern for other trucking agreements, as well as spilling over into either related industries or other sectors also organized by the Teamsters. And to the extent that the pattern is followed in these other sectors (such as food warehousing), it sets an example for related occupations (such as meatcutters and retail clerks) that are a part of that retail-food wage structure. In fact, one of the main interests of the Labor-Management Committee in Retail Food, a private carry-over from a similar committee established by John Dunlop under the Cost of Living Council, is analyzing the continuing impact of the NMFA on the entire retail food sector.

The Teamsters bargain and sign a total of nearly 60,000 agreements. The extent to which most of these significantly duplicate the NMFA is unknown, as are the terms those agreements would have were there no NMFA pattern. Without very detailed research only rough tendencies can be observed, and these trends might well be explained by general

Table 2

**International Brotherhood of Teamsters,
Selected Agreements, 1976-77**

Date	Parties	Terms
4/1/76	National Master Freight; Chicago Area Agreement	65¢ in 1976, 50¢ in 1977, and 50¢ in 1978, plus uncapped COLA; higher pension contribution; and work condition changes.
8/76	Teamsters and National Auto Transportation	Similar to NMFA
12/9/76	Teamsters and United Parcel Service—15 State Regional Conference	Similar to NMFA
11/76	Teamsters and Eastern Area Tank Haulers	Similar to NMFA
1/19/77	Teamsters and Produce Trade Association	$1 in wage increases over 3 years, plus benefit and other increases.
3/77	Teamsters and Eastern Area Cement Haulers	Similar to NMFA
5/1/77	Teamsters and Drayage and Household Moving Agreement (Seattle)	Similar to NMFA

economic conditions as much as by the pattern set in the NMFA. Nonetheless, the rigid adherence to the details of the NMFA settlement in other contracts—in auto hauling, for example—does show a pattern, regardless of how this is interpreted. By 1978, this pattern put substantial cost pressures on small trucking firms in local cartage and regional or metropolitan markets. Due to lack of ICC control over entry in some markets, these firms face much more nonunion competition than the very large over-the-road companies which have dominated in national bargaining. Over the past decade the number of union firms in these local markets has declined precipitously, as has the employment of union teamsters. There are strong pressures by the smaller trucking firms to break out of the NMFA structure and to bargain separate economic settlements in local contracts. Indeed, some local unions even voted to forego the 1978 increases in the current contract in order to save some firms from bankruptcy, but these exceptions were disallowed by the International.

The URW and the tire and rubber industry

After the longest major strike in 1976, the United Rubber Workers (URW) settled consecutively with each of the Big Four tire and rubber companies. The settlement began with an "understanding" with Firestone, the "target company" in the strike, but the first contract was signed with Goodyear on August 24 and then similar contracts were signed with

Firestone, Uniroyal, and Goodrich. The agreement consisted of a large first-year increase of 85 cents, to be followed by increases of 25 cents in two subsequent years. The first-year increase was a catch-up provision made necessary by the lack of a COLA in the previous contract. Other provisions of the 1976 agreement were the inclusion of an uncapped COLA to begin in 1976 and increases in pension and other benefit provisions.

The strike had begun on April 15, two days after Peter Bommarito, the URW president, announced that Firestone was to be the target company. The strike was called to begin immediately upon the contract expiration—even before the URW had considered Firestone's final offer. Despite the publicly announced choice of a target company, a policy begun in the 1973 bargaining, Bommarito suddenly decided to strike the entire industry. Although production was shut down in most plants of the Big Four, only about 60 percent of the tire industry is organized and the unorganized 40 percent includes some plants of the Big Four, so tire production was not completely stopped.

The fact that the strike took place and that it lasted so long was apparently due to miscalculations on each side. The companies felt that the union could not support a long strike; the union felt that the tire and auto industry, then booming, could not afford a strike. But due to tire stockpiles and to workers' outside economic support, the strike took place and continued until federal intervention and mediation.

One key issue for the companies was related not to the size of the wage settlement itself but to the structure of bargaining. Since the early 1950s the tire industry had been involved in two types of patterns. One of these derived from the original decision by the companies to permit company-wide bargaining on economic issues. Because the companies are diversified across types of rubber products, this company-wide bargaining was to cause difficulties later. The second pattern arose under the War Labor Board in 1951, when both the companies and the union justified a contract settlement on the basis of their "tandem" relationships with the auto industry. What the United Auto Workers had previously received from the Board, the United Rubber Workers wanted.

By the 1960s these pattern relationships were under heavy economic pressure. Due to domestic and foreign competition in the tire business, the companies felt they could not continue to sustain the tandem relationship to autos. During bargaining in the sixties there was an attempt to break out of this pattern and this was finally achieved in 1968 after strikes of varying lengths at some of the companies. But in the late 1970s the companies were still trying to break out their non-tire facilities from the overall tire bargaining. This concern was largely due to the heavy competitive pressures they faced in these product markets from lower-wage firms. The union's intransigence on this issue forced the strike but the strike was settled without its resolution. As a result the Big Four companies are continuing to close many of their non-tire plants. (Ironically, not only have URW members voted down moderate wage settlements in the face of plant closings, but in at least one case a company closed a plant and then reopened it and hired back many former workers at lower wages.)

Thus, in 1976, the central bargaining issues in the rubber industry included: (1) exceeding the NMFA settlement, because of the lack of any COLA in the URW agreements, and (2) refusing to alter an internal relationship between tire and non-tire wages.

The UAW and the auto, agricultural implement, and aerospace industries

Bargaining by the United Auto Workers (UAW) in the auto and other industries provides an example of a union that undertakes differentiated bargaining, reaching settlements in the four large auto companies, in many of the large and small parts suppliers to the auto industry, in UAW plants in the large truck and agricultural equipment sectors, and in some companies and plants in the aerospace industry. Of course, with the growing diversification of many large unions across manufacturing sectors, this kind of differentiated bargaining is becoming more common. Because the UAW has been involved in this kind of multiple product, firm, and industry structure since its inception, its history and experience in this regard may be of some general interest, in addition to being important for an understanding of the nature of bargaining and wage patterns within the industries organized by the UAW.

Figure 1 suggests the apparent wage interrelationships in these industries. It shows the level of hourly wage rates for one job classification within each sector: auto assembly, agricultural implements, and two aerospace firms—one organized by the UAW and the other by the International Association of Machinists and Aerospace Workers (IAM). Over the twenty-year period, the similarity in rates of change in three of the rates is striking; this is what is called the "Auto-AgImp-Aerospace pattern." At the same time there are obvious exceptions, for example, the relatively slower growth of wages in the UAW aerospace company and the jump in IAM/Boeing aerospace rates due to the large first-year increase in their 1974 agreement.

This theme of a basic similarity in agreements, but with exceptions and variations, runs through the history of UAW bargaining. In the 1976-77 negotiations, the following examples can be observed:

1. The usual successive, newly identical settlements with Ford, General Motors, and Chrysler. The Ford agreement set the pattern for the others, its major breakthrough coming in the area of extra days-off (the

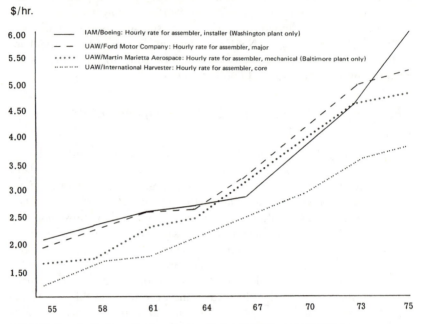

Figure 1

Hourly Wage Rates for Similar Job Grades in Auto Assembly, Aerospace, and Agricultural Implements 1955-1975

$/hr.

6.00 ——— IAM/Boeing: Hourly rate for assembler, installer (Washington plant only)

      — — UAW/Ford Motor Company: Hourly rate for assembler, major

5.50 • • • • • UAW/Martin Marietta Aerospace: Hourly rate for assembler, mechanical (Baltimore plant only)

      ········· UAW/International Harvester: Hourly rate for assembler, core

SOURCE: Compiled by the author from Bureau of Labor Statistics wage chronologies.

Scheduled Paid Personal Holiday Plan). This pattern was not followed at American Motors, however, due to its weaker financial situation. AMC obtained a one-year contract extension and later settled on substantially lower terms, both in wages and benefits.

2. Settlements at International Harvester, Caterpillar, and Deere for an economic package very similar to the Big Three auto agreements but with substantial differences in various benefit provisions, including time-off. In fact, the Deere contract had set a precedent for extra days-off late in the 1973 negotiations, but that settlement required that the time be earned through attendance criteria. This *quid pro quo* was dropped in the 1976 auto negotiation (although the auto companies tried to obtain it) but continues in the agricultural implements contract in various forms.

3. Settlements at the major parts manufacturers, such as Eaton, Budd, and Bendix, on terms virtually identical to the auto agreement. In contracts with the smaller parts suppliers major variations continue to occur in relation to the individual size and circumstances of each company. Yet the UAW, while it bargains with considerable attention to these differences, cannot separate these settlements entirely from the level of the major auto agreements. If it did so, it would influence the make-or-buy

decisions of the Big Three, perhaps to the detriment of the employment of its membership in those companies. Many of the smaller parts companies simply do not have a large enough work force to fund insurance programs such as SUB (supplemental unemployment benefits). For these reasons, such benefits do not "spill over" into supplier contracts.

4. Differences in agreements continue to occur due to the nature of the work force, job structure, or employment conditions in different industries. For example, there has been little emphasis placed on SUB plans in aerospace because of the substantial decline in employment in that industry. Rather, some companies have extended lay-off benefits that are funded on an individual basis and include direct worker contributions. Also, the agricultural implement firms have an Income Security Plan in their contracts, which guarantees wage payments at a previous hourly rate if a worker is bumped down a job grade due to lay-offs. This plan does not exist in autos because their job structure is more horizontal and thus there is little loss of pay due to grade reduction.

In sum, the UAW bargaining shows a similarity in wages and increases where feasible, with significant differences to fit distinctive industry and firm characteristics. The recent bargaining has focused almost entirely on benefit issues, leaving wages to increase at a trend rate of roughly 3 percent (the "annual improvement factor") plus cost of living. But the benefit plans are not seen by the union as new demands designed to capitalize on temporary advantages in market power. The benefit issues in the 1976 bargaining (health care, funding of SUB, and time-off) run through every negotiation from the early 1950s onward. Past experience, and indeed, long-run union goals for job and income security and full health-care coverage, affect particular negotiations as much or even more than the particular market conditions under which they occur. In addition, the union is well aware of auto business cycles, particularly their impact on employment and profits. The recession of 1975-76, although it caused massive lay-offs of auto workers and near exhaustion of SUB benefits, did not "moderate" union goals for increases in total compensation. The "Collective Bargaining Statement" prepared for discussion at the union's special bargaining convention early in 1976 noted the impact of the recession of 1975 on company profits, but also looked ahead to the considerably brighter picture for the companies in 1976 and after, i.e., once volume recovered from the recession. The UAW noted:

> Looking at the 28-year period from 1948 through 1975, GM's profits after taxes represented an average annual return of nearly 19 percent on stockholders' investment, even though periodic recessions and strikes reduced earnings substantially in several of these years. Profit rates of this size indicate that GM could easily absorb significantly higher costs or significantly lower prices or both, and still earn a rate of return well in excess of the average for all manufacturing.

Finally, the UAW convention noted the increases gained in recent settlements by other unions. But in doing so it included an analysis of how the different cost-of-living formulas in other contracts affected the size of the settlements. The UAW program commented: "The difference in COLA provisions is merely one illustration as to why we will not look to the patterns of other unions in shaping our own collective bargaining goals." (See Table 3.)

The USW and the basic steel, aluminum, and metal container industries

The United Steel Workers (USW), now only a large but a very diversified union, bargains for workers in a wide range of industries. Its main industry conferences include basic steel, nonferrous metals, aluminum, metal containers, founderies and forgings, and chemical and

---

Table 3

The United Auto Workers and the Auto, Agricultural Implement, and Aerospace Industries: Selected Settlements, 1976-77

Date	Parties	Terms
10/5/76	UAW and Ford	Three percent of base rate (plus 20 cents in the first year); increase in SUB contributions and guarantee; Scheduled Paid Personal Holiday Plan.
11/5/76	UAW and Chrysler	Same as Ford.
11/8/76	UAW and Deere	Similar to Ford: 3 percent in wages; bonus time-off for attendance; and pension funding increases.
11/19/76	UAW and General Motors	Same as Ford plus letter on organizing neutrality.
11/19/76	UAW and International Harvester	Similar to Ford and Deere.
12/20/76	UAW and Caterpillar	Similar to Ford and Deere.
1/77	UAW and Budd	Similar to Ford.
1/77	UAW and Mack Trucks	Similar to International Harvester.
1/77	UAW and Borg-Warner	No wage increase in Warner Gear Division.
2/77	UAW and TRW	Similar to Ford.
2/15/77	UAW and American Motors	Three percent plus 17 cents, but no roll-in of COL escalator in base rate and no increase in benefits (one-year agreement).
3/77	UAW and Eltra	Larger first-year and smaller second- and third-year increases plus two extra holidays.

NOTE: Some agreements signed between the Allied Industrial Workers (an old faction of the UAW) and some transportation and equipment firms also followed the Ford pattern.

---

allied products. Since the bargaining structure in each of these industries is different, though each has tended to evolve toward more centralization over time, the USW presents examples of different kinds of pattern bargaining.

Three of the largest conferences are usually said to represent one of the most significant interindustry wage patterns. These are basic steel, aluminum, and can (or metal containers). The usual sequence in this bargaining has traditionally put the can industry first and basic steel last, but this order was modified in the 1970s due to particular conditions affecting the negotiations in the individual industries. Within each industry, however, settlements reached by joint bargaining with many companies (as with the ten-member Coordinating Committee Steel Companies) or with one company (as with Alcoa in aluminum) usually set a rigid pattern for other agreements in the same industry. Interindustry patterns, however, are usually limited to similar levels of wage increases, since changes in benefits, as well as their level, coverage, and cost, can vary significantly between sectors. Within industries, however, much more uniform contracts are negotiated, exceptions being due to the special circumstances of some firms.

The major issues in the 1977 negotiations were in some respects carried over from the previous round of bargaining in 1974. In that year, the first year of the Experimental Negotiating Agreement, Alcoa led the bargaining sequence because the aluminum companies wanted to avoid bargaining after basic steel and the risk of following a settlement imposed by an arbitrator. Then can and containers followed and basic steel bargained last. Following the auto negotiations in 1973, the USW spent weeks trying to interpret the gains and costs in that agreement. The UAW had emphasized major improvements in "front-loaded pensions" (i.e., early retirement with full pension in the "30 and out" plan), but this approach was not needed or desired by the USW membership in aluminum. So they bargained toward improving benefits and pensions for workers retiring at 62 and older. This emphasis in aluminum on benefits and pensions then became central to the USW can and steel negotiations.

In 1977 the key issue in the basic steel bargaining was "lifetime job security." Contract provisions called the Employment and Security Program increased job security by improving SUB benefits to last 104 weeks (with full insurance coverage), increasing SUB "short week" benefits, and guaranteeing payments in the Earnings Protection Plan. The characteristics of the subsequent aluminum settlement were very similar, the only major difference being the broader eligibility of workers in aluminum for SUB and benefits provisions. The can industry negotiated last, largely because of major weaknesses in the unionized part of the industry due to competitive pressures from other containers and from "captive" bottlers and canners. The major issue in the can agreement was not job security, since can already had provisions such as 260 weeks of SUB coverage for their senior employees. Rather, the can negotiations centered on noneconomic issues involving work scheduling to permit efficient operation of the new continuous-processing canning technology for two-piece cans.

In the late 1970s one of the major problems for the USW in pattern bargaining appeared to arise not from the interindustry relationships but from intraindustry difficulties in basic steel. Within the steel industry the UAW has the policy of "we're all steelworkers" and thus all are entitled to the same level of increases. However, within the fabricating divisions of the ten largest companies, and for many smaller fabricating firms, pattern wage increases are becoming harder to sustain. Yet attempts to provide variation in wages for different companies, particularly the smaller companies, face resistance from both the USW membership and the biggest steel firms, whose fabricating divisions compete with these small companies. Several years ago, for example, Bethlehem Steel closed its fabricating division because it could not successfully bargain a concession of one dollar an hour less than the compensation levels in the basic steel agreement. Due to political pressures for equity within the USW, such adjustments are difficult to make, even though other, smaller firms in the industry may have lower labor rates in their contracts.

Another indication of the tremendous political appeal of equal conditions in union contracts is exemplified by the iron ore strike by USW locals in northern Michigan. This very costly strike was initiated by local union leaders, supporters of Ed Sadlowski, in order to get an incentive pay plan in ore production similar to that in basic steel. In effect, it was an attempt by a local dissident group to better the economic terms supposedly settled in national bargaining. But it also represents a wage relationship (in this case, the spillover of similar incentive plans) being created by political forces rather than being instituted or modified by product market pressures.

The CWA and the Bell System

The Communications Workers of America (CWA) is organized largely around the eighteen different companies in the American Telephone and Telegraph (AT&T) system. It also includes members grouped in two other bargaining conferences: one for independent telephone companies, who usually follow the Bell pattern, and the other for public employees. The CWA bargains nationally on economic issues for all eighteen units; separate local agreements follow on noneconomic issues.

In the 1976 wage round, the CWA bargained after many of the other agreements. All of these (auto, steel, rubber, electrical, and trucking) were studied by the CWA research staff and an analysis was presented to the union's bargaining council. Wage increases are rarely a major factor in these comparisons. As with many other major contracts, the CWA has received a base wage increase that has always run between 2.5 and 3 percent each year. If some settlements are substantially out of line with a perceived pattern, they are studied and explained in the context of problems in that particular industry. And despite the mild similarity of the work done by some Bell technicians and by building trade electricians, very little impact is felt from International Brotherhood of Electrical Workers (IBEW) settlements in the construction industry. Because of major differences in job security and perceived social status, telephone employees do not look to craft wages for comparisons.

In 1977 CWA interest focused mainly on the job security provisions in the auto and steel contracts. While this would not have been of comparative interest in years past, antitrust decisions and technological change were now threatening to cause a substantial decline in employment in telephone communications. The CWA is not resisting these changes but is studying the mechanisms that have been introduced into collective bargaining contracts in other industries to protect displaced workers.

In response to attacks by the chief AT&T economist, who described the CWA's goals as "inflationary," the CWA also analyzed the relation between its recent settlements and productivity. In this, the CWA contrasted the figures on increases in average hourly earnings in the industry between 1971 and 1976 (76 percent) with actual wage rate increases for operators in their contracts (52 percent over the same period). The discrepancy comes from the upward bias in average hourly earnings data due to compositional changes in the work-force. Overall, the CWA estimated that Bell workers received real wage increases of about 2 percent per year during the last two years of the 1974-77 contract, while labor productivity in the industry was rising at a rate of 6 to 10 percent a year. However, despite this lag of wages behind productivity increases—hardly a cause of inflation—there is a sense in the CWA that the link between manufacturing and operating wages within the Bell system may not be sustainable. Although each Bell division has a different wage and occupational structure, both have been receiving the same percentage increases. Due to the new competition permitted in the manufacture of telephone equipment, Western Electric may have to be separated from this internal pattern.

Other settlements

Wage patterns are also evident in industries not described above. Bargaining across the country in the apparel industry, while split between men's and women's clothing and their respective unions (the Amalgamated Clothing and Textile Workers and the International Ladies' Garment Workers' Union), generally followed settlements made early in 1976 in New York City. In 1977 and 1979, the Oil, Chemical, and Atomic Workers signed contracts with one major refiner which were then taken up by the other firms in the industry. In the electrical equipment industry, similarities can be observed in the settlements by different unions with the major consumer and industrial product firms (Westinghouse, General Electric, etc.), while significant deviations occur in electronics subsectors tied to aerospace contracts or suppliers to the auto industry.

It is worth noting briefly that two of the major agreements in the last years of current wage round, the longshore and the coal-mining, were dominated by issues peculiar to conditions in each industry. The relative sizes of wage increases in these industries in comparison to other settlements were not major difficulties as such. Rather, the longshoremen's agreement faced renewed difficulties in providing income guarantees to workers unemployed due to technological change (containerization), and the coal industry confronted problems in funding pension benefits and in reducing work days lost due to strikes.

Whether the high coal settlement would in turn set a pattern for 1979 negotiations was unknown at the time of this writing. There were some attempts to isolate it by COWPS and other government economists, calling attention to the particular conditions of a strong demand and local union militancy in the industry. However, the same government economists also labeled other 1978 settlements, such as rail or postal, as sure to set patterns if not moderated in the public interest. This arbitrary use of the pattern-following concept for the purpose of jawboning was criticized by some as only adding to the visibility and pressures on particular negotiations, perhaps making it more difficult for union leaders to make concessions. And, after the coal settlement, Teamster president Frank Fitzsimmons was quoted as saying that his members would accept nothing less than a similar gain of "39 percent" in their 1979 NMFA negotiations. Later, he denied ever making such a remark. Apparently, the designation of a settlement as a "pattern-setter" can be manipulated politically by government officials and union presidents alike.

A wage pattern?

Without a very detailed analysis of the provisions and costs of the whole package of wages and benefits in each agreement, it is difficult to identify patterns in bargaining across industries. Nonetheless, as a tentative beginning of this kind of comparative study, Table 4 presents the average annual increase in wages (including COLA), total compensation, and unit labor costs in most of the industries reviewed above. It should be emphasized that although comparisons of wage and COLA increases are relatively straightforward, estimates of changes in total compensation are very rough due to differences in employee age mix and funding provisions for pension benefits, and to the unpredictable costs of contributions to SUB funds and earnings protection plans. Changes in unit labor costs, which are a function of estimates of both total compensation and productivity per man/hour, are therefore doubly suspect. With all of these provisos, the

Table 4

Average Annual Increases in Wages, Total Compensation, and Unit Labor Costs in Major 1976 and 1977 Collective Bargaining Agreements (In percent)

Industry	Wage and COLA[a]	Total compensation	Unit labor costs[b]
Trucking	9.7	10.4	7.9
Electrical equipment	9.9	NA	10.0[c]
Tire and rubber	11.7	11.0	10.0[c]
Autos	8.4	9.8	5.9
Telephone	7.7	9.5	3.3
Basic steel	9.1	9.3	7.2
All manufacturing (1976)	NA	8.8	NA

SOURCE: Compiled by author from Council on Wage and Price Stability reports.
[a]COLA increase assumes 6% change in the Consumer Price Index.
[b]Based on COWPS estimates of productivity change.
[c]First year of settlement only.
NA=Not available.

comparison of changes across contracts does show that annual average changes in total compensation were remarkably similar, while the impact of these on unit labor costs across industries was quite diverse. If, in fact, the similarity in percentage increases in compensation is due to pattern following, the results might be interpreted as moderating some settlements in industries with relatively high productivity increases (e.g. telephone communications) and raising the costs of agreements in other industries with lower rates of productivity change (e.g., basic steel).

The similarity of rates of change in total compensation should not obscure the extreme diversity in the composition of that compensation across and even within industries. While major unions are well informed about and aware of settlements by unions in other industries, they are by no means unsophisticated in their interpretation. In their analyses they appear to pay less attention to wage changes as such than to mechanisms or innovations, such as pension escalators or job security measures, that may represent new breakthroughs in bargaining. The actual rate of wage change in major contracts is, in fact, rarely at issue: most large unions get "annual improvement factors" approximating long-run productivity trends in the manufacturing sector of the economy. As a result, innovations in benefit programs receive much more attention. Yet, due to the sometimes substantial differences in labor market characteristics between major industries, these benefit programs will not be duplicated exactly. For example, although dental plans are dental plans in all contracts, pension plans or "job security" mean and cost something quite different in autos than in basic steel. And, of course, peculiar conditions in other industries, like

129

containerization for the International Longshoremen or an uncapped escalator for the United Rubber Workers, can dominate bargaining more than adherence to a simple pattern of compensation change.

Nonetheless, there are substantial similarities in the basic benefits problems dealt with in current major contracts. To a large extent these problems revolve around three central issues: (1) protection against unanticipated inflation in order to protect real wage gains; (2) financing the costs of medical care; and (3) providing income and employment security. The exact provisions incorporated into contracts to deal with these issues vary, but the motivation and pressures for them are virtually identical. Gains made by one union on any of these issues are closely watched by others for possible incorporation, in some form, into their own contracts.

Interpretation and implications

Just this cursory examination of the settlements in various industries over the three years 1976-78 does lend some support to even a simple theory of pattern bargaining. In the area of wage change, at least, there are substantial similarities between many contracts, particularly within one industry or within one union across manufacturing sectors. However, even a superficial reporting of the contract terms shows that the patterns of fringe benefits and other compensation issues (ignoring completely the questions of work rules) can vary considerably. Despite the complexity and variability of the interrelationships among contracts, the patterns do not seem to be "idiosyncratic." Rather, there seem to be fairly consistent sets of relationships or channels of influence among certain contract settlements, but the nature of these interrelationships varies for different unions and industries, and in some cases over time. Even if a pattern is only a theme on which subsequent bargains appear as variations, the basic structure of wage relationships can be deciphered on the basis of firm and industry perceptions.

Types of pattern bargaining or spillover effects

For all its faults, the Phillips curve literature still represents a coherent theory of wage determination, coupled with a rigorous quantitative analysis of the determinants of wage change. More "institutional" theories of wage dynamics, such as wage contours or pattern bargaining, have perennially suffered either from a lack of theoretical elaboration or from a dearth of empirical verification. What is now essential in a theory of wage interdependence is differentiation between market and institutional (or political) forces that work to create similarities in the rate of wage change. As Robert Hall noted, "Wage increases in related industries are . . . highly correlated, but this can be explained by their similar responses to fluctuations in the labor market they share."[2] If the existence of wage patterns can be explained solely by the coincidences of market forces, then their denomination as "patterns" or "contours" adds little to the theoretical understanding of wage determination. While a weak version of a theory of wage interdependence might be rescued on the basis that it is only through institutional actions of comparison that apparently disembodied "market forces" can be reified, a strong version of the theory must be based on the hypothesis that the creation, maintenance, and persistence of patterns can occur in direct opposition to labor and product market forces.

As a first step toward developing this stronger version of a theory of pattern bargaining, the types of wage and benefit relationships which were perceived to exist among contracts in the 1976-78 wage manual are summarized in the matrix in Table 5. The columns of the matrix represent what may be two distinct types of institutional forces: interunion comparisons of relative wages in the first column and intraunion linkages in the second. The former are based on more general considerations of relative equity, while the latter are engendered by specific internal union considerations of political solidarity.[3] The rows of the matrix represent two distinct product market contexts, within one industry or across industries, which may provide substantially different climates of labor demand for the operation of the institutional forces of interdependence.

In general, it might be expected that the pattern bargaining which is congruent with intraindustry market forces would prove to be the strongest (with the usual exceptions for special cases of some firms within industries), while the wage comparisons made across industries would tend to be more fragile. As a result, the potency of the institutional forces may vary a great deal depending on the structure of bargaining. In some cases, as in a single product or labor market, institutional and competitive forces do operate jointly. In other cases, as in intraunion, interindustry bargaining, the institutional forces may retard competitive adjustments. Although, as Harold Levinson found, intraindustry wage patterns tend to be strong while interindustry relationships are less robust (due largely to the conjunction of product market conditions with the former and not the

---

Table 5

Examples of Market and Institutional Structures in Bargaining

	Interunion	Intraunion
	1	2
Interindustry	Auto, steel, rubber	Aluminum, can, steel companies
	Trucking, warehousing, retail food unions	Autos, agricultural implements, aerospace firms
	3	4
Intraindustry	Construction building trades	UAW: Big Three auto firms
	Electrical equipment unions	ILGW: Apparel firms
		OCAW: Refining and chemical companies

latter), all intraunion relationships appear to be very binding even under the most extreme market pressure.[4] It takes great efforts at what one union director called "democratic leadership" to get a union to break out of an internal pattern and to differentiate wages or wage changes across product markets. Union leaders have to work to educate their membership, changing their expectations from the shorthand of referring to other agreements to the incorporation of new market factors.

In sum, each of the cells in the matrix represents a different bargaining context. The task of a contemporary economic history of collective bargaining is to develop data and interpretations showing how the forces in wage determination work in each of these contexts. Cells 3 and 4 of the matrix often represent clear cases of wage and compensation interdependence, due perhaps to the coincidence of market and institutional forces. The interindustry patterns in cells 1 and 2 are more complex: the wage and benefit interrelationships are more subtle and may evolve over time. More importantly, they may be created and persist in the face of rather different firm and labor market conditions (as appears to have occurred in the spread of the basic steel pattern across industries organized by the United Steelworkers, for example, or in the spillover of wage increases from the National Master Freight Agreement to contracts in the retail food industry).

It is precisely these interindustry spillovers or patterns which have the greatest implications for a theory of wage inflation. High settlements in one sector of the economy may indeed spread, through specific well-established channels, into other industries. As yet, there is little other than circumstantial evidence that there is an economy-wide wage contour of major contracts as is suggested by the supposed link between the auto, steel, and rubber agreements noted in cell 1 of the matrix. But recurrent attempts at wage controls, such as the 1978 voluntary program of guidelines, rediscover (or re-create) these linkages. Indeed, the proposals for administering the 1978 guidelines speak of permitting some wage increases to exceed 7 percent if they are "in tandem with" previous agreements. Unfortunately, COWPS has not yet established precisely what the "tandem" wage relationships are in the economy. If future economic research on wage determination took a more sectoral and institutional approach, these questions of wage interdependence might be fully articulated and even partially resolved.

Notes

1. O. Eckstein and T. Wilson, "The Determinants of Money Wages in American Industry," *Quarterly Journal of Economics* (August 1962); Eckstein, "Money Wage Determination Revisited," *Review of Economic Studies* (April 1968).
2. Robert Hall, "The Process of Inflation in the Labor Market," *Brookings Papers on Economic Activity* (Brookings Institution, 1974), p. 2.

3. Internally, unions usually seek to create more uniform job and wage categories, thus reducing the firm and even industry wage dispersion. Externally, some unions may seek to maintain "customary differentials" with other unions or reference groups.

4. H. M. Levinson, *Determining Forces in Collective Wage Bargaining* (New York, Wiley, 1966).

Fragments of a "Sociological" Theory of Wages

2

BY MICHAEL J. PIORE

THIS PAPER REPRESENTS an attempt to sketch some elements of a "sociological" theory of wages. I use the term "sociological" as it is generally used in economics as a shorthand for other social science disciplines but without the pejorative connotations that economists some-times attach to it. Such a theory of wages is implicit in models of labor market stratification which, by hinging upon nonwage factors as determin-ants of the allocation of labor, free the wage from its traditional role in economic theory and open the way for noneconomic determinants. Several economists in recent years have also alluded to "sociological factors" in a somewhat different context to explain rigidities in the income distribution or the wage structure.[1] But in none of the discussions which have come to my attention has the role of these averred sociological factors been explicitly developed.

I conceive of the problem as one of specifying "sociological" forces in such a way that one can understand how and when they will prevail in a relatively competitive market economy. I mean by such an economy one where most families have a strong desire to substantially increase their income levels and where most managers feel pressured to minimize cost. This is the view of economic motivation which underlies conventional models of wage determination. The record of such models in tracking the economy, particularly in recent years, does not exactly compel one to operate within this framework. But in the course of my own research, I have had a lot of discussions with workers and managers about labor market decisions, and the conventional view does seem to be a fairly accurate, albeit incomplete, picture of what emerges from their comments. Another important element in organizing the impressions of the labor market gathered in this way is the set of institutional models of wage determination developed by labor economists in the 1940s and 1950s.[2] Indeed, as I will try to argue, the "sociological" and "institutional" forces are closely related; at root, perhaps, they are the same thing.

"Sociological" forces

The key to an understanding of the role of "sociological" forces in wage determination lies, I believe, in an appreciation of the nature of on-the-job training and its significance in the development of job skills. The latter point is now, I think, generally accepted by labor economists of all persuasions, and need not be labored here.

The nature of the training process is less widely appreciated. My own research suggests that for blue collar workers, it occurs within informal social groups and may be understood in terms of what sociologists call "socialization," *i.e.*, the adaptation of the individual to the norms and role patterns of the work group. It is literally socialization in that a good deal of what is required to perform effectively on-the-job and is involved in the improvement in productivity during the "training" period is the understanding of the norms of the group and of the requirements of the various roles which are played within it and conformity to the generalized norms and to the specialized requirements of the particular role or roles to which one is assigned. But, even when the training involves the acquisition of skills which can be distinguished independently of the social situation where they are displayed, the learning process involves the imitation by the new entrant of older inhabitants of the work place. Such imitation is a psychological phenomenon very similar to that through which the individual conforms to a social group. Learning by imitation, moreover, generally involves at least the acquiescence, and often the active participation, of the older members. Either of these is likely to be withheld unless the new entrant finds the kind of initial acceptance, and cements it through the kind of efforts at conformity to group norms, which are involved in socialization.

Groups of the kind in which such learning occurs have a tendency to develop a set of norms governing not only the way in which work is performed and individuals relate to each other in the work process but a wide variety of other features of the work place as well. Such norms appear to be essentially what economists and industrial relations specialists have generally referred to as custom. They form a kind of customary law analogous to that which prevailed in the feudal manors of medieval Europe.[3]

Space does not permit an elaborate discussion of the origins of custom. Its chief attribute, however, appears to be a dependence upon past practice. Customs tend to grow up around existing practice. The practice may initially be dictated by economic considerations; or it may be imported into the work place from the larger community from which the labor force is drawn. But once it has been regularly repeated in a stable employment situation, people develop an independent attachment to it. In the eyes of the work group it acquires an ethical aura. Adherence to it tends to be viewed as a matter of right and wrong, and violations are seen as unfair and immoral. The morality of adherence to custom may co-exist with some other higher and conflicting morality. Thus, in the medieval period, custom was often in conflict with the precepts of the Church and yet custom frequently prevailed in courts of law and, one may infer, even more so in practice. In the modern work place, there is a dual allegiance to the morality of custom on the one hand, and the individualistic ethic of the market place which sanctions management's pursuit of economic efficiency and the individual's pursuit of his own welfare, on the other hand.

The moral character of custom permits the work group to punish violations through the imposition of sanctions which the moral code of the larger society proscribes and which the workers themselves would normally adjure as illegal and unethical. When directed against management, the available sanctions are legion. They range from petty individual sabotage to massive job actions. The vulnerability of society to attacks of this kind, particularly industrial sabotage, need hardly be emphasized today.[4] The cost of such attacks to a recalcitrant management are overwhelming. The costs to the individual who undertakes them depend almost completely upon the willingness of his fellow workers to deter such actions through group pressure and to cooperate with legal authorities. We are dealing here, in other words, with a range of weapons distinct from those invoked in the normal course of industrial relations. They are distinct because the extreme imbalance of costs makes it impossible to build them into a stable industrial relations system. For that reason also, there is no effective external deterrence. The real deterrence is in a set of restraints internal to each individual and associated with the underlying moral consensus upon which the society is founded. It is these restraints which custom, in providing an alternative moral code, relieves.

I have placed such heavy emphasis upon custom because among the rules which tend to be governed by it are those which determine wage rates. Although custom has never achieved a place in the formal analytical apparatus of economics, its role in wage determination has been recognized by virtually every student of the labor market from Adam Smith to J. R. Hicks. Its continuing influence today is suggested by the ethical phraseology which surrounds the wage setting process in the modern shop and appears in the vocabulary of management as well as labor.

In the medieval period, where the market forces were weaker, custom often determined the wage rate itself. In a modern economy, where the wage rate is subject to continuous revision, the precedents required to establish a customary fixed wage rate do not arise. The structure of wage rates, *i.e.*, the relationship between wages on different jobs, is not, however, subject to such frequent revisions. It thus does tend to become customary, and it is that customary set of relative wage relationships which is what appears to be, at least on the micro economic level, the "sociological" determinant of the wage.

Thus, in sum, the environment in which on-the-job training can successfully occur is one in which a customary law tends to develop and prevail. Among the tenets of the law are a series of relationships among the wages of the members of the group and between the group members and other workers. These relationships generally establish a fixed structure of relative wages. They can, but usually do not, govern the level of wages (*i.e.*, the base upon which the structure is built) and the magnitude and timing of changes in the wage level. The structure is imposed upon individual management by the moral commitment of the work group to it and their willingness to undertake actions in its support which would otherwise be deterred by law and by a commitment to a higher morality and code of behavior. But the structure achieves its larger economic significance from the fact that the commitment to it is intrinsic in the process through which the supply of labor is generated and, hence, it is difficult to generate a set of competitive pressures which will undermine it.

Institutionalization

There is relatively little literature on the kind of shop custom in which we are arguing "sociological" wage relationships are embedded. There is, however, a much more extensive body of literature on institutionalized wage structures, embedded in collective bargaining contracts and the administered wage and salary structure of most large white collar organizations. In the limited space available here, it is impossible to develop the relationship between these two sources of rigidity in the wage structure, but I do believe that they are closely related and, at a certain level of analysis, one and the same thing. American trade union organizations are grounded on the shop level. They thus encompass within them the informal social groups in whose domain custom lies. Craft unions in the United States have been built up out of such informal groups. Industrial unions tended to be organized from the top down; but this has meant "with union organizers sent out from the international." The shop remains the basic unit of union organization even in national policies. The National Labor Relations Act, through its definition of the bargaining unit and its procedures for certification of union representation through majority rule within that unit, virtually mandates that this be the case, and collective bargaining agreements have thus tended to embody existing shop custom and supplement ad hoc group pressures with formal institutional sanctions.

The incorporation of the informal social group within a larger organization had also had certain consequences, however, for the evolution of custom. It has generally imposed requirements for certain kinds of consistencies among the customs of the units of the organization. And an important strand of trade union history involves the process of reconciling conflicting customs among interrelated organizational units. This process is very nicely documented by Lloyd Ulman for craft unions where it was closely connected to the problem of the mobile craftsman, whose travel took him from his home locale to a variety of other jurisdictions.[5] There is a strong parallel between efforts to resolve these conflicts and the process through which a national common law evolved in medieval Europe from a separate series of manorial customs. The national unions, like the emergent European nation states, try variously to apply to each man the custom of his home locale, then the locale in which he is working, and finally for certain customs, are forced to develop a standard which supersedes local precedents. I think it can be argued that a similar process occurred within industrial unions, although it has not, so far as I know, been carefully documented. In both the craft and the industrial case, the forces driving toward some kind of national organization, and hence requiring a reconciliation between conflicting customs, are economic in character. It is less clear that economic forces dictate the kind of custom which ultimately emerges.

This brief discussion of institutionalization suggests two conclusions. First, that institutionalized rules are closely related to custom. Second, that the effect of building the informal social groups which generate custom into larger, more formal, institutions is to reconcile conflicts between customs and to make certain customs, at least, uniform throughout the economy.

Economic considerations

There are several possible ways of examining the relationship between the customary wage structure and a structure derived from more conventional economic considerations. One of these is to use, as the point of comparison, the structure which would prevail in a perfectly competitive economic system. This does not, however, appear to be a very meaningful approach. We are asserting a wage structure, which despite its sociological and institutional foundations, is economically compelling. The economy cannot operate without its skilled labor force, and the skilled labor force will not let it operate independently of the wage structure to which it has a customary and moral commitment. The assertion is, in other words, that there cannot *be* a perfectly competitive labor market in the sense that it is generally envisaged in theory.

An alternative approach is to examine the relationship between the customary wage structure and the competitive pressures generated by the economic system. As noted in the introductory comments, such pressures are as characteristic of the observations out of which this paper grows as the attachment to custom. Any attempt to model an economic system which generates such pressures immediately points to conflict with custom and such conflicts in the real world do occur. The interesting thing is that they do not occur more often and the question is why they do not. This is not a question which can be fully explored here. But the following observations appear appropriate.

The wage structure must perform two economic functions. It must insure that the training process occurs, and it must allocate trained workers effectively so that their scarce skills are utilized. In a competitive economy, it will have to perform these functions to survive. Most of our expectations about what kind of structure is required for the first of these functions, *i.e.*, the training process, derive from Gary Becker and are based upon the assumption that the training process carries a cost.[6] Given that assumption and relatively weak assumptions about competitive pressure, the wage structure must adjust so as to distribute these costs between labor and management for there to be any training at all. The requisite wage structure thus allows relatively little scope for such outside factors as custom (although as Peter Doeringer and I tried to show, there is more scope than in Becker's original model even under the assumption of "cost").[7] However, if training is basically a socialization process (or, simply, involves imitation), it is largely automatic, and its costs may be trivial. The critical function of the wage structure is then not to distribute the cost of training. Rather, it is to insure the variety of exposure to work situations in which the training for some jobs consists. This exposure requires certain patterns of labor mobility. Obviously, not all wage structures will be consistent with these patterns but the requirements for consistency are not those upon which we have previously focused. The range of consistent structures, moreover, is expanded by two considerations sometimes overlooked: a) In certain jobs, the requisite movement for "training" is forced by the limited duration of the job (the outstanding example is construction), and b) the socialization process through which training occurs and the workers acquire attachment to the customary wage structure will also tend to affect job preference in such a way as to make preferences for different jobs consistent with the requisite movement between them.

The tendency for the socialization process to affect preferences should also reduce the conflict between the customary wage structure and its second economic function, that of allocating scarce workers.

There is another, possibly more important, factor working to reduce that conflict, however, in the costless nature of the training process; if the training process is indeed costless, there is no particular reason to expect trained personnel to be scarce. They may generally be in excess supply, and, indeed, the prevalence of seniority and other devices for rationing scarce jobs suggests that this is indeed the case.

Still, even if trained workers were generally in excess supply, one must expect occasional labor shortages and in a dynamic economy such as ours, operating close to full employment, one would expect those shortages, however exceptional, to occur with some frequency. There would then be pressure to attract new sources of labor, not "trained" or fully socialized to the environment in which they were entering. The employment of such "new" workers would thus impose costs, which adjustments in the wage structure should be required to accommodate. Competition would also generate pressure to raise the relative wage of older workers now in short supply.

Here again, without wishing to deny that conflicts with a customary wage structure will never occur, it may be noted that they do tend to be reduced greatly by the underlying processes involved. When a flow of labor between two previously separate environments occurs, there should be a tendency for the environments themselves to evolve toward each other in such a way that the amount of adjustment required to move between them declines. To the extent that this is true, the cost of movement between two previously isolated jobs should decrease rapidly with the amount of movement, and the circumstances of costless training and permanent excess supply might be swiftly restored.[8]

Two additional, relatively obvious but nonetheless important points about competitive pressures on a customary wage structure can be made. First, such pressures will be reduced to the extent that the customary structure is the same across all firms in an industry. To derive from the idea of a customary wage structure the propositions about the constancy in the aggregate wage structure alluded to in the introduction requires some assumption about uniformity. One factor—but probably not the only one—tending toward such uniformity is, as the preceding discussion suggests, institutionalization. A tendency for workers and management to import a customary wage structure into new plants from other work situations would also work for uniformity. Second, economic pressure to change a fixed wage structure of the kind which we are describing will depend to some extent upon how much of that structure is contained within a single firm. When all of the jobs in the structure are represented within the firm, a change of any one wage will be deterred by the leverage which that change would exert upon the wages of the firm's other jobs. When each firm, however, has only one job, there is no deterrence of this kind and the firm should be more willing to respond to changes in economic conditions. (This is a point of particular relevance in analyzing the inflationary potential of the economy since if a response to economic conditions does not succeed in changing the wage structure and instead simply levers it upward, its inflationary impact is substantial.)

Finally, conflicts between a customary wage structure and competitive pressures may be resolved through adjustments in the customary wage norms. These norms are essentially little more than a reflection of past practice and if a new practice can be instituted and maintained, it should itself become the governing norm. Even the most casual inspection suggests that many existing norms reflect some earlier market relationship. This relationship presumably dictated the practice, which subsequently become customary. There is obviously scope within the system for developing new norms in this way: ambiguities in existing norms can sometimes be exploited for this purpose; occasionally employers are able to wait out employee resistance or negotiate changes with employee representatives in a way that circumvents such resistance. Firms embodying older norms may be driven out of business by new enterprises without past practices that block a wage structure appropriate to market realities. If adjustments of this kind were frequent, however, the customary wage structure would be a minor "friction" in an otherwise competitive system: it might be useful to recognize for some purposes but would hardly command the attention I am devoting to it here. It certainly would not explain something so fundamental as the constancy of the income distribution. The logic of the argument we are developing here then is that it is these adjustments in custom which are the frictions (or marginal features) of a system whose basic properties are reflected in the other adjustment mechanisms.

Labor market strata

The theory of a customary wage structure which I have just described is not a generalized description of the wage setting process. It is characteristic of only one strata of the labor market: elsewhere I have termed that strata *the lower tier of the primary sector*. It is characterized by regularity and continuity of employment. The jobs tend to involve a set of relatively specific skills in the learning of which schooling is unimportant and training on the job critical. The employees tend to be what sociologists term *working class adults*. They are attached to a life style or subculture which places a premium upon stability and routine and is centered in an extended family unit the support of which is the primary function of work.

There are other segments of the labor market where the wage structure is unlikely to be governed by custom. In the secondary sector, for example, which is dominated by youth and by the "disadvantaged," turnover tends to be too rapid to permit the formation of the social groups in which custom is embedded, and even when such groups do manage to form, the essentially unskilled nature of the work reduces the employer's dependence upon them and their norms. Professional and managerial employments are also unlikely to generate a customary wage structure. The norms for these jobs tend to be internalized by individual workers; workers in these jobs have a greatly reduced commitment to the work group; general education plays a more important role than on-the-job training in the development of skills; and wages and salaries are generally private matters which employees are relatively guarded in discussing with each other.

An examination of wage setting patterns in these other strata would take us well beyond the allotted space and time. To use the theory as developed thus far to explain the aggregate phenomenon with which we started out, one has to make rather restrictive assumptions about these other patterns. To explain the constancy of the income distribution, for example, would require the assumption either that wages in the other strata were somehow parameters of the customary wage structure or that these other strata dominate the extremes of the income distribution, which when examined closely would turn out not to be as stable as the center portion. Neither assumption seems farfetched but neither have they been closely examined.

Conclusion

The title of this paper was chosen with some deliberation. But I am under no illusions about the ability of terms like "fragments" and "sociology" to cover the departure from the standards of rigor to which the economics profession has become accustomed. The justification for this departure must be found in the light it sheds upon important policy issues. One of the issues is that of the income distribution to which I alluded in the body of the paper. I think that it is appropriate to conclude with reference to a second such issue, that of wage inflation.

The kind of customary wage structure I have described is one with tremendous inflationary potential. Since relative wages are fixed, pressure at any point in the system (in the strata where custom prevails or in some other strata whose rates are parameters of the customary structure) exerts a leverage upon all wage rates. But it is also a system whose inflationary potential lends itself to a viable long run system of wage controls. Both economists and industrial relations specialists have tended to frown upon controls, particularly as a permanent policy; the latter because of the threat which the imposition of controls pose to industrial peace; the former because of the instability and inefficiency of a controlled wage system. Controls are presumed to produce allocative distortions which eventually undermine the control structure and in the meantime result in a loss of potential output. A system which follows the contours of the customary structure, however, should be open to neither of these traditional criticisms. Because it is in accord with the prevailing norms and values, it is a structure—possibly the only structure—which should induce workers to forgo the exercise of economic power. And since it embodies the structure which would prevail in any case, it is unlikely to be any more inefficient or unstable. Indeed the very concept of inefficiency as applied to wage controls seems to ignore the processes of labor market adjustment which allow customary wage relationships to survive at all.

Such a system of controls would be very different from any which have been tried, or for that matter seriously thought about. (With the possible exception of the present construction industry stabilization program in the United States). The understanding of the detailed customary relationships required to administer such a system may turn out to be too much to expect from ordinary men. But it does seem to me sufficiently promising to justify further research.

Notes

1. Lester C. Thurow and Robert E. Lucas, *The American Distribution of Income: A Structural Problem* (Washington, D.C.: Joint Economic Committee, March 17, 1972); and Bernard Ducros and Jean Marchal, *The Distribution of National Income* (New York: St. Martin's Press, 1968).
2. Arthur M. Ross, *Trade Union Wage Policy* (Berkeley and Los Angeles: University of California Press, 1953); and George W. Taylor and Frank C. Pierson, eds., *New Concepts in Wage Determination* (New York: McGraw-Hill, 1952).
3. Marc Bloch, *Feudal Society*, trans. by L. A. Mangon (Chicago: University of Chicago Press, 1964); and Peter B. Doeringer and Michael J. Piore, *Internal Labor Markets and Manpower Analysis* (Lexington, Mass.: D. C. Heath, 1971).
4. For example, see Richard Walton, "How to Counter Alienation in the Plant," *Harvard Business Review* (November-December 1972).
5. Lloyd Ulman, *The Rise of the National Trade Union* (Cambridge: Harvard University Press, 1966).
6. Gary S. Becker, *Human Capital: A Theoretical and Empirical Analysis* (New York: Columbia University Press, 1964).
7. Doeringer and Piore, op. cit.
8. Michael J. Piore, *Notes for a Theory of Labor Market Stratification*, Department of Economics, MIT, Working Paper no. 95 (October 1972).

Pricing Rules 3

BY MICHAEL J. PIORE

THE REASON ECONOMISTS ARE attached to unemployment as a cure for inflation is that the relationship derives from the concepts of supply and demand, concepts that form the foundations of scientific economic theory. Theoretically prices will rise when demand exceeds the capacity of the economy to produce goods and services, and they will fall when supply exceeds demands. Unemployment is interpreted as a measure of under-utilized productive resources, and hence, of the gap between overall supply and demand.

The idea that prices are determined by supply and demand rests on certain assumptions about the behavior of individual economic agents. These assumptions are plausible, and probably correct in some markets where prices are set by impersonal forces so strong and so compelling that each individual has no choice but to accept the market price or go out of business. The market for most agricultural commodities is of this kind. So is the stock market. In other markets, however, the assumed behavior of prices rests heavily upon certain calculations that people are thought to make in order to maximize their economic welfare. The theory more or less assumes that people estimate the demand and supply curves for their products and use these to set prices and wages.

There have been some studies of the way in which prices and wages actually are set in those markets. The studies do not support the hypotheses of conventional economic theory. People do not appear to make calculations on the basis of anything like estimates of supply and demand. Instead they apply a set of pricing rules. These rules tend to impose a fixed structure of wages and prices. In wage setting, in fact, they seem to do exactly this.

Price-setting rules are generally a little more complicated than wage setting, but the basic tendency to impose a fixed structure of relative prices is much the same. Thus, for example, in retailing it is common to use a fixed percentage mark-up over cost. This guarantees that the relationship between the wholesale and retail prices will be constant whatever the state

From "Curing Inflation with Unemployment," *The New Republic,* November 2, 1974. Reprinted by permission of *The New Republic.* © The New Republic, Inc.

of supply and demand in the two sectors. Car prices, to give another example, are set as a certain percentage of the median income and thus they rise automatically with wage increases.

The existence of widespread fixed-rule pricing means that there are essentially two modes of wage and price setting: one governed by supply and demand, in which individual prices rise and fall in response to scarcity or surplus; the second, or rule-determined sector, in which prices and wages are *set relative to each other* in order to maintain a fixed price structure. The two modes of price setting create the possibility of *structural* inflation.

Normally one would expect even in a relatively prosperous economy wide differences in market conditions. Some markets would be in surplus and others would have scarcities. If everybody responded directly to their own market, the prices of scarce commodities would rise; the prices of surplus commodities would fall. Overall these contrary trends should tend to cancel each other out and lead to price stability.

When you have fixed-rule pricing and wage setting in one sector of the economy, however, this balancing will not necessarily occur. It will specifically not occur if the scarcities are concentrated in the market-oriented sectors while the surplus is concentrated in the fixed-rule sectors. Under these circumstances the prices and wages in the market-oriented sectors will rise. Those price increases will feed into the rules of the other sectors, and their prices will *also* rise. This is structural inflation.

It should be noted that structural inflation need not be set off by market forces. It could be triggered by a union political situation that upsets the wage structure, as appeared to be the case in the construction industry in the late 1960s. It might be initiated by the creation of many new plants, without an established place in the existing structure, as tends to happen in an economic boom. It could be triggered by the creation of a new monopoly that seeks to change the position of its product within the national price structure. This in fact occurred in oil after the Arab-Israeli war and is indeed one of the causes of inflation in the United States and abroad. But, in addition, in the last year and a half we have had what appears to be the classic conditions for a structural inflation: major shortages of market orientated raw materials balanced by surpluses in rule-set prices for manufactured commodities and labor.

How will such structural inflation respond to the conventional remedy of unemployment? Does this characterization suggest alternative economic policies? The answers to these questions depend very much upon how one interprets the commitment to the rules in the fixed-rule sectors. The approach of conventional economists has generally been to dismiss the rules as shorthand or a "rule of thumb" for the more elaborate calculations that are assumed to take place. The people who use these rules, the argument goes, actually are responding to the economic reality described by demand, supply and profit maximization procedures of economic theory, and when the gap between the rules and that more fundamental reality becomes important, people will abandon the rules and respond to the market directly. If this interpretation is correct, one can argue that higher unemployment will eventually break up even a structural inflation. The surplus will make it very costly to adhere to the rules and in this way force firms to abandon them in favor of market pricing. The reality of fixed rule pricing appears, however, to be somewhat more complicated than this conventional interpretation suggests.

In the case of wage rates, the rigidities in the wage structure appear to be a product of a moral commitment on the part of the labor force. Rank-and-file workers tend to view the process of wage determination in moral or ethical terms: they describe their wage rates as *just, fair* or *equitable*. And they are willing to go on strike to ensure that a *just* wage is received. Workers are not, of course, motivated by concepts of justice alone; they are deterred from striking by high unemployment rates, and they are not above pressuring for a wage that is a little more than "just" in a favorable economic climate. But the just wage is a standard. People are a good deal more willing to strike to preserve it, even in periods of high unemployment, than to better it, and it acts as a restraint upon wage demands even in a tight labor market.

A good deal less is known about the process of price determination than about wage rates. The process is more private; academic analysts have never been as intimately involved in its operations as they have in wage setting through collective bargaining; the rules that create rigidities in the price structure seem more complex and more difficult to explain. Still a part of their compulsion also seems to be moral, especially in those situations where buyer and seller have regular, personalized relationships. Both parties come to expect certain pricing patterns to be maintained, and think of any departure from those patterns as unjust and slightly immoral. It is the kind of breach of trust that causes a buyer to look elsewhere for new suppliers, if not immediately then later when the market is slack. And of course the fact that a buyer is likely to see things in this way causes the seller to adhere to the rule, even when he would like to take advantage of a favorable market to boost his margins.

But in the case of pricing, there is a technical as well as moral reason for adherence to conventional rules: there's no really sound alternative. The market forces that economists assume determine relative scarcities are impossible to *know*. The relative scarcities for many commodities, and hence their relative market prices, in fact remain pretty stable over long periods of time. A lot of the changes that do occur are temporary, attributable, for example, to managerial shakeups, the politics of industry, government relations or just a mistake. They tell nothing about the underlying market conditions but do confuse the picture. Thus the kind of variations in market conditions that might reveal something about the structure of demand and supply is missing. And, as any first-year graduate student will tell you, without that variation it is simply *not possible* to estimate the kind of relationships upon which the calculations assumed in economic theory are predicated.

This last explanation is a little bit like the conventional interpretation of the rules as shorthand calculations but with a critical difference. The conventional interpretation assumes that there is some deeper reality behind the rules, of the existence of which economic agents are at least aware, and that the major surpluses created by increasing unemployment will both induce people to seek out that reality and enable them to find it. However the alternative interpretation suggests that neither of these things is the case. For most price and wage setters the structure embodied in their rules *is* reality: nothing in their experience leads them to be aware of the deeper market structure that economists postulate.

If this is the nature of fixed-rule pricing, what is the likely effect of high levels of unemployment? High unemployment will create large surplus in virtually all markets. Such surpluses would confront price and wage makers with a reality lying completely outside the realm of their experience and not encompassed within the constructs through which that experience is understood. Such a confrontation might predispose people to redefine reality. But even if it did the higher levels of unemployment would not provide the needed information about the underlying structure of supply and demand. And it is not at all clear that high unemployment would in fact predispose people to reconstruct "reality." Psychological studies of people suddenly confronted with situations that do not fit their world view suggest they more often ignore the incongruity than revise their view. Economic agents, of course, cannot easily ignore the situation. Probably they would be forced by the threat of bankruptcy—or bankruptcy itself—simply to abandon established norms of price and wage behavior, and cut prices willy-nilly in some blind effort to shore up demand. They would then be behaving as economic theory says they should, in direct response to market forces, and this would presumably halt the inflationary movement. In this sense unemployment might be a cure.

There is a catch here, inherent in the phrase "abandon the established norms." In any other social setting the kind of wholesale abandonment of established norms of behavior upon which the "unemployment" cure to structural inflation rests would be interpreted as *anarchy*. It would probably be viewed as anarchy in economic activity as well. The orthodox story, in interpreting conventional rules as shorthand expressions of the laws of supply and demand, fails to appreciate this prospect. In that story unemployment merely forces people to recognize that the shorthand is no longer appropriate and to respond *directly* to market forces. From the agent's perspective the traditional rules of price and wage setting represent the *best* construction they can make of economic reality: they don't see any higher, more basic set of forces from which those rules derive. And when the rules are no longer appropriate, they feel that they have lost their grasp on reality. Add to this the vaguely moral flavor surrounding such rules, particularly in wage setting, and one does have anarchy.

What does economic anarchy imply? A panic, perhaps. Probably a prolonged depression. It is extremely unlikely that in the climate of uncertainty that would prevail the private sector would be willing to undertake the kind of investment upon which economic prosperity depends. And the capacity of the government to move fast enough and far enough in increasing its own spending to cover the shortfall in private demand is questionable.

If unemployment won't produce the required adjustments in the wage-price structure, what will? If, as we are arguing, the rules that impose the existing structure are indeed an effort to interpret economic reality, they will probably be revised eventually without a severe deflation. It is difficult to say exactly how this will be accomplished because nobody has taken these rules seriously enough as real economic mechanisms to study the processes of formulation and revision. However one can guess: the attempt of goods in the market-oriented sector to break out of the wage-price structure may be frustrated by existing rules, but it is not without its impact. Relative prices do change at least temporarily, before the rules reassert themselves and other prices catch up. To the extent that prices do not change, shortages occur. All of these things are indicators of a change in relative scarcities. They will make it more profitable to reduce the markups in pricing rules. And price makers should eventually find this out, if not by direct calculation, at least by accident. The fact that increases in food and fuel prices are still generating inflationary pressure probably reflects, as much as anything else, a basic skepticism that these crises were generated by permanent changes in the world economic system rather than transitory events—war, famine and the politics of détente.

In the case of wage determination, the argument is even more straightforward. There the commitment to a fixed structure rests almost entirely upon past practice and precedent. The leads and lags inherent in the wage setting process mean that a wage or price forced out of line by market pressures will prevail for at least a time. That period becomes a weak precedent. If the wage keeps jumping out of line each time efforts are made to restore it, the precedent becomes stronger and stronger. It then becomes something of an independent moral force capable of competing with the traditional wage structure.

It may be possible to facilitate these adjustments in the wage-price structure through public policy. Certain government agencies may, for example, be in a position to get people to recognize the changes in market conditions and revise their decision-making rules accordingly more quickly than people could or would do on their own. The moral authority of governmental institutions, and particularly the presidency, might be brought to bear to excuse people from the moral compulsion inherent in the traditional wage-price structure. In fact this view of the inflationary process points, in many respects, to a program of wage and price *controls*. The conventional distrust of such controls springs from the belief that they would suppress changes in the wage-price structure and, in so doing, forestall adjustments in supply and demand necessary to relieve the inflationary pressure. But if, as we have argued, the structure is rigid and wage-price changes set off an inflationary spiral, the structural changes won't occur anyway, and controls at least prevent the spiral from developing. The case for such controls would seem especially strong when combined with other policies designed to convince people directly of changes in economic conditions. Since the price structure has difficulty changing on its own, there is also a case for direct government interventions to expand supply or suppress demand. This is particularly true in sectors of the economy where the price is set by rules, but it is true even in market-oriented sectors, which act to set off the inflationary spiral elsewhere.

All of these interventions constitute an incomes policy of sorts. But it is not a simple matter of announcing—or even enforcing—a single wage-price standard. It is in fact a much more subtle approach to inflation that sees, as the central problem, the revision of a set of decision-making rules, which in turn reflect a particular construction of reality. The specific interventions then must be tailored to the particularities of the rules, which must be revised, and the specific markets in which those revisions occur. Ultimately the policymaker is trying in some sense to get into the heads of the economic agents themselves.

PART THREE

Labor Market Structure

Editor's Introduction
to Part Three

THE READINGS IN THIS SECTION examine various aspects of labor market structure. The first of these, by Roger Kaufman, contrasts the structure of the labor market in North America with that in Western Europe and Japan, and traces differences in the level of unemployment in these two groups of countries to differences in the institutions through which jobs are secured against fluctuations in demand. The following piece, by Charles Sabel, introduces the concept of industrial marginality and shows how the market, structured by the characteristics of the demand for labor, uses various marginal groups to adjust to these structural conditions. The third reading explores the implications of the behavior of these marginal groups for wage determination, and shows how the characteristics of marginal workers produce unexpected patterns of wage behavior even in a competitive market. The last three pieces examine particular groups of marginal workers: youth, foreign workers, and welfare households. Each of the last three pieces is directed at the particular policy issues surrounding the groups with which they are concerned: unemployment in the case of youth, extralegal immigration in the case of foreign workers, and public assistance legislation in the case of welfare households. But they may also be read as particular illustrations of the general class of individual labor to which Sabel's essay is devoted.

The work in this section is relatively homogeneous in its theoretical approach. It is all conceived in terms of the dual labor market hypothesis, which was outlined and discussed in the Introduction. Some consideration was given to the inclusion of selections from the theory of structural unemployment, prominent in the late 1950s and early 1960s. The leading proponent of this view was Charles Killingsworth. Despite the common use of the term "structural," however, the theoretical orientation of this volume is very different from that of the earlier literature. The earlier hypothesis about structural unemployment was concerned with the structure of the labor force and, to a lesser extent, the structure of jobs. It saw unemployment as indication of a mismatch between these that rendered the unemployed *incapable* of filling job vacancies. The mismatch was attributed to the fact that either demographic trends or technology or both were evolving autonomously of market control. The structure with which this volume is concerned is the structure of the economy in the broadest sense of the term. Unemployment is the outgrowth of the role that particular workers play within the structure, and so it is "structural" in that sense; but it is not necessarily indicative of a malfunction or inability to participate in the system. Moreover, to the extent that there is a mismatch between unemployed workers and job vacancies, it has to do with the aspirations of workers, not their qualifications.

Why the U.S. Unemployment Rate Is So High

1

BY ROGER KAUFMAN

ANY CASUAL OBSERVER of the unemployment data of industrialized nations will make the rather shocking discovery that U.S. and Canadian unemployment rates throughout the 1960s and early 1970s were almost double those of most Western European countries and Japan. Although most countries have experienced sharply rising unemployment rates during the recent worldwide recession, the disparities have generally persisted.

For many years, American economists and statisticians explained these differences by asserting that U.S. unemployment statistics were more comprehensive than those of foreign countries. Whereas U.S. unemployment data are compiled from intensive household surveys, many European governments have used registrations for unemployment insurance benefits as their official estimates of those unemployed. These differences in measurement techniques were investigated in 1962 by the President's Committee to Appraise Employment and Unemployment Statistics. The Committee discovered that many foreign countries also conducted household surveys similar to the one in the United States. The Department of Labor has collected these survey data and adjusted them to conform to U.S. concepts. (A person is counted as unemployed in the U.S. survey if he or she did not work at all for pay or profit during the survey week but actively sought work within the preceding four-week period. Workers on temporary layoff and people waiting to begin a new job within thirty days are counted among the unemployed even if they have not actively sought other employment.) These adjusted unemployment rates appear in Table 1.

The U.S. and Canadian unemployment rates have typically been far greater than those prevailing abroad, even after these adjustments have

From *Challenge*, May-June 1978, pp. 40-49. © 1978 by M.E. Sharpe, Inc. Support for this research was provided by the Sloan Foundation through its grant to MIT on Public Control of Economic Activity.

Table 1

Adjusted Unemployment Rates, 1959-1977 (As a percentage of civilian labor force)

Year	United States	Canada	Japan	France	West Germany	Italy	Sweden	Great Britain
1959	5.5	6.0	2.3	2.1	2.0	5.0	NA	2.9
1960	5.5	7.0	1.7	1.8	1.1	3.8	NA	2.2
1961	6.7	7.1	1.5	1.6	0.6	3.2	1.4	2.0
1962	5.5	5.9	1.3	1.5	0.6	2.8	1.5	2.8
1963	5.7	5.5	1.3	1.3	0.5	2.4	1.7	3.4
1964	5.2	4.7	1.2	1.5	0.4	2.6	1.5	2.5
1965	4.5	3.9	1.2	1.6	0.3	3.5	1.2	2.2
1966	3.8	3.4	1.4	1.9	0.3	3.8	1.6	2.3
1967	3.8	3.8	1.3	2.0	1.3	3.4	2.1	3.4
1968	3.6	4.5	1.2	2.6	1.4	3.4	2.2	3.3
1969	3.5	4.4	1.1	2.4	0.9	3.3	1.9	3.0
1970	4.9	5.7	1.2	2.6	0.8	3.1	1.5	3.1
1971	5.9	6.2	1.3	2.8	0.8	3.1	2.6	3.9
1972	5.6	6.2	1.4	2.8	0.8	3.6	2.7	4.2
1973	4.9	5.6	1.3	2.7	0.8	3.4	2.5	3.2
1974	5.6	5.4	1.4	3.0	1.7	2.8	2.0	2.8
1975	8.5	6.9	1.9	4.2	3.7	3.2	1.6	4.7[a]
1976	7.7	7.1	2.0	4.6	3.6	3.6	1.6	6.4[a]
1977[a]	7.0	8.1	2.0	5.2	3.5	3.3	1.8	7.0[a]

SOURCE: Private communication with Joanna Moy, U.S. Bureau of Labor Statistics, September 1977. *Economic Report of the President, 1978.*

[a]Preliminary estimates based on incomplete data.

156

been made. Over the past eighteen years, the U.S. unemployment rate reached a nadir of 3.5 percent in 1969. From 1959 to 1974, however, the highest unemployment rates experienced in Japan, France, West Germany, and Sweden were 2.3, 3.1, 2.0, and 2.7 percent, respectively. Until recently, 4 percent unemployment was considered to represent "full employment" in the United States. That figure, however, is considered to be extremely high in Europe and Japan, where "full employment" is often taken to be 2, and even 1 percent unemployment. The fact that the adjusted unemployment rates abroad, especially in France and Great Britain, have recently risen to levels approaching and even exceeding those in the United States lends further support to the hypothesis that their normally lower rates are not merely the result of less comprehensive surveys.

There has been surprisingly little research on the huge disparities in national unemployment rates, largely because of the numerous economic, political, sociological, and cultural factors involved. In the discussion that follows we shall consider various economic "explanations." After casting doubt on several commonly held beliefs, we shall introduce a new explanation of these differences by focusing on the sharp contrasts in the job security and job continuity arrangements among the various countries.

It should be noted that five or ten years ago one would undoubtedly have transformed all the following "explanations" into propositions about each country's Phillips curve, which is a functional relationship describing a trade-off between wage (or price) inflation within a country and its unemployment rate. Recent experience and theoretical research, however, have shown that such trade-offs are more short-lived and complicated than was heretofore believed. Many economists now prefer to speak about a country's "natural rate of unemployment." Whenever the actual unemployment rate falls below the "natural rate," it is postulated that the inflation rate that has prevailed begins to accelerate; conversely, whenever the actual unemployment rate exceeds the "natural rate," inflation presumably begins to decelerate. These theorists would view this article as a discussion of the reasons why the "natural rate of unemployment" appears to be higher in North America than in Western Europe and Japan.

Overplayed theories

Contrary to the expectations of some of the adherents of the so-called "structural" or "technological" views of unemployment, the North American economies have generated substantial amounts of new employment during the past quarter-century. Between 1960 and 1972, civilian employment grew at a faster rate in the United States and Canada than in such countries as Japan, France, West Germany, Italy, Sweden, and Great Britain. In the previous decade, the U.S. performance in employment creation was exceeded only by Japan and West Germany.

Table 2

Participation Rates

Country	$\left(\dfrac{\text{Total labor force}^a}{\text{Population 15–64 years}}\right) \times 100$		$\left(\dfrac{\text{Total male labor force}^a}{\text{Total male population 15–64 years}}\right) \times 100$		$\left(\dfrac{\text{Total female labor force}^a}{\text{Total female population 15–64 years}}\right) \times 100$	
	1961	1972	1961	1972	1961	1972
United States	67.0	67.9	91.4	86.4	43.1	50.0
Canada		65.3		87.2		43.2
Japan	75.8	71.3	92.5	89.8	59.9	53.5
France	69.2	67.3	NA	86.1	NA	48.3
West Germany	70.9	68.9	95.5	91.7	49.3	47.5
Italy	63.5b	54.6b	92.3	81.9	36.6	28.4
Sweden	73.3	75.2	93.1	88.1	53.3	61.9c
Great Britain	73.7	71.9	98.9	92.6	49.3	41.5

SOURCE: OECD *Labor Force Statistics*, various issues.

aIncludes military personnel. The total labor force data for 1972 are very close to the adjusted data discussed in the text.

b14–64 years old. Note, however, few Italians over 55 years old remain in the labor force.

cThe Swedish data are slightly misleading because of the unusual composition of the Swedish population. The percentage of the Swedish labor force which is female is only slightly higher than in the other European countries.

Despite these large increases in employment, North American unemployment rates have remained high because our civilian labor forces also grew at relatively high rates. This was the result of an increase in working-age populations and rising labor force participation rates (Table 2). According to neoclassical economic theory, labor force growth should have little effect on the unemployment rate. In economies experiencing large increases in their labor forces, wages would merely be bid down to new equilibrium levels. Thus, economists who argue that increased labor force growth will have a deleterious effect on the unemployment rate are implicitly assuming either that wages are not perfectly flexible in all sectors or that some other market imperfection is present.

As mentioned previously, 4 percent unemployment was regarded as full employment in the United States during the 1950s and much of the 1960s. Many economists, however, now believe that a 4 percent goal is impractical, that 5 or even 6 percent unemployment rates are more reasonable targets. They base their conclusions partly on the fact that women and teenagers now comprise a significantly larger portion of our labor force than in the past. These groups presumably have fewer skills and looser attachments to their jobs than prime-age (25- to 54-year-old) males. Allegedly, they tend to search longer for "good" jobs after entering the labor force because they are not usually the principal breadwinners in their families. Similarly, they may feel less compelled to find alternative employment before quitting their jobs.

Female labor force participation has definitely been rising sharply in the United States and Canada, as shown in Table 2. Nevertheless, as late as 1961, female participation rates were lower in North America than in any of the other countries listed except Italy. Even by 1972, our female labor force participation rates were not especially high in comparison with Western Europe and Japan, yet those countries had managed to keep their unemployment rates well below 3 percent. The fact that female labor force participation has increased hardly explains these international differences.

The post-World War II baby boom did swell the ranks of teenage labor force participants in the United States, but this did not occur until the 1960s. In 1960 a smaller proportion (7 percent) of the U.S. civilian labor force were teenagers than in any of the other countries listed in Table 2. By 1972, however, the U.S. proportion had risen to about 10 percent, while the European percentages had declined to below that figure, largely due to expanding enrollments in secondary and university education there.

U.S. unemployment rates for the various age groups and by sex are typically two to three times higher than those in Europe and Japan. Nevertheless, the ratio of the teenage unemployment rate to the adult unemployment rate was relatively high in the United States throughout the 1960s. In the past, economists have attributed this to an overly general educational curriculum, an inferior prevocational counseling system, minimum wage laws which do not exempt teenagers, and the relative dearth of apprenticeship programs in America. It is also worth noting that the overwhelming majority of teenagers in European labor forces are full-time participants; relatively few work while they are still in school, partly because many European governments provide stipends to all students. In America, on the other hand, most teenage workers are also students, and this may reduce their job attachment. These arguments, however, are now suspect because the ratios of teenage to adult unemployment rates have recently risen sharply throughout Europe.

Unemployment benefits

It has also been alleged that excessive unemployment compensation allows American workers to refuse job offers or extend their "job search" and thereby remain unemployed for longer periods than is desirable. Many people overestimate these effects; careful study (by Stephen Marston) has revealed that the American unemployment insurance system may add between 0.2 and 0.4 percentage points to the U.S. unemployment rate. In addition, unemployment benefit programs in Western Europe and Japan are typically more generous than those in the United States, which vary from state to state. Constance Sorrentino and Joanna Moy of the U.S. Department of Labor calculated the "replacement ratios" for unemployed manufacturing employees in eight nations in 1975. These data appear in Table 3.

A replacement ratio is the average unemployment benefit taken as a percentage of the average after-tax earnings. Theoretically, the higher the replacement ratio, the easier it is for unemployed workers to maintain their previous standard of living while remaining unemployed. As Table 3 illustrates, European replacement ratios are generally higher than those prevailing in most American states. Although the Canadian system also appears to be relatively generous, North American unemployment benefit replacement ratios are not high by European standards. (We should note, however, that the percentage of the labor force covered by unemployment compensation is relatively high in the United States, primarily because a larger portion of the foreign labor forces are employed in small firms and in agriculture, which are often exempted.)

Consonant with these results, the Department of Labor has discovered that the average duration of unemployment appears to be significantly greater abroad and, more recently, in Canada. These data indicate that the higher U.S. unemployment rate results from greater flows of people moving into and out of employment, rather than from a given number remaining unemployed for a longer period of time.

Before proceeding to a discussion of the roles of job security and job continuity, we should note that many other hypotheses have been suggested to explain the international differences in unemployment rates: the contributions and effects of guest workers in Europe and illegal aliens in the

Table 3

Unemployment Benefit as a Percentage of Average Earnings, Manufacturing Workers in 8 Nations, Mid-1975

Country	Single worker	Married worker with 2 children	
		Unemployment benefits	Unemployment benefits and family allowances
United States[a]	50	50	50
Canada	63	63	68
Japan	60	62	62
France			
Regular system			
First 3 months	56	63	69-77[b]
Subsequent months	50	57	63-71[b]
Supplementary benefits			
system[c]	90	90	96-104[b]
Germany	60	60	66
Great Britain			
First 6 months[d]	38	60	63
Next 6 months[d]	19	41	44
Italy			
Flat-rate benefits	9	22	22
Earnings-related scheme[e]	67	80	80
Sweden[f]	62-72	62-72	67-79

SOURCE: Constance Sorrentino, "Unemployment Compensation in Eight Industrial Nations," *Monthly Labor Review* (June 1976), pp. 18-24.

[a]Figures shown are representative of the majority of States.
[b]Lower figures relate to family allowance payable to family with more than 1 wage earner; higher figure includes single wage earner allowance.
[c]For workers under age 60 laid off for cyclical or structural reasons.
[d]Means-tested public assistance payments can substantially raise these ratios.
[e]Industrial sector employee at the same enterprise for 3 months.
[f]Trade union system. Numerical ranges due to trade union funds.

United States; structural unemployment; unionization *per se;* the relative ethnic and racial heterogeneity of the U.S. and Canadian populations; public employment and other manpower efforts in the various countries; and even the low voting incidence among the U.S. electorate.[1]

Job security and job continuity

We now turn to an issue which has been practically neglected by economists until recently. Figure 1 shows that job losers have comprised the largest category among the U.S. unemployed since 1967, when these data were first collected. In January 1975, the number of unemployed

Figure 1

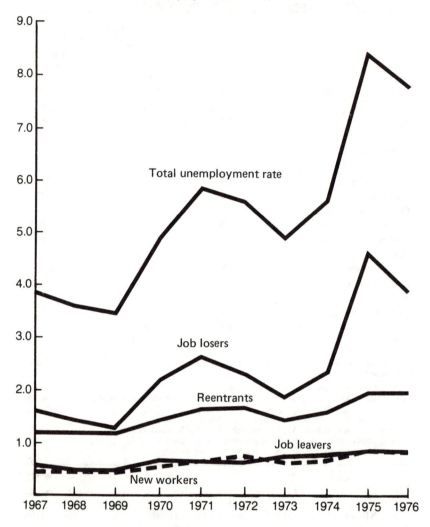

U.S. Unemployment Rates: By Reason

Total unemployment rate

Job losers

Reentrants

Job leavers

New workers

persons in the United States who had lost their previous jobs reached 3,800,000. These job losers included those temporarily as well as permanently laid off.

In contrast, layoffs occur much less frequently in Europe and Japan. Table 4 gives the available separation rate data in seven countries. These data have been adjusted to represent the number of separations per month per 100 employees in manufacturing or in all industries. Variations in definitions and data collection procedures make comparisons of the data across nations very unreliable. Nevertheless, the U.S. and Canadian rates exceed those of the other five countries by an order of magnitude which might be diminished but probably not eliminated by any further adjustments. One major problem in interpreting separations data is that they

Table 4

Monthly Separation Rates Per 100 Employees[a]

Year	Canada	United States	France	Great Britain	Sweden	Japan	Italy
1953	6.9	5.1	N.A.	2.7	N.A.		N.A.
1954	6.6	4.1	3.7	2.9	N.A.		N.A.
1955	6.4	3.9	3.7	3.1	N.A.	1.8	N.A.
1956	6.9	4.2	4.2	2.8	N.A.	1.8	N.A.
1957	6.9	4.2	4.0	2.8	N.A.	1.9	N.A.
1958	6.1	4.1	3.6	2.4	1.7	2.0	2.2
1959	6.2	4.1	3.3	2.4	1.9	2.8	2.2
1960	6.2	4.3	3.5	2.7	2.4	2.1	2.4
1961	5.9	4.0	4.2	2.6	2.7	2.5	2.6
1962	6.0	4.1	3.8	2.5	2.5	2.4	2.8
1963	5.9	3.9	3.7	2.5	2.6	2.3	2.8
1964	6.0	3.9	3.7	2.7	2.8	2.6	2.7
1965	6.2	4.1	3.4	2.8	3.1	2.3	2.0
1966	5.9	4.6	3.5	3.0	3.0	2.2	2.0
1967	N.A.	4.6	3.4	2.7	2.5	2.2	2.1
1968	N.A.	4.6	3.6	2.7	2.5	2.4	2.3
1969	N.A.	4.9	N.A.	3.1	3.2	2.3	2.4
1970	N.A.	4.8	4.0	2.9	3.2	2.3	2.1
1971	N.A.	4.2	3.8	2.9	2.4	2.2	2.4
1972	N.A.	4.2	3.7	2.3	2.1	1.9	2.2
1973	N.A.	4.6	N.A.	2.7	2.2	2.0	2.2
1974	N.A.	4.8	N.A.	2.8	2.4	1.9	1.4
1975	N.A.	4.2	N.A.	2.3	2.1		1.1

SOURCES: Canada: Dominion Bureau of Statistics, *Hiring and Separation Rates in Certain Industries,* Ottawa, June 1968.
United States: U.S. Department of Labor, *Handbook of Labor Statistics* (Washington, D.C., passim).
France: 1967-1968, 1970-1972: Chabanas, N., and Volkoff, S., *Les Salaires dans l'Industrie, le Commerce et les Services,* Les Collections de l'Insee, passim. 1963-1966: Insee, *Etudes et Conjonctures,* passim. 1954-1962: Insee, *Etudes Statistiques,* passim.
Great Britain: 1969-1975: Great Britain Department of Employment and Productivity, *Department of Employment Gazette,* passim.
1953-1968: Great Britain Department of Employment and Productivity, *British Labour Statistics: Historical Abstract 1886-1968* (London: Her Majesty's Stationery Office, 1971).
Sweden: 1968-1975: Statistiska Centralbyran, *Statistiska Meddelanden,* Series Am., passim.
1958-1967: Konyankturinstitutet, *The Swedish Economy,* passim, reprinted in Flanagan, Robert J., *A Study of International Differences in Phillips Curves,* unpublished doctoral dissertation, Berkeley, Calif.: 1970, p. 120.
Japan: Ministry of Labor, *Yearbook of Labor Statistics* (Tokyo, passim).
Italy: 1965-1975: Ministero del Lavoro e della Previdenza Sociale, *Rassegna di Statistiche del Lavoro* (Rome, passim).
1958-1964: Ministero del Lavoro e della Previdenza Sociale, *Statistiche del Lavoro* (Rome, passim).
[a]Definitions and coverage vary significantly across nations. Details may be obtained from the author upon written request.

include voluntary as well as involuntary separations, that is, job quits as well as layoffs. There is a substantial amount of additional evidence, however, which suggests that layoff rates in North America are substantially higher than those abroad.

How do these differences in layoff activities affect aggregate unemployment rates? In answering this question we have found it useful to distinguish among five sectors of the civilian economy. We shall currently ignore two of these: the self-employed, for whom job security is meaningless; and public employees, who typically enjoy a great deal of job security in all countries. Because of space limitations we shall also disregard the "transient" sector, which consists primarily of temporary jobs, and shall focus our attention on the "secure" and "open" sectors, each with its own unique features.

The secure sector consists primarily of workers in highly unionized industries within manufacturing. For our purposes the relevant characteristics are: relatively high wages; a fluctuating demand for the final product; work which requires skilled and semi-skilled labor; and the presence of a collective bargaining agreement. In the United States most workers in the "secure" sector enjoy a considerable degree of job security as a result of the seniority provisions in their collective agreements. It appears, however, that these workers experience a relatively high degree of job discontinuity; they are frequently laid off for one or more weeks. People in the "secure" sector are less likely to accept lower-paying jobs while on temporary layoff, partially because of the unemployment and supplemental unemployment benefits which are often available to them. Instead, they often remain unemployed, awaiting their recall. In contrast, foreign firms in the "secure" sector tend to retain their workers during temporary downturns. There is some evidence that foreign employers also try to allocate production more evenly over the course of the year in order to avoid abrupt changes in labor requirements.

Neoclassical theory suggests good theoretical reasons for these apparent differences in layoff rates. For instance, firms will be more likely to lay off workers in a loose labor market, where they can rehire them as needed. Foreign layoff rates, however, do not appear to rise as much as those in the United States, even during economic recessions. Furthermore, foreign reluctance to lay off workers seems to be primarily motivated by national job security legislation and public and worker attitudes. To the extent that foreign firms in the "secure" sector continually employ a greater percentage of the labor forces which are "attached" to these firms, the unemployment rate will be lower in the "secure" sectors of Western Europe and Japan.

The "open" sector of the economy includes workers in smaller unionized and nonunionized manufacturing plants, and many white collar and service employees. The essential characteristics are: relatively low wages; few provisions for job security (at least in the United States); a

Table 5

Constraints on Layoffs in Seven Countries

	Japan		France		Italy		Sweden		Great Britain		Canada		United States	
	"Secure" sector	"Open" sector	"Secure" sector	"Open" sector	"Secure" sector	"Open" sector	"Secure" sector	"Open" sector	"Secure" sector	"Open" sector	"Secure" sector	"Open" sector	"Secure" sector	"Open" sector
Layoffs must be preceded by permission of government authority			X	X										
Layoffs must be preceded by consultation with worker representatives			X	X	X	X	X	X	X	X	X			
Layoffs must be preceded by advance notice of at least one week	X	X	X	X	X	X	X	X	X	X	X	X		
Employers' unemployment insurance contributions are experience-related													X	X
Layoffs will probably incur extreme union and/or worker opposition			X	X	X	X			X	X				
Layoffs are contrary to custom and tradition	X	X	X	X	X	X								
Layoffs will probably be followed by severe and widespread public criticism			X	X	X	X								
Layoffs involve the payment of mandatory severance benefits			X	X	X	X	X	X	X	X	X		X	
Employers must seek outside approval before scheduling overtime			X	X	X	X	X	X						

fluctuating demand for the final product; and jobs which require labor that is either unskilled or semi-skilled, or that is readily available both within and outside the labor force. A large number of workers in this sector are women, members of ethnic and racial minorities, and youth. In comparison with the "secure" sector, a greater proportion of total separations in the "open" sector are permanent terminations rather than temporary layoffs. Since jobs in this sector tend to be less well-paid, firms do not have "captive" labor forces, as do firms in the "secure" sector. When workers are discharged in the "open" sector, they do not await rehiring. They usually search for different jobs, drop out of the labor force, and/or content themselves with collecting unemployment benefits.

Aside from anti-discrimination laws enforced in most of these countries, job security provisions in the "open" sector are relatively rare in the United States and Canada but common throughout Western Europe and Japan. Table 5 summarizes the job security and job continuity arrangements in the "secure" and "open" sectors of seven countries. The two main arrangements in the United States, aside from seniority, are the mandatory payment of severance benefits included in most collective agreements, and the U.S. system of varying employers' contributions to the unemployment insurance fund according to the amount of benefits received by past and present employees. In addition, a handful of American companies unilaterally grant extensive job security and job continuity to their nonunion employees, partly to forestall union organizing efforts.

Although none of the European or Japanese unemployment insurance systems is "experience-rated" to as great an extent as in the United States, many of these countries have enacted widespread legislation which inhibits layoffs. All of them require elaborate prenotification periods of a minimum of six days for most employees, and layoffs of more experienced employees may require prenotification of several months. In the United States, only 12 percent of those employees covered by major collective agreements in 1970 were entitled to advance notice exceeding six days.

In many European countries, terminations must be preceded by consultation with works' councils or similar worker representatives, who may suggest alternatives. Worker, union, and public opposition to layoffs also appears to be significantly greater abroad. Worker takeovers have followed announced plant shutdowns at the LIP watch factory in France and at the Upper Clyde Shipyard in Great Britain; Italian employers have expressed fears that the government will nationalize their plants if they close down.

By law, European employers must pay almost all employees substantial sums if they are laid off.[2] Moreover, Italian firms frequently offer additional *de facto* severance payments to obtain a worker's "voluntary" resignation in order to avoid an industrial dispute over his termination. (Since the labor unrest of 1969, it has become extremely difficult to lay off employees in the "open" and "secure" sectors in Italy.) During the recent recession, German employers also offered their employees this "golden glove" option. In 1975 the British government introduced Temporary Employment Subsidies, which subsidize employers for each redundant worker they retain.

In France, job security has been increased considerably. French employers must receive approval from the Minister of Labor before dismissing anyone for economic reasons, and refusals appear to have become more frequent. French textile firms are obliged to find places for their displaced employees in other firms, and even in other industries.

In an extensive international study conducted by a Chicago law firm (see the volumes by Seyfarth, Shaw, et al., published by University of Michigan Press), most European employers reported that they felt unable to schedule overtime during periods in which some employees were on layoff. The vast majority of U.S. employers in the study felt no similar constraints. (Only 9 percent of those U.S. employees covered by major collective agreements in 1970 were protected by clauses limiting overtime during slack periods.) Work-sharing as an alternative to layoffs is also more prevalent in Western Europe and Japan. On the other side of the coin, James Medoff has presented evidence suggesting that unionized workers in the United States actually have a preference for temporary layoffs over alternative adjustments to slack demand.

Many readers are familiar with the Japanese system of *sushin koyo*, in which designated workers are guaranteed continuous lifetime employment until the normal retirement age of fifty-five for men and fifty for women. (Many of these people continue to work on renewable one-year contracts beyond the official retirement age.) These rigidities are alleviated, however, by the fact that Japanese employers are allowed to shift workers from one job or one plant to another. The Japanese system of job security is also unique in that it emanates more from tradition and implicit agreements than from Japanese law or collective bargaining agreements. Nevertheless, the prevalence of lifetime employment in Japan is often exaggerated. Only 30 to 40 percent of the nonagricultural labor force in Japan is thus protected. Even so, temporary layoffs and permanent discharges appear to be much less frequent in Japan than in North America. Although some Japanese employers were forced to lay off employees during the recent recession, many others retained their excess labor. There are numerous stories of Japanese companies sending excess production-line workers out to sell their products door-to-door or to do landscaping around the factory.

We have already mentioned how the relative absence of job security and job continuity arrangements may raise the unemployment rate in the "secure" sectors of the United States and Canada. In the "open" sector, their absence also acts to raise the unemployment rate, but in a different fashion. This is due to the fact that employees do not become "attached" to firms in the "open" sector, as they do in the "secure" sector. In the "open" sector in North America, lower layoff costs lead to more job creation, more job elimination, and more unemployment. The last occurs because employers in this sector tend to recruit new workers from outside the labor force, and these recruits do not leave the labor force immediately after their jobs are terminated. People "incur" fixed costs, both psychic and monetary, when they enter the labor market. These include the costs of changing one's mode of life and that of one's family, the cost of overcoming one's fears of ineptitude, and the cost of acquiring new clothes and perhaps an automobile in order to begin employment. After these fixed costs have been incurred, a person is likely to remain in the labor force for an extended period of time rather than exiting as soon as his or her first job is terminated.

We also believe that the availability of significant unemployment benefits is likely to increase the duration of "search" or "between-job" time for people who have been discharged. This will result in a higher "frictional" rate of unemployment in the country where involuntary turnover is greater. We do not believe that the availability of substantial unemployment benefits increases quit rates to a great extent. Many people who quit their jobs do not even file claims for unemployment insurance benefits. Between 1973 and 1975, people who voluntarily quit their previous jobs and applied for unemployment benefits represented only about 10 percent of all those newly eligible for such benefits. To those who have been laid off, however, unemployment compensation is probably viewed as a right rather than a privilege. Inasmuch as their terminations were involuntary, these people may feel justified in extending their "job search." Thus, the generosity of unemployment insurance systems abroad may not significantly increase foreign unemployment rates in the "open" sector because layoffs and discharges are greatly inhibited. In the United States, however, these benefits do increase the unemployment rate significantly.

International differences

For more than two decades, U.S. and Canadian unemployment rates have been persistently higher than those prevailing in Western Europe and Japan. Many of the explanations offered in the past to account for these differences have been shown to be either fallacious or of minor significance. We have suggested a new explanation, one which focuses on international differences in job security and job continuity. In doing so, we are not arguing that the implementation of measures which enhance job security and job continuity will automatically lower a country's unemployment rate. Instead, we believe that in a comparison of "full employment" unemployment rates (or "natural rates of unemployment"), *ceteris paribus*, the unemployment rate in the country with greater job security and job continuity will be lower. The United States and Canada have been shown to have relatively few arrangements for job security in the "open" sectors in their economies. They also appear to have high layoff rates in the "secure" sectors.

The relative absence of these provisions in the United States can also explain why we have experienced large increases in employment and labor force participation amidst high unemployment rates. It also helps us understand why many European countries were late victims of the recent worldwide recession (as measured by their unemployment rates) and why they seem to be late in recovering. Foreign employers suddenly found themselves with surplus workers whom they could not easily lay off. These labor surpluses are gradually disappearing, but employers are now cautious about taking on new employees. In an international comparison of so-called Okun's Law (which relates the level or changes in the level of the unemployment rate to current and past changes in GNP), the author found that the unemployment rates of Western Europe and Japan were less sensitive to macroeconomic fluctuations in the short run than were the U.S. and Canadian unemployment rates. Over a period of three years, however, the reactions appeared to be fairly similar, with the exception of Japan. The international differences in job security and job continuity, coupled with the recent recession, may also contribute to an explanation of the severe youth unemployment problems currently facing many Western European governments. The traditional institutional arrangements to alleviate Europe's youth unemployment problems in the past appear to be vulnerable. It seems that many European employers are now wary of hiring any new employees until they utilize the surplus labor they are now holding and become more confident about the future.

Finally, as a result of the job security and job continuity arrangements which prevail abroad, a greater portion of foreign labor costs are what economists call "fixed costs," which is to say they cannot be avoided through layoffs if production falters. (Even in the United States the experience rating of the unemployment insurance system acts as a deterrent to layoffs.) As a result, during periods of slack demand foreign firms may be more likely to sell their products at whatever prices they can get, especially on the international market. It may be rational for them to "dump" products at prices which do not fully cover their costs, if they do not have the option of laying off their workers and curtailing production.

Notes

1. For a more complete, but by no means exhaustive, survey of these and other issues, the reader is referred to the author's dissertation (An International Comparison of Unemployment Rates: The Effects of Job Security and Job Continuity, M.I.T., 1978).
2. Although workers who are temporarily laid off do not qualify for these "redundancy payments" in Great Britain, workers who quit after four consecutive weeks of layoff (or six weeks of layoff within the past thirteen weeks) are eligible if it is deemed unlikely that normal, full-time employment lasting continuously for thirteen weeks will be offered within the next four weeks.

169

Marginal Workers in Industrial Society

2

BY CHARLES F. SABEL

FROM THE START, theories of labor market segmentation have been concerned with the problem of marginal economic groups—the low-skilled and poorly paid workers in menial or routine jobs who are the first to be fired during recessions. This is hardly surprising, since the new theories were first conceived as an alternative explanation of the persistent poverty of blacks and Puerto Ricans, who tend to occupy just such jobs in our society.

The orthodox view of poverty focuses on problems of education: because of a combination of discrimination, ignorance, and their own shortsightedness, it is said, the poor simply fail to acquire a sufficient stock of economically valuable skills. The argument is that these workers are paid little because they in fact contribute little to the economy. Conversely, if they had more skills employers would pay them more—an assumption which is at work in the current Comprehensive Education and Training Act program (CETA).

But during the 1960s, many researchers became convinced that the problem of education, at least in the way it was posed by the dominant school, was a red herring. They found that regardless of the skill level of the available work force, employers were creating jobs which required nothing more than a minimal education. One implication of this finding was that even if all workers were well-trained, employers would still be offering a certain number of low-skill and low-paying jobs. Raising the skill level of the poor, in other words, would not eliminate poverty. Someone, after all, would have to take the low-skill jobs if no better ones were to be had. Moreover, the researchers found that marginal workers had motives for their behavior which did not square at all with the picture painted of them in the orthodox theory. They seemed to have complex reasons for putting up with jobs most of us would never want to do; and these reasons seemed to influence, in important though obscure ways, their reaction to attempts to help them escape poverty.

From *Challenge*, March-April 1979, pp. 22-32. © 1979 by M. E. Sharpe, Inc.

But what, precisely, could make employers determine to go on offering low-skill jobs? And what, beyond powerlessness, ignorance, or laziness, could be the motives of the workers who, however reluctantly, accepted them? This brief essay offers some answers to the second question. But before the story of the marginal workers' motives can be told, a word must be said about industrialists' interest in preserving menial jobs in the first place.

The double origin of low-skill jobs

Two quite distinct considerations lead managers to create jobs requiring a minimal level of skills. The first has to do with the rationalization of work and the pursuit of efficiency in the technologically sophisticated or primary part of the economy; the second concerns the problem of market uncertainty in the more backward or secondary economic sector.

In firms which use a great deal of machinery to produce large amounts of goods for relatively stable markets, there is a tendency to try to cut the costs of production by subdividing tasks. The theory (and often the fact) is that if two whole-widget makers working separately can make a hundred widgets in a day, then a top-of-the-widget maker working together with a bottom-of-the-widget maker can produce substantially more than a hundred widgets in the same time. The upshot of this process of the subdivision or rationalization of work is that the productivity of the work force goes up at the same time the skill level, in at least some of the groups of which it is composed, declines. (Rationalization does of course create some jobs requiring new machine-tending skills and can even lead to the upgrading of certain craft skills, especially those required in maintenance; but how and to what extent this occurs is beyond the scope of this essay.) So the progress of large industry—think of the automobile assembly line—is one source of unskilled work.

The second source of supply of unskilled jobs is, paradoxically, the failure of the secondary sector of industry to progress to the point where the introduction of machinery on a large scale becomes profitable. Before industrialists will invest large sums in capital equipment, they need to be assured that their prospective product faces good long-term chances on the market. The thought of paying off the loan necessary to buy some piece of machinery while the machine stands idle for want of demand will obviously give pause to any rational investor.

But there is only so much demand for any given product. The first-comer to the market for that product can make a conservative estimate of the minimum which is likely to be demanded in the worst of times. He builds a plant using modern machinery and rationalized methods of work which allow him to turn a profit even when operating with some slack capacity in times of lowest demand. What about the late-comer manufacturers? It makes no sense for them to invest in the same kind of plant, because if the first-comer was right, in bad years the machinery would be idle. But in good years the late-comers might still profit by meeting the demand in excess of the amount supplied by the early birds even operating at full capacity. To make use of this opportunity they will want to set up production in a way which requires a minimum of capital outlay (to cut losses in a recession when equipment cannot be used temporarily or must be sold), *and* a minimum investment in worker training (to minimize the time it takes before the new firm can start to meet the transient demand and again to reduce the losses associated with going out of business if the inevitable slump is particularly severe).

Typically, the firms which go into business to satisfy this fluctuating kind of demand will start by buying up some old, cheap, and rather inefficient machinery. Next they hire a few craftsmen to patch the machines together; finally they hire a much larger group of unskilled workers to man the equipment. With respect to the latter the manufacturers are drawn in contrary directions. Because the machinery is relatively inefficient, they would like the workers to make up for its defects by learning to use it skillfully; but at the same time they, the manufacturers, are unwilling to invest time or money in training the work force. In the end, they will prefer minimally skilled inefficient workers to more skilled and efficient ones: so long as demand is exceptionally high, so are prices; and high prices will compensate for the relatively high costs of production.

Notice that in introducing this analytic distinction between economic sectors, I am arguing that most unskilled work in our society derives from these two sources, not that every firm in the economy employs significant numbers of unskilled workers. Extremely capital-intensive primary sector plants like refineries or nuclear power obviously do not; neither do small engineering firms which develop and apply the latest technology, nor do precision tool shops specializing in one-of-a-kind jobs. (Strictly speaking, neither of these last two examples should be included in a discussion of the manufacturing sector at all: the first is more like a laboratory, the second more like an artisan's shop than a factory.)

By itself, furthermore, the distinction says nothing about the division within any given industry between production for the primary and secondary sectors, or about the institutional form that division will take. Typically, *some* production in almost all manufacturing industries will be organized according to the principles of the secondary sector; and no less typically, some firms will try to operate in both sectors at once by combining within a single legal framework quite different and often geographically distinct production divisions. An electronics firm in West Germany, for example, might have its central plant and highly skilled work force located near a large city. During boom periods it will establish a radio assembly plant in an old building in a rural area. Or a machine shop might turn out prototypes for a local aerospace firm and take on larger orders for automobile parts during business upturns. To establish the actual distribution of production between sectors, there is no substitute for empirical investigation.

The analytic framework does, however, suggest a conclusion which is crucial to the present discussion. It is that despite an important difference, unskilled jobs in what seem to be radically different kinds of factories are fundamentally similar.

The difference between the two kinds of jobs I have been discussing, is that unskilled work in the primary sector of the economy will tend, *ceteris paribus*, to be more secure than unskilled jobs in the secondary sector. (More will be said about this later.) The similarity is that both are monotonous and empty; both are dead ends: no one encourages either the man on the automobile assembly line or the woman in the radio assembly plant to learn new skills.

Perhaps the surest sign that both kinds of jobs are fundamentally alike is that identical kinds of workers can be found doing both. In Western Europe, for example, a Turkish or Algerian migrant laborer can be found working on an automobile assembly line or on construction; his wife might be found assembling radios for a large company or sewing buttons at home for a very small one. In the United States, a Chicano migrant may be working in a steel mill or picking fruit; his sister may be assembling radio parts for General Electric or pieces of a doll for a fly-by-night toy company; and so on. To see why workers see these jobs as similar, it is necessary to know what they see in them at all; and that brings me to the next part of the story.

Why do workers put up with unskilled work?

The obvious answer to this question, it would seem, is that they have no choice about it: they put up with unskilled jobs because those are the only jobs to be had. Surprisingly, however, there is much empirical evidence showing that this is not so. Immigrants, for one example, frequently prefer relatively high-paying low-skill jobs leading nowhere to relatively low-paying jobs which offer the chance to learn skills and have a future. Agricultural workers, for another, often prefer work in the immediate communities at low-skill jobs to moving or even commuting to the city in order to do more promising work. And, to take a third and final example, there are many cases of low-skill workers who, having more or less accidentally revealed some extraordinary aptitude for their work, are offered a chance at a career—and refuse it.

This evidence against the thesis that the unskilled choose their jobs for lack of a real choice might be interpreted as supporting the orthodox view of the unskilled as ignorant of the possibilities open to them or simply lazy. (In a society in which working hard is considered a virtue, to say someone prefers leisure to work is to say politely that he is lazy.) But here, as is so often the case elsewhere, such accusations will only embarrass those incautious enough to make them. Anthropologists thought the "natives" ignorant and incapable of logical thought until they, the anthropologists, realized that they had been ignorant of the natives' system of logic. The same thing may already be said of the economists and sociologists who study the poor. For what the evidence does show is not that the poor have confused ideas about their opportunities, or that they dislike work, but rather that they work quite hard in pursuit of precise ends which happen to differ systematically from the ones the orthodox school imputes to them.

Specifically, the evidence is that a great mass—perhaps, though it is hard to say, the largest part—of the workers doing unskilled industrial jobs do not want to become full participants in industrial society. Rather, they have taken the jobs they have in hopes of earning the money they need to establish themselves and their families in the pre- or, to stretch the meaning of the word a bit, the post-industrial areas of the economy. Some examples will make their standpoint more intelligible.

Consider a peasant with a plot just a bit smaller than the minimum required for subsistence. Think next of an artisan or small shopkeeper whose shop is just a bit too small to make a go of it in the local market; or for that matter, think of a young person who quit school early and now is trying to save enough to buy a car or to pay for the additional schooling he needs to get a good white-collar job. Finally, imagine both a housewife whose husband earns just a shade less than is required to pay a mortgage on a new house, and her younger sister, just out of school, who has to support herself until she decides on a husband or a career. All these are in a situation where a little extra income will allow them to carry on in pre- or post-industrial occupations. The peasant could return to his plot, the artisan and shop-keeper to their shops, the woman to her home.

The adolescents are in a somewhat different, but fundamentally analogous situation. Some of them will be self-consciously biding their time in factories until they can afford to return to school. Encouraged by the leisure-time industry to think they are on a lifelong consumption trip, the rest may have no clear ideas about their future work at all. But when these latter do seriously consider how they will spend their working lives, they too think of leaving the factories, be it to return to school; to go to work directly in the service sector; to set up a small business; or, in the woman's case, to work at home. The irony of the situation is that the only source of the income necessary to accomplish the adolescents' ends no less than those of the peasant, artisan, or housewife, is industrial work.

Hence the indifference of many unskilled workers to an industrial career derives not from rejection of the idea of a career, but from rejection of the idea of a career in industry. They view industrial work from a vantage point outside it. They have what has been called an instrumental relation to factory work. They see themselves using industrial work solely as a short-term means to what they hope will be a long-term end.

They want to exchange their effort for the highest possible short-term wage. If work is defined as an activity expressive of the meaning of one's life, then inside the factory, these workers do not work at all: they toil or exert themselves. The sooner they save the requisite amount, the sooner they can go back to or begin doing what they consider to be their *real* work. Starting at a low-paying job at the bottom of a career ladder in industry would therefore make no sense to them: they don't want to climb as high as they can on the career ladder; they want to get off it as soon as possible. Since many of the workers who hold this view of industrial work have been farmers, or (as is often the case in Europe) actually continue to farm small plots part-time while they hold factory jobs, I will call all workers of this type peasant workers regardless of their origins or ultimate intentions.

The peasant worker's attitude

Notice first that peasant workers are not simply collective victims of a pipe dream. Many of them may never scrape together the money they need to escape industrial work. Looking back, they would have to admit that they gambled and lost. But most adolescents who are determined to continue their studies can do so. Less frequently, but still often enough to be noticeable, housewives do succeed in returning to the home; and many peasants do earn enough to make a new start in their native communities. To take one extreme, but hardly unique, example of the extent of the circular flow of migrants: between 1907 and 1911, according to Italian statistics, the average annual number of immigrants who returned to Italy from the United States was 150,000, or 73 percent of the total who left for America in those years. And the success of some encourages the hopes of the others.

Notice too what a tremendous convenience—necessity is probably the more precise word—peasant workers are to employers offering low-skill dead-end jobs. Almost all blue-collar workers *do* demand careers in the sense that they value the opportunity to demonstrate and develop technical prowess on the job. Indirect but substantial support for this claim is provided by studies done in the United States, France, and Great Britain of unskilled workers who, unlike peasant workers, consider themselves part of the industrial labor force. The studies show that these workers are ashamed and insulted by what they take to be the official accusation of incompetence implied in their job rating. The reaction to this offense is to try to discredit management's verdict by having their work reclassified as semi-skilled; by passing whatever qualifying tests are necessary to advance in the skill hierarchy; or, if attempts to secure promotion fail, simply by disrupting production as a way of demonstrating how indispensable their cooperation is to the smooth functioning of the plant. In a word, these workers respect the confidence of the skilled and want to show they are the latter's equals. For this reason I will refer to them as would-be craftsmen.

In contrast, for all the reasons mentioned earlier, peasant workers do not want industrial careers. And not wanting them, they are not likely to bother management by demanding promotion, or by flexing their collective muscles at the expense of the production schedule.

Secondary sector employers, moreover, cannot even offer job security. But in this regard, too, peasant workers are likely to be more tolerant than other workers. Once more their attitude is rooted in their dual economy identity. During business downturns peasants and artisans can return to their original occupations and survive by working extremely hard under subsistence conditions or relying on family or friends in the home community. An out-of-work adolescent can often go on living in the same place he lived in when he had a job—his parent's house; and a jobless working wife can rely on her husband's income for a time.

This mesh of job characteristics and attitudes toward work explains the large concentration of peasant workers in some parts of the economy. In France and West Germany today, for example, virtually all production workers in the automobile industry are either foreign migrants or recruits from agriculture. In Italy, about which I will say more later, the same was true until the late 1960s, with the bulk of the work force being migrants from the South of the country. In the United States, foreign immigrants and black and white migrants from the South have all been crucial to Detroit's success in the past. (Today, with the northern automobile plants dominated by men who do not think of themselves as peasant workers, the industry has begun to migrate south in search of a new labor force.) In all these countries women make up a very large part of the production line work force in the home appliance, electronic parts, textile, and garment industries. On the extremely conservative assumption that only the *Gastarbeiter* or foreign workers in Europe and their homologues, the undocumented aliens in the United States, should be counted as peasant workers, a rough estimate would be that the least desirable 10 percent of the jobs in the advanced industrial societies are done by workers who reject the idea of a life at industrial work.

But for all the overlap between the peasant workers' attitudes and the industrialists' requirements, it would be wrong to conceive of the former merely as the tools of the latter. Peasant workers come to the job with fixed moral ideas, that is, with reasonably clear ideas about what is or is not appropriate in relations between managers and workers. In this they are like craftsmen or any other kinds of workers. These moral ideas permit a kind of collaboration between peasant workers and industry; but they also impose important limits on this collaboration. In other words, the same set of ideas about work which lead the peasant workers to accept the authority of management can, in certain circumstances, lead them to reject it as well. Two of the limits set by the peasant workers' sense of honor to their compliance with authority are of particular importance, since they offer a first hint of the potentially subversive role of these marginal workers in industrial society.

In the first place, with regard to factory work the peasant worker has no pride of craftsmanship. He does take pride in living up to his obligations; but as he conceives of it, his obligation is to do what he is told, not to worry about the results or lack thereof of his obedience. Now in theory—the theory, that is, of industrial engineers and managers—an unskilled worker is required to do no more than obey instructions. The rules are supposed to be constructed so carefully that following them blindly produces a perfect product every time. But ten minutes inside any factory will convince a neutral observer that industry is no different from the rest of life: in factories as elsewhere reality is so complex and rapidly changing that no plan can be comprehensive enough to be a completely reliable guide to action. In manufacturing this means that the worker, even the worker who is officially unskilled, cannot simply follow orders. If he doesn't show initiative from time to time in adjusting to the unforeseen, production will suffer. So the first disadvantage of the peasant worker, from management's point of view, is his relative lack of initiative: because he does not care about what is produced, the peasant worker is much less likely than, say, a craftsman, to throw his inventiveness into the breach when the plan fails.

The following incident, reported in a study of unskilled workers in a French metal-working factory, illustrates in an unusually dramatic way the significance of this attitude from management's point of view. In the factory studied, the workers were required to produce a given number of "minutes" a day, a "minute" being defined as a given number of work pieces on each of several different machines. In some cases the equation of work pieces to "minutes" for a particular machine was set so that even the best worker working his hardest could not produce his quota; on the other machines anyone could exceed it almost effortlessly. This disparity in the rating of machines would have caused more bitterness in the shop than it did but for one circumstance: workers were seldom penalized for failing to meet their quotas.

One group of workers, however, took great pride in fulfilling the quota as a proof of their physical stamina and honesty. All of these workers had been born, raised and, at the time of the study, lived in nearby agricultural villages, where some of them continued to farm small plots. Of these peasant workers, one in particular was especially intent on producing the norm. On those days when he was assigned to a machine which yielded few "minutes" he would simply stop what he was doing and, disregarding the consequences of his actions on the whole flow of production, start work at a more favorable post. Consider for a moment how mutually dependent the departments of a modern plant are, and you begin to understand why management must consider a work force which cheerfully executes the letter and never the spirit of industrial law a mixed blessing.

This indifference to the quality of production is of course only an inconvenience, though perhaps a major one, to management. The second implication of the peasant worker's instrumental attitude toward factory work is more radical: it amounts to an indirect challenge to the way industrial work is organized in our society.

The central justification for a hierarchy of wages in factories (and not just there) is that people are rewarded according to their actual contribution to production. In this sense the orthodox view of poverty as resulting simply from a lack of skills only echoes and reinforces a popular conception: in asking for a raise, electricians, maître d's, and college teachers all lay great stress on the presumably factual assertion that they are worth more to the company than they are getting.

The peasant worker, however, is not disposed to make any such claim when he asks for a raise. The idea of an exchange of effort for a wage excludes the idea of an appeal to productivity as much as a concern for the quality of production. What counts for the peasant worker is effort, not the value of the product of his exertions. His honor requires that he try his hardest—and no more. He works a full day for a full day's pay, with both the amount of work and the amount of pay being defined in reference to the collective experience of the particular group of workers to which he belongs. Where the craftsman says, "Pay me more because of the value of my product," the peasant worker says, "Pay all those who try hard equally." At bottom the peasant worker is expressing the idea, widespread in pre-industrial society, that all those who participate actively and fully in the community are entitled, in virtue of that very fact, to a decent life.

This implicit rejection of meritocratic ideas goes far in explaining the demands raised by striking peasant workers (most of them foreign migrants) in Europe over the last decade. Peasant workers on strike in France, Italy, and Germany have thus demanded collective raises for whole groups of workers regardless of differences in their jobs; and they have tended to justify these demands by reference to their fundamental needs as people and their good faith efforts as workers.

Migrant workers, for example, have frequently gone on strike for equal raises for all workers, and better living quarters (even when they were not living in company housing), as well as additional days of vacation in order to allow for visits to distant homes. Striking women have demanded "family days" or free time each month to do home chores. If such demands seem self-evident given the particulars of these workers' situation—namely, that uniform percentage wage increases discriminate against the lowest-paid, and working women hold two jobs—then it is worth noting that neither management nor other workers have viewed them that way. Their reaction was rather to see demands linking work life and home life as solecisms reflecting complete ignorance of the etiquette of industrial relations. Frequently, for instance, in the same factory in which a group of peasant workers struck for a general and equal wage increase and additional vacation time, a group of would-be craftsmen would go on strike to have their particular job classification upgraded or to get time off as compensation for hazarding their health on the job. The logic of the would-be craftsmen's demands tended to reinforce the idea of a meritocratic wage hierarchy and to better their position within it; while those of the peasant worker tended to undermine the hierarchy as such.

To this point I have treated the personality of the peasant worker as an unchanging given. To take the full measure of his potential to disrupt, not to say transform, industrial society, it is necessary to consider the ways in which the core element of his personality, his attitude toward work, changes in time. And by examining the sea changes which occur in the peasant worker's identity, I will be able to say something as well about the origins of another kind of marginal unskilled worker in our society.

Coming to grips with industrial society

There is no hard and fast rule which determines when a peasant worker will give up the idea of himself as a temporary factory worker. Mere exposure to the practices and artifacts of urban factory life, at any rate, does not produce this result. People, in other words, do not change their fundamental beliefs about themselves because of what they see on television. Instead, in rethinking his relation to factory work, the peasant worker does what we all seem to do when we make complex choices with essentially incalculable results based on insufficient information: he cautiously confronts some of the key presuppositions of his global view of his situation with his best assessment about the relevant facts. So long as there is a fair fit between expectations and reality—and every group of workers, no less than every group of scientists, will have some common standards for judging which fits count as fair—the assumptions hold; otherwise they give way to new ones. In practice this boils down to saying only that if peasant workers really have no chance to live out some substantial part of their original life plan, they will eventually realize it—and change plans.

In what follows, I will limit myself to illustrating this point and the themes which flow from it by referring only to the experience of peasant workers in the strict sense of the term, that is, to workers who themselves have been or whose immediate ancestors were peasants. By way of a conclusion, I will take up the question of the applicability of the distinctions used to capture the experience of these workers to the situation of one of the other groups which make up the category of peasant workers.

In the modal or most frequently observed case, the change in attitudes awaits the succession of generations. Fathers go to a foreign country or to a distant city in their native land in search of work. They may live more than half their lives away from their original home. But they have seen too many of their friends and relatives return home for good—they themselves may have gone back and forth more than once—to be able to give up the idea of doing so as well. For their children, however, the foreign country *is* home.

179

They can see how farfetched their parents' hopes have become; and they break with their family's past by defining themselves with respect to the factories and streets where they live. Many second-generation Americans have known this experience well: for many of them, home was not just the most familiar, but also the most alien spot in the world. Children of the Turks who came to Berlin or Frankfurt in the 1960s are having this experience now.

Sometimes, however, an immigrant group will succeed in virtually colonizing a part of town and a cluster of factory jobs. If economic conditions are stable enough, a kind of rustification of industrial life can take place: for a period of several generations, the group will be able to lead some version of its traditional social life in the new setting; affairs in the factory will be regulated according to the rules which prevailed in the home village. So even without being able to return to the mother country, the group will not be forced to cast off its old self-conception. Something of this sort seems to have occurred in some cities in the northeastern United States during the last part of the nineteenth and the first part of this century. Logically enough, rustification of factory life also seems to be quite typical of the early phases in the industrialization of third world countries, when the owner and the workers of a particular factory are likely to have known one another first as landlord and tenants.

Yet a third variant of this development can be seen in postwar Europe. Here government support to agriculture and the decentralization of industry have helped to keep the peasant on the farm and bring the factories to the country. One result has been to encourage peasants to supplement their income from farming with the proceeds of a factory job not far from home. The earlier description of the behavior of the peasant workers in the French metal-working factory suggests that this combination of income can perpetuate the peasant worker's instrumental attitude to work.

Alternatively, migrants can enter industrial work already half convinced that they are going to remain at it. This occurs when disruption of an agricultural community is so longstanding and pervasive that everyone who is forced to emigrate from it knows that he is probably leaving home for good. Under these circumstances, a kind of urbanization of the countryside takes place: agricultural work is scorned as old-fashioned; city ways become fashionable; young women look down on the young men who want to become farmers; young men in search of brides have to go to the city or dress and act as though they already lived there. Coming from this kind of community, a young worker who finds an industrial job thinks he has taken a step up. This, for example, is the attitude of many native Puerto Ricans who have recently begun working in the mainland United States. Italian and Spanish sociologists noted a similar development among some rural migrants in the 1960s.

There is, to repeat, no ticking sociological clock which determines when the peasant worker's self-conception will break down. Everything depends on the circumstances he faces. But however he comes to realize that, like it or not, he is an industrial worker for good, this realization is likely to have explosive consequences for the surrounding society.

Starting from the bottom

So long as the peasant workers hold to their original self-conception, they do not think of competing with the native workers. Either the peasant workers consider themselves to be completely outside the hierarchy of industrial society (which would be consistent with the notion of an industrial job as dead time); or they think of *any* industrial job, even the most menial, as superior to any job in traditional society (which is consistent with the idea of an industrial job as a step up). But once the peasant workers come to see themselves as part of industrial society, they realize that they are at the bottom of the dominant hierarchy. Worse yet, just as they discover that they are nobodies, they realize that they are doing jobs that lead nowhere. Neither discovery pleases them; both together seem to lead, within a surprisingly short time, to significant changes in the peasant workers' behavior.

One preliminary reaction to the reappraisal of the situation is to become more security-minded. As long as they thought they had no future in industrial work, peasant workers were relatively oblivious to the greater security offered by primary as compared to secondary sector unskilled work. Once they realize that they will be permanently dependent on the income from factory work, they begin to migrate to the primary sector in hopes of insuring themselves in a minimal way against economic fluctuations.

The peasant worker's heightened need for security is also accompanied by a redefined idea of dignity. He refuses to do the work traditionally reserved for peasant workers precisely because such work is defined in the society at large as beneath the dignity of a truly competent worker. The fact that many employers and fellow workers persist in taking his surname, skin color, accent, or address as signs that he will not object to such work makes him all the more assertive in rejecting it.

Whether peasant workers with this new-found dignity will be assimilated as individuals into the larger society, or whether they will act collectively to try to transform it, will depend in a complex way on the labor market situation they face and the political ideas and institutions available to help form and express their frustrations. If relatively skilled workers are in short supply, for example, each peasant worker, who by now is acting like a would-be craftsman on his way to the top, can solve his problem by himself: most anyone determined to have a career will be able to get the training and a job necessary to have one. Through the 1920s many second-generation immigrants in this country were integrated in this piecemeal way into the core of the labor force.

But if the labor market is slack and there are no places for the career-minded, the peasant workers must turn to collective solutions. Mass, public action, anticipated and colored by earlier communitarian strikes replaces or complements private efforts. Through the political parties and in workplace organizations, peasant workers as a group press for reforms which will give them some say in the decisions to hire, fire, and promote, which so vitally affect them. Out of this process of collective contractualism can emerge a set of institutions and techniques for regulating industrial conflict which can have serious long-term consequences for the development of the national economy. Thus in the 1930s, millions of second-generation Americans (often they were the descendants of Slavs or Poles) became active supporters of the Democratic Party and legal members of the new CIO unions. By their militance they created the preconditions for restructuring American industrial relations according to the principles of the Wagner Act. More recently, the Southern Italian migrants seem to have produced the analogous shakeup of their country's bargaining system when they rejected second-class status in the late 1960s.

If anything, the upheaval in Italy seems to have had more radical consequences than the equivalent episode in America. The Italian Communist Party and the Communist unions did more to shape, and were more shaped by the original egalitarianism of the peasant workers than were the Roosevelt Democrats and their union allies. The idea of pay according to need is less alien to communist doctrine than to the ethos of yeoman democracy which dominates so much of American political life. The result was that the peasant workers' spontaneous challenge to the idea of hierarchy was lost from sight in this country, while in Italy it led to a serious and prolonged, if still inconclusive, debate on the legitimacy of the meritocratic wage structure.

Ghetto workers

Scarcely any disadvantaged group gets anything without fighting for it; but not every disadvantaged group that puts up a fight gets what it wants. So far I have been considering the winners, the fortunate peasant workers who create career ladders for themselves, as Polish Americans did in the automobile industry; or who help redefine the very idea of an industrial career, as did the Southerners in the Italian automobile plants. What about the unfortunate peasant workers, the ones who lose the struggle for place and remain at the margins of the industrial work force? What becomes of them?

Given the scantiness of the relevant evidence, any answer to this question must be largely speculative; but an empirically plausible speculation would be the following: the peasant worker—he might be the son of an agricultural worker who migrated to a city—who is stuck in a dead-end job quickly becomes demoralized. He has no hopes of returning to the land; at the same time he accepts society's judgment that no one who is capable of anything better does the work he does. His own record on the job, moreover, soon convinces him that he is no exception to the general rule. He moves from job to job, sometimes pulled by the attraction of slightly higher wages (since he is learning nothing that will pay off in the future, he thinks only of the present), sometimes pushed by layoffs. All his friends are in the same situation: none of them has any long-term plans. Before his wife and children he is embarrassed by his incapacity to be the steady breadwinner which society and his own conscience demand he be. Failure at home and failure at work echo and amplify one another. Fatalism gets the upper hand. The peasant worker sees himself trapped in a world where *all* human relationships are provisional and fragile. Trusting no one's steadfastness more than his own, he gives up the search for a better job. His passivity becomes a lesson for his son, who follows his father in anticipating failure even in those rare cases where he might in fact succeed. In this way children of peasant workers can become trapped for generations in the ghetto of their own despair.

The situation I am describing is of course related to the widely discussed idea of a culture of poverty as the chief obstacle to the economic-emancipation of the ghetto blacks and Puerto Ricans in big American cities. The view put forward here, however, differs in two ways from the culture of poverty argument as it is usually presented. First, the standard argument is subtly linked to the orthodox economic view of poverty, inasmuch as it suggests that the ghetto poor really do not want to work: they are supposed to have become so corrupted psychologically, so enslaved to their need for immediate gratification, that they lose all respect for steady work. I think it is closer to the truth to say that the ghetto poor have become dejected. They do not think they can ever get steady work—but they would be glad to get it if they could, and anxious to defend it if they did. Studies of the attitudes of the long-term unemployed and the militance of ghetto workers who do get decent jobs tend to bear this out.

Second, my argument is much more restricted in scope than the standard culture of poverty notion. The latter sees all those living in the ghetto trapped in the same miasma of despair. I think it is more accurate to say that at any one time only a relatively small group of former peasant workers—the real losers—are caught up in the fatalist trap. Of course, one reason the culture of poverty argument has been applied so broadly and not, as I am suggesting, treated as a residual category, is simply because in any community of peasant workers it is in fact extremely difficult for outsiders to tell the real losers from everyone else.

Suppose, to use an old-fashioned but brutally direct and revealing phrase, I go slumming in a Puerto Rican ghetto one afternoon. On every street corner I see unemployed men. Because of the similarities in their dress and demeanor, I conclude that they belong to a single social class. In fact, there are, and they themselves know there to be, important differences among them. Some are without a job because, having just arrived from Puerto Rico, they have not had the time to find one. Others just quit work in order to be able to return to the Island. Among those who grew up in the United States, some are jobless because they have gotten picky about the work they will accept. They have had decent jobs and been laid off. Now they insist on having a job that leads somewhere—and such jobs are hard to come by. Others of the native-born are in the street because that seems to be where they always wind up. An early reputation as street fighters made it natural to start fights on the job; and a history of fighting on the job did not make it any easier to get hired. By the time they were no longer proud of being street fighters, they had a reputation for being losers. Getting last crack at the good jobs and being fired for the first mistake only convinced them that they deserved their reputation. It didn't make it any easier to support a wife and child, either. Now they work when they have to, and rely on welfare and petty theft for the rest of what they need.

Of all these men, of course, only those in the last group begin to fit the description of the lost souls caught in the culture of poverty. The others can just as obviously be described in terms of the preceding discussion of peasant workers. Indeed, the evidence on which the Puerto Rican example is based suggests that it is more fruitful to see ghettos as way-stations for peasant workers coming to, departing from, entering, or failing to be admitted into the larger society, than as self-renewing centers of moral debility. But the evidence is inconclusive. Exactly how importantly the culture of poverty figures in the life of urban ghettos, it is at present impossible to say. A precondition to fruitful research on the question, however, is surely to drop the assumption that all those without work in the ghetto have a common preference for leisure, and that this preference has a common psychological cause.

Conclusion

Mutatis mutandis, the arguments I have made about peasant workers in the narrow sense apply to other groups of marginal workers. A brief discussion of how this is so in the case of women will serve to illustrate this general point and summarize what has gone before.

Think back to the earlier example of the woman who takes a temporary factory job to help pay the mortgage on her house. In the first place, it is clear that, like the immigrant looking to save some money in a foreign country, she may always deny to herself that she truly is a factory worker; but then again, she may not. A series of accidents, some of them rather likely accidents in our society, might force her to keep working at the same time as they reinforced her convictions about the temporary character of the job. Thus, after the birth of a child, she might want to continue working, first to help pay for some home improvements, then to buy a second car, and finally to tide the family over when her husband is laid off or sick. By accident, convinced all the time that she is about to go back to being a full-time housewife, she may have done a lifetime of factory work. But suppose next that she is divorced or her husband dies. There is evidence that a caesura of this kind forces the woman to take stock of her situation on the labor market. Even if she wants to remarry, she faces the prospect of supporting herself over a long period through factory work. This realization changes her relation to her job.

She becomes more interested in job security than the housewife who may reasonably regard being laid off as half a respite from a double burden; she also becomes more interested in learning skills which will be useful to her later. She may become interested in unions which protect her from discrimination as well. In a word, she becomes a more or less militant would-be craftsman. At least that is what she becomes if she is relatively lucky. Bad luck means she loses her job and has trouble finding another. After losing that one too, she winds up on welfare, and has trouble getting off. This end to the story recalls the fate of the loser in the ghetto.

If allowance is made for this variety of possible endings, the story of all kinds of marginal workers has been the same through much of the history of industrial society. It is the story of workers who come to factories more than half-convinced that they are not going to stay there; and of employers who are eager to have them as long as they do not intend to stay. Since the motives of the latest factory recruits and the most up-to-date managers are the same as the motives of marginal workers and managers in the past, the story seems to be a timeless one. But to see it in that way is to take a superficial view of the matter. In every country, certain generations of marginal workers in the very act of ceasing to be such have set important institutional limits on management's power to organize work. The CIO in the United States and the trade unions in contemporary Italy are two monuments to their efforts. Perhaps successive generations of marginal workers, with the help of other groups in society, will so totally transform the organization of the factory and the labor market that employers will neither have reason to supply, nor find anyone willing to accept, marginal jobs. The story of that transformation, though it is hardly near its end, has now progressed far enough so that it should begin to be told.

The Structure of
the Labor Market for
Young Men

3

BY PAUL OSTERMAN

YOUTH UNEMPLOYMENT HAS BECOME a major public issue. The reason for this is not hard to find: youth unemployment rates are remarkably high. In 1978 the unemployment rate of 16-to-19-year-old whites was 13.5% for males and 14.4% for females. For blacks the figures were a staggering 34.4% and 38.4%.

High as these rates are, their welfare implications are not clear. For whites (but not for blacks) the current unemployment rates are not out of line with past experience, as measured by the ratio of teenage to adult unemployment. It is also not clear whether teenage unemployment has important long-term consequences. Almost half of the 16-to-19-year-old unemployed are in school and seeking only part-time work. Most live with a parent or adult relative. Two-thirds of the unemployed teenagers are either looking for their first jobs or looking again after a spell outside the labor force. Unemployment for these new entrants and reentrants is not unexpected; finding a job when one has never worked or has been out of the labor force for a while takes time. In addition, teenage unemployment falls with age. This does not necessarily imply that teenage unemployment is not a problem or that all teenagers will emerge from unemployment with good prospects. It does mean, however, that the high unemployment rates of teenagers today do not augur later unemployment for most of them.

These ambiguities in the interpretation of teenage unemployment suggest that it would be worthwhile to step back and examine the process of labor market entry. We do not have a clear picture of how the youth labor market works, and without this we cannot evaluate the real meaning of youth unemployment.

© Paul Osterman. The research reported here was supported by the Ford Foundation through a grant to the National Committee for Full Employment. The views expressed here are not necessarily those of either organization. This is an abridgement of a longer paper with the same title.

In order to understand the process of labor market entry, one needs more textured data than are available from conventional sources. I therefore conducted interviews with a variety of participants in the youth labor market. One hundred and fifty interviews were held with noncollege young men in two Boston communities: East Boston, a white working-class area, and Roxbury, a black area. In addition, I interviewed executives of thirty-five firms that employ youth, and over fifty other individuals such as school officials, youth workers, and staff in training programs. What follows is a description of some of the findings that emerged from these interviews.

The school-to-work transition

When young people leave high school and enter the labor market, they are generally not at once in a state of mind to be stable, reliable full-time employees. Rather, for many youths, sex, adventure, and peer group activities are more important than work. Jobs are viewed in purely instrumental terms, as ways of getting money for these other activities.

Young people who exhibit this pattern of behavior can be characterized as being in a *moratorium* stage. They have weak labor force attachments, frequently moving in and out of jobs as well as of the labor force itself.

For most young people, this moratorium period terminates in the late teens and early twenties; they move toward settling down. Some of the incentive to do this comes from the prospect of higher wages and lower unemployment rates. But noneconomic considerations are also important. In part, simple aging—the maturation process—makes youth prone to settle. Marriage and family formation provide additional pressure. There is also an important peer group effect: as friends begin to settle, the pressure builds on other members of the group to follow suit in order to maintain comparable lifestyles and hence friendships.

Thus, entry into the labor market comes in stages; it is a process of adjustment that takes time. The "school-to-work transition" does not happen quickly. However, these behavioral stages are only half the picture. It is also important to examine the nature of jobs in which young people work.

Labor market entry: secondary jobs

The jobs that young people hold in their early years in the labor market, during the moratorium stage, are usually casual and unskilled— jobs that some economists call *secondary*. Settling down frequently occurs in a different employment environment, in firms where jobs involve greater skill, better long-term prospects for advancement, and greater job security. These jobs can be characterized as *primary* labor market jobs.

In descriptive terms secondary jobs can best be understood by contrasting them with primary jobs. Michael Piore has made the distinction in these terms:

> The primary market offers jobs which possess several of the following traits: high wages, good working conditions, employment stability and job security, equity and due process in the administration of work rules, and chances for advancement. The secondary market has jobs which, relative to those in the primary sector, are decidedly less attractive. They tend to involve low wages, poor working conditions, considerable variability in employment, harsh and often arbitrary discipline, little opportunity to advance.[1]

Primary jobs thus tend to have strong internal labor markets and offer opportunities for training and for stable employment. They are the jobs into which most young men settle. By contrast, secondary jobs involve few skills and offer few opportunities for skill acquisition. Since workers make few investments in acquiring specific skills in secondary jobs, and firms make few investments in these workers, there is little incentive on either side to encourage job stability. In a sense, from workers' viewpoints all secondary jobs are alike since there is little to choose among them.

It seems fairly clear that many, and probably most, youths spend their initial years after school in secondary jobs. It is difficult to be exact about this proposition since there has been considerable disagreement in the literature about how to identify primary and secondary jobs in large data sets. In addition to the pattern observed in my interviews, other studies using national data sets have found that substantial numbers of youths start off in secondary jobs.[2]

An important reason why moratorium youths work in secondary firms is that these firms find them to be a quite satisfactory source of labor while primary firms do not. We will discuss the motivations of primary firms below, but for now it is enough to note that the unstable behavior of young people in the moratorium stage makes them a risky investment for firms that put resources into training. Secondary firms do not have this problem since they, almost by definition, provide little training. Nor are they overly concerned if their employees do not stay very long on the job. These firms are interested in an assured supply of low-wage unskilled labor. They also prefer to hire employees who will be passive, i.e., not likely to unionize in the face of unstable employment, for example. Youths fit these requirements quite well. They are plentiful and thus provide an elastic source of labor. Because they view their employment as temporary they are unlikely to be "troublesome" employees. In fact, young people provide such a satisfactory source of labor that some secondary firms organize their production schedules to recruit them. For example, one candy factory I visited, which employs large numbers of Spanish-speaking adults, also ran a special after-school production shift in order to employ youth. Large retail establishments also organized work shifts to attract youth.

For young people these secondary jobs quite adequately meet the requirements of the moratorium period. The jobs are casual and unskilled.

Little penalty is attached to unstable behavior since all jobs are similar and none lead to career ladders. The jobs provide spending money with very little responsibility or long-term commitment.

The East Boston interviews suggest that there are three major types of secondary employers: large firms, "mom and pop" stores, and "under-the-table" jobs. The major examples of large secondary firms were security firms, supermarket chains, cleaning companies, and a gum products company. All of these firms are large, employing well over one hundred workers each. They all paid the minimum wage or very close to it and hired youths into jobs that essentially involved no skills. The young people who worked in these jobs reported either that they already knew the job through common sense or that it took one week or less to learn it. These firms also hired "walk-ins" (i.e., youths who simply came in off the street and asked for work) more frequently than did other firms. This is indicative of the unimportance of stable work behavior to the firms. These firms were widely known in the community for having casual, low-paid jobs available. Many unemployed youths indicated that they could always find a job in one of these firms. A remarkably high percentage of young men in the sample (29%) worked in these firms at one time or another, usually in the first two years after school; but a considerably smaller fraction of youths older than twenty still worked in these firms.

Another category of secondary firms is small, family-owned operations. Examples are bakeries, small construction contractors, newsstands, restaurants, gas stations, and auto-service operations. The key characteristic of these firms is that they are small, located in the neighborhood, and family-owned. They also provide low-paid, casual, unskilled work without a future, but in a quite different atmosphere than the large secondary employers. Although many of the young men who held these jobs characterized the work as boring, there was very little of the bitterness about personal relationships, supervision, and working conditions that showed up repeatedly in the descriptions of large secondary employers. As might be expected, conditions in the small firms are much more paternalistic and relaxed. Finally, these jobs are virtually always found through personal contacts. Because of the family nature of these small firms, the few available jobs go to relatives and friends. And, except for the occasional son destined to take over the business, youths soon leave these jobs in search of better-paying work with a possibility of advancement.

The third category of jobs is "under-the-table" work. This phrase is used to describe odd jobs that are not reported to tax, unemployment insurance, and welfare authorities. Young men who characterized themselves as being unemployed often indicated that they received some income from occasional jobs such as housepainting, repairing cars, or construction. Except for the "off-the-books" aspect these jobs are similar in structure to the second category: they are neighborhood based and found almost exclusively through family and friends. However, they are very unsteady in the sense of being one-time opportunities, i.e., they end when the house is painted or the project is over. Casual criminal activity, which half a dozen youths in the sample hinted at, also falls in this category of odd jobs undertaken during spells of unemployment.

Labor market entry: primary firms

For young men who are successful, the end of moratorium comes with the acquisition of a job in a primary firm. These are firms that provide stable, long-term jobs with reasonable opportunities for promotion and advancement. They are typically large enterprises with well-articulated internal labor markets.[3]

These firms generally prefer not to hire young men just out of high school who are engaged in moratorium behavior. Obviously this preference is modified by business conditions, and patterns of settling vary with the business cycle. However, on average the firms prefer to hire youths who have already had some experience in the labor market. This section will examine why primary firms have this preference and will explore their hiring practices in some detail.

An important characteristic of these firms is that once a person is hired (and passes a probationary period, if there is one) he is likely to stay with the firm for a long time. Because the firm invests resources in training, and because the employee too invests time and resources, both parties have an incentive to maintain a stable relationship. Internal labor markets promote this stability: the worker naturally moves up through the internal labor market as he acquires more skills and as openings become available. From the firms's point of view it is expensive and disruptive to train an individual (either formally or on the job) and promote him to an important place in the production process—and then have him leave.

Because of the importance of stability in employment, the key issue in understanding the hiring process is how firms judge who will and who will not become a stable worker. Because this concern is often more important to firms than prior skills or relevant experience, they will seek to evaluate the reliability and maturity of a job applicant.[4] The other important issue firms consider is the individual's ability to learn future jobs, since the job he is being hired for is simply the bottom rung of the internal ladder.[5]

These considerations explain why a rather nebulous attribute of job applicants, their "attitude," was consistently cited by firms as the most important factor in the hiring decision. This term seems to encompass several attributes: a neat appearance and respectful manner during the interview, a clear interest in the proffered work, willingness to learn the job, and a general alertness. Virtually every firm interviewed cited attitude as the central consideration in hiring.[6]

Because firms engaged in hiring have to make judgments about the potential stability of an applicant and his ability to mesh well with the work group, it is not too surprising that attitude is such an important determinant of hiring. In effect, attitude is a proxy for maturity and is a way of screening out moratorium stage applicants and others judged unlikely to be stable and reliable. Proper attitude is of course likely to be age-related, and its importance implies that moratorium stage workers are less likely to be hired by primary firms. This inference is supported by the findings of other studies of industrial hiring practices.[7]

The reluctance of primary firms to hire young workers plays a central role in shaping the youth labor market because it forces youth into the secondary sector where their natural tendencies toward unstable behavior are reinforced. Without doubt this hiring pattern on the part of primary firms is the central structural characteristic of the youth labor market. It is this reluctance to hire potentially unstable workers that dominates the youth labor market, and not, as is frequently argued in the popular literature, youngsters' lack of entry-level skills.

Most of the employers I interviewed did not exhibit a strong preference for hiring youths who already knew how to do the job.[8] There are two explanations for this attitude. First, a great deal of production is in reality very firm-specific in its technology. Two firms may produce the same product with machinery which, to an outsider, looks identical. However, the layout of the machines, the organization of the steps, and a myriad of "small" details that add up, can make the production process as experienced by a worker quite different from one firm to another. Thus the advantage of previous experience is diminished. In addition, firms with internal labor markets generally cannot hire from the outside into skilled jobs. Rather they hire into unskilled entry positions and train and promote from within. This greatly reduces the advantage of previous skills. Thus, inadequate previous experience cannot be adduced to explain the inability of youth to find jobs.

Patterns of labor market adjustment

Our interviews in East Boston and Roxbury provided some quantitative information on the nature of the jobs held by the young men in the sample. In fact, a special effort was made to elicit information on the employing firms because most national surveys tend to focus on individual characteristics and ignore the nature of jobs.

As a first step in the quantitative study of the relationship of primary and secondary jobs to labor market adjustment, it was necessary to classify the various jobs held by the youth into the two categories. I did this "by eye," examining the nature of the job and making a decision. However, the criteria were not self-evident. At first, wage level seemed the obvious candidate, since a clear intuitive message of the dual labor market argument is that primary jobs pay well while secondary jobs do not. But, whatever the merits of this criterion for adults, it is clearly inadequate for young people. An entry position in a firm that provides training and a future may pay no better than some casual labor jobs, but we would not want to classify the former as secondary. Employment stability is another criterion; yet a variety of skilled jobs, such as those in construction, are frequently unstable. The best criterion seems to be the presence or absence of career lines or internal labor markets in the firm. Firms that have progression paths, in either the craft or industrial sense, provide the sheltered employment which is intrinsic to the notion of dual labor markets. Employment stability and good wages are generally associated with industrial-type internal labor markets because of the firm-specific training which becomes embodied in the worker. Craft labor markets provide less stability, but the skills involved typically provide the worker with a stable career.

The interviews included two questions that sought to measure the presence of internal labor markets. The youths were asked what jobs they could expect to be doing after two, three, and five years in the firm. They were also asked what promotions they had already received. It was hoped, and generally proved true, that the answers to these questions would enable me to discern the presence or absence of career lines in the firms.[9]

Tables 1 and 2 provide data on job-finding techniques and a variety of

Table 1

Distribution of Job-Finding Techniques

	Primary jobs (in %)	Secondary jobs (in %)
Friends	19.7	36.2
Parents/relatives	30.8	19.7
Ads/walk-in	24.6	19.7
Institutions[a]	12.3	16.4
Other	12.6	8.0
Total	100.0	100.0

[a]Institutions include private employment agencies, schools, the state employment service, and manpower programs.

Table 2

Characteristics of Primary and Secondary Job Holders

	Primary	Secondary
Mean number of friends	.75	2.05
Mean number of parents/relatives	.63	.33
Mean number of promotions	.55	.11
Mean number of months to learn job	4.3	0.8
Already knew job (in %)	41.6	58.4
Learned new skills (in %)	60.6	39.4
Continue to learn (in %)	58.7	31.5

characteristics of primary and secondary job holders in the sample. The first set of issues involves the social relations of production, in the sense of how the young men found jobs and who they knew on them. Table 1 shows that most jobs are found through personal contacts. We will take up this point in more detail when we come to racial differences, but here the key issue is that secondary jobs are much more likely to be found through friends while primary jobs are more frequently found through parents and relatives. Similarly (Table 2), we see that secondary jobs average over two friends per job and .33 parents or relatives. In primary jobs we find fewer friends than in secondary jobs but more parents and relatives (the questions that elicited these responses referred to persons who were *already* on the job when the respondent arrived).

The heavy emphasis on friends in secondary jobs confirms the nature of these jobs as I described them. They tend to be either neighborhood small retail or contracting operations, which are likely to employ youths from the same area who know each other, or larger firms such as security and cleaning companies that have reputations for hiring youths, where a young person is likely to find some friends already at work.

Primary firm jobs are different in that they are more often found through relatives and there are more relatives than friends already on the job. This is to be expected given our understanding of the hiring practices of these firms. They are largely interested in stability, and while friends are likely to be poor sources of referrals in this respect, relatives and parents are likely to be better since they can exercise some control.

A more general, but striking, point is that when friends, parents, and relatives per job are summed, the jobs in our sample average well over one previous acquaintance per job. Although the Boston area is very large, these young people do not move in an impersonal labor market. This is not simply a neighborhood phenomenon, since 67 percent of the jobs in the sample were outside the neighborhood. Clearly, part of the answer to the question of how youths enter such a large dense labor market and find their way, is that they move through channels already traveled by people they know.

Additional characteristics shown in Table 2 refer to how job skills are acquired. The pattern of these variables conforms to our notions about the distinction between secondary and primary jobs: a large fraction of holders of secondary jobs already knew the job; fewer learned new skills when they took the job; it took less time to learn the skills required in secondary jobs; and fewer holders of secondary jobs continued to learn new skills.

The main lines of our argument are thus confirmed by these learning patterns. It should be noted, however, that the pattern is more complex than a simple version of the theory would imply. Secondary jobs are not always without learning opportunities, and there is clearly some continued learning on the job. It is possible, at least up to a point, to improve on even the most straightforward jobs and it is even possible to learn new skills. Of perhaps greater interest is the pattern in primary jobs. Almost 60% of the youths in primary jobs had not known how to do the work beforehand. This would not be surprising except for the recurrent arguments in the popular literature, and in some professional writing as well, that a major cause of youth unemployment is that entry skill requirements are rising while the schools are failing to produce competent workers. In fact, as I have already noted, most people do not know how to do the job when they are hired. The firm trains them. Hence preexisting skills are not centrally important. These data bear out our earlier observation.

Problems of black teenagers

The staggering unemployment rates of black teenagers and the racial differentials in these rates (cited at the beginning of this paper) obviously require a separate analysis of the labor market problems of black youth.

Any explanation of the racial differential must deal with two issues: why black youth unemployment rates are higher than those of whites and why the differential has been widening in recent years. The latter trend is especially troublesome because there is good evidence that in other respects—wages and occupational attainment, for example—the situation of black youth has been improving. One obvious explanation lies in the baby boom; the black teenager cohort has grown more rapidly than the white group, and we may be observing the inability of labor markets to absorb this influx. However, this explanation is incomplete. Even if the number of redheads in the labor market grew relative to blondes, if the two groups were alike in all other respects, we would expect the unemployment rates of both groups to be equal. Hence there must be something else at work. One possibility suggested by my interviews is racial differences in job-finding techniques.

Most workers, and especially young people, find jobs through personal contacts. The white youths I interviewed landed a job because a friend who was working at a firm told them of an opening, or because a parent or relative or neighbor knew someone who could make a job available. These networks of job contacts completely dominated all other sources of job acquisition for the whites.

One might expect that the heritage of past discrimination would leave today's black youth at a disadvantage with respect to this method of job acquisition, since they would lack family, relatives, and friends who had access to good jobs (though they might know of unstable, low-wage jobs). The interviews showed this to be true. For young blacks, the dominant source of job-finding was formal agencies—schools, employment agencies, and manpower programs—and walk-in search off the street.

These methods are neither as efficient (in terms of time expended) as the informal routes, nor are they as likely to lead to good jobs. Thus, even in the absence of overt discrimination, differential outcomes are likely to persist because of the heritage of past discrimination. Furthermore, young blacks are much more dependent than whites upon government services, such as schools and employment programs. The well-known difficulties and problems these agencies have in providing high-quality service has a differentially adverse effect upon the fortunes of blacks.

Another explanation might lie in racial differences in behavior. If young blacks have unrealistic aspirations, if their reservation wages are too high, or if they are more "difficult" employees, then these differences would result in higher unemployment rates. However, I have been unable to find evidence that supports any of these hypotheses. It is true that racial differences in background characteristics such as education and training may play a role. My research suggests, however, that these factors can explain at most 50% of the racial difference in annual weeks of unemployment.[10] I would thus accord an important role to discrimination (along with the problem of job contracts). In part, this discrimination is manifested in a simple reluctance to hire young blacks, given a plentiful supply of white youth as well as adult women, whose labor market participation rate has been increasing sharply.[11]

Finally, it should be understood that the problems of black teenagers are not simply a consequence of the youth labor market; a substantial racial differential in unemployment holds for adults. Just as racial discrimination persists in other areas of society—housing, for example—so does it in the labor market. The unemployment problems of black youth will not be resolved until we are ready to confront the continuing problem of discrimination in our society.

Notes

1. Michael J. Piore, "The Dual Labor Market," in *Problems in Political Economy*, ed. David Gordon (Lexington, Mass.: D. C. Heath, 1971), p. 91.
2. Martin Carnoy and Russell Rumberger, *Segmented Labor Markets*, Center for Economic Studies Discussion Paper no. 75-2 (Palo Alto, 1975); Paul J. Andrisani, "An Empirical Analysis of the Dual Labor Market Theory," doctoral dissertation, Department of Economics, Ohio State University, 1973.
3. Peter B. Doeringer and Michael J. Piore, *Internal Labor Markets and Manpower Analysis* (Lexington, Mass.: D. C. Heath, 1971).
4. As Richard Lester pointed out in his study of hiring in Trenton, New Jersey: "Managements with a fairly long perspective tend to consider an applicant, not in terms of his qualifications for an initial job, but for the job he (or she) is likely to hold during his working life with the firm, and to emphasize psychological traits, such as cooperativeness, dependability, adaptability, and loyalty to the firm." Richard A. Lester, *Hiring Practices and Labor Competition*, Princeton University Industrial Relations Section (Princeton, N. J., 1954), p. 28.
5. The importance firms assign to the "trainability" of the applicant is the driving force behind the "queue theory" of income distribution. In this model firms rank applicants on the basis of their ability to learn the jobs within the firm at the lowest training costs. See Lester Thurow, *Generating Inequality* (New York: Basic Books, 1975).
6. The importance of "attitude" indirectly supports the proposition argued by Bowles and Gintis (which in turn is based upon work by Edwards) that a major function of the school

system is to inculcate a proper attitude in young people, and that this attitude is an important determinant of labor market success. However, the results I have presented here also raise a serious difficulty for this proposition. Since there tends to be a period of several years between school leaving and entrance into primary firms—much of which is spent in the secondary labor market where attitude is not so important—there is something of a mystery about how the lessons of school get translated to the workplace. It appears to me that the labor market experience of young people, particularly their inability to get primary jobs without the proper "attitude," plays at least as important a role as the schools in creating "proper" personality characteristics. See Samuel Bowles and Herbert Gintis, *Schooling in Capitalist America* (New York: Basic Books, 1976); and Richard C. Edwards, "Individual Traits and Organizational Identities: What Makes a 'Good' Worker?" *Journal of Human Resources,* vol. XI, no. 1, pp. 51-68.

7. See Lester, op. cit.; and Theodore F. Malm, "Recruiting Patterns and the Functioning of Labor Markets," *Industrial and Labor Relations Review,* vol. 7, no. 4 (July 1954), pp. 507-25.

8. Lester also reports a disinterest on the part of most firms in prior skills.

9. Both questions, however, suffer from one important problem since they represent the worker's perception of the firm and his possibilities rather than an objective appraisal. An overly optimistic worker (or an unduly pessimistic worker) may convey a misleading impression. In part this is mitigated by the objectivity of the past promotion question, but even so we still face the problem of an unusually good or bad worker or a worker who has not been on the job long enough to receive a promotion. The ideal solution would be to examine more closely each of the firms involved, but in the absence of this we must accept the limitations of the interview approach.

10. Paul Osterman, "Racial Differentials in Male Youth Unemployment, in *Employment Statistics and Youth,* eds. Robert Taggert and Naomi Berger Davidson (Washington, D.C.: U.S. Government Printing Office, 1978). I say "at most" because it is not clear whether differences in, say, education are legitimate sources of labor market differentials or whether they are used by employers as devices for screening out blacks.

11. Paul Osterman, "The Causes of the Worsening Employment Situation of Black Youth," Report to the Assistant Secretary of Labor for Policy, Evaluation and Research, May 1979.

Wage Determination in Low-Wage Labor Markets and the Role of Minimum-Wage Legislation

4

BY MICHAEL J. PIORE

NOT ALL WAGES IN MODERN industrial economies are governed by wage contours and orbits of coercive comparison. The observations on which these concepts are based and the theoretical notions that have grown up around them suggest that such patterns will tend to prevail only in stable social groupings or in institutions with formal wage-setting procedures. There are two strata of the labor market where their relevance to actual wage-setting procedures is dubious. One is the stratum composed of professional and managerial workers, particularly that portion of the professional and managerial labor force which works outside the government (where wages are determined by civil service regulation) and for whom private practice or entrepreneurial activities are viable employment alternatives. The other is the stratum of low-wage workers, defined in the dual labor market hypothesis as the secondary sector. The latter is of particular interest from the point of view of public policy because of the role of the minimum wage. This essay, drawing upon two case studies of low-wage labor markets, summarizes some observations about wage determination in that sector.

At first glance, one would expect the wages of low-wage workers, to behave more like the prices of nonlabor commodities than like the wages of workers above them in the job hierarchy. The institutions that govern wage determination in other sectors of the economy, such as unions and large

This material is drawn from Michael J. Piore, *Labor Market Stratification and Wage Determination*, a report prepared for the Office of the Assistant Secretary for Policy, Evaluation and Research of the U.S. Department of Labor (October 1974).

corporations, appear to be less prominent in the low-wage sector; high turnover among low-wage workers discourages the development in the work place of coercive social groups that might attempt to substitute social for market criteria in wage determination. Low-wage workers, moreover, seem to resemble the *homo economicus* of economic theory more closely than do other members of the labor force. They tend to be drawn from groups that define themselves in terms of nonwork roles or for whom employment is instrumental, a means to ends inherent in their self-definition: women who think of themselves as housewives and work to finance consumer durables that facilitate their activities at home; peasants who think of themselves as farmers and work in industry or services to expand their landholdings or purchase farm equipment; youth who are students or in what Paul Osterman calls the moratorium phase working to finance their education or a Saturday night out.

To the extent that such workers behave in this way, one should be able to understand wage determination in terms of conventional supply and demand analysis. Were supply and demand in this market to operate as they do in most commodities markets, institutional interference—through a governmentally imposed minimum wage, for example—would be either irrelevant or a generator of unemployment. It would be irrelevant if the institutionally determined wage were set below the wage that equated demand and supply; it would create unemployment if it were set above that wage and more people were willing to work than could be profitably employed. This is very conventional economic theory—and the basis for the suspicion of the minimum wage among professional economists.

However, the very characteristics of low-wage workers which suggest they will behave like the *homo economicus* hypothesized in conventional theory, also imply that the supply curve will not take the form of a "normal" commodity. One reason it will not is that such marginal workers are "target" earners; they are working to accumulate a fixed sum of money, often to buy a particular commodity. Once they have "made their target" they tend to withdraw from the labor market. The result is that their individual supply curves are backward bending: the higher the wage, the smaller the amount of work required to meet the target. As a result, as the wage rises the amount of labor supplied declines. The market supply curve could reflect this and be backward bending as well. If this were the case, an increase in the wage would act, perversely, to reduce supply; and a decrease, to increase it. A market with such a supply curve could be very unstable. It is not at all clear in such a market that a minimum wage would have the effect of creating unemployment; its effect could in fact be quite the opposite. And indeed, one way of understanding the introduction of a minimum wage is that it is welcomed by employers as a means of stabilizing the market and alleviating the uncertainty about labor costs.

A second analytical problem is that it is quite unclear what the supply curve for marginal workers actually is. It appears that the supply of most marginal groups is extremely sensitive to employers' recruitment efforts. Historically, when supply has been short at the bottom of the labor market, employers have been able to generate new flows of migrants from rural areas or to recruit part-time workers from among housewives and youth who had not previously thought of working. It is possible, therefore, to think that in the long run the supply is infinite at any wage. It is clear, for example, that the prevailing wage does not equate the demand and supply for migrants from rural Mexico and the Caribbean, any more than it did 15 years ago before employers started seeking out these workers. The sensitivity of the labor supply to recruitment efforts is also likely to increase the instability and uncertainty of wage rates in an uncontrolled market, and work like the backward-bending supply curve, making the statutory minimum wage attractive to both workers and employers as a means of stabilizing market conditions.

Wage setting in the secondary sector

Very little is known about wage setting in the secondary sector. To fill this gap, wage-setting procedures in two labor markets were examined. The first included low-wage employments in Boston and some surrounding communities that had been selected as part of another study on Puerto Rican migration into Boston.[1] The chief criterion for selection was that the firms were reported by community leaders to employ relatively large numbers of Spanish-speaking workers, or were in industries or communities where other plants were reported to employ these types of workers. Wage-determination questions were attached to an interview designed to investigate Spanish-speaking employment (employers seemed more willing to talk about Spanish workers than about wage-setting procedures, so questions about the latter were inserted into interviews about the former). Low-wage employments in Boston have been subject to continuous investigation by researchers for a period of about eight years. Although not specifically focusing on wage determination, these other investigations picked up enough information about that process to provide reference points for a check of our findings, in what is necessarily a very impressionistic research procedure.

The second labor market visited for this study was a small town in western Louisiana. This site was selected to shed some light upon the finding in Boston that most low-wage employers felt they were operating in a labor-shortage economy and very few paid the minimum wage. A labor-surplus region with a good deal of minimum-wage employment was therefore sought. (The particular site was chosen because there was an especially good research contact there.) As it turned out, the town selected was a dumping-off point for off-shore oil drilling. This had generated a considerable boom in new industries connected not only with oil but with shipping and with construction, and it was hard to characterize the area as one of genuine labor surplus. On the other hand, the traditional industries related to sugar cane and shrimping were still very active, and these industries paid the minimum wage.

The principal findings of these case studies are as follows:

1. Wage determination in the secondary sector of the Boston labor market appears to divide into two broad patterns. A number of the jobs are part of the wage-determination patterns of the lower tier of the primary sector. The jobs themselves possess the characteristics ascribed to the secondary sector in terms of job security, advancement, supervisory techniques, and the like. But for one reason or another they are attached to the institutional mechanisms of wage setting in the lower tier. The reasons vary. The most common one appears to be attributable to a bimodal job structure, in which there are numbers of unskilled, menial jobs at one extreme and highly skilled jobs at the other, with very few intermediate positions through which one might progress from one mode to the other. The whole of the enterprise is, however, organized by a single union and that union negotiates one wage structure, the components of which move together as if they were all in the lower tier. Union organization, on the other hand, does not appear to affect other job characteristics. It is common, for example, to have a formal bidding procedure for jobs in the skilled mode and for movement among the few intermediate jobs that lead out of the unskilled mode and into the more desirable jobs. But the allocation of the jobs in the unskilled mode and at the ports of entry into the skilled mode is the prerogative of the foreman, who makes the decisions on his own and without union review.

Other examples of secondary jobs built into primary wage structures occur in dispersed industries such as trucking or garment manufacture, where the union generally organizes whole industries and imposes a single standard contract on all firms, whether or not they are part of the industrial core to which the union organization is adapted. It is impossible to estimate the size of that part of the secondary factor tied into primary patterns of wage determination on the basis of this study alone. It is noteworthy, however, that these patterns seem to be linked to the existence of trade unions, and that one study of Puerto Rican employments in Boston— almost all of which can be classed for our purposes as secondary—reports that one-half of the employed labor force are union members.

2. Wage determination in that section of the secondary labor market which is not tied into the lower-tier wage structure appears to be characterized by *stagnation* rather than competition. One gains the impression from the interviews that wages in these firms very seldom change despite variations in labor market conditions, and that when they do change it is most often under the impetus of changes in minimum-wage legislation. This is an impression that could be checked by collecting

continuous time series from single plants or industries, but we were unable to do this within the confines of the present study.

The explanations as to why wages seemed to stagnate followed very closely those outlined in the discussions of the previous section: both workers and firms in this labor market have a marginal commitment to it. The work force is dominated by youth, women, and temporary migrants, who are seeking a target income and wage increases that will enable them to reach their target more rapidly. Wage increases thus are thought by employers to have a perverse influence on individual labor supply. On the other hand, the total labor supply is responsive to special recruiting efforts, which substitute for wage increases as a means of increasing the pool of labor (and have no impact upon those already working). Recruiting was especially noticeable among employers of Puerto Ricans in Boston. In fact, the whole Puerto Rican migration was apparently stimulated by direct recruitment in rural areas of the island by employers experiencing a shortage of the black workers who had traditionally filled these jobs.

The other side of the story is the marginality of the employers. These people are often in exceedingly competitive industries where the labor is a high proportion of total cost, and employers therefore feel unable to raise wages even in the face of labor shortages. Whereas in Boston the marginality of the labor force was most frequently cited as an explanation for wage stagnation, in Louisiana it was the marginality of the firms. In fact, the labor force explanation was equally plausible in both areas. In Louisiana, however, there was considerably greater day-to-day variation in the amount of work available; work in the chief industries, sugar and shrimp, was highly dependent upon the vagaries of the weather. The women and youth who constituted the marginal work force seemed to have target incomes, but the targets were measured over a year or more and the uncertainty was such that even with a couple of months of very high incomes, it was difficult to be sure that targets would be reached.

A single industry, shrimp packing, dominated our observations of secondary employers in Louisiana. Each packer was small (some employing no more than eight women) and both bought and sold in a very competitive market. The firms were all physically close to each other. Aside from the raw meat, which was cleaned and frozen, labor was the only major component of variable cost and it thus became the critical determinant of profitability. All of this forced employers to hover around the statutory minimum wage. The statute in fact seemed to stabilize the market; employers who paid above it were under considerable social pressure, and although several claimed that given labor market conditions they would have liked to pay more, they reported themselves forced by their competitors to await changes in the statute. The employers in Boston were not under this kind of pressure. All operated with at least slightly differentiated products in apparently much less competitive product markets, and in none were labor costs as critical to profitability. Many, but by no means all, the employers were marginal but the wage was not the sole control variable over their profitability.

3. The third element in the structure of wage determination in the secondary sector is the role of the minimum wage. It is very hard to know what to say in the context of the present theory about the minimum; in some ways, the two markets reviewed for the present study might lead one to consider the minimum more rather than less of a mystery. The following points about the minimum may be made:

a. In Boston the effective minimum wage is a social rather than a statutory minimum. While the statutory minimum at the time of the study was $1.60, it was generally agreed that work much below $2.00 was unacceptable. A few jobs with lower wage rates existed, but workers in them were thought to be exploited. For example, a firm in Providence reportedly was recruiting workers in Puerto Rico for $1.65 an hour. Community leaders in New England refused to help this firm locate labor and insisted that workers who came to take these jobs left them as soon as they became acclimated to the area.

It is clear from conversations with workers, with employers, and with other market actors (community leaders, employment service counselors, school placement officers) that the social minimum is a moral standard. Work below that wage is considered an indignity to the person who performs it and exploitation on the part of whomever pays it. In this sense it is an equitable wage, very much like that prevailing in the lower tier. It thus appears to be interpretable as a social norm, a norm embedded not in a local work group—such groups do not exist in the secondary sector—but in the low-wage community as a whole. It is probably enforced upon employers by worker pressure in the form of resistance to supervision and work discipline (much as are equitable norms in the lower tier); the only people who willingly accept jobs below the norm are those who have not yet been integrated into the local community, such as the recent immigrants who work at the Providence plant. The ability of a secondary work force to exert such pressure is amply demonstrated in Boston by the behavior of the black work force in secondary jobs, which ultimately led employers to replace blacks with Puerto Rican recruits.

The only real alternative hypothesis is that the social minimum reflects a true competitive equilibrium. What makes this difficult to accept is not only the tone and terminology in which it is discussed by the market participants but the extreme elasticity of the local labor supply in response to employers' recruiting efforts. Given the apparent availability of labor, one would expect the prevailing wage to lie much closer to the statutory wage.

The missing piece in the social minimum theory, however, is an explanation of how it is established and how it changes. As noted, the dominant feature of this labor market is stagnation: most observers of the

Boston scene seemed to believe that the social minimum has not changed much from the $2.00 level over the last eight years. On the other hand, in our own interviews there were some signs that employers paying at this level were in the process of adjusting their base rates up in anticipation of an increase in the statutory minimum. This suggests that the social minimum is linked to the statute, perhaps in the way that wage differentials are fixed in the lower tier of the primary sector. An alternative hypothesis is that the social minimum is linked to lower tier wages, probably not directly but through a kind of demonstration effect. As the average level of consumption rises, low-income workers feel pressures to follow suit, and these pressures generate changes in the standards of equity by which they judge their own wages. This, however, seems unlikely for at least three reasons. First, there is little evidence that desired levels of consumption affect standards of equity, although they may well affect behavior in other ways. Second, given the fact that many secondary workers have target incomes and a less than full-time labor force commitment, it should be possible to meet pressures on consumption by working longer periods of time. Third, insofar as Puerto Ricans are concerned, a socially acceptable standard of living is defined by reference to the island and not the prevailing wage in Boston.

b. Louisiana presented a fairly sharp contrast to Boston with respect to the statutory minimum. There was no evidence of a social minimum wage distinct from that established by statute. There are several possible explanations for this difference. Perhaps the one most consistent with conventional wisdom is that Boston is a tight urban labor market whereas the Louisiana labor market is a loose one with a large agricultural labor reserve. As has already been noted, however, there is little evidence to support this conventional view. The Boston labor market is drawing off the rural labor reserve of Puerto Rico, and low-wage employers in Louisiana talk about the tightness of the labor market in language distinguished from that of Boston employers only by accent and certain regionalisms in their vocabulary.

A second possible explanation for the difference is the central role of sugar cane in the low-wage economy of Louisiana. Sugar cane is covered by a special federal wage statute that sets minimum wages for various different occupations in that industry. This procedure is of long standing. The current minimum for the lowest-paying sugar cane job is substantially above the federal minimum in industry (let alone in agriculture) and at about the level of the social minimum in Boston. One might argue that the politics of the sugar minimum reflects the industry's own socioeconomic conditions. In that sense it is probably closer to a collectively bargained wage, and perhaps responds to social standards in the areas where cane is dominant in a way that the broader national statute, applying as it does to such a mixture of industries and geographic areas, cannot. The plausibility of this explanation is enhanced by the fact that the U.S. sugar market is

completely controlled: governmental regulations assure domestic producers not only a given price but also a market for their crop at that price. This
would seem to relieve pressure for the labor statute to accommodate
product market constraints and free the industry to set the wage in
response to worker attitudes and labor market pressures.

On the other hand, one might expect the relatively high wages paid for
even menial, casual labor in sugar—particularly if those wages were
themselves a reflection to the social minimum—to infect workers' attitudes
toward other low-wage work; but this was most certainly not the case.
People who worked for $2.00 as casual labor in cane when work was
available there, spoke with equanimity about jobs at $1.60 in shrimp
packing or hospitals, and even lower-wage household day work which they
performed at other times of the year.

A third possible factor for the lack of a distinct social minimum is the
competitive nature of the shrimp industry, which after sugar was the major
low-wage employer. Given the tight product market competition, the wage
was effectively forced down to and held at the level of the statute. Thus, to
the extent the social minimum is a kind of custom dependent upon practice
and precedent, product market competition made the statutory minimum
customary and prevented the development of an alternative set of wage
norms.

Personally, I find most plausible an altogether different explanation,
which is that the low-wage labor market in Louisiana is qualitatively
different from the secondary sector in Boston in the same sense that the
secondary sector is qualitatively different from the primary sector. The
major low-wage employments in Louisiana, sugar and shrimp, are traditional employments; they have existed in the area for several hundred
years. Each has a distinctive pattern of work and of work relations.
Shrimping is an individualistic industry in which each man is an independent entrepreneur; people on the shrimp boats do not receive a wage, they
receive a share. Sugar, however, is a plantation industry. The labor
relations in the shrimp-packing factories seem to duplicate those on the
plantation; they also draw plantation labor.

It is typical of the plantation industries that all lines of authority are
vertical. The worker has a direct, personal allegiance to his boss, and that
allegiance is such as to discourage the development of horizontal al-
legiances among members of the work groups. The nature of that
allegiance—and its effect upon wage payments—is illustrated by the fact
that, in contrast to other manual occupations, many plantation workers told
us that they did not know what their fellow workers were paid and they
were not *supposed* to know. That was a matter between each worker and his
boss. The vertical relationships at work are also reflected in political
relationships. The politics of the region is very similar to that prevailing in
other traditional economies, such as in southern Italy. It would take us too

far afield to develop this theme here. It is of some more general interest, however, because traditional agriculture of this kind constitutes the original economic base for most of the immigrants into the low-wage sector of the Boston economy.[2]

For the limited purposes at hand, the chief conclusion to be drawn from the preceding discussion is that the statutory minimum is imposed upon an altogether different wage-setting system in an economy like that of Louisiana than it is in Boston. The duration and pervasiveness of statutory regulation in Louisiana make it difficult to say what the unregulated payment might have been. But on the basis of what is left of the old plantation system in Louisiana and of the prestatutory system on cotton plantations in Mississippi, I am inclined to believe the wage was previously set at what the plantation owner conceived to be subsistence, supplemented by certain suprasubsistence rewards to faithful retainers. Evidence for this comes from the large percentage of income received more or less in kind. On the plantations we visited this still included a house and a garden plot, both of which moreover varied in size and condition depending upon the relationship between the worker and the boss. In outlying plantations there is still a plantation store, and thus, irrespective of the wage, purchasing power is also controlled and one can well argue that the plantation owner effectively controls the consumption pattern of the work force.

In such an economy, the effect of statutory regulation is to substitute state control for the control of the individual patron. This is the continental European system. The wage statute in sugar, which is not just a single floor but a whole wage scale, more closely resembles the minimum-wage systems in France, Italy, and Puerto Rico than it does the system prevailing in, for example, Boston.

Summary

Thus, our observations in the secondary labor market suggest that wage determination is somewhat less distinctive than it is in the primary sector. A considerable part of the secondary wage structure is tied into the primary sector, largely through union organization. The floor for the structure is also set institutionally, through minimum-wage legislation. In Louisiana the wage structure in the major low-wage industry is also fixed by statute. The determinant of the wages above the statute and outside the lower-tier wage structure remains something of a mystery. The chief attribute seems to be stagnation rather than competition. Employers believe that individuals in the labor force have a target income and will react perversely to a wage increase by reducing work effort. At the same time the total labor force seems to be perfectly elastic at the current wage. In Boston, moreover, that wage seems to represent something of a social minimum below which it is considered undignified to work and exploitative to hire. The determinants of the social minimum remain unclear: they could be tied either to the primary wage structure or to the statutory minimum, but what evidence there is argues in favor of the second reference point. In Louisiana there is no social minimum distinct from the statute. Product market competition, and more broadly, the desire of employers for stability and certainty in the face of this competition, is an effective deterrent to payments above the minimum. The minimum-wage structure in Louisiana, moreover, appears to substitute for a subsistence wage in a very traditional and paternalistic industrial relations system.

Notes

1. Michael J. Piore, "The Role of Immigration in Industrial Growth: A Case Study of the Origins and Character of Puerto Rican Migration to Boston," Department of Economics Working Paper no. 112, May 1973.
2. Herbert Gans, in developing the sociological foundations upon which a good deal of the labor market typology used here builds, makes much of this relationship, particularly with reference to southern Italy. Fortuitously, our research contact in Louisiana had just returned from a year studying peasants in southern Italy and was also very conscious of the parallels. See Herbert J. Gans, *The Urban Villagers* (New York: The Free Press, 1962).

Foreign Workers   5

BY MICHAEL J. PIORE

RECENT IMMIGRANT GROUPS have seldom been popular in America, particularly when their native language is not English and their skin is not white. Hence it is not surprising that the present wave of immigration from Mexico and other Latin American countries has touched off political controversy. The fact that many of the immigrants come without proper papers—making them "illegal aliens," in the unhappy phrase of the moment—only exacerbates the situation. Conservatives fear for American purity. Unions fear for American jobs. Well-intentioned reformers wonder how to do justice to the undocumented immigrants who are already here without inadvertently opening the floodgates. President Carter's recent proposal to legitimate the status of some aliens while strengthening border enforcement is a politician's accommodation to these conflicting pressures.

Most of the worry and most of the good intentions, however, are misplaced. In the current debate, illegal immigration is frequently seen as an oversight; if the laws were better enforced, Americans could calmly provide for limited legal immigration and protect themselves from an uncontrollable influx of foreign workers. That is a bit like thinking that illegal liquor during Prohibition was an oversight. If people want something that is prohibited by law badly enough, a black market will develop. Extralegal immigration seems to reflect the fact that legal immigration quotas don't let in as many immigrants as the American economy needs. In this we are not alone. Europe too has an immigration "problem."

Industrial societies seem systemtically to generate a variety of jobs that full-time, native-born workers either reject out of hand or accept only when times are especially hard. Farm labor, low-level service positions like dishwasher or hospital orderly, and heavy, dirty, unskilled industrial work

Reprinted with permission from *Working Papers for a New Society,* March-April 1978, pp. 60-69. © 1978, The Center for the Study of Public Policy, Inc. This article, originally entitled "The 'Illegal Aliens' Debate Misses the Boat," was condensed and adapted from *Birds of Passage and Promised Lands,* a manuscript prepared for the National Council on Employment Policy, September 1977. The research on which it is based was supported by the Ford Foundation through a grant to the National Committee for Full Employment; by the Alfred P. Sloan Foundation; and by the U.S. Department of Labor. The author is solely responsible for the views expressed in this article.

all fit into this category. Jobs like these—referred to by manpower analysts as jobs in the "secondary labor market"—offer little security, opportunity for advancement, or prestige. Often they are seen as degrading. Finding people to fill them poses a continual problem for any industrial system.

Long-distance migrants from relatively backward rural areas provide one way of solving that problem. Indeed, most industrial countries have employed immigrant workers in these jobs almost since the beginning of the industrial revolution. Such immigrants typically view their stay in the industrial area as brief and purely instrumental. They plan to accumulate some savings quickly, return home, and invest their earnings there. They are untroubled by the lack of job security and promotion opportunities in secondary jobs because they do not plan to remain long enough for either to matter. They are unaffected by a job's menial status because their industrial work is well removed from the social setting of their home, where they derive their status and self-image.

The problem with temporary immigration as a solution to the low-status job problem is that, although the migrants do not plan to remain long, many nonetheless stay. Some develop permanent commitments to the industrial society. They have children who are born or raised in the industrial setting. The children, whatever their legal citizenship, view the labor market with the same eyes as other native-born workers. They "belong" to the industrial societies, and the work they perform there defines them as social beings. They thus feel degraded by low-status work, and they care deeply about matters like job security and advancement.

Nothing in the migration process, however, ensures that this second generation will be able to move up to higher level jobs. Indeed, industrial societies appear consistently to disappoint second-generation expectations in this regard. That disappointment has in turn led to enormous social tensions. The sit-down strikes of the 1930s, which sparked the industrial union movement in the United States, stemmed at least partly from the resentment of workers whose parents had immigrated just prior to World War I. Similarly, the ghetto disturbances of the 1960s can be seen as a revolt of black migrants' children against a society bent on confining them to their parents' jobs.[1]

A process that generates such tensions also creates myths and misconceptions. It is widely believed, for example, that immigrants replace native-born marginal workers—notably young people and women with families—thereby increasing unemployment among these groups. At some times in the past that may have been true. As Paul Osterman suggests, however, there is no evidence that the opportunities available to American-born marginal workers have changed significantly since the current wave of immigration began in the late 1960s (see "Understanding Youth Unemployment," *Working Papers*, January/February 1978). Women and youth who take low-level jobs are typically willing to work only in certain places and during certain hours; many don't want low-level jobs at all. So they are poor substitutes for immigrants.

Another misconception is that temporary immigration invariably benefits the migrants' home countries by generating a flow of income from the more developed society. Migration does have a variety of effects on the migrants' places of origin, and in some instances may stimulate economic development there. But it also raises expectations among the people back home, and over time begins to change the structure of values. Traditional activities are degraded, people become less willing to perform them, and in some cases traditional industries are destroyed altogether. Anyone looking at southern Italy, for example, would be hard put to say that the years of migration from there to the United States and more recently to northern Europe have uniformly benefited the home region. Nor would rural Puerto Rico be an advertisement for the salutary effects of continuous long-distance migration.

A third misconception is that poverty and population pressure in underdeveloped areas are the prime causes of large-scale migration. In fact, income differentials have existed for long periods of time without stimulating migration. Migrants themselves typically dislike the industrial areas. They are ordinarily interested only in the money that can be earned there, and then only if they are able to accumulate savings. When they cannot find a job quickly, they return home.

The true determinant of migration flows is the process of economic development in the industrial region, particularly the number and character of jobs available. Migrants frequently learn about jobs from recruiters for industrial employers. The current undocumented migration from Mexico and the Caribbean began in this manner in the late 1960s. Reserves of labor in the black South were being depleted, and what labor remained there was increasingly being absorbed by southern industry. In the North, the black labor force had come to be dominated by a second generation of workers intolerant of the jobs their parents had held. So employers went looking for Mexicans, Puerto Ricans, and other Latin Americans. (The black migration from South to North itself had originated in employer recruitment shortly after World War I. Businesses wanted to replace the European immigration flow interrupted by the war.)

A final misconception is that jobs held by immigrants somehow replace jobs held by native workers. In fact—though the evidence is not all in—the migrants' jobs appear to fall into two categories. In one category are jobs that complement, or indeed make possible, the "good" jobs held by natives. Some declining industries, for instance, provide good jobs but also depend on a supply of low-wage labor, without which they would go out of business or move abroad. The shoe and textile industries in New England are examples of this: white Americans work as cutters or machine repairers while poorly paid immigrants do most of the stitching, last pulling, warehousing, and the like. Other industries guarantee employment by transferring peak-demand work to subcontractors who employ immigrants and other low-wage labor on a temporary basis.

In the second category are jobs that don't necessarily complement native-held occupations but which contribute to the standard of living of better-off groups. Household workers typify this second category; so do some groups of restaurant workers, delivery people, and janitors.[2]

There are some native-born workers, of course, who share the secondary labor market with immigrants. The impact of immigration on these workers is uncertain. Their primary interest, presumably, is in advancing to higher-status, more secure jobs. If the jobs they share with migrants are improved when there are fewer workers to fill them, then native-born workers might well be better off with less immigration. But if the jobs are essential to the continued functioning of the system—and if they can't be upgraded without radically changing the system—then the society will look for other ways to maintain the labor supply. In the medical-care industry, for example, which is now hard pressed to meet demand, it seems unlikely that hospital orderly and other low-level jobs will suddenly become first steps on a career path that leads to nurse or doctor. In heavy industry, it seems unlikely that we will do away with peak-demand subcontracting to nonunion firms, particularly when workers in unions are beginning to demand lifetime job guarantees. It seems much more likely that we will seek to curtail the upward mobility (through discrimination or other means) of groups that presently hold low-level or temporary jobs and to expand that traditional labor force by changing institutions like unemployment insurance and welfare benefits.

Given all these considerations, an ideal immigration system from a policy maker's point of view should seek several objectives. It should minimize the number of jobs for which migrants are required in the first place, since large-scale immigration disrupts the migrants' places of origin (and may in fact generate unfulfilled expectations on the part of the migrants themselves). It should minimize the degree of competition between nationals and foreign workers in the first generation, since too much competition means both groups will suffer. It should aim at keeping the second generation as small as possible, since the expectations held by the children of immigrants are particularly unlikely to be realized. And finally, it should maximize the chances of upward mobility for whatever second generation does emerge.

Evaluated in these terms, existing policy is nowhere near the failure it is presumed to be; in fact, it is a more rational approach to the problem than any of the protagonists in the current debate is willing to admit. Ironically, the principal institutional feature that makes the system work well by these lights is the very feature that makes it appear so irrational: the fact that it is underfunded. The Immigration and Naturalization Service (INS) has a budget so small in relation to the magnitude of immigrant flows that it cannot possibly enforce the law as written. That fact, plus the fact that it has never received any congressional guidance on priorities in spending, means that the INS has tremendous discretion as to when and where the law is enforced. On the whole, the service seems to utilize this discretion to minimize the competition between undocumented aliens and other workers, and to realize some of the other objectives outlined above.

Patterns of enforcement activity are revealing. For example, the INS seems to give priority to apprehending undocumented workers, as opposed to other undocumented persons, and to those workers in relatively high-paying, high-status jobs. The lowest level, most menial job categories—like household help—receive virtually no attention. Also, the service concentrates its enforcement activities in the Southwest. That is ostensibly because of the heavy traffic from Mexico there, but the effect is to drive undocumented Mexicans out of a region where they are in direct competition with Mexican-American and toward Los Angeles, San Francisco, and the Midwest. There, the native wage scales are higher, and low-wage labor is scarce.

Some INS offices make a practice of varying enforcement activities seasonally so that alien workers in effect complement native-born youth in the labor market. When school lets out in June, the Service raids various restaurant and hotel jobs to open them for young people; when school resumes in the fall, enforcement is relaxed. Enforcement also varies with the business cycle in some industries. In the 1974-75 recession, for example, the service actively pursued Canadian workers in the construction industry. But it had tacitly allowed them to enter during the preceding boom when there had been a shortage of skilled Americans.

INS agents recognize the power that the current institutional framework puts in their hands; they are anxious to justify the way they exercise that power, and they speak quite freely of their enforcement philosophy. Their rationale is complex, with implications extending beyond the immediate issues at hand. But the goal of maintaining a labor force that complements native workers under varying economic conditions is a prominent part of it.

The present system is least effective in its handling of permanent settlement and the second generation. To the extent that undocumented workers are indeed illegal, one would expect them to live at the margin of society, minimizing their children's exposure to the institutions and experiences that would help them advance in the U.S. labor market. For example, parents are often afraid to send their children to school or to seek out medical attention for fear of making their presence known to authorities. Again, however, these effects are greatly mitigated by the way the law is enforced. The chances of getting caught are in fact small; enforcement patterns depend more on the labor market than on immigrants' utilization of public services; and the INS already has so much more information than it can possibly act on that it pays little attention to the kind of data aliens fear.

The other mitigating factor is that the de jure immigration system is not nearly as divorced from the prevailing de facto system as the term "illegal" suggests. It actually provides a variety of channels through which those who become permanent settlers and have children can regularize their status. Several mechanisms (which from another perspective are highly invidious and inequitable) operate here. The most important is the system, termed in the business "equity," whereby people with close relatives in the United States are given priority for immigration visas. Together with the fact that children born in the United States are automatically accorded citizenship, this system has assured that immigrants who have children in the United States, return to their home countries, and then apply for legal entry will almost certainly be granted legal status.

A second procedure, which enhances the value of equity as a means of regularizing one's status, in voluntary departure. A record of illegal entry into the United States would normally preclude subsequent entry through legal channels. However, few aliens apprehended by the INS undergo the formal deportation procedures necessary to invoke this legal barrier. Most leave through voluntary departure, a kind of nolo contendere device in which the illegality of the previous entry is never formally established. The INS prefers this procedure since it saves a good deal of time and expense; it also preserves equity. (I have seen immigration judges grant voluntary departure in place of formal deportation for no reason other than that the defendant had an American-born child.) Voluntary departure also means that an immigrant need not wait for his documents at home, a wait that can be extremely long. It is apparently quite common for people to enter without documents, work, establish the relationships on which equity is built, return home to file papers, reenter without documents, continue working until notified that the papers are ready, return once again to pick up the papers, and finally reenter the United States as legal immigrants.

While the combination of voluntary departure and equity appears to have been the most important method of legitimating undocumented workers, other procedures work toward the same end. For example, it is relatively common for the INS to parole an undocumented worker whose papers are in process, so that an apprehended alien whose status seems likely to be regularized need not leave the country even temporarily. Another common practice is for immigrants to obtain work permits for "labor-scarce" occupations; frequently the jobs in question were acquired by the immigrants when they were undocumented workers, and the main proof that an immigrant is required to fill the job is the fact that he or she is already holding it.

The success of the system in terms of the goals outlined is evident from available statistics. It works best for Mexican immigration on the West

Coast. Most Mexicans appear to enter the country simply by crossing the border illegally. Many are apprehended and quickly returned to Mexico. There, by all reports, they simply turn around and reenter, in most cases successfully. The immigration is temporary: the best available data suggest that the average Mexican returns home every six months, and that the total length of stay averages two-and-a-half years.[3] Family formation, which may be taken as both an indicator of permanent settlement and a measure of the size of the second generation, is low. Only 11 percent of apprehended aliens in one sample had a spouse in the United States, though 50 percent were married; similarly, while 50 percent had children, fewer than 10 percent had children in the United States. Most Mexicans seem to work in the kind of secondary jobs that complement native workers; penetration into higher-wage employment has been slight. The equity system works as described to legitimate those who do acquire permanent attachments in the United States. It also presumably facilitates their children's access to the institutions that will help them advance.

The system operates somewhat less effectively for non-Mexican workers from the Western Hemisphere. Most of these immigrants seem to enter as visitors or tourists, with documents but without the right to work. They violate the terms of their entry first by taking a job and then by staying in the United States after their visas have expired. The migration of these workers also appears to be essentially temporary, with relatively low rates of family formation, and they too are concentrated in the secondary sector of the labor market. But each of these characteristics is decidedly less pronounced than with the Mexicans. Migrants from elsewhere in the hemisphere go home less frequently than Mexicans (every 22 months, on the average); a larger proportion (28 percent) have families in the United States; they send less money back to their places of origin; and they have advanced farther up the occupational hierarchy into positions competitive with native workers.

Once we recognize the way the present immigration system actually operates, it is evident that certain minor changes in obscure characteristics of the system can produce substantial gains in terms of the goals outlined. Other proposals, which at first glance seem beneficial, are likely to have negative results.

The most obvious defect of the present system is the disparity between the experience of Mexicans and that of other Western Hemisphere aliens. No single explanation accounts for the difference between the two populations, but discussions with workers themselves suggest that a major factor is simply the relative difficulty of reentry. Mexican workers have little trouble moving back and forth across the border. Other workers, who must enter on regular documents, have great difficulty in doing so. The documents are difficult to obtain in the first place: the State Department officials who issue them are highly suspicious of would-be entrants' motives. The migrants fear that, once they have violated the terms of their entry, they will be unable to obtain entry again. Hence many feel obliged to stay on much longer than they originally anticipated. In the process, they develop attachments—often in the form of second families—that they never intended, but which make it still more difficult to leave.

This paradoxic effect of a tight entry policy upon the size and character of the migrant population is not unique to the population of visa violators in the United States. Western European countries experienced similar effects in the last several years when they tried to curtail immigration by restricting entry. Workers already in the country feared that they could not reenter, and so delayed departure, often illegally. The result was that both inflow and outflow declined. The net effect may well have been an increase in the total population of aliens; certainly the size of the second generation has grown.

One obvious improvement in existing immigration policy would therefore be to issue tourist visas for relatively long periods of time, and to allow unlimited trips between the United States and the home country. Such a change need not affect the State Department's screening of applicants to exclude potential violators. It would simply recognize that a mistake in the screening process cannot be rectified after the fact, and that trying to do so will simply aggravate the problem. On the Mexican border, by the same token, attempts to "enforce existing policy" by tightening the border may achieve precisely the opposite of what is intended. Increased difficulty in crossing the border may simply cause those migrants who enter successfully to stay longer, and thus increase the rate of permanent settlement.

Three other troublesome changes, also likely to create more problems than they solve, are the recent restrictions on the number of legal entrants and on the exercise of equity conferred by U.S.-born children; the denial of public services to undocumented workers; and proposals to penalize employers for hiring aliens. The restrictions on legal entry and the exercise of equity were introduced by Congress last year as part of a revised distribution of immigration quotas. The reform was supposed to allow more equitable treatment of Western Hemisphere countries relative to European nations. In the process, though, Congress put a limit of 20,000 on immigration from any single nation, substantially below the roughly 70,000 immigrants who were being admitted at the time from Mexico. Congress also made it impossible for parents of U.S.-born children to regularize their status immediately. Since legal immigration and equity constitute the principal channels through which permanent settlers can regularize their own and their children's status, both restrictions may hurt the second generation's chance for advancement significantly.

That is especially likely to be true in light of recent trends at the state and local level to limit undocumented workers' access to public services. The most destructive of these efforts is the movement in New York City to bar the children of illegal aliens from the public schools. Given past difficulties even among those immigrant children with access to public education, it is hard to exaggerate the potential damage of this policy to the individuals involved and to the social stability of the city itself. Education is a sine qua non for any kind of upward mobility. Other services are important too. The lack of health care, housing programs, food stamps, and the like will certainly increase the number of second-generation immigrants with frustrated aspirations. To be sure, services are thought to attract even more migrants, and to encourage permanent settlement. But the evidence suggests that this kind of conscious economic calculation plays a minor role in people's decisions about migration. Social variables are far more important.

The proposal for reform that has received the greatest public attention recently would make employers liable for hiring illegal aliens. Here too the solution appears likely to do more harm than good. The issue of employer liability is related to the broader question of the size of the secondary labor market and the possibility of controlling its size through public policy. However large the secondary labor market currently is, its size seems to be limited by a network of legislative restrictions imposing minimal health and safety standards and mandating a minimum wage. The market for undocumented workers lies more or less within these standards. The survey cited above, for example, found that more than 75 percent of apprehended aliens were paid at least the minimum wage. Of those who worked in manufacturing, almost 90 percent earned at least the minimum. According to the same survey, the market for undocumented workers also generally respects a number of other legal standards involving income, social security, and unemployment taxation. It is somewhat less effectively controlled by union organization, but it is not totally beyond the unions' purview either.

Why the market for undocumented workers respects these standards is not clear. Such workers are an easily exploited group; they are afraid of being reported to authorities and are often willing to work for less than prevailing wages under substandard conditions. There is a lot of money to be made by forcing them to do so. One could easily imagine a market in which employers, by evading taxation and letting working conditions deteriorate, were able to make a higher profit while paying workers essentially what they take home now. It is possible that the market is already drifting in this direction: we have no good data about alien job characteristics over time, and the limited violations found in some recent one-shot studies may be the first signs of a long-run deterioration.

A chief factor in limiting abuse by employers, however, must be their legal situation. They risk nothing in employing the aliens; they risk substantial financial and criminal penalties for tax evasion and violations of labor and work standard laws. If penalties were imposed for hiring aliens, this balance would be upset. Many employers might feel that, having placed themselves in jeopardy by hiring aliens, they might as well take full advantage of the profits to be made. In many industries employing aliens, only a few employers need make this calculation to put the remainder under strong competitive pressure to follow suit.

To argue that the present immigration system meets some unrecognized goals, and that many reform proposals are misguided, is not to argue that the system is ideal. Three major reforms seem desirable: first, restrictions on the now-legal entry of higher level manpower; second, a concerted effort to reduce the size of the secondary sector; and third, the legitimation of the migrant labor force required to fill the jobs that remain.

The proposal to restrict higher level immigration follows directly from the analysis outlined above. Labor shortages in an industrial society are concentrated in low-level occupations. The trouble with migration as a solution to these shortages is a lack of opportunity in higher level positions for immigrants' children. Americans already have an accumulated obligation to black workers that we are unable to meet, and we simply cannot afford to allocate what high-level positions we do have to foreigners. Indeed, it appears that in a number of areas (notably medicine) immigration has provided a kind of safety valve against expanding domestic employment opportunities. Importing foreign doctors, for example, helps undercut pressure to expand medical-school enrollments in this country.

The idea of restricting the secondary labor market's size is less controversial. But many believe we can do so simply by restricting the number of unskilled immigrants. That, as noted, is a dangerous notion. If the restrictions are successful but the work cannot be dispensed with, social pressures will tend to create a labor force by restricting the upward mobility of native workers or immigrants of a previous wave (blacks, Mexican-Americans, etc.). The extreme limit of this process would be the reimposition of the kind of racial caste system that once prevailed in the South. If the restrictions on immigration are unsuccessful—and history tells us they are likely to be—the immigration becomes clandestine. It is then likely to escape legal restrictions upon the size of the secondary sector, and the sector will begin to expand beyond its present limits. Eventually, social forces will presumably react to check the expansion. But by that time we may have grown accustomed to the expanded standard of living that immigration permits, making it difficult to reverse the process. Efforts to curtail the secondary sector by curtailing the labor supply are therefore likely to have the opposite effect from what is intended.

The wiser course is to approach the problem directly by tightening the legal standards that limit the secondary sector. At present, that means at least three types of reform: (1) an increase in the minimum wage; (2) more stringent health and safety standards, particularly for low-paying jobs; and (3) encouragement and protection for union organization. In this sense, current proposals to repeal Section 14(b) of the National Labor Relations Act, to extend to agricultural workers the right to organize and bargain collectively, to restrict employers' unfair labor practices, to index minimum wages, and the like, are tightly bound up with immigration policy and ought to be considered in combination with it. Finally, to make all of these laws more effective, the INS should be prohibited from responding to employer complaints about undocumented workers in their establishment once a union campaign is in progress or whenever an employer is found in violation of a labor statute.

The arguments against curtailing the secondary sector by restricting immigration lead to my final proposal: regularizing the status of existing immigrants. So long as the labor supply represented by these immigrants is extra-legal, there is a danger that the labor market will escape its present limits and begin to expand. Available data suggest that this has not happened yet, at least on a large scale, but the violations that have been found would be disturbing if they are the beginning of a trend.

Proposals for legitimating the existing migrant labor force have recently been outlined by the Carter administration. In evaluating them, it is useful to distinguish between more or less permanent settlers on the one hand and temporary workers on the other. The objective with permanent settlers should be to legitimate their status and that of their children as completely as possible, thus maximizing access to channels of advancement. For temporary workers, on the other hand, the objective should be legitimation without encouraging any permanent attachment. Because some temporary workers are likely to develop permanent attachments in any case, however, and because any administrative process is likely to make mistakes in its initial classification, there must be some mechanism by which temporary workers can convert to permanent status.

Carter's proposals handle this problem through a "two-tier" amnesty. One tier covers people who have been in the United States for over seven years. They would be granted immigrant status, enabling them to bring their families from home or to regularize the status of family members already here. The second tier would cover workers in the country as of last January who have been here less than seven years. It would give them legitimate status in the United States but would provide no rights for their families at home. The distinction can be viewed as corresponding to the distinction between permanent and temporary migrants. The correspondence is imperfect, since some permanent settlers will have been here less than seven years, and a number of temporary migrants could acquire immigration rights as relatives of those who fall under the seven-year amnesty. But it may be the best possible.

The chief problem is that no provision is made whereby current temporary migrants could convert their status. Conversion of this sort could be handled easily by giving temporary migrants priority in the allocation of existing immigration quotas, with the order of priority based on length of stay in the United States. People should be able to exercise this priority at any time in the future; that would minimize the incentive for immediate conversion. It may also be desirable to expand existing immigration quotas to accommodate these adjustments in status, or to create a special quota for this purpose. At a minimum, the Mexican quota should be raised either permanently or temporarily to the rate of 60,000 to 70,000 a year that prevailed before the 20,000 limit was established by Congress in 1976.

Current proposals presume that, if the alien population can be legitimated, further entry can be handled through more effective law enforcement. Indeed, the amnesty program has been justified on essentially humanitarian grounds: making up for past errors. If the program is seen instead as a means of bringing an essentially irreversible process under some form of legal control, one is forced to face the distinct possibility that illegal entry will continue after amnesty.

Illegal entry will initially be limited: the secondary labor market itself is limited, and so long as sufficient legal labor is available the attraction of illegal labor is not great. Over time, however, one would expect the pool of legal labor to decline, through the return of some temporary migrants to their places of origin and through upward mobility of others. It would be desirable, then, to have some means of expanding the available labor pool. One such measure, which would introduce a safety valve in the system without creating the open-ended immigration that the public seems to fear, would be to establish a temporary work permit. The permit would go to those who, because of their status as relatives of present aliens, would eventually become eligible for permanent immigration, but who are now barred by the quota and by administrative delays from immediate entry. Over the long run, this proposal would not expand the number of people with immigration rights, but it would enable us to adjust the time at which those rights are exercised in accord with the requirements of the economy.

There are two major issues of immigration policy that are largely untouched in this article, and a brief comment on each will have to suffice. One is unemployment. It is frequently alleged that it would be possible to solve our unemployment problem were it not for the presence of large numbers of undocumented workers. But it is hard to imagine that immigrant workers are really to blame. The principal cause of U.S. unemployment is the low level at which first Ford and now Carter have chosen to run the economy. Unemployment could be eliminated through policy instruments readily available to the president and Congress. These instruments have not been used, allegedly for fear of the inflationary pressures they would generate. I believe that this fear is greatly exaggerated. In any case, none of the theories that purport to justify the fear of inflation suggests that inflationary pressures would be less under a policy that sought to expel alien workers.

A second important point concerns the fairness—or lack thereof—of the present immigration system. However the failings of the current system have been exaggerated, it is hard to exaggerate either the system's unfair and inequitable features, or how far it departs from conventional standards of justice and due process. The INS's discretion may be very good for control of the market to preserve job opportunities for Americans, but it leads to an erratic and personal manner of dispensing jobs and it penalizes those who attempt to respect the law. The proposals in this essay will not greatly improve things in this regard; in some respects they may make them worse. I am not unmindful of this nor untroubled by it.

To argue the issues involved would require a separate article. But it does seem to me that the civil rights and civil liberties issues here have consistently been fought on the wrong turf: in the battle for substantive legislative changes rather than in the battle for the budget through which substantive provisions would acquire some force. I also believe that the advocates of equity and due process have never faced up to the conflicts of values inherent in the situation. To give meaning to the philosophy expressed in the current de jure immigration system would probably require either a Berlin Wall on the Mexican border or a national identity card. It might well require both.

Notes

1. In the United States, the internal migration of blacks from the Deep South to northern cities in many ways resembled the international immigrations that are the subject of this article. When black migration is being discussed, of course, the phrase "native-workers" refers to natives of northern urban areas.
2. Both categories fall into the secondary labor market of low-wage, low-skill jobs with frequent layoffs and high turnover. Legislative standards establishing minimum wages and working conditions apparently set a floor on the secondary labor market, and these standards probably respond to the need for workers in the first category. If minimum standards are set too high, then some "supportive" secondary jobs will be eliminated and the employment of native workers threatened. If they are too low, employers will be tempted to transfer more work into the secondary sector of subcontractors and the like; again, more native workers would be out of a job. Demand for workers in the second (standard-of-living) category is probably not so important a factor in determining the size of the secondary labor market. Given the ease with which new migration streams appear this must be the case, or there would be no limit to the menial labor the American economy absorbs.
3. This and subsequent data referred to in this article are drawn from David S. North and Marion F. Houstoun, *The Characteristics and Role of Illegal Aliens in the U.S. Labor Market: An Exploratory Study* (Linton & Company, March 1976).

Work and Welfare 6

BY BENNETT HARRISON

IN RECENT YEARS, an important new view of labor market structure and functioning has emerged. This theory of "dual" (or, more generally, segmented) labor markets grew out of the institutionalist tradition in economics (the work of Clark Kerr, Charles Myers, and John Dunlop), and out of the political writing by blacks in the sixties (in books such as the autobiographies of Malcolm X and Eldridge Cleaver). Many of its creators were also actively involved in the civil rights and anti-war movements of the decade, and sought to fashion an analysis of the labor market which integrated the tenets of economics with their experiential insights into the political process.

One part of the new view—developed by such economists as Barry Bluestone, Peter Doeringer, Michael Piore, Marcia Freedman, and David Gordon—posits the existence of a class of jobs collectively referred to as the "secondary labor market." These are jobs characterized by low productivity or earnings, high turnover and seasonal or cyclical instability, weakly structured internal promotion systems with little on-the-job training, and a more or less permanent excess supply of low-skilled labor. Both entry into and exit from the secondary labor market, as well as mobility into the "primary" labor market of higher-quality jobs, are believed to be only partially related to education, training, experience, or other factors that are so important in orthodox labor theory. Instead, emphasis is placed on ascriptive traits like race and sex, which employers use as criteria in terms of which to practice discrimination. Age is also used as a measure of the ability and willingness of young workers to settle down into a stable job situation.

An important question posed from within the "dualistic" perspective concerns the mechanisms for the social reproduction of the secondary labor market. What forces act to lock people into such low-wage jobs without

From *Challenge*, May-June 1978, pp. 49-54. © 1978 by M. E. Sharpe, Inc. This research was supported by a grant from the Center for the Study of Metropolitan Problems in the National Institutes of Mental Health.

either permanently impairing their utility to employers or eroding their willingness or ability to work—to such an extent that labor shortages might eventually force employers to raise wages? In the context of studies of the urban ghetto in the 1960s, several authors have advanced the concept that programs like public welfare and subsidized government training (as well as quasi-legal to potently illegal "hustling") have become "irregular" institutions upon which ghetto dwellers can draw to supplement their earnings from work in the secondary labor market. No one of these institutions would allow sufficient dependable income to free the typical recipient from ultimate dependence on work, however. Louis Ferman, Stanley Friedlander, Daniel Fusfeld, S. M. Miller, Frances Fox Piven, and Martin Rein have all contributed to this formulation.

Following this line of inquiry, we are concerned with the hypothesis that welfare helps to reproduce "secondary" labor—low-income workers and low-wage, high-turnover jobs—by systematically reinforcing such modes of work. How many households are connected to both the world of work and the world of welfare? How do they differ from otherwise similar households which do not bridge these two spheres of what Gunnar Myrdal long ago called the "periphery" of the economy? And finally, to apply the analysis to an urgent matter of contemporary public policy, what are the implications of our findings for the Carter administration's proposals for welfare reform?

Some operational definitions

In principle, the relationship of welfare to the labor market can be direct, indirect, or nonexistent. There will be a direct relationship if people receive wages and welfare within the same time frame, either simultaneously or by moving back and forth between the two over time. There will be an indirect relationship if, whether or not welfare recipients actually work, labor market conditions significantly affect the extent and timing of their utilization of welfare.

In this study, the unit of analysis is the household, rather than the individual. Other researchers have looked at the behavior of individual welfare recipients, especially women who head their own households. Studies conducted by Barry Friedman and Leonard Hausman, and by Frank Levy, have contributed much to our understanding of short-run phenomena and the caseload dynamics for households where, throughout the period of analysis, the women *remain* the heads. But we need a different viewpoint for those households where the "headship" changes over time. This is an important segment of the population: within any five-year period, of those women who will ever experience divorce throughout their lifetimes, over a third will begin and end their first marriages and two-thirds of the divorcees will remarry. And these data greatly undercount the turnover in female household "headship," since they exclude changes associated with a spouse's death, as well as both legal and informal separation. Yet these situations, too, can force a woman to become a self-supporting head of household.

Our own study focuses on women aged 24-54 in 1968 and on their households during the subsequent five years, whether or not those women were heads of households. (Younger and older women were excluded, in order to avoid the additional complexity of processes like school-to-work transition and retirement.) There were 35 million such households in the United States in 1968. The data come from the first five years of the University of Michigan Survey Research Center Panel Study of Income Dynamics, which studied the income patterns of a sampling of households over an extended period.

All welfare income accruing to the household from Aid to Families with Dependent Children (AFDC), AFDC-Unemployed Father, or state General Assistance is included, regardless of which member receives it. With respect to earnings, however, only the work of household *heads* is counted, since the data source did not provide complete information on the working conditions of spouses or children. Any household whose head ever reported any earnings was considered to have demonstrated involvement in the world of work.

The mixing of work and welfare

The probability that a given household would receive welfare was small for any single year, but the data allowed us to follow the sample households (adult women and the people who live with them) over a five-year period. During this time, households could move from one location to another, in and out of welfare, or in and out of work. Over the same period, households could also change their heads as well, thus potentially changing their need or eligibility for welfare.

The long-run cumulative probability of welfare receipt increases as a result of all this turnover. During 1968-72 the annual incidence of welfare utilization was 11.1 percent for the first year, 6.2 percent for the second, and 6.3, 9.0, and 9.3 for the next three years respectively, but the cumulative probability of ever having welfare was .177. That is, 17.7 percent of all households went on welfare at least once in the five-year period. (About 52 percent of these "ever-welfare" households experienced two or more discrete spells of welfare during the five-year period.) For minority households, the chances of going on welfare were much higher— over 40 percent. Among those households whose adult women were ever the head (a quarter of the cohort, or about 9 million households in all), one in three received welfare at least once during the five years. Of those households which were "permanently poor"—defined here as being in the lowest third of the cumulative five-year distribution of gross U.S. family income—45 percent received welfare one or more times.

In any one year within the sample period, the proportion of households receiving both earnings (from the head) and welfare was small—between 3.4 and 7.9 percent. (Because only the earnings of household heads were counted, the true figures are probably somewhat higher.) But the cumulative probability—the percentage of all households which received both earnings and welfare during the five-year period (not necessarily in the same year)—was 16.3 percent, again as a result of turnover in the labor market and in family structure. Mixing was much more prevalent among minority households: between 11.4 and 16.4 percent mixed wages and welfare in any one year, and one out of every three mixed work and public assistance over the course of the five years. Households that were headed by women during at least part of the period experienced about the same cumulative probability of mixing (32.6 percent). For those households I have called permanently poor, the odds of receiving both earnings and welfare over the period 1968-72 were the highest of all: fifty-fifty.

But let us now turn to the two questions of greatest interest in the study of mixing. First, what proportion of those who ever received welfare also worked at some time? The probability (p) of ever having earnings ("everwork"), given that the household ever had welfare ("everwel"), is equal to

$$\frac{p \text{ (everwel and everwork)}}{p \text{ (everwel)}} = \frac{p \text{ (mixing)}}{p \text{ (everwel)}} = \frac{.163}{.177} = .921$$

Clearly there is an enormous amount of cumulative mixing: 92 percent of those adult women who ever had welfare also either worked themselves at some time during 1968-72 or lived in households where another adult (the "head") worked. The conditional probabilities for the various subgroups of the population were all about the same.

Second, what proportion of those households whose heads ever worked also received some welfare? I found that 97.7 percent of all households had wage income in at least one of the five years. Therefore the probability of ever having welfare, given that the head ever worked, is

$$\frac{p \text{ (everwork and everwel)}}{p \text{ (everwork)}} = \frac{.163}{.977} = .167$$

Thus, having a job *per se* was not sufficient to keep a household off welfare. Even with earnings coming in, one out of every six households went on welfare at some time during the period.

The importance of looking at the cumulative experience of welfare-eligible people over time, rather than at the kinds of momentary snapshots that have governed most welfare policy design and evaluation in the past, is illustrated in Figure 1. In any one year (the year 1970 is shown here), 93.2 percent of all households had heads who worked. Only 6.2 percent received welfare. About 4 percent received neither wages nor welfare, relying instead on social security, workmen's compensation, gifts from relatives, or other sources of income. But there was considerable overlap, shown by the shaded area. A little over half the welfare households also had earnings coming in (.034 ÷ .062). Over time, as households changed composition and as their eligibility for welfare and their search for jobs also underwent changes, this overlap became much greater. Over the whole five-year sample period, more than nine-tenths of the welfare households had heads who worked (.163 ÷ .177).

That those who mix earnings with welfare tend to work in the secondary labor market, when they work at all, seems incontestable from the evidence. Eighty percent of the sample households in the survey fell into the upper two-thirds of the five-year distribution of U.S. family incomes, so the sample is clearly not biased toward poor people. Yet 44 percent of those households that ever mixed work and welfare were in the lowest 33 percent of the long-run distribution. In the same years that their households received welfare, heads had average earnings of $2,400 a year, and were almost always employed in unskilled jobs. Even if they had worked full-time, the best wage they could expect to have earned—given

Figure 1

Long-Run and Short-Run Probabilities of Receiving Income from Work and Income from Welfare: All Households (n = 2,688)

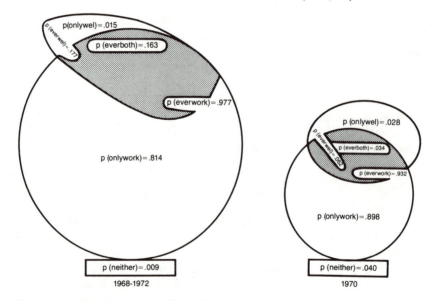

p (onlywel)—probability of receiving welfare at some time, never wages
p (everwel)—probability of receiving welfare at some time
p (everboth)—probability of receiving welfare and wages at some time
p (everwork)—probability of receiving wages at some time
p (onlywork)—probability of receiving wages at some time, never welfare
p (neither)—probability of receiving neither wages nor welfare

the prevailing demand for all workers with the same age, race, sex, and education—was only in the range of $4,300 to $5,400 a year. The low wage is a property of the jobs themselves as much as it is an indication of disproportionately low productivity among these particular individuals. This is demonstrated by the fact that the national average wage in the industries and occupations in which these welfare household heads worked was itself only about $4,000. Conditions for women, especially those heading welfare households, are even worse. According to Levy, who looked at the year 1971 using the same data as I did, employed female household heads with children averaged about 1,100 hours of work in that year (the full-time equivalent would have been 2,200 hours), and earned only about $1,500, implying an hourly rate well below even the legal minimum wage. These are clearly secondary labor market workers.

The labor market and welfare utilization

Among the many statistical models with which I was able to experiment, I usually found the same variables to be the best predictors of whether or not a woman and her household received welfare, whether or not they experienced multiple spells (that is, received welfare for several periods of time), and how much welfare was received, both absolutely and relatively to the head's earnings. The number of dependent children, whether the household was located in a county with high unemployment (average rate more than 6 percent), whether the head belonged to a union or was a military veteran, the economic status of the head's parents, and the national average wage for the industry and occupation in which the head worked, were all important factors. The education, training, and age of the head seemed to be of greater importance in predicting who used welfare more than once than they were in explaining who ever used welfare at all, or how much welfare the users received.

Implications for welfare reform

Political leaders in the United States consider the welfare caseload to be unacceptably large, both because it is costly and because the prevailing ideology has it that people should earn their incomes. The last four administrations have all struggled to find a solution for this problem which would be both politically popular and economically feasible.

In congressional testimony and in legal briefs on welfare rights, some experts have argued that the distinction between "employable" and "unemployable" recipients is a function of the tightness of the overall demand for labor and the society's commitment to creating enough work to go around. Nevertheless, the leadership in Congress and in the White House continually insist upon trying to fashion a more streamlined HEW transfer payment program for those deemed unemployable, sending the rest over to the U.S. Department of Labor to fill existing job vacancies or new job slots created especially for them, mainly through federal grants to state and local governments (public service employment). These "employables" would, of course, have to be paid at less than prevailing wages, both to make the policy less expensive and to create an incentive for the employables to seek better-paying jobs outside this subsidized sector. This two-tiered tracking solution to the "welfare mess," which basically characterizes every idea that has been seriously considered in Washington since the late 1960s, has now reached its most sophisticated expression yet in the current welfare reform plan put forth by President Carter and HEW Secretary Joseph Califano.

The two-tiered plan, like all other such welfare reforms, turns crucially on what one assumes about the true magnitude of the "employables" category. Here the administration is caught in a dilemma. If relatively few on welfare are in fact employable, then no work relief program is likely to have more than a trivial impact on the costs of welfare. Califano himself used to make this argument during the Johnson era. On the other hand, if most of the caseload are employable, then work relief is going to be intolerably expensive and administratively massive, except perhaps at very low wages and with minimal policing. The two-tiered strategy thus rests on the assumption that there are enough employables on welfare to matter, but not so many that the economic and political costs of forcing them to work will offset the hoped-for savings in welfare payments and administration.

My research on this subject has focused on the extent to which, over time, the heads of ever-welfare households also have at least some attachment to the labor market. I have implicitly defined as "employable" any head of household who ever received at least some earnings over a five-year period. (Of course, since my data allowed me to consider only the work activities of heads—and only their reported work activities at that—the true count of employables must be even larger than that which I found.) I learned that the vast majority of adult women on welfare either work themselves at one time or another, or live in households whose heads work at one time or another. Specifically, over a five-year period, the chances that an ever-welfare household containing an adult woman (whether or not she is the head) will also bring in earnings from work in the secondary labor market are better than nine in ten. Even for the most welfare-dependent group of all—very poor households whose head is always a woman—Friedman and Hausman have estimated the odds at four in ten. My own research has also shown that, even for those who participate in the welfare system from time to time without themselves actually working, labor market conditions (in the country, and in their home counties) significantly affect the timing and the extent of their utilization of welfare. If these findings are generalizable—and I think they are—then a major assumption underlying the two-tiered approach to welfare reform is seriously called into question. If a sixth of the households with adult women are likely to go on welfare (at least once), and if 90 percent of these households also contain heads who sometimes work, then 15 percent of the cohort are likely to include "employable" heads. That's 5.25 million people.

Neither sloth nor exploitation of the taxpaying middle class by those on welfare stands up as an especially good explanation of these findings on the incidence of welfare receipt or on the extent to which people mix earnings and welfare. The jobs to which welfare recipients and their households have access are too insubstantial to permit anyone to survive—let alone to support families—without additional supplementary income from such sources as the welfare programs. Between 1970 and 1972, the average annual wage that the heads of welfare households could expect to earn under the most optimistic assumptions was less than $5,000. Jobs were typically part-time or part-year, providing little on-the-job training or access to career ladders.

The best way—probably the only way—to reduce the welfare rolls is to reduce the need for welfare by creating jobs that provide alternative sources of income to households presently subsisting on welfare. Unionization tends to upgrade jobs to a certain extent; therefore the encouragement of unionization would also reduce the need for welfare. Policies which tighten labor markets, at both the national and local levels, will reduce the utilization of welfare.

The extent to which a policy of job creation promotes a permanent substitution of work for welfare depends, however, on the quality of the new jobs as measured by such factors as remuneration and stability. Unless such jobs are competitive with existing welfare grants, many welfare recipients will—quite rationally—choose not to make the substitution. In any case, if the jobs are unable to provide people with a subsistence income, those people will have no choice but to continue mixing work and welfare. For the given number, kinds, and locations of jobs in 1968-72, most of those households with welfare *did* have heads who worked at some time or other, and yet did not, could not, or would not stay off welfare. Apparently there weren't enough good jobs around.

Thus, policy that adds to the stock of jobs in the secondary labor market will promote more mixing of work and welfare, not a permanent, durable substitution of work for welfare. To the extent that secondary jobs erode productivity and promote unstable work behavior, the deliberate use of public resources to increase the supply of such jobs is actually a formula for retarding long-run economic well-being and the development of human resources.

The implications for welfare reform policy are therefore clear—and will be difficult to swallow, especially for Washington planners. But there is no escaping them. The unexpectedly high incidence of work-welfare mixing by the recipients of public assistance in the United States, combined with the finding that national and local unemployment are the most consistently important determinants of the likelihood that a household will have to go on welfare, tell us clearly and forcefully that any program to reduce dependency in America will have to be very expensive. We must increase the capacity of the economy to absorb the extra labor at wage levels that permit family support. Then—and only then, in my judgment—will it be feasible for us to implement a simple, efficient negative income tax at reasonable cost, for those who are truly "unemployable," or for those who suffer by occasional displacement from the economic mainstream.